What Have I Done?

25/6/2016

25-5-17

ALSO BY AMANDA PROWSE
FROM CLIPPER LARGE PRINT

Poppy Day

What Have I Done?

Amanda Prowse

W F HOWES LTD

This large print edition published in 2013 by
W F Howes Ltd
Unit 4, Rearsby Business Park, Gaddesby Lane,
Rearsby, Leicester LE7 4YH

1 3 5 7 9 10 8 6 4 2

First published in the United Kingdom in 2013
by Head of Zeus Ltd.

A CIP catalogue record for this book is available
from the British Library

ISBN 978 1 47122 876 6

Typeset by Palimpsest Book Production Limited,
Falkirk, Stirlingshire
Printed and bound in Great Britain
by MPG Books Ltd, Bodmin, Cornwall

What Have I Done? *is dedicated to
every woman who lives under the cloud of
control. You will find happiness when you find
the courage to set yourself free . . .*

I will gather up all the little pieces that you have chipped away, hidden in drawers, swept under the carpet and shoved behind cushions and I will rebuild myself. I will become all of the things that I thought I might. All the dreams I considered before you broke me, I will chase them all.

TEN YEARS AGO

Kathryn Brooker watched the life slip from him, convinced she saw the black spirit snake out of his body and disappear immediately through the floor, spiralling down and down. She sat back in her chair and breathed deeply. She had expected euphoria or at the very least relief. What she couldn't have predicted was the numbness that now enveloped her. Picturing her children sleeping next door, she closed her eyes and wished for them a deep and peaceful rest, knowing it would be the last they would enjoy for some time. As ever, consideration of what was best for her son and daughter was only a thought away.

The room felt quite empty despite the blood-soaked body lying centrally on the bed. The atmosphere was peaceful, the temperature just right.

Kathryn registered the smallest flicker of disappointment; she had expected to feel more.

Having changed into jeans and a jersey, she calmly stood by the side of the bed on which her husband's pale corpse lay. With great deliberation and for the first time in her life, she dialled 999.

It felt surreal to put into practice the one act that she had mentally rehearsed for as long as she could remember, although in her imagination the emergency had always been a child with a broken leg or a fire in a neighbouring empty building, nothing too dramatic.

'Emergency, which service do you require?'

'Oh, hello, yes, I'm not too sure which service I require.'

'You are not sure?'

'I think probably the police or ambulance, maybe both. Sorry. As I said, I'm not too sure . . .'

'Can I ask you what it is in connection with, madam?'

'Oh, right, yes, of course. I have just murdered my husband.'

'I'm sorry, you have what? This is a terrible line.'

'Oh, I know. I'm sorry, I'll try and speak up a bit. It's always a terrible connection from here, even if I'm phoning someone locally. It's because I am up in the main bedroom and the reception is very bad. My son thinks it may be because of all the big trees around us; we did cut them right back one year, but I can't remember if it made any difference. Plus we get interference from the computers in the next building; we've been meaning to get it looked at, but that's by the by. Right, yes. I said, I have murdered my husband.'

Kathryn blinked at the humming strip light that winked overhead; the bulb needed to be replaced.

It was a distraction that could easily become annoying.

'Did you do it?'

Roland Gearing rested his weight on splayed fingers, his hands forming little pyramids that, incredibly, supported his muscular frame as he leant over the table. He lowered his voice an octave; this was the one question he knew he had to ask and yet he was fearful of her response.

'Did I do it?'

'Yes, Kathryn, did you?'

He held her gaze, hoping to instil trust, trying to tease out the honest answer. He knew a lot about lying and relied on his gut instinct. Years on the job had taught him to monitor the interviewee's pupils carefully.

'It's a question that I wouldn't normally ask quite so early in proceedings, but as your friend – as Mark's friend too – I feel I have to. Is that okay?'

'Yes, yes of course. I understand.'

She gave a fleeting smile as her index finger and thumb looped her hair behind her left ear and then her right.

Her calm composure rattled him; there was none of the hysteria or fear that usually characterised these encounters. Women in similar situations were often almost insane with terror, rage or the dread of injustice. Kathryn, however, appeared placid.

She remembered her husband's glassy eyes. The way his fingers slipped and missed as they struggled with an invisible tourniquet that stopped the breath in his throat. Her nose wrinkled; her nostrils still carried the faintest trace of the iron stench of Mark's seeping blood. It had repulsed and comforted her in equal measure. It was as if she could taste it at the back of her throat. She hadn't sought to ease his discomfort in his dying moments, nor had she offered any words of solace. She had in fact smiled, as though he would manage, was still the strong, capable man who could cut wood, paint walls and raise a hand.

She may have even hummed, as though she wasn't hovering, desperate to witness the demise that would mean the end of the whole sordid chapter. When she had spoken, her tone had been nonchalant.

'Take your time. I've got hours, nowhere to go and a whole lifetime ahead of me. A promise is a promise.'

Her flippant pragmatism hid a heart that groaned with relief.

'I haven't got long.'

His voice had been a waning whisper. His final words coasted on fragmented last breaths.

'Too slow, painful. You'll pay.'

She mentally erased the words before he had finished. She would not share, recount or remember them.

'Oh, Mark, I have already paid.'

Bending low, with her face inches from his, she breathed the fetid air that he exhaled, sharing the small space where life lingered until the very end. Kathryn marvelled at the capacity for human animals to cling to the 'now'. It was quite impressive, fascinating even, despite the obvious futility.

'Yes. Yes, I did it, Roland. It was me. Me alone.'

There was a hint of pride in her admission, as if she were commenting on an achievement. Roland found it most disconcerting. He shook his head. Disbelief clouded everything, even after having seen and heard her confession. He looked at the neat, middle-aged woman with the pretty face sitting opposite him. The same woman who had handed him canapés on doily-decorated platters, served him percolated coffee and proffered homemade cake. The facts would simply not compute. She had been married to Mark Brooker, a man that he liked and admired. A man he had trusted with the education of his only daughter.

Roland exhaled slowly and scratched his chin where his stubble was at its most irritating. The hot, stress-filled environment of the interview room did nothing to help his sensitive skin. He wanted to go home and shower. Better still, he wanted to rewind the day and not pick up the 3 a.m. call that would disturb his family's rest and destroy the community as he knew it.

Kathryn sensed his irritation, knowing he was the sort of man who cherished his sleep. She pictured him at home earlier that evening, enjoying sea bream with steamed vegetables and a chilled white, after having spent an hour in the gym, maintaining that flat stomach. Neither could have guessed that his Sabbath would have ended like this, with him facing her across the table inside Finchbury police station at this ungodly hour, trying to figure out what the hell was going on.

'Are you sure you want to talk to me?' he prompted.

His jacket fell open, revealing the hot-pink silk lining of his handmade suit. She imagined his fellow police officers taking the mick, but knew enough about Roland and the care he took with his appearance to realise that he wouldn't pay them any heed. He would never be seen in the cheap, crumpled brands that some of his contemporaries wore. Kathryn recalled a conversation she had overheard between him and Mark in which he'd lamented the loss of his uniform, an inevitable consequence of climbing the ranks and becoming chief inspector. He had taken such pleasure in polishing buttons, shining boots and removing specks of lint from the wool of his tunic. She watched as he ran his palm over his abs, clearly enjoying the feel of himself against the inside of a crisp, white shirt.

'Yes.'

'You are absolutely certain that this wouldn't be easier with a stranger?'

She noted the flash of wide-eyed hope.

'I am positive, Roland. Thank you for asking, but there is no one else that I would rather talk to and I appreciate you coming and giving up your sleep, I really do.'

It was as if she didn't get it, as if she had invited him over, rather than the fact he had been hauled from his bed in the early hours in response to the first suspected murder on his patch in eighteen years. There was no quaver to her voice, no hesitation or apparent nervousness. Her hands sat neatly folded together in her lap. She looked as calm as someone waiting for a doctor's appointment.

Roland had been a police officer for twenty years. He had seen things – gruesome, unjust and amusing things. But this? It made no sense; it was shocking. It had stunned him, shaken him.

'You seem very calm, considering your current situation.'

He wondered if she was in shock.

'Do you know, it's funny that you should say that, because I do feel calm. I feel very calm.'

'That worries me greatly.'

'Oh, Roland, there's no need to worry, no need at all. It makes a pleasant change for me, this feeling of serenity. I had almost forgotten what it was like! In fact I don't think I have felt like this since I was a child. That was a lovely time in my life, when I had absolutely nothing to worry about and I was very much loved. I had a wonderful childhood, a wonderful life. I wasn't always this way, you know.'

'What way?'

'Oh, you know . . . afraid, edgy, contained. I was quite determined. Never racy or wild, but I had

7

a quiet belief that I could set the world alight, blaze trails. I thought I would achieve so many things. My parents always told me that the only limit to my achievements was my imagination and I believed them. They are both gone now, and I don't think about them too much.'

'Why not?'

She exhaled deeply.

'To tell you the truth, Roland, I have always thought that the dead might watch over us in some way, even have the capacity to protect us. If my parents have been watching over me, then I am ashamed for all that they have had to witness, mortified by what I have become. On the other hand, if they were able to protect me from their viewing gallery on high, why didn't they? I've lost count of the number of times I've asked for help, prayed for help, all to no avail. So I tend not to bother. It's far too confusing and that's one thing that I haven't needed any more of – confusion.'

'If you did it, Kathryn, then it begs the question, why? Why did you do it?'

With the small smile of one uncertain of where to begin, yet aware that she had to, Kathryn slowly formed her response.

'It's quite simple, really. I did it so that I could tell my story, unafraid.'

'Your story?' Roland was baffled.

'Yes, Roland. I needed to tell my story to my children, to our family, our friends, even our community, without fear.'

'Fear of what exactly?'

He had been listening to her for a while now, yet was still no nearer to understanding.

A small laugh escaped her lips. At the same time an unbidden tear rolled down her face.

'Oh, Roland, I don't know where to begin! Fear of pain, death, but most importantly fear that I would disappear inside myself and never resurface. I don't know where I have gone, you see. I don't know where the person that used to be me is any more. It's as if I have become nothing, like I have been living outside society even though I am within it. My life has felt so inconsequential, as if it doesn't matter what happens to me. I have become invisible. Very often I speak but no one hears me. Earlier today something happened that changed me, Roland. I can't say that it was a big, momentous or even a particularly memorable thing, but something happened and I knew that I had had enough. It was time, it was my time.'

He contemplated her words and decided not to ask just yet what that 'something' was that had changed her.

'You need to consider what you are saying, Kathryn. I want you to think very, very carefully about what you say and who you say it to. Your words and actions from now on can dramatically affect how things turn out for you. Every scrap of information that leaves your mouth will be recorded and will affect your future.'

Again the small laugh.

'Oh my goodness. My future? That's another funny thing: the fact is I don't have to think about anything very carefully now. I've already thought about it. I've had years to think about it.'

Roland paused and weighed up the options, trying to decide on the best course of action. His eyes widened suddenly. There was one possible way out for the headmaster's wife.

'I think it would be a good idea for you to see a doctor, Kathryn. For your own good.'

'Ah, yes! A psychiatrist, I assume? That would be fine. You will see that I am very good at acting on suggestions, agreeing with statements and following orders. In fact, I can't tell the difference between them any more! But I should warn you that after careful assessment and diagnosis, he or she will write you a long-winded, expensive report that will tell you I am one hundred per cent sane, rational and in full control of all my faculties. The fact is, I acted alone and with complete knowledge and understanding of both my actions and their consequences. But you go ahead; get this confirmed by someone with a gilt-framed certificate hanging behind their comfy swivel chair, if it makes it easier for you.'

'It's not about what is easier for *me*! Jesus Christ, Kathryn, I can only assume that you've had some kind of breakdown and that your actions are the result of some form of madness, temporary or otherwise.'

She laughed then.

'Temporary or otherwise? I like that. The fact is, Roland, I am speaking the truth and I do so from a lucid mind. Can I tell you something?'

He prayed for some revealing rationale, a fact or piece of trivia, anything.

'Yes, yes of course.'

'There have been times over the last two decades when I could quite easily have lost my marbles, times when things felt so bleak and sad that I wondered if it wouldn't be easier to let myself sink into depression and opt out. Two things stopped me from giving in to that, no matter how tempting. Dominic and Lydia. They have been my reasons for keeping sane and keeping going. I would have been no use to them if I'd gone a bit loopy. It's been a battle, though, I can't say it hasn't. I would stare at my distraught face in the mirror day after day and wonder how long I could keep up the pretence. Turns out for quite a while!'

She laughed in a short, unnatural burst.

Roland stared at her, convinced she really had lost her reason, despite her protestations.

'I have to say, Kathryn, that as a friend, and not as a chief inspector, I am worried about you, very worried about you.'

Her laugh interrupted him. She sighed, rocking slightly as she retrieved a damp square of kitchen roll from the sleeve of her cardigan and blotted her eyes and nose.

'I am so sorry, Roland. I shouldn't be laughing,

I know. I'm a tad emotional. It's been a difficult forty-eight hours.'

Neither of them commented on the gross understatement.

'The reason I laugh is that I have been wanting someone to worry about me and help me for the last eighteen years. But now, for the first time since the day I got married, I don't need anyone to worry about me because I am finally safe.'

She placed her palms flat against the table, as if taking strength from its solidity, to emphasise the point that she could stand alone now.

Roland stood and paced the small police-station interview room; his hands were on his hips, his arms sticking out at right angles. He was starting to lose his patience, his frustration level rising in direct proportion to the lack of progress. He had the feeling that their conversation could meander like this for hours and that was time he didn't have to waste.

'Okay, Kathryn, I am going to level with you. I find myself in a very difficult position. I don't mean professionally, but psychologically. I am having great difficulty in understanding what is going on with you. I have known you and Mark for . . . . how long? Nearly ten years?'

Kathryn pictured the arrival at Mountbriers Academy of his daughter Sophie at the age of eight, with her little leather satchel, frightened eyes, freckles and swinging plaits. She was now a confident sixteen-year-old who had not only caught the eye of her own son, but every other boy in the year. Kathryn nodded. Nearly ten years.

'And in all that time you and Mark have always been seen as a very close couple, a devoted couple. He speaks – spoke – very highly of you, Kathryn, always. So can you understand why this seems . . .?'

Roland stared up at the ceiling momentarily, steadied himself, and tried a different tack.

'God, Kathryn, I am struggling to word this politely, so I'm going to stop trying and cut to the chase. Mark is . . . was . . . a much-respected and loved member of this community. He was the headmaster, for God's sake! Only recently nationally recognised, well regarded by all. And you expect me . . . everyone, in fact . . .to believe that for the last eighteen years you have been living a life of misery behind those high flint walls and sash windows? When all we have seen is a strong, happy couple who appeared devoted to each other? Do you see why people might have some difficulty with this?'

She smiled her hesitant smile and chose her words carefully.

'I can see that some people will only ever see what they want to see, Roland. I do know that. But it's also important to recognise that some people are great deceivers. Mark was a great deceiver and, to a certain extent, so was I. He was a monster who pretended to be otherwise and I was a victim and pretended I was not. Guilty as charged.'

'Kathryn, do try not to use that phrase, please.'

She didn't know if he was joking.

'Okay, Roland. The point that I'm making is that it doesn't really matter to me what people think or what people think they know. I know the truth and one day my kids will know the truth, and that is the *only* thing that matters to me. The fact is, I *am* guilty, and I do expect to pay the penalty. You should know that for me there is no punishment that would match the life that I have lived as Mark's wife. None. I am not afraid, not any more.'

Roland sat down on the opposite side of the rectangular table. He stretched out his legs and crossed them at the ankles, clasped his hands behind his head and sighed. His mind flitted to the numerous times that he had sat at the table in the Brookers' warm family kitchen, Kathryn wearing her floral apron and serving tea from a dotty pot. Mark would hold court and dish out the banter after Sunday service, debating the latest on the cricket while Classic FM hummed quietly behind the delicate clink of china on china.

None of it made any sense. Roland was fully engaged and prepared to listen. It was essential that he listened because he needed to hear. More importantly, he needed to understand.

He ran his hand over his face and finished by raking his scalp and patting his side parting.

'I have been in this job for a long time and I

know that things can happen. Sometimes on the spur of the moment; bad things, accidents—'

'I think I know where you're going with this,' Kathryn interrupted, 'but I should stop you right there. This was no accident. Not that I planned and plotted or anything like that, but it wasn't an accident. I intentionally stabbed Mark and as I held the knife in my hand, I wanted to kill him. Thinking about it, I've probably wanted to do it for a long time, deep down. So whilst it was "spur of the moment", as you say, it really wasn't an accident.'

Roland shook his head; she wasn't exactly helping herself.

'I tell you what would help me greatly . . . why don't you give me some examples?'

'Examples?'

'Yes, anything that will help me to fully comprehend what you have been through. Give me something typical.'

'Something typical?'

'Yes. A snapshot, if you like. Paint me a picture to help me get it; tell me exactly how it was. Explain to me what he did to you that was so bad. Enlighten me in simple terms as to what he put you through. You talk of fear and torture, but I need you to make it real. Tell me what he did that made you so afraid. Tell me what he did that pushed you to take his life.'

Roland had abandoned the friendly angle and was now in full copper mode.

15

'You want a snapshot?'

'If you like, yes.'

'Let me think. A snapshot, things that were typical . . .'

She paused.

'It's difficult to know where to start, how much to give you.'

'Give me anything, Kathryn, other than the phrase "my husband was a monster", which is a bit too generic and dramatic to be of real use. Give me something tangible, something that will help me to understand, any detail that will help me explain it to others.'

'Righto. There is one thing that I would like to say before I start, and that is that I will neither exaggerate nor understate the facts. I have told you and will continue to tell you only the whole truth and nothing but the truth – is that the phrase?'

Roland nodded. 'Yes, that's close enough. Ready when you are.'

Kathryn breathed in sharply and used her left thumb to spin her wedding band around her finger. It hadn't occurred to her to remove it, but she now decided to do so as soon as she was alone. She pushed the gold sliver upwards and briefly pondered the groove it had notched into her finger, wondering how long it would take for the tiny track to disappear. That would mark a big step towards her emancipation.

'Well, Mark was very fussy, obsessive, really. I

16

wasn't allowed to wear jeans or trousers, only skirts. Every minute of my day was more or less accounted for; there was very little time for free choice. I could decide what route to take to the supermarket or what veg to prepare for supper, but that was pretty much it. How and where I stored the groceries, when I served dinner, these things were all prescribed. I had to complete a round of chores every day, often pointless and repetitive chores that were designed to exhaust me and break my spirit . . .'

Roland pinched his eye sockets with his thumb and forefinger. He could just picture those words being repeated in court: *'I killed my husband because he was a little bit fussy, preferring me in skirts. And I had to do household chores.'* Jesus, if she got away with it, most of the women in the country would have justification. He hoped she had something better than that.

'At the end of every day, we would climb the stairs together. With only a plaster wall between me and my children, I would kneel at the foot of our bed and Mark would allocate me points according to how badly he thought I had executed the chores that day. Extra points would be added if I had done anything to irritate or anger him.'

She had his attention.

'These points would be on a scale of one to ten and depending on how badly I had scored – ten being bad – would determine what came next.'

Kathryn's tears snaked their way into the waiting

17

square of kitchen roll. Her breath stuttered in her throat, her distress as much for the shame in telling as for the memory of the events.

'Points?'

Roland shook his head. Kathryn couldn't gauge whether this was in pity or disbelief.

'Yes. And then he would hurt me.'

This she whispered. Roland strained to hear.

'How long had he been doing this to you, Kathryn?'

She coughed, collected herself and continued quite brightly, as if she could fool herself that all was well.

'Well, looking back, I can see that I was bullied from the moment we met. It was little things at first: criticising the clothes I wore, the way I styled my hair, and disliking all of my friends. He put a halt to my career as an English teacher, which was a shame. He broke or threw away anything that I had owned prior to meeting him, monitored my calls, that sort of thing. I was slowly alienated from my family. All his actions were designed to desta-bilise me and make me more dependent on him, cutting off all my allies and destroying my self-esteem so that when he started the real abuse I was already a victim and quite alone. I had become unable to confidently make a decision, such was my confusion. I had no voice. At least that's how it felt.'

'And what you term as "real abuse" – how long had that been going on?'

'Oh, let me see . . . since I was pregnant with Dominic.'

'Who is now sixteen?'

'Yes, that's right, although it doesn't seem possible! Sixteen . . . it goes so quickly, doesn't it? You must find that with Sophie. Sometimes I feel as if I was chasing a chubby toddler around the house, then turned my back for a second to find he's suddenly become this invincible life force, "a teenager". Sorry, Roland, I'm going off-piste a little, aren't I?'

She watched his expression, understood his predicament. Kathryn knew that it didn't sound plausible; it sounded completely bonkers that she had been talking about Mark Brooker, the head-master! She knew that Roland and every other parent would only ever be able to picture Mark offering a firm handshake and a clever quip. They would all agree that the whole affair was most shocking. What would Mark's PA, Judith, make of it all? Kathryn smiled to herself as she considered the woman's reaction, she could just imagine her statement: *'Mark didn't look like a nasty man, in fact he was quite gorgeous . . .'*

Kathryn hoped that in time and once all the facts had been revealed, people would ask them-selves one important question: if her life had been as perfect as Roland and everyone had thought, why would she have done it? Why would she fabricate the whole nightmare and then ask for punishment if it weren't true? Unless she was crazy, of course. And Kathryn was determined to prove that she was anything but.

Roland took a deep breath and prepared to repeat his questions.

SEVEN YEARS AGO

Marlham prison was never, ever silent. If it wasn't the droning TV with its endless cycle of mind-numbing soap operas, then it was the screams of derangement, shrieks of laughter and shouted expletives which apparently could not be delivered without the volume turned right up. Kate, as she was now known, knew from experience that the vilest prose was far more menacing when spoken quietly, slowly and in close proximity, forcing you to really listen and absorb the meaning. Shouting was for amateurs.

There was no peace even at night, when the cells were haunted by the inescapably noisy sobbing of the young and uninitiated. Kate found it heartbreaking. She could not stop herself superimposing the image of her daughter, Lydia, onto their weeping faces and she longed to make them feel better with a hug and a kind word. Their howls were punctuated by the bangs of desperate, angry hands as shoes and hairbrushes hit metal bars and bed frames, tapping out a rhythm that was Morse code for 'Get me out of here, I want to go home. Please let me go home.'

In the wee hours, unsympathetic warders and tired inmates barked instructions to 'Quieten down, shut up and turn out the bloody light!' When the inmates finally fell silent and the warders had taken refuge in their office, the building itself came alive. The Victorian plumbing creaked and groaned, radiators cracked and popped, light bulbs fizzed in their sockets and wind whistled through the gaps between pane and frame.

For Kate, the relentless noise was one of the biggest challenges of prison life, something she had not anticipated. She had steeled herself for the loss of freedom and the tedium, but it was the small things that had the biggest, most unexpected impact. Kate's yearnings and frustrations grew from the tiniest of privations. Having to squeeze her toes into over-dried, stiffened socks was a daily sufferance. But not being able to make herself a cup of tea dampened her spirits to the point of depression. The cool, milky brew that she was served three times a day was the exact opposite of how she liked it and even after three years she still hadn't got used to it. Not that she ever longed to be back in the head's kitchen at Mountbriers – not once, never.

When she first arrived, it was quite exhausting learning the timetable, rules and lingo of the strange environment. Most of her education came from watching the other inmates and imitating their responses to bell rings and indecipherable shouts.

She noticed that new residents fell into two categories: those who raged against the system that had unjustly removed them from a life they loved, taking any opportunity to holler, protest or lash out; and those, like herself, who conducted themselves with a level of serenity that suggested prison might in fact be a refuge from whatever had harmed them on the outside.

In the early weeks of her incarceration, Kate had to remind herself of where she was and why she was there. It was just as someone had once suggested to her: a kind of madness, temporary or otherwise. She had become single, widow and killer in a matter of hours. She was separated from her children and Mark was dead.

The kids were with her sister in Hallton, North Yorkshire. At various times of the day and night, Kate would have sudden panics about their welfare. Had she ever told Francesca that Dominic was allergic to cashew nuts? Supposing she inadvertently fed him some, did he have his EpiPen? Fear of the potentially fatal consequences pawed at her for days; she could think of nothing else. A logical mind would have reassured Kate that her son was a teenager and perfectly able to remind his aunt about his allergy, but this was not a logical mind; this was the mind of someone trying to cope with the enormity of being separated from her children.

When sleep was slow to arrive, Kate would ask herself some pertinent questions. *Do you regret it?*

Do you ever think that maybe it would have been better to have kept quiet, to have kept your hand out of the apron, left the knife in your pocket? Wouldn't it have been better for everybody, Kate, to have continued living your life the way you always had? At least you got to see the kids every day. At these times she would open one of her sister's letters and devour her words.

Francesca always started with '*Hey, Katie*', which turned back the clock to a time when they were young and close, a time before Mark Brooker had left his bruise on the sweet young girl who had very little to worry her. It was, however, more than a time-travelling term of endearment; it was also an acknowledgement that that was the last time the girl who married Mark Brooker had acted of her own free will and not as a frightened puppet. '*Hey, Katie*' was for Francesca a term of forgiveness now that she was finally able to understand what had lain behind her sister's cold and stilted behaviour over the years. It was a way of saying, 'all is forgiven, slate cleaned, onwards and upwards'.

Kate read and reread the snippets of information about her children, thankful beyond expression that her sister had, at Kate's time of direst need, simply scooped them up and taken them to safety, just as she had known she would. Equally gripping were the dropped hints of ordinary life carrying on regardless – '*Must dash, shepherd's pie in the oven!*' – enabling Kate to picture the family around the table, chatting and eating her sister's signature dish. And then there were the bigger details: Lydia having *'been accepted at art college to take her foundation course'* and Dominic *'helping Luke and his dad design the interior of a new business venture he is working on, a boutique hotel, no less! He's coming up with some great ideas and slowly, slowly the business is finding its feet again, thank goodness.'*

Having reread Francesca's latest news, Kate could answer her own questions without hesitation. No, it would not have been better to have kept quiet, to have left the knife in her pocket. Mark would have killed her eventually, of that she was certain.

It had taken almost three years inside before Kate realised that her confidence and self-esteem were slowly returning. During her marriage she had barely registered their absence, but now she was beginning to feel that she was actually worth something, that she had something valuable to say. She could at last say 'no' without feeling guilty – could say no to anything, in fact, be it an invitation to tea, or an aggressive sexual demand. She finally understood that to say no was her right.

Kate knew, however, that she would always carry her experiences in every fibre of her body; she would drag the person she used to be inside her like a waterlogged sponge. Given the choice, she would have preferred a spike of emotion, an obvious grief that after a brief and explosive hysteria would have left her cleansed. But that was not how she operated. Instead, she hauled along a low-level misery that, while suppressed, would shape the rest of her life. This she accepted with a certain resignation. The fear of Mark had gone. In its place lurked a ghost that might appear over her shoulder in the bathroom mirror or creep under the duvet to spoon against her in the dark of night. These momentary jolts, these shiver-inducing memories were entirely preferable to the abject terror in which she used to live.

The loss of contact with her children sat on Kate's chest like a dead weight. The pain of their absence was instant and sharp; it made breathing difficult and eating nearly impossible. Memories stalked her dreams and she regularly woke in tears, bereft at the recollection of the dimple in Lydia's toddler finger, Dom's blue woollen mitten discarded on the icy garden path. The deep, gnawing hunger she felt for them distracted her from everything she tried to do. It was debilitating and ever present, insistently there during every chore at every second of every day. Yet, like someone thirsting for water in the desert, she wasn't able to fix the problem. Words of apology and explanation hovered on her tongue, but with neither child listening, it felt hopeless, and the frustration drove her frequently to tears. Hard as she tried, her jailers couldn't or wouldn't understand that it wasn't prison per se that bothered her, it was that she needed time alone with her children, just an hour or two in which she could explain to them, comfort them. Could someone not force them to visit her? *Please . . .*

An image of her feeding them as newborns, each baby tiny, perfect and adored, sat behind her eyelids, never more than a blink away. She pictured their minute fingers splayed against her stretched, white skin, where tiny blue veins meandered towards their seeking, rosebud mouths; she watched their eyelids fall slowly in long, lazy blinks, tummies full, ready to doze. Her gut would contract with the familiar feeling of yearning, not unlike when she was feeding. If she could only go back to that time and find the courage . . .

The steady slap of flip-flops on the linoleum floor told Kate it was time for the post. The slovenly girl whose job it was to deliver the mail slowed her cart as she approached and flicked through a stack of manila envelopes. Kate could always sense when a letter was heading her way. She smiled as she pictured her sister scribbling at her little desk in between mouthfuls of coffee and the wiping down of counter tops. Lovely Francesca.

The post-girl flung an envelope through the open door and onto Kate's bed. Having never received one herself, the girl had little idea of how much joy and distraction a letter could bring.

'Thank you.' Kate was sincere.

The girl gave the briefest of nods. She wasn't in it for the thanks; it was all about the few pence she received for her troubles.

Like a connoisseur savouring a fine wine or a good cheese, Kate had learned not to rush the process. She always delayed the opening, holding the envelope, scrutinising the seal and feeling the weight before examining the spidery script of the address. She discreetly put her thumb over her prison number written in black ink in the top left-hand corner; she ignored the thin strip of glue that had already been lifted so that the contents could be scanned and the word 'AUTHORISED' stamped in red ink across the flap. For a second or two, she could dismiss the thought that a prison official had already devoured gossip intended only for her and pretend she was somewhere else, receiving news and enjoying the connection with the rest of the world.

Kate turned the innocuous brown rectangle over in her palm until it lay flat against her hand. Her heart jumped. It wasn't the meandering script of her sister's fountain pen that stared back at her, but the unmistakable tiny, precise strokes of her daughter's hand.

'Oh! It's from my daughter!'

Kate didn't know who she was shouting to, her words were almost involuntary. The joy bubbled from her throat.

'Good for you, love,' came the indifferent reply from a neighbouring cell.

It was only the second letter she had received from Lydia in three years. Kate had all but worn out the thin sheet of its predecessor. This precious new talisman would provide her with hours of reflection. Each word would very quickly be committed to memory, but the text and its meaning were not enough. To hold the piece of paper and trace the words that her little girl's fingers had rested on connected her in a way that recall alone could not. To inhale the paper which revealed the vaguest hint of her daughter's fragrance, transferred from the lightest touch to her wrist, was an indescribable pleasure. Kate read and reread the two pages at least twenty times that day. Other readings on future days would become part of her routine.

Gosh, Mum,

Nearly three years, it's gone so quickly. Francesca's still completely bonkers, but brilliant and reminds me a lot of you. I can see some of your traits in her and vice versa. I guess I'd never spent enough time with her before to notice. She has the same voice as you and when I first came here, if I heard her on the phone or she'd call me down to dinner, I'd get really upset. But I'm used to it now and sometimes I make out it is you downstairs cooking my tea and it makes me smile.

Kate stopped reading to mop at the tears that fogged her vision. She pictured the countless times she'd called up the stairs, *'Supper's ready, kids!'*, to hear them thundering down either laughing or arguing. How she missed dishing up their meals, hearing their moans, watching as they tucked into their food, spilt drinks on the tablecloth and scraped their shoes against the wooden floor.

College is amazing! Learning loads and when they set me new assignments I think, oh goody! Whereas a lot of my friends just get pissed off with the workload. I think this means I love it more than them. They say I'm quite good, particularly my painting, which makes me happy!

I know I haven't written for a long time. I start a lot of letters, but I don't finish them. Hope I finish this one. If I don't, then I'll try again in a while. I find it hard, Mum, I really do. I don't know how to write to you, if that makes any sense.

'I know, darling, I know it's hard, but don't stop, Lydi. It means the world to me.'

Kate was unaware she had spoken out loud.

'You got visitors in there, girl?' her neighbour shrieked across the corridor.

Kate ignored her; she was talking directly to her daughter.

It's taken me this long to realise that what happened really happened and wasn't just a bad dream. That's how it all felt for a long time. I've been seeing a kind of counsellor in York and it's helped. (Didn't think it would, but it has. Dom won't go, but I think he should.) It's helped me understand that Dad was my dad no matter what he did or didn't do. I miss and mourn him because he was my dad and before this all happened he was a great dad. I was proud that he was the Head. It made me feel special at school. I can only remember being really happy when I was with him, never anything else. I also mourn you too, Mum. You were my 'background noise' – always there and always doing something, and now my world feels silent because I've lost you. I have lost you both.

'No you haven't, darling. I'm right here!'

Kate's voice was a strained whisper, her vocal chords taut with distress.

Dom and I talk about it sometimes, not all the time as you might expect, but sometimes. It's like we have a secret and when we discuss it we do it in a whisper. If we can work it out with dates and stuff, we will try and come down to see you at half-term.

I miss you and I love you as ever,

Lyds xx

Kate held the paper against her chest and hugged the words to her breast. She knew Lydia was right: your dad was your dad no matter what he did or didn't do and she would never try to influence her beautiful kids one way or another. She had

31

protected them their whole lives and she would continue to do so.

One sentence burned brighter than any other: *'we will try and come down to see you at half-term'*. The very idea of seeing the kids made her feel giddy. Her stomach muscles clenched with anticipation. She was allowed two sixty-minute visits every four weeks. She had only ever had two, one from a court-appointed chaplain and one last year from Francesca, who had travelled the length of the country to sit for an hour in the strained confines of the visiting room. Kate had assured her that her time would be better spent in Hallton, making things as comfortable as possible for Dom and Lydi. The hour had passed in minutes and the two had grasped each other's hands awkwardly and whispered inadequate goodbyes through their tears. It had been horrible.

Four weeks passed, then six, then eight. Kate stopped counting. They weren't coming.

Kate now accepted that the more time passed, the less likely they were to visit. It was as if the cavern they would have to cross grew wider and more treacherous with each passing day. The only visitor she could rely upon was her best friend, Natasha, whose first trip to Marlham was one that she would never forget. It had been some weeks into her sentence, when she was alerted by the particular squeak of the guard's rubber soles.

'You've got a visitor, Kate.'

'What?'

She had heard perfectly, but was so stunned by the words, she wanted them repeated for confirmation. The warder pushed open her cell door. Kate was momentarily confused. It was so rare for her to have a visitor she had forgotten the drill. She felt a split-second flicker of dismay that her reading was about to be disrupted; Paulo Coelho would just have to wait. Her heart beat loudly in her chest, her mouth went dry.

Lydia, Dominic, or both: who had finally decided to come? *Oh please let it be both*, she prayed. Her hands shook inside her smock pocket. She teased her fringe with her fingertips as she paced the corridor, impervious to the fact that the state of her hair would be the least of her children's worries.

The visiting room was functional and austere, smaller than she had imagined. Square tables and plastic chairs like the ones in the Mountbriers school hall sat uniformly in three rows of four. Security cameras blinked from every corner. The linoleum floor had been polished to a high shine. *God help anyone in socks*, thought Kate as she peered through the safety glass at the top of the door.

The visitors were already in situ, with some of her fellow inmates seated opposite them. It was fascinating for Kate to see the women she lived with interacting with their families and friends. A brassy, blonde scrapper called Moll was crying as she squinted at a photograph. *Not such a tough nut after all.*

Jojo, a neighbour of Kate's, was wearing a vest, her wasted addict's muscles on full display. She was slouched in a chair across from a woman who was unmistakably her mother, decked out in pearls and wearing a flashy watch. The older woman sat with lips pursed, eyes darting continually to the clock on the wall, disapproval and disappointment dripping from every pore.

Kate scanned the rest of the tables. *Where are you, where are you?*

Her eyes lighted on a familiar face. It was Natasha, the art teacher at Mountbriers and Kate's one and only friend. She smiled widely to hide her disappointment. Not her children, not today.

Natasha sat cleaning and admiring her nails, before twisting the beads on her chunky bangle to best show off their pattern. She surveyed the decor as though she were rendezvousing in Costa Coffee on a sunny day rather than visiting her jailbird friend. Natasha looked as if she had stepped from a pavement cafe in St Tropez. Her skin held the burnish of a recent tan. Silver and diamante clips attempted to hold her unruly hair at bay, which she had grown to shoulder length. Her vest sat snugly over her slender, bra-less form and a multi-coloured patchwork skirt pooled in a fan around her chair. Kate knew it would not have occurred to her friend to opt for demure or depressed.

Kate took the seat opposite Natasha and worried momentarily how they would start. But Natasha hardly blinked, as though it had been a few minutes and not many months since they had last seen each other.

'Okay, so I once stole a bottle of Panda Pop when I was twelve, but was too scared to repeat the exercise, so I gave up thievery there and then. Every time there was an early-evening knock at the door I thought it was the police coming to get me! I used to hide, sweating under the duvet until my dad sent them away.'

Kate shook her head, trying to pick up the thread.

'It was more of a dare and not my thing at all. Oh, and I also sneaked a look at your notebook once, when you left it on the kitchen table at Mountbriers. I read a list of chores, all quite standard, and saw a picture of a flower that you had scrawled, which wasn't very good, your perspective was all wrong. I remember thinking, God, I hope this is a bloody code for something deviant and exciting – no one's life can be this boring! And finally, *drum roll please*, I did have a teeny tiny crush on Cattermole, the school chaplain. I think I saw myself in some *Thornbirds*esque illicit love affair, with the poor chap caught between his devotion to the church and his lust for me.'

Natasha raised one of her elegantly arched eyebrows and flashed Kate a wicked grin.

'So, there we have it, Kate, my confession to

35

you; things I didn't share but probably should have, knowing that you wouldn't have judged me and that you'd have loved and helped me no matter what. Now it's your turn!'

Kate laughed until the tears gathered.

'Oh, Tash, I never told anyone. I couldn't.'

'I'm teasing you, honey. We've got all the time in the world.'

'I guess we do. I hated pretending to you, to everyone, but especially you. I reached a point where I just couldn't do it any more.'

'Do you know what, mate? I knew something wasn't right. He was a pig of a man in a number of ways, but I had no idea of the extent of your suffering. I guessed at a bit of bullying, but when I heard the full detail . . .' Natasha paused to compose herself. 'I think you are a remarkable woman, Kate. Stronger than anyone I know, to have shouldered what you did just to keep it secret from the kids. I admire you greatly.'

'I didn't feel like a strong person, quite the opposite, even now.'

'Well you should. Most people would not have been able to function, let alone put on that brave face and make things "normal" for everyone else. You are amazing.'

Kate smiled, unused to discussing her feelings in this way, let alone taking a compliment.

'How are you doing now?' Natasha looked concerned.

'I'm . . .' How was she? It was hard to phrase.

'I'm okay. I like the peace I have in here, I can read. But obviously I miss . . . I've had a couple of letters from Lyd, but I haven't heard from Dom. She said they might . . . I thought they might . . .' Kate's eyes stung, her nose ran, and her mouth twisted into the ugly angle of one in distress.

'I've seen them.'

Her friend's words cut and soothed in equal measure.

'Oh! Oh, Tash!'

She had so many questions that bubbled on top of the jealous bile that rose in her throat. *They are my kids, my kids! How come you've seen them and not me?*

'They are alternately angry and confused, as you would expect, but they are doing great. Lydia is expressing her thoughts through her art and is very centred, determined; she has your strength. Dominic is more of a loose cannon, but then he always was.'

Both women thought briefly of their time at Mountbriers.

'It will not always be this way, Kate, and your sister is doing a great job. She keeps you present every day in little ways – the odd comment, and an easy patter about your childhood, that sort of thing.'

This was good to hear. 'Thank you.'

Her words slid between mucus-smeared lips. Her heart ached with longing. *My babies, my children . . .*

★　★　★

Kate fixed her smile and entered the classroom. Eighteen months into her sentence and with a record of model behaviour, she had been asked to run an English Literature class for her fellow inmates. Incarcerated English graduates who were willing to teach were thin on the ground.

Her fellow convicts were a varied bunch, but largely came from backgrounds that were quite alien to Kate. Over eighty per cent were addicts, jailed for crimes they'd committed to feed their habits. These women often wanted to tell her their stories. They ranged in age from eighteen to sixty, but their tales were remarkably similar. All spoke of the vice-like grip of addiction that meant scoring the next hit took precedence over every aspect of their lives. They would sell anything, including themselves, and stop at nothing to get their hands on their drug of choice. Most had been in and out of prison so many times they may as well have fitted a revolving door with heroin or crack on one side and their cell on the other. Prison seemed to give them the respite they needed, enabling them to think clearly and make promises they knew they would be unlikely to keep.

Kate felt especially sad for the younger women, most of whom seemed to have been dealt a losing hand. She felt certain that with a little more direction and a lot more kindness, they could have been heading off to study art or design hotels like her own children, rather than watching mind-numbing

TV for twelve hours a day and sneering at their lookalikes from the other side of the room.

The first time Kate taught a class, she felt an overwhelming sense of achievement. It wasn't quite the environment she had envisaged when she qualified twenty-odd years ago, but nevertheless, she was now a teacher, she was finally a somebody. Her class had grown in popularity and was now at full capacity. She entered the room with gusto.

'Right, girls, *Hamlet* beckons! If you would like to turn to where we left off last week, where Ophelia is very sadly starting to lose her marbles, we can crack on!'

The assembled 'girls' all had a thirst for learning and escape, needs that Kate understood only too well.

'What do we think of Ophelia? Do we think she *is* mad? Or is there something else going on here?'

'I think she's mad, yeah – to put up with all Hamlet's shit!'

This succinct summing-up caused a ripple of laughter around the room.

Kate laughed too; there were no right or wrong answers in here, only sound opinion.

'I like that, Kelly. You are right, of course. Ophelia seems to be at the mercy of all the male figures in her life; she's a victim. Hamlet himself uses her to wreak revenge. I think she suffers because of how the men in the play view women; even her father and brother rule her life. Do we

39

think it's the guilt she feels at Hamlet's supposed madness and her father's murder that sends her insane?'

Kate paused and looked around the room, her palms upturned, inviting interaction.

Jojo sat forward. 'I can't believe that even in the olden days, like Hamlet time, women were still treated like dirt. It's like nothing has changed in hundreds of years.' She shook her head.

Kelly was not going to accept this. 'Speak for yourself, Jojo. I've never put up with shit from a bloke. It's weak, man. If a bloke treated me badly, I'd leave, every time. Ophelia should have done a runner.'

Kate was used to this, the meandering from the text in hand to real life and back again. She could never have envisaged such rich and current debate. It was wonderful.

'Every time, Kelly?' she prompted. 'What if there are circumstances that stop her leaving, other factors?'

'Like what? There's nothing that would make me stay with some fucking shit-head bastard, nothing.'

'Okay, let's try and cut the language a bit – although Shakespeare was a big lover of cussing! I guess we are talking about two different things. Ophelia was trapped both by the time in which she lived and by her circumstances and you are saying that in today's world you wouldn't have to put up with that level of oppression, is that right?'

'Yep.' Kelly nodded. That was exactly what she was saying.

'What I'm asking you to think about, Kelly, is what if you had reasons to stay, whether others thought those reasons were valid or not. They could be self-imposed reasons, like guilt or duty. Or practical reasons: nowhere else to go, poverty, no roof over your head . . .'

The girls stared at her. Kate realised that many if not all of them had themselves faced poverty and homelessness; these aspects of life were accepted, to be expected, even. The bar was set so low. She decided to change tack.

'What if you had kids; what if you needed to stay to take care of them?' She pictured Lydia and Dominic at seven and eight, tucking them into bed, kissing their foreheads, switching on their night lights.

'You'd have to be some sort of moron to have kids with a bloke that's no good in the first place!' Kelly wasn't done.

Jojo piped up, looking directly at Kelly. 'I had kids with someone like that. Trouble was he was all right at first, suckered me right in, but he turned out to be a really bad man, class A shit, a liar, total bastard.' Jojo instinctively wrapped her arms around her torso, administering a self-soothing hug.

Kate smiled at Jojo. They had more in common than the girl could ever have guessed. She thought she might have found a kindred spirit.

'Did you stay because of the kids?'

'No, I stayed because of the drugs. My kids were

41

in care within a year of him moving in. I don't see them no more.'

Jojo spewed out her words with bravado. But Kate saw the flash behind her pupils and the flush in her cheeks at the mention of her children. She had noticed the way Jojo unconsciously and momentarily cupped the left breast that had fed those children. It told her she would have loved to have been a good mum had circumstances been a little kinder.

Kate looked at the book in front of her: '*Frailty, thy name is woman . . .*'

She sat in the chair at the front of the class, aware that all eyes were upon her. It broke her heart, the very idea, the waste. Kate felt a sense of futility; what would teaching these girls about Shakespeare achieve? Would it bring back Jojo's kids, help Kelly reach stability? Of course not. Was it more about her stupid, self-indulgent desire to teach?

Kate was aware she had to do something. She swallowed hard and closed the text. Her voice was soft.

'Sometimes it's easy to judge others in the cold light of day or to say how you would react in a certain situation, but I think the one thing we all have in common is that we know how hard it is to make the right decision when your mind is so scrambled with tiredness, fear or drugs. We judge Ophelia just like people will be judging us, all of us, and they will probably never know what it's like to walk in our shoes. I know that I can't even make a cup of tea without crying when I'm feeling a bit lost, when I'm that worn down, let alone make a good choice. I guess what I'm saying is that life is not always straightforward or easy, but I don't have to tell you lot that.'

There was a faint ripple of laughter, but generally there was a hush as each considered the bad choices that had led them to that strip-lit classroom in Marlham's women's prison.

The scrape of metal chair legs against the floor made everyone turn their heads. Janeece had been sitting at the back of the class, listening intently and making copious notes as she always did. Kate had thrown her an olive branch when she had first arrived and Janeece, who had never known support of any kind, had grasped it with both hands.

She stood slowly, tugging at the hem of her grey T-shirt, trying to cover her ample stomach. Then she addressed the class, an act which took all her courage.

'I think sometimes leaving is the easy choice. It takes courage not to bugger off. It must be harder to stay in a situation that is scary or horrible than to go. My mum left as soon as anything got tough. She kept leaving until one day she just went for good. I was six. Things were quite shitty when she was there, but they got a whole lot more shitty when she'd gone. It would have taken balls to stay and sort the mess out. Ophelia says, "we know what we are, but know not what we may be". I

43

think this means that we can all make good choices if we try and that we can be whatever we want to. It's up to us.'

Kate beamed. If she had given Janeece the confidence to stand up in public and quote Shakespeare then maybe her role wasn't so self-indulgent after all.

She and Janeece had come a long way since their first encounter. At the time, Kate had been just a month into her sentence. She was happy that her first weeks had passed without event. She had managed to keep to a routine of sorts and was sleeping all right despite the night-time noise levels.

She was sitting at the large table in the communal area on the ground floor as she did most afternoons. Most of the women were either clustered around the television, playing pool or knitting, but as usual she had her nose in a book. That day it was Thomas Hardy's *Under the Greenwood Tree*. Her hair was still neat in its immaculate bob; years of cutting it herself to keep it tidy and pretty would certainly pay off in here. She felt a prod in her back and swung round to face an enormous, acned teenager of mixed race.

'Yes, can I help you?'

The girl's response was swift and hostile.

'You is in my seat!' she snarled through gritted teeth.

'Oh, right, and who might you be?'

Kate had years of practice at hiding fear and

44

remaining calm; she knew it best not to rise to any provocation. Her heart beat loudly against her ribs nonetheless. Was this going to be her first sticky moment? She smiled at the girl as though she were engaging a lost six-year-old she had found wandering alone in the local supermarket.

'Janeece.'

'Well, Janeece, it is very nice to meet you. I'm Kate.'

She held out her hand.

The girl reluctantly unfurled her own fingers and extended her palm. Kate shook it and Janeece quickly pulled away, not used to physical contact.

'Firstly, Janeece, I think that this seat belongs to anyone that wants it, and secondly, you say, "you *are* in my seat" and not "you *is* in my seat"; do you hear the difference?'

Struck dumb, Janeece appraised the middle-aged woman who looked like a teacher and spoke like Mary Poppins. She nodded.

Kate continued. 'I'm just about to start *Under the Greenwood Tree* by Thomas Hardy. Have you read it?'

Janeece shook her head.

'Nah. I don't *do* readin'.'

'Well, that is a great shame, Janeece. You are missing out on a million different worlds that you could visit, which when your own world consists of these grim walls, might be a good thing to do. Why is it that you don't "do" reading?'

The girl stared at her and, without responding,

bit her bottom lip, angry, embarrassed and ashamed. Her likely response floated into Kate's mind as surely as if Janeece had spoken the words out loud: *'Because I'm not very good at it. I don't read because I can't read very well, I don't know all the words . . .'*

'Did your mother or your teacher never read you a book? My daughter used to love that.'

Janeece shook her head slightly, to indicate 'no' and also to banish the image of her mother, the slapping flat hand with the long nails that scratched, her voice like a machine gun in her head: *'You are a fat, useless piece of shit; you are nothing and you will always be nothing, just like your shit of a father.'*

'Would you like me to read it to you?'

Kate showed her the cover.

'Wha'?'

Janeece pulled her head back on her shoulders. Was this woman mad? Did she look like a baby that wanted story time?

'I said, would you like me to read it to you? It's a lovely story, I think you'll like it! But, Janeece, be warned, once you fall in love with Hardy it can become a bit of an addiction. We would then have to progress to *Far from*, and *Tess* of course.'

Without speaking, Janeece sloped around the table and pulled out the chair opposite Kate's.

'How much of it are you goin' to read?'

Maybe she would listen, just for a bit.

'Oh, Janeece, I am going to read all of it, cover to cover, word for word; all of it! Not eighty or so words here and there, but all of it and then, if I

46

like, I might go right back to the beginning and read it all over again!'

'But you'd already know what 'appens!'

Janeece shook her head as though it was Kate that had misunderstood the concept of book reading.

'Oh, I've already read it many times. But that's the lovely thing about books; they are never the same twice. Every time I read this story I picture something different, learn something new, and the ending always takes me slightly by surprise. It's like heading to a particular destination, but taking a different route each time you go. That way you see and feel new things each time you travel, and when you arrive, it's always a bit of a mystery quite how you ended up there! So, Janeece, would you like to go on this journey with me?'

The girl considered this.

'Awright. But most people in here don' mix with me cos I'm dangerous.'

'Well, I am not most people and I think we can all be a bit dangerous, when provoked. Now, are you sitting comfortably, as they say?'

'What you in for?'

'Janeece, are we going to start this book or not?'

'Yeah, but I wanna know what you's in for. I wanna know who I'm mixin' wiv.'

'I don't know why it is important, but if you insist. I am here because I killed someone. I stabbed my husband with a very sharp knife and I watched him bleed to death. I just sat and watched until he gurgled his last breath. He tried to ask for help, tried to beg, but I didn't listen to his pleas and I certainly wasn't going to help him.'

Kate was trying to earn her stripes.

'Why d'you do that?'

The girl was all ears. Bingo!

Kate leant across the table and whispered conspiratorially, 'He wasn't very nice to me, Janeece.'

Janeece had nothing more to say.

Kate began:

To dwellers in a wood almost every species of tree has its voice as well as its feature. At the passing of the breeze the fir-trees sob and moan no less distinctly than they rock; the holly whistles as it battles with itself; the ash hisses amid its quiverings; the beech rustles while its flat boughs rise and fall. And winter, which modifies the note of such trees as shed their leaves, does not destroy its individuality.

Remembering the day she introduced Janeece to reading always gave Kate a small swell of pride. Yes, she was in here, her skin slowly greying from the lack of fresh air and good veg, but that really didn't matter in the great scheme of things. What mattered was each small difference she could make to someone else's life.

Her cell door was ajar and Kate became aware of a presence in the doorway. Janeece's Herculean form stood blocking the light, a piece of A4 paper clutched in her hand.

'Is everything all right, dear?'

It was rare for the girl to come to Kate's cell; the two usually met in the reading room or in class. Kate couldn't accurately read her expression.

'I did it, Kate! I bloody did it!'

Janeece's tears clogged her nose and throat; she hadn't cried in years. Her childhood had taught her that crying was futile, but this was different, these were tears of joy.

Kate jumped up, knowing instantly what she was talking about.

'Oh, my love! Well? What did you get?'

The excitement bubbled from her.

'I got an A star in English and an A in French and a B in Maths. I did it, Kate! I can't believe it, but I bloody did it!'

Kate rushed forward and took the girl into her arms, cradling her bulk as best she could. She spoke into her scalp.

'I am so proud of you, Janeece! I really am!'

'I find it hard, but that won't stop me. I'm going to be the very best that I can, even if it isn't easy.'

'Nothing worth having ever is, love, and when you leave here, Janeece, you have a very bright future. It's like you said: if you try, you can be whatever you want to be. It's up to you now. All the hours you have worked, it will all pay off. You have conquered the hardest part, believing in yourself! Look at how much you have changed, how far you have come. The rest should be a walk in the park and you won't be alone. I'll be there for you.'

'It's all because of you, Kate. You changed my life, an' it's all because of you. I had nothing and now I have something. I'm gonna go to university and I will be someone and it is all because of you.'

She whispered into her teacher's shoulder, the words inaudible to anyone else, but Kate heard them, loud and clear.

TEN YEARS AGO

'Morning, Mrs Brooker.'

'Good morning, Mrs Bedmaker.'

The boys spoke simultaneously – only a knowing ear could decipher or distinguish between the two greetings. Both boarders smiled through their fashionably long fringes. Kathryn had much preferred it when regulations had required boys' hair to be worn above the collar and over the ear, feeling that this better prepared them for the conformity of the workplace. But she knew enough about teenagers to keep such thoughts to herself.

The two ambled along in no hurry to get to wherever they were heading, vigorously bumping shoulders in order to send the other skittering off the path, which made them laugh. If one were to topple over, that would be hilarious. With grubby, dog-eared books in hands, shirts hanging outside their trousers, ties a little too loose about the neck and jersey sleeves rolled up, it told her all she needed to know about how they viewed her.

Had it been Mark or one of the stricter masters outside that morning, they would have been tucking and smoothing, hiding and straightening. Not for her, though; no such courtesy for her.

She smiled at them: two sweet boys. They had been at Mountbriers since they were in single digits and she had watched them grow into these teenagers full of life, fun and promise. As ever, a flurry of emotions swirled through her: she was happy that they saw her as 'soft' and felt relaxed in her presence, but sad that they felt able to mock her by calling her 'Mrs Bedmaker', probably considering her too slow to notice. They were wrong; she always noticed. Always.

She removed the dolly pegs from her mouth and smiled as though oblivious.

'Good morning, boys! Lovely day today. On your way to lessons?'

They nodded.

'What have you got first period, anything interesting?'

'Classics, worse luck. Really boring.' Luca answered for them both.

None of the trio heard Mark tread the shingle in his soft soles; he approached the washing line at which his wife laboured with something bordering stealth.

'*Boring*, Mr Petronatti? Did I hear you refer to a fine and informative subject like Classics as *boring*?'

'No, sir! Well, yes, I did, sir! It is, but not when you teach it!' Luca scrambled to verbal safety using flattery as his rope and harness.

'I am jolly glad to hear it, Luca. Am I right in assuming that you are both heading back to your boarding house to get properly dressed? Not sure Mr Middy would like to hear of extra duties being handed out to Peters House boys for inappropriate dress, and I'm quite sure he would not have let you come over to main school so shabbily attired. What did you do? Wait until he had finished roll call and then leg it out the back door after breakfast?'

The boys sniggered into their palms; that was *exactly* what they had done.

'Thought as much.' Mark nodded in jest.

Without a word, they turned a hundred and eighty degrees on the path. With straight backs and heads held high, they began retracing their steps.

'Did you catch the match last night, boys?' the headmaster shouted at their backs.

They turned their heads as they continued walking away.

'Oh, sir! It was gutting. We were robbed!'

'Aha! Just goes to show that even with all that fancy Italian footwork, we can still whoop you!'

'You got lucky, sir, that's all!'

'Is that right? And by the way, boys, if you are trying to use the correct football lingo, it is "we *was* robbed" – only ever "we *were* robbed" if talking cricket. Got it?'

The two laughed even harder as they quickened their pace towards the dorms. They loved him. All the kids did.

Mark brushed past his wife and wandered towards the rose bed that formed the waist-high perimeter at the back of their private garden. With hands on hips he surveyed the scene in front of him. The house sat as a separate wing to the Upper School, with a large patch of immaculate lawn overlooking the main sports fields. The school itself was Gothic in places, but largely Georgian in construction. The main administration block reminded Kathryn of an oversized doll's house with its four large, symmetrically placed square windows and panelled front door with lion's-mouth knocker. She sometimes imagined removing the front completely and moving the little dolls around inside. The classrooms were spread around two main quadrangles and there was a beautiful early-nineteenth-century chapel.

It was one of those fine English establishments whose every angle offered a postcard opportunity and whose character and history were far more impressive than the day-to-day running would have you believe. It had a reputation for being elitist, proud and superior, and with good reason. Mountbriers Academy was a centre of excellence in many subjects, from science to art. Its alumni included high-ranking military men, prime ministers, scientists and medics of note; attending the school therefore carried its own pressures.

The school's elaborate gold emblem, with eagle wings spreading behind it and the Latin motto beneath – *Veritas Liberabit Vos*; Truth Shall Set You

Free – adorned not only all sports kit and blazers, but also bags, vehicles and even the school bins; everything was similarly stamped. The school did not miss an opportunity to advertise the elitist symbol that set its pupils apart. In Finchbury and its surrounds it was instantly recognisable as a badge of privilege that few could aspire to. Not that the paying parents minded; it was all part of a carefully orchestrated PR campaign to keep the fees rolling in.

Gone were the days when it was all down to a recommendation from an old boy and a strenuous entrance exam; days when many a titled family would pace their panelled hall and snap at the staff, waiting anxiously for the cream, crest-embossed envelope whose contents would either smooth their son's path through life or hamper it.

Nowadays it was all very different. As long as your parents had the requisite bank balance, you too could run amok wearing a rugby shirt that would normally cost fourteen pounds, but once embroidered with the Mountbriers logo had to be purchased from the school shop for a shade under forty.

A more shocking fact for many Old Mountbrierens was that the school now allowed the female of the species to attend. The offspring of newly moneyed families desperate for social elevation, the children of oligarchs with their eyes on European prizes, and Trustafarians whose Right Honourable parents wore extra jerseys to stave off the damp in their crumbling, country piles – all now rubbed shoulders along the portrait-lined corridors and ivy-clad walkways, each step reinforcing just how very fortunate they were.

Mark hummed an excerpt from his favourite Tchaikovsky overture, 'Romeo and Juliet', the only one he knew. Stepping forward and removing a pair of nail scissors from his inside pocket, he snipped the head off a full-bloomed rose. It was one of Kathryn's favourite varieties, a blushing pink called 'Change of Heart'.

Kathryn tucked in her lips and bit down, a physical trick she employed to stem the words of dissent that often gathered behind her tongue. It was easier that way. She quietly winced, calculating that the flower would have remained beautiful for another week or so, maybe ten days at a push, without a rough wind to shake its darling buds. It would now wither and die within the hour. Mark tucked the cutting into his button-hole and lifted his lapel to inhale the scent; satisfied, he bent again and with great deliberation removed a second flower. Turning to his wife, he held out his hand, presenting her with the gift.

'*Amor vitae meae*.' His voice was low and clipped.

Love of my life. Kathryn didn't lift her eyes from the ground, but took the proffered flower between her thumb and forefinger. Mark placed his index finger under her chin and raised her face until she looked him in the eye.

'That's better, my wonderful wife. Now I can see your lovely face properly. What do you say?' he prompted. 'What do you say for the gift of a rose?'

'Thank you,' she offered in a whisper.

He lowered her head and kissed the top of her scalp.

'Oh my God, you two lovebirds, get a room!'

Their fifteen-year-old daughter mimed retching as she walked past, weighed down beneath a rucksack full of books. Her skinny legs appeared to dangle in their black tights, and her long, dark hair was full of knots and styling product; again, the correct look of the day, and not to be remarked on.

It amused Kathryn to see how far the children would go to push the limits of 'acceptable uniform wearing'. To the untrained eye, even with a sleeve rolled up, a tie in an unconventional knot or a pair of non-regulation tights, all the pupils looked identical. No matter how scruffily they dressed or how they slouched and swore, they couldn't shake the stamp of privilege and the whiff of money that followed in their designer-styled wake.

Kathryn ignored her daughter's comment.

'Are you home for supper, Lydia, or have you got art club?'

'Dunno. I'll let you know.'

'Okay, darling. Fine. Have a great day. And please make sure you eat lunch.'

'I'll walk with you, Lyds. Hang on a mo, I just need to fetch my case.'

Mark was happy for the opportunity to catch up with his little girl. His hectic schedule meant time alone with either of their children was precious.

'No, please don't, Dad. I'm meeting Phoebe and it is just too uncool to arrive at lessons with you.'

'Uncool? I've never heard anything like it!' He feigned hurt. 'I'm a very hip and happening dad, I'll have you know!' He laughed at her scorn.

'Oh my God, please shut up! If you were either of those things then you would know not to say "hip" and "happening" for a start! You are both so embarrassing, firstly snogging in public and then trying to be my mate; it is just so cringey! Why can't I have normal parents? Just for once I'd like a boring mum and dad like everyone else's, ones that didn't make everything so awkward!'

Her mother interjected. 'It was hardly snogging, Lydia.'

No one heard her.

The head and his daughter disappeared around the corner. The echo of their playful banter drifted back in fragmented syllables, interspersed with squeals; it was all jolly good fun. Kathryn tucked in her lips and bit down hard.

Left alone in the garden to continue with her chores, Kathryn wondered what it must be like to have a place that you needed to get to – an office, a shop, a classroom – and what it might be like to be the kind of person that people would miss if you disappeared.

Aware of the flower in her hand, she squeezed

the rose until the sap dripped from the petals and ran down her wrist, its heady perfume offering her a few seconds of joy. It wilted in the middle of her scrunched-up palm. Walking to the flower bed, where its siblings and cousins stood proud and tall, she scooped out a handful of soil, placed the rose in the hole, and buried it.

With her hands now free and wiped clean on her apron, she turned her attention to the laundry. She secured one corner of the sheet, then pulled the other end taut and fastened it with another wooden dolly peg.

The peg was one of a set that she had owned for ever, possibly since she was a little girl. She didn't know for certain when they had been passed on to her, but she knew they came from her mother's pantry. She could clearly picture the metal box in which they had been kept, with its image of straight-backed, marching toy soldiers on the lid. Her mother had in turn been given them by her own mother. For some reason Mark had allowed her to keep them; they were probably too insignificant to warrant his attention.

Over the years she had acquired and discarded many a set of lurid plastic pegs with fiddly little springs which often perished before the end of their useful life, but these long wooden splints with their bulbous heads and precision, hand-cut splits would outlive them all. She would in time hand them on to Lydia. The thought made her chuckle; she could imagine Lydia rolling her eyes at the prospect of inheriting a set of pegs. As a little girl, Lydia had shown an interest in them once, carefully selecting a random peg and using a big, fat, black felt-tipped pen to draw two dots for eyes and the upward curve of a smile. Kathryn had named that particular peg Peggy, and it still made her smile on a daily basis. Maybe when Lydia was older she would feel differently; goodness knows, her own views were now so very altered from when she had been her daughter's age.

In the early days of her marriage, Kathryn remembered feeling comforted by the knowledge that she was probably the third generation to handle these funny little objects. She often considered the clothes that had been held fast; three generations of garments in which her family had slept, worked and loved. She would finger the end of the splint, wondering if it had touched her grandpa's work shirt or her mum's silk slip.

She often wondered if her mother and grandmother had derived as much joy as she did from a line strung full of clean laundry. The anticipation of gathering it in huge armfuls and inhaling its fresh, blown-dry scent was itself a unique pleasure. The folding and smoothing of clean garments was satisfying and used to give her a feeling of great contentment. The washing and ironing of clothes had been tangible proof of a family life lived in harmony.

The pleasure she used to take in doing the laundry had, however, been removed from her the day she got married, seventeen years and five months ago. These days there was no joy in this daily ritual, none at all. Apart from her two children, there was very little joy in her life, full stop.

Kathryn knew that her nickname was Mrs Bedmaker; she had known it for some time, having heard it muttered behind cupped hands and seen it scrawled in chalk and pen on various surfaces, including the underside of a desk and the back of a loo door in the junior common room. She was called it regularly by the more daring children, each hoping that she would not hear and would not comment. Of course she never did 'hear' or comment, giving them the confidence to continue. She didn't mind too much; she had more to worry about than that on a daily basis, much more.

On better days, she could find humour in the fact that the rumour mill among the pupils had it laid down as fact that she was a sex maniac who insisted on indulging in a wild and frantic love life on a nightly basis. Why else would there be the constant need for the laundering of bed linen? Nudge, nudge, wink, wink . . . Saucy Mrs Brooker, lucky Mr Brooker. Was that why she always looked so exhausted, so weak, and he so happy, so smug?

She would sometimes stare at her reflection, pondering her skinny frame and nervous expression, her pale demeanour, the dark circles under her eyes, her cellist's fingers with their square-cut nails and her blunt-bobbed haircut. Pulling her olive-coloured cardigan over her linen skirt, she would think, *That's me, a regular sex kitten.*

Kathryn wandered back into the kitchen, reluctantly abandoning the warmth of the early-morning sun, and started to clear the breakfast things from the scrubbed pine table that dominated the room.

A marmalade-smeared plate and an empty coffee mug were the only evidence that her son Dominic still lived under their Georgian roof. Their interactions were minimal, so she welcomed these little reminders that he was still around, living in the same space, even if she hadn't actually seen him. At the moment he appeared to be playing the role of a reluctant lodger who sought the solace of his own room at every opportunity. The truth, she suspected, was that he was probably sneaking off to the comfort of someone else's room at every opportunity, someone in the girls' dorm. She was pretty sure it was Emily Grant who was the latest object of his affections, but there was no point commenting or getting involved – it would be another identikit, glossy-haired lovely in a few weeks' time. This seemed to be how it worked nowadays.

There were many aspects of her son's life, not just his courtship rituals, that Kathryn simply did not understand. Far from disapprove, however, she was in fact happy for him, happy for both of her children. Delighted that they were living busy, joyful lives, full of fun and excitement, with a host of possibilities ahead. She needed to know that this was how it was and that there was a whole world out there for them to grab with both hands and run with; otherwise, what was the point?

The Brooker family had lived in the house for seven years, having moved there in the September when Mark had been promoted from head of year to headmaster. It was a wonderful achievement, the youngest head of school ever to be appointed. It meant a happy life for her and her family; this had to be true because everyone had told her so, even her sister, Francesca. Kathryn had detected the vaguest hint of jealousy and for Francesca to be jealous, it most certainly had to be true.

She knew that the outside world saw her as the fortunate Kathryn Brooker, living a fulfilling life in a lovely two-hundred-year-old house with her perfect family and a rosy future. Many envied her charmed existence, her prestige and her material wealth. Not to mention that she had bagged the rather hand-some Mark Brooker – the girl had definitely been punching above her weight on *that* day. This amused Kathryn, knowing that if they walked in her sensible shoes for a day and a night, they would be clam-ouring to escape, clawing at the flint stones until their fingernails ripped away, scrambling over the walls until knees were raw, and digging with bare, bloodied hands at the very foundations to make a tunnel. They would try anything and stop at nothing to be free of the charmed life she led.

There was something about living in a school house on school grounds in a building that was

63

joined on to the school that meant that she never quite felt like it was hers. Which was quite right – it wasn't. The majority of the time, Kathryn felt more like a curator or custodian than a home-maker. She took extra care of the blackened range, original window cording and parquet flooring, as if she would be judged on the state in which she kept this venerable property and the state in which she handed it back. This of course is exactly how history would have judged her, had some other more significant and somewhat more shocking event not occurred, rendering the cleanliness of her windows and their dust-free cording quite irrelevant.

The children had been young when they moved in and it had taken a while for them all to get used to the new set-up. Lydia could no longer run around 'nudey dudey' after her bath, not with masters and pupils dropping in unannounced. And Dominic had had to say a reluctant goodbye to his beloved pet chickens, Nugget and Kiev; the prospect of having to repeatedly retrieve them as they pecked around the cricket crease could not be countenanced. Once had been enough to cause much annoyance to the visiting Millfield eleven, who to this day were convinced it had been a clever tactic to divert and conquer.

Those youngsters were now teenagers, Lydia fifteen and Dominic sixteen. Being the headmaster's children meant that you were either extremely popular or unpopular for all the wrong reasons.

Thankfully for the Brooker children, they had already been at the school for a number of years prior to their dad's appointment as head honcho, so they were established and accepted. It also helped that they were both considered attractive by their peers. They had inherited Kathryn's rangy physique and the striking face of their father translated very well onto those sharp, young cheekbones. They were funny, cool kids who were well liked, regardless of their parents' status.

Mark, of course, flourished in such an environment, constantly in character and always ready to perform. He engaged in banter with the children and displayed the jovial camaraderie that made him a hit with the masters. He appeased and buttered up the parents, offering a firm handshake to the wealthy fathers and all the time in the world to discuss minutiae with the coiffed and toned mummies. He was in complete control of all he surveyed, a very happy man.

Kathryn, however, upon taking up residence in the 'big house', had felt her refuge diminish until it was non-existent. Earlier in Mark's career, when they had lived in rented accommodation in Finchbury, she at least could spend the daytimes away from his obsessive gaze. Until he returned from school, there was no one to watch her, no eyes waiting to see how she did things, what she wore, what she said or ate, who she sat with, spoke to, when she arrived and when she left. Life in the head's house was very different; the list of things that were forbidden, permitted and expected was long and ever changing. It was in this fluid environment of constant scrutiny that she existed. 'Existed' was the word Kathryn used when thinking about her situation – 'lived' would imply that she had a life, and she did not. Kathryn had no life at all.

As she scraped the breakfast detritus into the bin and loaded the plates into the dishwasher with the rest of the china, her mind flitted back to the early hours of that Thursday morning in June, nineteen years ago. She had been twenty-one, her sister Francesca nineteen. They were both still living at home with their parents, occupying adjacent bedrooms in the cramped, semi-detached house.

Kathryn had padded into Francesca's room and gently shaken the blanket-wrapped shoulder of her sleeping sibling. She hadn't wanted to wake her, but knew if she didn't share the news that was threatening to burst from her, she would very probably explode.

'Francesca, are you asleep?'

'Mmmmnnnn . . . Go away . . .' Francesca mumbled.

'Wake up! I really need to tell you something.'

Even in her semi-conscious fog, Francesca knew from her sister's tone that resistance was futile. She reached out an arm and snapped the lamp on the bedside table into life.

'For God's sake, Katie, this better be good.'

Rubbing her eyes, she focussed on her sister's blushing face.

'Well, go on then!'

Francesca's irritable prompting rather robbed her of her moment, but she proceeded nonetheless.

'Guess what?'

'What?'

'Francesca, you're supposed to guess! Come on!'

'For God's sake, Katie, you're really annoying me now! We're not children any more; it's three o'clock in the bloody morning. I've got to be up for work in three hours. So, you either tell me now why you've woken me up or bugger off and leave me alone!'

'Okay, grumpy, you are not going to believe this, but Mark has asked me to marry him!'

Kathryn clapped her hands together and let the news hang in the air. Francesca reached over and located her glasses, perching them on the tip of her nose. She leant forward as though improved visual focus would help her mentally focus as well.

'He has asked you to *marry* him?'

'Yes! Can you believe it?'

Her sister thought for a few seconds. 'Frankly, no. I thought you were going to say you'd shagged him.'

'Oh for goodness sake, Fran, you are so gross! Isn't it wonderful?'

'Truthfully, honey? I don't know.'

'What do you mean, you don't know?'

'I mean . . . Look, Katie, I love you, but you are a bit like a character in a *Famous Five* novel who doesn't realise that there is a big bad world out there. Even though I'm the youngest, I've always felt as if you needed my protection. We all do, in fact.'

'Do you?' It wasn't exactly news to her that Francesca felt that she was a total idiot, but her parents as well?

'Yeah, kind of. And this Mark . . . It's great that you're so happy, but he's your first proper boyfriend, you've only known him five minutes, and you haven't even, you know . . . Sex is very important!'

'Oh for goodness sake, there has to be more to a relationship than sex!'

'There does? Okay, don't look like that, I'm kidding, kind of. I am happy if you are happy, but I don't think that you should be rushing into anything.'

'Actually we have been going out for three and a half months and I love him, Fran, and he loves me.'

Kathryn chose not to divulge the frenzied kissing and aggressive smooching that left her more excited and alive than she had ever felt. This she knew boded well for a satisfying love life in the future.

'Blurgh! Pass the bucket!'

Kathryn punched her sister on the arm.

'I'm truly chuffed for you, sis, but there's

something about Mark that I'm not quite sure about . . .'

'What do you mean?' Kathryn's voice was a high-pitched squeal, she looked close to tears.

Francesca decided to backtrack.

'Oh, I don't know. Maybe it's just that I haven't got to know him yet or maybe he isn't relaxed with us because it's all new for him as well.'

These words caused Kathryn to brighten again. Yes, that would be it.

'All I am saying is, Katie, why don't you have a long engagement, get the sex out of the way, get to know each other a bit and see how it works out. Worst-case scenario, you get to keep the rock; best-case scenario, you end up with the love of your life!'

'I don't have to wait or have a long engagement. Mark *is* the love of my life, he is so gorgeous and he feels the same, we just know.'

'How do you "just know"? Do you remember how much you loved jacket potatoes when you were little and then you discovered pasta and *that* became your favourite? Maybe Mark is your jacket potato?'

'Oh for God's sake, he is not my jacket potato! I can't explain it, but we *do* know. Mark says why wait if we have found what we would only spend our future searching for. It would be like wasting years, only to reach the conclusion that we were right all along!'

'Well, mate, when you put it like that!'

'I know you're taking the mick out of me, but I don't care, Fran, not tonight.'

'Katie, I am pleased for you, but can't you just have a nice little love affair and see if it wears off? Just in case?'

'Mark says we should jump in while the water's warm!'

'"Mark says", "Mark says . . .". Blimey, Katie, you want to be careful there.'

'What do you mean, "be careful"? Why?'

She couldn't hide the slight irritation in her voice; she was in the first stages of love and any negativity directed at the object of her desire felt like daggers being plunged into her heart.

'Because you are a strong, smart girl and I don't want you to lose any bit of yourself, ever. No man is worth that.'

This was a phrase that Kathryn replayed in her mind many times in the coming years. She should have listened to her baby sister, wise and prophetic beyond her years. She wished she had listened.

She replayed it now as she studied the hand-painted mug in her hand. *'I don't want you to lose any bit of yourself, ever.'* What would she say to her sister now? She imagined trying to phrase the words. They saw each other so infrequently that when they did meet up, there was always an awkward hour or so when they had to relearn how to act in the other's company. It was so different from being with a friend or a colleague; being with a sister was unique.

It didn't matter what either of them achieved or how much time passed, it was hard for Kathryn to play the role of contented grown-up, to deceive. Not when they shared so much history. Francesca knew her sister back to front, inside out. There were so many fond memories that they used to retell over and over until they became hysterical with laughter. Kathryn's favourite was about one night during a childhood holiday, the two of them top-to-toeing in a rusty Cornish caravan, aged six and eight. They had eaten so much chocolate that Kathryn threw up out of the window, only to discover that the window was closed. Her parents spent the best part of the next day hosing Caramac from the velour interior of their rented home.

Part of their awkwardness now was down to the fact that Mark never left them alone for a second; it was as if he was monitoring them, making them mindful of their conversation. He was careful to steer them onto topics that he felt were appropriate, and he was always slightly anxious until after her sister left. His nerves were not obvious to anyone else, but Kathryn noted that he spoke a little quicker than usual and laughed a little too loudly. He needn't have been concerned; she could never have told. She would never have told.

It was all too difficult. What would she like to say to her sister? *'You were right, Fran, I should have listened to you because I haven't just lost a bit of myself, I have lost all of myself. I wish I'd listened to you, but I didn't, did I?'*

It was so easy with the wonderful gift of hindsight to be the judge and juror of her past decisions and choices. So easy to look at the person that made those decisions and the person that she had become and spot the cracks, pondering on how she might have done things differently. *Of course I should have listened to my sister! But I thought that I knew different, I was giddy, blinded and thought that I knew best.* What would hindsight say? It would say, *'You definitely did not know best, Kathryn, you could not have known best, you were too busy fighting a tide of raging hormones and infatuation.'*

Kathryn closed her eyes tightly to try and erase the memory of the last telephone call she had had from her sister. Three weeks later, it still weighed heavily on her mind and she wondered if she would ever be able to repair the damage.

'Kathryn.' Mark's voice had summoned her.

She had been peeling the potatoes for supper, but instinctively she rose from the chair at the sound of his voice, a soldier trained to stand to attention upon the arrival of a superior. After all these years it was now automatic.

'It's your sister on the telephone.'

He flashed a short flickered smile that appeared and disappeared in a matter of seconds. It told her that he was not happy to have Francesca on the end of the telephone at all and was even more irritated to have had his 'study time' interrupted by having to answer the call and come and inform her.

She nodded and walked over to the wall-mounted phone above the dishwasher.

'Hello?'

She waited for the click of the receiver being replaced into its cradle in the study, but it never came. Mark was listening and would continue listening to their entire conversation, as was customary. It had been two months since the sisters had been in touch and now with her husband's monitoring, Kathryn knew that the conversation would again be stilted and uncomfortable as she would have to censor all that she said. She knew her sister would pick up on this and think that she was being aloof. Kathryn once again felt trapped and more than a little tearful.

Francesca had accused her of being a bit 'off' in the past, which had rendered Kathryn dumb, unable to explain that there was so much that she wanted to say, but couldn't, for many reasons. The first being that their conversation was never private; Mark would be listening and, more importantly, judging.

'Oh, Kate, I had to call you—' Her sister's voice immediately broke away in a sob.

'It's okay, it's okay. Oh goodness, Francesca, don't cry! What on earth is the matter?'

Kathryn could hear rain against a window and the whoosh of water as tyres sped along wet tarmac. She pictured Francesca sitting in her car with her cardigan around her shoulders to ward off the North Yorkshire chill.

She waited while Francesca blew her nose loudly.

'Oh Kate, something terrible has happened!'

'What's happened? Is Luke all right?' Kathryn's first thoughts were always of her own children; the worst thing that could happen would be something affecting them, and so naturally she thought immediately of her sister's child.

Kathryn recognised in her sister the slight guilt of a mother who had pushed her son to achieve; it was always with a dose of pressure that he would be encouraged to study for exams and cram for extra credits. The fees that they paid quarterly for his education were hard to come by and his time at school was for them in lieu of foreign holidays, new carpets, even trips to the hairdresser.

Kathryn admired the sacrifice but knew that Francesca wanted something in return: good grades, a place at a top university or at the very least a voice that was crystal clear with rounded vowels, and the correct pressure of handshake in the right circles. Luke didn't disappoint, he was diligent and industrious, a lovely boy.

It would be unfair to describe Francesca as jealous, but Kathryn knew she was conscious of her own position as wife of the head teacher at one of the country's top public schools. It was important for her sister to feel every bit her equal when they chatted about school life in general at any gathering, knowing that her Luke was just as good as his cousins.

Kathryn laughed at the idea that her family considered her to lead a charmed life in her subsidised house with her attentive man and her perfect children. If only they knew . . .

'No . . . No, thankfully it's nothing like that, no one is hurt, but the business has folded. We tried so hard, Katie, we've been keeping the bank and all the suppliers at arm's length for a while and it's finally collapsed. I'm so disappointed for Luke, for us all. Gerry and I thought we were building for his future, but we have lost everything.'

Francesca paused to gulp back a sob.

'We sank every penny into the new building company. We thought Luke would step into his dad's shoes when the time was right, we thought it was going to set him up for life, but the developer was a charlatan, Kate, a total con artist. I still can't believe it! We might even lose the house . . .'

'Oh, Fran! That's terrible; I know how excited you all were . . .'

Kathryn knew that her sister's share of their parents' legacy had been the primary funding for Gerry's business. Their dad had worked so hard all his life. Infrequent trips to the seaside at Abersoch were his treat, but beyond that he had saved and saved to finally own a three-bedroomed semi-detached slice of Croydon, now all gone . . .

What to say next, Kathryn? What she wanted to say was, *'My poor darling, my poor little sister, that is the most terrible news. Come here for a few days,*

75

all of you and let me look after you and spoil you. We can drink tea and make a plan. Nothing is as bad as it seems right now and whilst I can't make it all go away, it will be good if you can get away from it all. Luke can spend time with Dom and Lyds and we can stay up late like we used to and drink wine and chat. It will all be okay, darling, because I am your big sister and I can make it feel better . . .' Instead, she heard a faint sigh from Mark, losing patience at the end of his receiver in the study, and she heard herself speak, staccato and automatic.

'Well if there is anything you need, *do* shout. Mark and I will of course do anything we can to help.'

Kathryn used Mark's name to ingratiate herself, hoping he recognised her loyalty. She listened to her sister's silence. She could picture Francesca replaying her words in her head with incredulity: '*Do shout?*'

She tried to fill the void with the first thing that popped into her head.

'What's the weather like in York?'

Her words were banal and regretful. A small tear trickled down her cheek. She willed her baby sister to hear her unspoken apology.

Francesca could not contain her surprise or disappointment.

'*What's the weather like in York?* Did you not hear what I said, Kathryn? We have lost everything! Everything! And you want to talk about the bloody *weather?*'

76

'I . . . I . . .'

Kathryn's tears fell thick and fast as she tried to find the words, the words that would please everyone, the words that would appease and comfort her darling sister in her moment of need and would not incur the wrath of her husband. Sadly, there were no such words.

'You know what, Kate, forget it, forget I called and forget my news. We will manage just fine. You sit tight in your four-bedroomed Georgian splendour and enjoy your bloody coffee mornings and your view of the cricket pitch and we will figure this out for ourselves!'

'Francesca, I—' She tried to interrupt her sister.

'No, don't bother saying another word. I am finished with you, not that either of us will notice much difference. You haven't been there for me for years; I guess I'm not in your league. Do you know what, Katie? I never thought that I would say this, but you think you are so high and mighty. You may have an idyllic little life, but I really don't like who or what you have become . . .'

Francesca let the phrase hang in the air as she ended the call. One small push of a button and she was gone, just like that.

Kathryn held the receiver between her palms and hung her head forward. She whispered through her tears, though no one was listening.

'Neither do I, my darling. Neither do I.'

Mark came through into the kitchen and placed his hand on her shoulder, alerting her to his presence and causing her to stand up straight and swallow her tears.

'Is everything all right, Kathryn? That sister of yours not been upsetting you, has she?'

She stared at his face, which did not betray the slightest indication that he had heard the whole exchange, and shook her head.

'No, Mark.'

'Well I'm jolly glad to hear that. We are very busy people with a great deal of responsibility and I don't want you worrying about anything that doesn't directly concern us.'

It was almost an instruction. He leant forward and kissed her long and hard, crushing her to him with his arm across her lower back. Her tears had caused her breathing to lose its natural rhythm; she had no choice but to hold her breath while he covered her mouth. Her head felt light, the threat of a faint pawed at her senses. It felt endless.

Finally, he released her.

'I tell you what, darling, why don't you pop upstairs and make yourself look neat and pretty and then you can put the kettle on and we shall have a cup of tea.'

Again she nodded, knowing that his suggestion was actually a direct order. She slowly climbed the stairs and tried to stem the flow of tears. Taking up her position at the dressing table, she replayed her sister's words in her head, *'You may have an idyllic little life, but I don't like who or what you have become.'* Oh yes, thought Kathryn. *I have an idyllic little life.*

'Only me!'

Judith's voice interrupted Kathryn's reliving of that dreadful phone call three weeks earlier. Mark's PA always announced her arrival in this way. She came through the back door and into the kitchen, which irritated Kathryn but was only one of a thousand things about Judith that irritated her. It was actually one of her smaller misdemeanours. Judith's chief offence was the way she referred to Mark as 'Headmaster', as though he were a person of such venerableness and status that he could be addressed in this way, like the Pope or Madonna. If only she knew what he was really like.

Judith was in her late forties, single and extremely overweight, but without any of the embarrassment or awkwardness that people of her size sometimes displayed. There was no clever dressing to minimise the contours, no opting for black, long or layered, oh no. Judith would happily wear a vest and a pair of khaki shorts, enjoying the stares and double-takes that came her way from pupils and staff alike. She would mistake their glances as interest and not revulsion.

'Morning, Kathryn! Lovely day!'

Kathryn nodded but didn't speak, looking up only briefly from the washing-up. She didn't feel like engaging, bantering with this woman about nothing. She didn't have the inclination or the energy; she figured correctly that the less she said, the quicker the exchange would be over.

'Headmaster has asked me to pop over to remind you that there is a masters' meeting tonight, *dans la cuisine*! So the usual, please: dips, chips, plonk et cetera and of course gluten-free for Mr Middy; we don't want a repeat of the swollen tongue and loose bowel episode that almost blighted the fifth-form careers fair last month. We've only just managed to get the carpet tiles in the junior common room replaced. Anyhoo, thought I'd better give you the heads up. All okay?'

'Yup, perfectly.'

It was the best Kathryn could offer. She disliked the way Judith treated her, as if she were an extension of Headmaster's retinue. It made her feel more like the hired caterer than the wife of said Headmaster. It didn't anger her any more; in fact she was almost glad of the diversion, knowing that to have her time filled with something – anything – was better than having time to think.

'Headmaster is in a rather jolly mood this morning. He's had several admiring comments about his floral accessory from the faculty. Whatever you gave him for breakfast, same again tomorrow please! Makes my life easier when he hasn't got his sore bear-head on!'

What should she say to that? *'It makes all our lives easier, Judith. You have no idea, Judith, of just how bad his sore bear-head can make my life. Leave*

80

me alone, Judith, you vacuous woman; leave me alone because you have no concept of what my life is like, of how I live.'

Instead, she smiled.

'Will do, Judith.'

She wasn't entirely sure what she was agreeing to, but knew that it would be enough to appease Judith, to make her feel that her errand and her messages had been understood, loud and clear.

In her meaner moments, Kathryn would think unpalatable thoughts about her unpopularity or her sickening fawning over Mark. This, however, would be quickly followed by, *How dare you offer up these thoughts when your own situation is so dire?* Then another thought would creep in: *I must be as thick as Mark says I am, otherwise how did I get myself into this bloody mess? I'm like one of those little bugs caught by a Venus flytrap and the irony is the more I wriggle the deeper I become entrenched. I am trapped.*

Kathryn wished that someone would offer her an escape, a way out. She often dreamed of freedom in a different time and place. She could only bear to contemplate a solution that was simple, having no capacity or inclination for anything complex. Yet no matter how hard she tried, a simple solution would not present itself. Every idea, every permutation, left her homeless and away from her children. Homeless she could just about manage, but living without her children and not being there to defend them, should . . .

if . . . *That* she could not manage. Her kids would always be an extension of her own heartbeat, the best thing she had ever done. She could not, would not contemplate a life without them.

Kathryn's grandmother had been an upright, slender harridan whose clothes and manner anchored her firmly in the Victorian era. Despite her humble beginnings and a life of hard graft in the East End of London, she exuded an air of grandeur that belied the poverty in which she had been raised. Kathryn remembered giving her the news that she was to marry Mark Brooker. Her granny's response had made her laugh although it didn't seem quite so funny now.

'My dear, think very carefully about this match. You should of course always make sure that you marry outside your postcode, but never outside your class. Your father went to university and that makes you a somebody. I'm afraid that just because young Master Brooker has ideas above his station does not instantly make it so. It makes things so much neater when you know the same people and have the same standard of table manners.'

It was still funny in one sense, that Mark's lack of understanding of what cutlery to use, that he regularly said 'tea' instead of 'dinner' and expressed a preference for UPVC over timber-framed windows was actually the least of her concerns.

Kathryn thought as she often did of Natasha; even the memory of her gave her mood a lift. Natasha had been a rare commodity in Kathryn's life.

For nearly three years, she had been her friend, her only friend. She was sure that it was Natasha's recent move to another school at the other end of the country that was partly responsible for the ever blackening cloud that seemed to hang over her head. She felt like a cartoon character who, when everyone else is bathed in sunshine, sits under their own portable rainstorm and, were it not for Acme umbrellas, would be soaked right through.

Natasha had gone to work in a school just outside York, teaching kids with special needs, helping them develop through expression in art. Kathryn thought it suited her much better than the jab and thrust of life at Mountbriers. She had moved to Alne and was living less than a mile away from Francesca. Something stopped Kathryn from putting the two in touch. It was partly that she did not want to share her friend with anyone, knowing that she would have found it unbearable to hear of them having fun together without her. But there was also the unacknowledged fear that the two might sit over a cup of coffee or a glass of plonk and discuss her life. They might compare notes and between them reach the conclusion that nobody wanted to hear, especially not Kathryn.

The day of Natasha's arrival in her life was one that she would never forget. It had been an assembly day and the great and the good had gathered in Big Hall for the headmaster's address and all the relevant notices. One or two pupils were decorated for achievements in music and foreign-verse speaking – the same four kids that were always honoured, in fact; kids whose talents were far reaching and renowned throughout the school. Kathryn was not convinced, however, that being able to speak Mandarin while fire juggling and completing a Rubik's cube in record time was adequate compensation for having no mates. Mark had been rambling so much, loving the sound of his own voice and a stage on which to use it, that he had lost the pupils and most of the staff after about fifteen minutes, and she couldn't recall the exact topic of his address now.

As the staff filed out of the double doors and into the quadrangle, Natasha made a beeline for Kathryn, who was standing by herself, loitering and unsure of how quickly she could scuttle off without seeming impolite. These things mattered in a school like this; one had to be seen to be doing the right thing, at the right time and in the right way. Timing was everything.

Kathryn watched the woman stride purposefully towards her and straightened her cardigan as she mentally prepared the answers to any questions that might be posed: *'Can you tell me where to find Art block C? What time is break? Where is the nearest staff loo?'* But their first interaction could not have been more surprising.

Kathryn saw both staff and pupils appraising Natasha as she walked away from them, quite unaware of the commotion she was causing – unaware or uncaring, Kathryn wasn't so sure now.

She wore a long, flowing, white cotton skirt and flat, clumpy sandals that looked like they had been made from recycled tyres and then painted pink. Her acid-green knitwear was unidentifiable as cardigan or jersey; it was more of a wool drape and was fastened at her shoulder with an enormous white flower. Her short brown hair was adorned with at least three hair clips, each with a sparkling butterfly attached – the sort of accessory you'd expect to find on a nine-year-old girl, but that was of no consequence to Natasha, who had seen them, liked them and so wore them. She was striking, different and fresh, and she looked lovely. It was as if she had not read the handbook of 'What teachers in a school like this are expected to wear' or, if she had, she had decided to disregard it. She made everyone and everything around her seem grey and dull and Kathryn would learn that this was something she achieved no matter what the occasion or the season. She was like light in a dark place.

'Hi there, I'm Natasha Mortensen. Today is my first day, Art and Design.' Her statement was confident and succinct.

'Oh, yes! I knew you were coming, well, not you per se, but a new tutor. It's very nice to meet you, Natasha. I'm Kathryn. Welcome to Mountbriers!'

The two shook hands briefly, both a little uncomfortable with such a masculine greeting.

'Thanks, Kathryn. I saw you in the hall and I have come to tell you that I've chosen you to be my friend because you look most like the sort of person that I would be friends with. Not like some of the antiques amongst that merry band. And what about that Mark Grade A Tosser Brooker! What an absolute arsehole! Does he ever shut up? Ye Gods – droning on and on. The kids were bored stupid, itching to escape, and I nearly nodded off twice! I can see that he and I are going to get along famously. Not!'

Kathryn was so taken aback with Natasha's directness that she couldn't think of anything to say. She wracked her brains, trying to remember what it was she'd overheard Mark saying about the new art teacher the night before. *'I'm rather over a barrel on this one,'* he'd complained. *'Max Whittington has asked me to give her a go; he thought she was the strongest candidate by far. I think he took a bit of a fancy to her and, as much as it grates, I can't risk him changing his mind about sponsoring the lower-sixth library refurbishment. Although if it was down to me, she wouldn't have made it past the gate; I've seen her sort before – a frightful and subversive lesbian.'* Kathryn thought he was probably right on that last point – for once. Though Natasha was clearly far from frightful.

Natasha continued, 'Don't look so stunned! I do that, Kathryn; I pick people to be my friends and they are stuck with me whether they like me back or not, I can't help it. I have always done it and the reasons that I pick my friends are often most spurious. If you don't believe me, you can ask Ellie

Simpson and Hannah Hartley. I picked them at primary school and they are still stuck with me now!'

'Why did you pick them?'

'Ellie has the most amazing smile ever and shared sweets with me, I now know that she will always share anything with anyone, she is pure goodness and Hannah has dimples and laughed like a drain, still does!'

'Why did you pick me?' Kathryn was curious.

'Mainly because you look like Mia Farrow, but more eye-catching. Plus you have something mysterious and aloof about you. Just by looking at your expression during assembly, I could tell that you felt the same as me about the whole carry-on; you looked like you wanted to be some-where else.'

Kathryn didn't reply, pursing her lips tightly to stop herself from blurting out that her new friend was absolutely right: she *always* wanted to be somewhere else. She laughed, however, in spite of herself. Mia Farrow? She could only think of her in the sixties, elfin and gorgeous, and that suited her very well. She took it as the compliment that it was intended to be.

Natasha hadn't paused for breath. 'So what do you teach, Kathryn, how long have you been here? Do you ever shorten Kathryn? It's a bit formal for a boho chick like you . . .'

'Kate,' she offered, as she was trying to work out which question to answer first, what a boho chick was and whether she liked being one or not. It was strange that the nickname of her youth sprang so readily to mind, reminding her of the person she used to be.

'Okay, Kate, yes, that's much better. So what do you teach, Kate?' Her new friend used the name twice, testing it out, making it familiar.

Kathryn brought her hand to her mouth in embarrassment. A familiar feeling swept over her: that she had no right to be there; she wasn't a teacher, she was merely an observer.

'Oh! I don't teach. Well, actually, I am qualified – English would be my subject – but I've never used it. Life kind of got in the way of my plans, babies and whatnot.' She gave a small giggle, hating how trite she sounded. 'No, I am in fact *Mrs* Grade A Tosser Brooker, Mark's wife.'

Most people would at that point have laughed, cried or covered their own mouth with embarrassment whilst apologising and over-explaining that it had all been a terribly misunderstood joke. But as Kathryn would discover, Natasha was not like most people. She put both of her hands on Kathryn's shoulders and looked into her eyes.

'Tough break, kid.'

And for that reason alone, although there would be many others quickly learned, Kathryn thought that Natasha was wonderful and was very glad that she had been chosen as her friend.

★ ★ ★

The rest of Kathryn's day was spent in a whirl of chores that included cleaning the French windows in the dining room, refreshing the flowers in the hall and study, buying and preparing the canapés for the evening masters' meeting and cooking the family supper. When these tasks were complete, Kathryn gathered her family laundry, ironed the sheets and placed them neatly in the linen cupboard to await their turn on the bed linen rota. By her reckoning, they would next be called for duty on Wednesday. Finally, just before 4.30 p.m., she sat at her dressing table and brushed her hair, then applied a little scent and rubbed some rouge into her pale cheeks. Then she changed into a rose pink linen skirt with a button-up cardigan, as per her husband's instructions to look 'feminine and understated' at all times.

Each afternoon at varying times, depending on the afterschool activity and season, Kathryn would sit at the white-painted dressing table with its triptych of mirrors and perform the task of making herself neat and pretty. The words of a sixties song would float into her head, unbidden, but with alarming regularity, like a pre-programmed alarm clock that she didn't know how to switch off:

> *Hey, little girl,*
> *Comb your hair, fix your make-up.*
> *Soon he will open the door.*
> *Don't think because*
> *There's a ring on your finger,*
> *You needn't try any more*

She practised her smile in the mirror. She did this too on an almost daily basis, because she hardly ever wanted to smile naturally. She had long ago lost the desire or fancy to do so.

Kathryn always expected to see her face sliding downwards on its bones, like Dali's soft watch or fried egg, slipping and dripping into an unhappy pool of misery. She was always slightly surprised to find her face still fixed on its anchors, in place and as it should be. It was only the smile that was the problem; she could grin from the nose down, but her eyes refused to cooperate, remaining fixed and frightened no matter how hard she tried. She would just have to try a little harder. *That was the answer, Kathryn: try a little harder.*

FIVE YEARS AGO

The lawyer's office was fusty, crowded with fat, dusty textbooks and what looked to Kate like ancient fishing gear. The wooden handles and woven holdall had both withered with age and looked entirely unable to cope with the thrash and slap of even the smallest fish. The window sill had become a magnolia-painted graveyard for spiders lying shrivelled on their backs like discarded currants. Particles of dust and minute fibres danced in the shafts of sunlight that crisscrossed the room.

Kate felt the specks of skin and other airborne matter tickle the back of her throat. She tried to keep her mouth closed, but resisted asking for the window to be opened. It was probably best not to invite in the dirt and fumes of central London and besides, she was enjoying the quiet of Mr Barnes' room.

Kate had been out for three days and six hours. A free woman, having served almost five years of her eight year sentence and ready to face the world. Her biggest joy thus far had been the peaceful state of silence in which she had found herself on three occasions: in the taxi that had collected her from prison, in bed at the Kensington hotel in which she was staying and now in this grubby office in Knightsbridge, facing the man that Mark had trusted with his most precious thing. His money.

The lawyer was old-school: red-faced, bloated and tweed-clad – and probably an Old Mountbrieren. The sort of man whose approval and friendship Mark would have courted. She could clearly picture this Mr Barnes retelling her story, trading it across the dining table between sips of claret and mouthfuls of game. She would be portrayed as that 'frightful woman' who had 'done in' the headmaster – an award-winning headmaster, no less.

Did she care? Only in so far as such gossip might reach Lydia and Dominic up in Yorkshire, which bothered her enormously.

Mr Barnes pushed his heavy, gold-framed spectacles up onto his bulbous nose and surveyed the papers in his hand. He was reading intently, as if the information contained within them was new to him. Maybe it was. It also provided him with the perfect opportunity to establish his superiority; he cared little that she might have other appointments to attend, or that her new-found freedom was being squandered in this dreary, airless room. He was happy to invite her to his offices and then let her sit in silence, waiting to learn of her financial fate, while he pondered the document. That he considered her so insignificant amused her. Unbeknown to him, she was quite content, not restless, keen or fidgety like others who'd sat in the same chair. She had all the time in the world.

Finally, Mr Barnes placed the papers face down on the leather-topped bureau and removed his glasses.

'I trust you are . . .'

Kate waited for him to finish the sentence; he didn't.

'Yes, yes I am.'

'Quite.'

He gave a flash of his ancient yellowed teeth. They reminded Kate of tusks, quite fitting for this walrus of a man. She smiled patiently at the meaningless exchange.

'Right, well, Kathryn—'

'It's Kate.'

'Excuse me?'

'I'm not Kathryn Brooker any more. I never was, really; that was what Mark called me. I was Kate or Katie as a girl and Kathryn was a label Mark gave me. He took every part of me, even my name. So now I am back to Kate and my maiden name of Gavier. I won't ever be Kathryn Brooker again.'

Mr Barnes stared at the neat woman seated in front of him. He stretched his neck by protruding his lower jaw – an ugly mannerism. She was clearly completely bonkers and no doubt one of those bloody women's libbers. In his day, a woman took her husband's name and was jolly glad to have it.

'Whichever. It's of little consequence—'

'To you maybe.' She wasn't going to let this go. 'But to me it's of huge consequence, so it's Kate from now on.'

'Yes, I got that. Shall we move on?'

'Please do.' She nodded.

Mr Barnes restored his reading glasses and turned over the papers. Kate smiled at the theatricality.

'Kate.' He paused after more or less shouting her name, point made. 'Mark has left you very well provided for. He not only had a sizeable pension that has performed rather splendidly, but was also prudent enough to have taken out life insurance, as well as a couple of other investments that we have redeemed on your behalf. Yours is a most unique situation and not one that I have been faced with before. There has been much discussion between myself and the insurance company in question and I confess to seeking counsel from more than one of my colleagues, but it would appear that all is in order in accordance with the law.'

She nodded. His tone was more than slightly accusatory and if she had to be honest, it did feel slightly odd to be the beneficiary of a life-insurance policy when it was she that had ended that life.

'Had you committed murder then things would

94

be rather different, but as it stands, I am *obliged* to inform you that the figure is as follows . . .'

The way he accentuated the word 'obliged' told her all she needed to know.

He slid the top sheet across the desk, his fingers sticking slightly, causing the paper to lift. His podgy digits were coated with the residue of a roast chicken lunch followed by a quick pee, after neither of which had he troubled to wash his hands.

Kate's eyes were instantly drawn to the bottom right-hand corner, where the numbers had been totted up. The total was just short of a million pounds. Kate felt her stomach clench in surprise. She had no idea, how had Mark managed to accrue such a sum? She felt her mouth go dry as her mind whirled with the possibilities of what this might mean for Dominic and Lydia . . .

'Is this in line with what you were expecting, Kate?' Again he almost spat her name.

She nodded and half shrugged, unsure of how else to respond. She had given little consideration to money matters while she had been in jail and never in her wildest imaginings could have guessed at such a considerable sum. Whatever the amount, a million or a billion, nothing could adequately compensate for the life that she had led with Mark and for her estrangement from her beloved children. She would have traded every single penny of it to have seen them at the prison gates upon her release.

Kate stood, indicating that the meeting was over.

'Do you have a plan for the money?' Mr Barnes' tone was sharp.

She found his comment impertinent and unnecessary. It was nothing to do with him, not any more. She really wanted to say, *'Yes – the whole lot on the two forty at Kempton methinks.'* But she didn't.

'Well, first on my agenda is a holiday with my kids, just the three of us whiling away the days in the sun. I can't wait. Thank you for asking, Mr Burns.'

'It's Barnes.'

'Whichever, it's of little consequence.' This she delivered over her shoulder as she left, relieved to escape the fusty atmosphere at last.

Kate lay on the bed in her hotel room staring at the ceiling. London traffic revved and hooted below. Her legs were crossed and rested vertically up the wall. She wiggled her toes inside her new, soft grey socks – one of many small luxuries that thrilled her. A cup of strong Earl Grey and two almond tuille crisps sat on a little tray beside her on the mattress. She wound the curly flex of the telephone handset around her fingers: it was fantastic to be able to just pick up a phone and make a call, exhilarating to have a window she could open, a door to walk through for a lungful of outside air.

'Hello, Yorkshire, we are all set!'

Kate's excitement bubbled from her as her sister answered the phone.

'Oh God, Fran, I can't believe it, I really can't. It's going to be so perfect, although to be honest I'd be happy to see them anywhere – Blackpool, Weston-super-Mare, you name it. It will of course be all the more perfect because we will be in the sunshine, but all that really matters is being able to talk, without distraction. I can't believe I'm going to see them! I can't believe it! Do you know what the best thing will be? Going to sleep under the same roof as Dom and Lydi and seeing them all sleepy and mussy-haired in the morning. Do you know how many years it is since I've done that! I feel like it's Christmas Eve, New Year's Eve and every single birthday all rolled into one—'

'Kate—'

'Can you tell them that I have all the factors and aftersun we need; might have gone a bit overboard. Lydi always goes brown as a berry, lucky thing, but Dom tends to do the whole several shades of lobster thing before tanning. I've got enough lotions and potions to last a lifetime.'

'Kate—' Francesca's voice was a little more insistent this time.

'I know, I know. I'm rambling, Fran, I can't help it! I am so excited! Did I give you flight times? I did, didn't I? I want to see them before we fly, obviously. I think I'll get a hotel room at Gatwick and they can either come down the night before or really, really early so we have a few hours to kind of get to know each other again before we take off—'

'They. Are. Not. Coming.'

Francesca delivered each syllable as though she were talking to a foreigner: louder than normal and over-enunciated.

'Oh, well, that's okay. It was just a thought. I can meet them at the airport and actually, thinking about it, that might work better. It might be easier for them with lots of people around, lots of distractions. In fact it will give us all a chance to just "be" together and by the time we arrive, talking will be easier. I don't mind, whichever is best.'

'No. Listen to me, Kate. They are not coming at all, not to the airport and not on holiday. They are not coming at all. I'm sorry, lovey.'

Kate allowed her legs to slide down the wall. Her babbling ceased and she curled into a small ball on top of the duvet, wrapped around the telephone handset.

'Is it the journey?' she whispered. 'I could easily come and pick them up. Or I could send money for the train fare, anything.'

'It's no good, Katie, they need more time.'

'More time? How much more time? They've had five years!' Kate squealed through a mouth contorted with sobs.

'I know, honey, I know . . .'

'You don't know, Francesca! You really do not know! I'm sorry, I know it's not your fault, but please, please, please bring them to me, please. Fran, please . . .'

'Honey, I have tried. I promise you, I have tried.

I have sat with them both and discussed the options. Bear with them, Katie, they just need longer. Having you out is yet another adjustment and we have to tread carefully.'

In prison Kate had been able to fool herself with many reasons for their absence: the distance from York, their hectic schedules, the fear of seeing her in a prison setting. Now, however, she had to face the reality. Not visiting her had been their choice. Worse still, even now, when they could simply jump on a train and be with her in a matter of hours, they still didn't want to see her. She could no longer conceal the unpalatable truth from herself.

'Please, Francesca, please!'

'It's not my decision, Katie. I know this is tough.'

Too tough, it's too tough. How do I get through this?

'Let's see how they feel when you get back. Don't cry, sis, it will all be okay. Please don't cry.'

My heart breaks every time. Every time.

The idea of a holiday hadn't occurred to Kate until she'd blurted it out to the nosy lawyer. But it made perfect sense: a chance for her and the kids to get reacquainted in a neutral setting, a chance to have them all to herself, to try and catch up after their time apart. She hadn't considered that they simply would not want to be with her.

This knowledge caused the tiny fracture in her heart to widen a little more.

Kate spent a long night torturing herself,

imagining her and the kids walking barefoot on sand, talking openly as the sun sank on the horizon. It was not to be. In the morning she surveyed the floor, now strewn with tear-soaked tissues, and she decided to go away anyway.

For the first time in her life there was nowhere that she needed to be, no house, job or family eager for her return. She might as well stay in a hotel abroad as a hotel in London, where she could gather her thoughts in peace and sit in the sunshine. St Lucia – even the name was exotic on her lips.

At Gatwick, she found herself filled with dread; it was as if everyone but her in the departure lounge knew the drill. The eighteen years she had spent isolated under Mark's control, then the time in prison, meant she was out of practice at being in a strange crowd. It was ridiculous really, that having lived with murderers and drug dealers for the last five years, she was now quite petrified of the backpack-wielding family whose haul of colouring books and wet wipes were spread on the bank of seats opposite her. Supposing they spoke to her? God only knew what she would have in common with the rather leggy mummy who sipped from her Styrofoam cup and occasionally stroked the muscular thigh of her husband.

Kate scrutinised the woman's face, watched her mouth, analysed her actions. She knew that you could never really trust first impressions. Was the woman scared? Restrained? Coerced? Kate had to admit she didn't look scared, restrained or coerced.

100

In fact she looked relaxed, comfortable and happy. Lucky girl.

Kate was saddened by her mistrust of people. Her confidence in being able to exchange small talk had vanished; perhaps with practice it would return. She allowed herself to imagine for a second what it might be like to choose a good man and live a lovely life. How had she got it so wrong?

She immersed herself in her book of Derek Walcott's poetry and tried to remain invisible. She was absorbed by one line that seemed impossibly apt, repeating it and revelling in the possibilities that it presented:

> *You will love again the stranger who was your self.*

She liked the idea of that very much.

The hubbub of a throng of boys jolted her from her musing. They ambled along in groups of four and five; a pack. Smart and polished, yet with the nonchalance and labels of boys she had once been familiar with, boys like Dominic. They were dressed alike, in tracksuit bottoms and hooded tops, with layered, long fringes and leather satchel bags slung over shoulders. She guessed they were aged between twelve and fourteen. They were polite but awkward in their as yet unblemished skin.

Much to her discomfort, the boys targeted the three empty seats next to her. They dumped their holdalls and clustered round, seemingly oblivious to the lady with her nose in a book. They exchanged banter about the rugby tour they were about to embark on, gate opening times and the fact that 'George' had been late, nearly missing the school bus. For this George was chastised and tagged with several politically incorrect names, although what his sexuality and a faulty alarm clock had in common was beyond her. Their tone was plummy and that they were comfortable in a large airport heading off without parents to the other side of the world spoke volumes.

It was almost simultaneous. As Kate lowered her book, one of the boys turned to face away from her, bringing the school crest on his back sharply into focus. Her breath caught in her throat, her skin was instantly covered in a thin film of cold sweat and her legs shook. It still had the power to do that to her, the gold emblem with eagle wings spreading behind, the Latin motto beneath: *Veritas Liberabit Vos*. Truth Shall Set You Free. It meant Mark, it meant torture, it meant prison. It meant that Lydia and Dominic were gone.

Kate reached for her bag and attempted to shove her book and bottle of water inside it. Her heart thudded loudly in her ribcage, her vision blurred. In her haste she dropped the book. A pair of young hands swooped to the floor and retrieved it.

The dark-haired teenager handed her the paperback.

'Excuse me, I think this is yours.'

'Th . . . thank you, yes it is.'

'He was a Nobel Prize winner, wasn't he? Any good?'

Kate looked up and into the eyes of Guido Petronatti. He had been nine the last time she had seen him. It didn't surprise her that he recognised a Nobel Prize winner when he saw one, smart boy.

She took a deep breath and decided she had nothing to lose.

'I've only just started it, Guido, but it's certainly showing promise. He writes some beautiful poetry. Do you still read a lot?'

Kate recalled the bespectacled young bookworm who had liked nothing more than to disappear into a quiet corner of the library with the latest Harry Potter. That was a lifetime ago.

The boy's eyebrows shot up in a confused upward slant.

'Yes, I do. Do I . . .? How did you . . .? Oh shit! Sorry, Mrs Brooker, I didn't mean shit, I mean . . .'

'It's okay, Guido. I understand.'

'Wow. I wasn't expecting to see you again, ever. Are you, like . . .? Did you . . .? Shit. Sorry.'

'How's Luca?'

She tried her best to calm the boy, who was clearly flustered, coming face to face with the infamous Mrs Bedmaker. Kate had always been fond of Guido's older brother, a friend of Dom's.

'He's studying medicine at King's. Mind you, I feel sorry for the person that ends up with him as their doctor, he's still a dickhead. I know Dom and he go out in London a lot; my dad's got Luca a flat, lucky thing.'

'Oh.'

Kate sat back down, winded by the mention of her son. London was close to her; he would travel that distance for Luca, but not her. It was fresh information, a new picture for her to mentally draw and colour in over the coming days. Dominic, her grown-up son, out in London with Luca, who always did have the makings of a playboy. The thought of the two of them made her smile. She was happy – cut by the latest revelation, but also happy. *Good for you, Dom, my beautiful boy.*

'Are you all right, Mrs Brooker? Can I do anything?'

Kate was unaware that she was now crying without restraint and that most of the group were staring at her. How she missed her kids, how she wished they were by her side. Their plane tickets nestled in her bag, just in case they had a last-minute change of heart.

'Oh, Guido, yes. I'm so sorry. I am fine. It's just that I haven't seen Dom for quite a while and I rather miss him and Lydia.'

The boy scuffed his trainer toe on the highly polished linoleum and stared at his feet.

'It was never the same after you, y'know . . .'

He squirmed, unsure if this was appropriate, but decided to continue anyway.

'That night . . . when Mr Brooker . . . Mountbriers became tougher, a bit meaner. I think

104

it's because you weren't there any more. I used to think you were like a spare mum; mine was always so far away, although come to think of it when she is with me, she's pretty rubbish. You used to sort my hair out before chapel and no one else ever did, like they didn't care. I cared that my hair was such a mess, but didn't know how to fix it myself.'

Kate's tears fell even harder.

'Right, boys! Quick huddle – don't want to leave anyone behind, do we?'

The young PE master's voice boomed across the space. Thankfully Kate had never seen him before; she couldn't have coped with the interaction. The group of lads jumped at his command.

Kate watched Guido saunter over to his friends. She whispered under her breath, 'Thank you, Guido. Thank you so very much.'

The globe seemed to have shrunk since Kate had last travelled. One long sleep, a meal and two movies later and she was in another world.

With her luggage carefully ensconced in the cubby-hole, the little red-and-yellow bus jumped and jolted along the grandly named Millennium Highway. It was a name that conjured images of multi-lane motorways with traffic whizzing in an orderly fashion between neon signs and flashing lights. Kate imagined the travelator on *The Jetsons*, but right there on earth. In reality the road was quite different, littered with gigantic potholes, some the size of a bath tub, and the odd obstacle. In England it would have been a B road at best.

Kate glimpsed a maroon velour sofa that had been dumped on a grass verge. Three scrawny dogs were curled asleep on its plump cushions, one of them with an eye half cocked and a leg dangling, as if waiting for the man of the house to come along and shush him onto the floor. A herd of goats, tethered together, had decided to take up residence in the middle of a bend. This was not a problem for the odd motorcycle and tiny Suzuki that darted past, but a much harder job for the unwieldy bus. The skilful, whistling driver did his best to navigate the small gap, as the right-hand wheels threatened to skitter on the gravel and plummet down the unguarded hill. Kate distracted herself by looking out of the opposite window until the danger had passed.

She marvelled at the multi-coloured housing, much of it built on stilts. It was clearly the only way to construct cheaply and safely into the slopes of the steep hills. From a distance the little wooden squares of soft purple, bright turquoise and sugar pink looked like marshmallow and gingerbread housing from a fairy tale. Close up, the faded paint on clapboard, the busy window boxes and fancy net curtains billowing in the breeze was even more enchanting.

Toothless old men in vests, whose lined faces told a million stories, and high-bottomed, mahogany-skinned women in curlers lolled on the rickety terraces. Huts selling Coca-Cola, rice and peas, and the local Piton beer were dotted along the route, all well patronised despite appearing to be in the middle of nowhere. Chickens and dogs meandered in small groups; they reminded Kate of characters from *Chicken Licken* out for a stroll or off to buy groceries. She did a double-take to check if any were carrying little baskets or brollies and wearing headscarves.

The heat was a warm blanket, soothing her joints and easing the knots from her muscles. In her stomach she felt a swell of excitement and anticipation at what her trip might hold. Banana trees and coconut palms fought for space in the dense roadside jungle. Each turn in the winding road revealed another stunning vista of mountains or tropical forest. This was exactly what Kate had hoped St Lucia would be like. She felt happy.

The thrill of the journey from the airport was not to last. One hour after hurling her bag into the bus's cubby-hole, Kate stepped into the huge, marble-floored reception of the Landings Hotel and instantly wanted to go home. But she didn't have a home to go to.

The place was beautiful. Marble pillars and floors shone. The great cathedral-like ceiling of arched wood reminded her of a tall ship. It was graceful, cool and expensive. These were only three of the reasons why she felt like a fish out of water.

The women, mainly American, who congregated on the over-stuffed sofas appeared to be waiting for nothing in particular. They all had with them the one accessory that instantly alienated Kate. A man.

As a group they were elegantly dressed, clutching Louis Vuitton bags and with sparkling diamonds around their wrists and twinkling from their lobes. Collectively they seemed to have decided that the appropriate attire for this green island was sheer, hot pinks, heeled sandals that clicked and clacked on the hard floors and a face full of filler. Sadly for Kate, no one had notified her of the dress code. She smoothed her palms against her thighs in an effort to remove the creases from her ditsy print frock and re-hitched her Sainsbury's raffia beach bag up onto her shoulder. She felt more school fete than Caribbean chic. West Indian men in navy Bermudas and pristine white polo shirts hovered with hands clasped behind their backs, waiting for a hand to beckon them, either to refresh their drink or offer advice on where to dine.

Kate quickly decided the best means of survival was to hide. She couldn't bear the thought of idling at one of the bars, bumping into these women or having to converse across a sun lounger:

'I'm Debbie. We're from New York, upstate. My husband? Oh he's in banking. Yes, two boys – one at military academy, he wants to fly, and the other a business major at Harvard. Our first time? No, our sixteenth. We just love the islands. You?'

'I'm Kate. From the UK. My first trip; I usually favour Padstow. My husband – he's deceased. Oh no, please don't be sorry, it was me that killed him. In fact I've only just got out of prison. My kids? Oh, not speaking to me because of the whole murdering their dad thing . . . Ooh, I love your bikini!'

She could see that this exchange would not result in the swapping of addresses and the issuing of Christmas cards. Instead, Kate sought out places other tourists shunned. Most wanted to be within a short, leg-stretching stroll of a paper-umbrella-adorned pina colada or an air-conditioned restaurant, but not her.

Kate spent the first two days venturing down to the beach, wandering the shoreline and then returning to the solace of her room. She lay on her vast bed and marvelled at the luxury that surrounded her. At night the chirp and peep of wildlife would serenade her to sleep. On day three she struck gold when she discovered Pigeon Island. It was the haven she had dreamed of: a quiet oasis with the ancient ruins of a British hill fort set among the junglescape.

The winding trail to the fort meandered upwards, allowing Kate to gaze in wonder at varieties of trees she had never seen before, trees with names like 'flamboyant' and 'lady's tongue'. She continued on to Signal Point without difficulty; the steep incline was a welcome workout after a couple of days of inactivity. Alone on a fortuitously placed section of wall in the midday heat, she watched the white boats bob on the ocean, pulling tiny water-skiers that bumped over the water like model railway dolls. She ran her fingers over the warm hunk of granite on which she perched. Sitting in its shallow, bottom-shaped well, she wondered at the many hands that had touched it during the two hundred years since it had been placed there.

Kate reflected on the super-human effort that must have gone into hoisting this gigantic boulder from the deck of a ship all the way to the top of the outcrop, some three hundred feet high. She pictured the tanned muscles slick with sweat, hauling and grunting under the relentless alien sun, maybe thinking as they toiled of ports and loved ones on the glistening, damp cobbles of their English home. It saddened her a little that their efforts were now diminished as this chunk of watchtower was reduced to providing a seat for weary bums.

It felt surreal that only weeks ago she was staring at shiny, white-painted walls, prison bars and bright blue carpet tiles whilst listening to the squeak of rubber-soled shoes as the guards patrolled the hallways after dark. It was difficult to imagine Marlham and its inmates going about their same daily routines, but without her there. She had felt similarly about Mountbriers after the huge cata-clysm that had occurred there, finding it hard to envisage the mechanics of the school continuing to grind. She decided that the sudden absence of a person or dramatic change in a situation was not dissimilar to a wound: the loss would be painful at first, but would eventually heal, closing over and growing anew, like skin.

On her way back from Signal Point, Kate stopped at the Jambe de Bois Café. The rickety wooden café was known for its bright local art work, cold drinks on hot days and the best home-made food under the stars at night, or so it claimed. She treated herself to a chilled Piton beer before settling on the tiny beach next to the jetty. She was having the most perfect day and could feel the warm glow of a tan spreading on her skin. It felt wonderful.

Kate drew long, slow breaths as though clearing her head, enjoying this new feeling of peace. She could do whatever she wanted. There was some-thing quite liberating about travelling alone for the first time in a foreign country; it made her feel adventurous, reckless and young. She could only imagine the amazing freedom that a gap year offered; there hadn't been such a thing in her youth, it was one of her many 'if onlys'.

A little girl wearing T-shirt and pants clopped along the shoreline, kicking up a spray and stop-ping only to paddle in the shallow waves that lapped at her chubby feet. Her hair was styled into coiled knots, each at the centre of a square, an intricate design that fascinated Kate. She put her age at around four. She was adorable. Her large eyes framed by thick, curly lashes sat in a heart-shaped face; her grin was wide and infectious. She ran towards Kate and stopped in front of her.

'Hello.'

The little girl smiled, but didn't reply. Stretching out her arm with her fist coiled tightly around a small object, she beckoned with her other hand for Kate to do likewise. Kate stretched out her arm and opened her palm under the girl's hand, just in time to receive a precious gift. It was a shell, approximately two centimetres long. Its end curled into a flawless point with a pale pink lustre that shone in the sunlight. It was perfect. Kate remembered finding a similar shell in Cornwall and giving it to Lydia when she was about the same age.

'It's the same colour as a rainbow, Mummy!' her daughter had squealed.

'Yes it is. That's because it's magic, Lyds.'

'What's it made of?'

'Tiny pink shells are made from mermaids' fingernails.'

Kate dug her toes into the sand and nursed the cool beer between her hands; she could hear the shouts from an impromptu ball game on the adjoining beach and the repeated thwack of a ball against a bat. The sounds of the children shouting and laughing with careless abandon took her mind back to that holiday when Dominic and Lydia had been small.

They had gone to Padstow for a long weekend, and to outsiders it must have looked like an idyllic summer break. The young family wandered the rock pools by day, caught tiny crabs in brightly coloured buckets, wolfed down fish and chips on the sea wall and ate every other meal al fresco. As the sun set and the temperature dipped, the children were tucked into miniature beds, exhausted by their seaside adventures.

By day, they made the beach their playground, lying on the sand, digging a hole, and making repeated trips to the shoreline to retrieve unwieldy buckets of freezing sea water that would be soaked up as soon as they were tipped in. Despite the futility, trying to fill their hole with water kept the kids occupied for hours. Their tiny feet pounded the mud-like sand back and forth, leaving smudged footprints that would be sucked back into the beach, disappearing in minutes.

It was only anyone close enough to hear who would have caught the unpalatable topic of conversation. As the family sat on the tartan blanket and shared sandwiches, Mark decided to open a debate with his baby children.

'So, Dominic, who do you love the most, Mummy or Daddy?'

The three others had looked on as his little face had crumpled in contemplation.

'Both the same!' the little boy declared as Lydia clapped her hands at this happy resolution.

If only it had ended there. Mark, however, was far from satisfied.

'No, Dominic.' His voice was firmer this time. 'You

can't say both the same; you have to love one of us more than the other, you have to love one of us the best. Is it Daddy? Do you love Daddy the best?'

Dominic had wrinkled his nose and looked from his mum to his dad and back again. His mummy was looking down at the ground and didn't seem to be joining in. This made his decision easier; he could give the answer that he knew his dad wanted to hear.

'You, Daddy. I love you the best.'

Mark was elated, jubilant; Dominic's reward was a tight hug in his daddy's arms.

'That's right, my clever boy! You love your daddy the best because your daddy loves you the best!'

This alerted Lydia, who even at a young age did not miss a nuance.

'Who loves Lydia the best?' she enquired.

Mark gathered her to him and kissed her face. 'I do, Lyds. Your daddy, I love you the best!'

'And who loves Mummy the best?' Lydia was not finished trying to analyse and understand the situation in which she found herself.

Mark looked her directly in the eyes. 'No one can love Mummy the best, Lydia, because she is a miserable, skinny cow. She wants to spoil all of our fun and make us all feel miserable with her miserable face and her miserable voice and we don't want that, do we, Lyds? We want to have fun! Do we want to be miserable?'

'No!' Of that and nothing else Lydia was sure; we didn't want that at all.

Kathryn had cried as she propped her head on her raised knees, keeping her face forward and looking out to sea so as not to alarm her children.

That night as the children slept soundly in their nautical-themed nursery, with anchors painted on the floor and billowing sails on the walls, Kathryn prepared to climb the stairs and meet her fate. She hesitated before drawing together all her courage. Reaching out, she touched her husband's arm.

'Mark?'

'Yes, Kathryn?'

'I want to ask you something.'

'Ask away!'

He said this with such joviality that for a second she wondered if she had imagined the whole horrid exchange. Such was his ebullience that if anyone overheard, it would be her that sounded unreasonable, with her formal tone and nervous, hesitant air. A miserable cow.

'I would like to ask you, Mark . . .'

'Yes?' He gave a slight nod, encouraging her to speak out.

'I . . . I would like to ask you not to turn the children against me.'

He didn't respond and it was this silence that she mistook for acquiescence. It gave her a small jolt of courage, enough to continue.

'I put up with a lot, Mark, and I don't care what you do to me, but I beg you, please, please do not be mean to me in front of the children because they are everything to me and it's not fair on them or me. They are all that I have and it's the one thing I can't cope with, I really can't.'

He moved quickly and without warning, striking her hard across the mouth with the back of his hand. It was the first time that he had properly struck her. Her mouth filled with the iron-tasting liquid that she recognised as her own blood and her lip felt enormous against her teeth as it swelled in response to its lashing. A round splat of scarlet stained the pristine floor.

Mark bent to where she had fallen at the bottom of the white-painted stairs with their thick, rope banister. He stroked her hair tenderly, removing the stray tendrils of her fringe that had stuck to the blood which oozed from her split lip. He shook his head gently from side to side as though placating a clumsy child who had hurt themselves by accident.

'I am very pleased that you don't care what I do to you and with that in mind you have got yourself a deal, missy.'

He reached out and gently took her hand before leading her along the narrow cottage corridor to their holiday room. Kathryn sat on the edge of the bed and slowly unbuttoned her shirt with trembling fingers. Shock rendered her numb.

Mark removed his socks from his feet and with almost choreographed precision he stepped forward and stuffed one of them into her mouth. She gagged, fighting to control the automatic reflex, knowing that if she were sick, she would surely choke.

He laid her face down on the mattress and whispered into her ear through gritted teeth. 'You are a very, very bad girl and you have amassed eleven points for offences too numerous for me to recount. But considering that you don't care what I do to you, this is all well and good, isn't it?'

He proceeded to punish her. Within seconds it was evident that he needn't have bothered with the gag; she wasn't going to scream or make a noise. She lost consciousness almost immediately.

When she awoke in the early hours of the morning, he had removed the sock from her mouth and for this she was grateful. Her lips were dry, her throat sore and parched. She stretched her hand out towards the glass of water that sat a fingertip's reach away.

'Would you like a drink, Kathryn?'

She nodded that yes, she would like a drink.

'I bet you would. But no. No drinks for you, my darling, not this morning.'

She tried to swallow, her tongue swollen, her spit thick with thirst, her throat raw from being suffocated and her lips swollen and encrusted with blood. She rolled onto her side and cried into her pillow, trying not to think about the pain in her thighs, not wanting to look at how he had damaged her this time.

★　★　★

Kate shook her head, trying to erase the image of that particular weekend. Every vaguely happy memory or event that she associated with her children was tempered by the dark shadow of her husband's abuse. It was as if she were an actress in a play: whilst on the stage, lots of wonderful and exciting things would happen to bring her joy, but she couldn't stay on the stage forever and as soon as she hit the wings, Pow!, dreadful things would befall her, things that she had no hope of avoiding, ever. All she could do, day after day, was face the audience and grin, trying to hide her misery whilst secretly hoping that one of them might see through her smile and rescue her.

Kate looked at the grinning child in front of her and pictured her own little girl placing the magic gift of a mermaid's fingernail inside her pocket to keep it safe. She blinked and swallowed the tears that threatened to spill.

'Thank you so much. Is this for me?'

The little girl gave a small nod.

'Well, this is certainly the best present that I have been given in a very long time. I shall treasure it!'

'There you are, Matilda!'

Kate looked up in the direction of the voice. The man strode towards them; he was tall and broad with braided hair hanging uniformly to the nape of his neck. His black skin gleamed under the sun, giving definition to each muscle; he was beautiful. He strode through the sea, which washed over his bare feet and soaked the bottom of his cargo pants. He was no stranger to beach life.

'Ah! I see she has made a friend!'

He smiled at Kate, revealing dazzling, perfect white teeth. Kate could see where Matilda got her smile from.

'She's fabulous.'

'Yes she is.' With his hands on his hips, he nodded in agreement.

'And she brought me a present; some treasure, no less.' Kate opened her palm to reveal her gift.

'Treasure indeed!' His eyes twinkled.

'I shall keep it forever; it will always remind me of here.' She meant it.

'That's good. You are obviously a person that recognises real treasure when you see it. Where you from?'

'The UK. Just here on holiday, three weeks of escape.' She laughed, aware that she sounded slightly giggly.

'What are you trying to escape from?' He looked at her earnestly.

'Oh, I don't know really.'

Kate chewed her bottom lip. Her tears threatened to fall despite her best efforts to control her emotions. The memories of her kids on the beach were so strong, it was agonising. She missed them so badly that it had become a physical ache and now that someone was being nice to her, it made it all the more unbearable somehow.

'I'm so sorry. Seeing you here with your daughter . . . I haven't seen my own daughter or my son in quite some while and it's the little things that remind me.'

He slumped down next to her on the sand.

'I'm sorry to hear that. Matilda isn't my daughter, but I do get to look after her and twenty-five like her.'

He stretched out his hand. 'I run the youth mission up at Dennery. My name is Simon.'

Kate shook his hand.

'It's lovely to meet you, Simon. I'm Kate Gavier, just Kate.'

She sniffed the creep of tears back to their source.

'Wow! Twenty-six kids? That takes some doing! Is it like day-care, a nursery?'

Simon smiled. 'It's a bit more than that. Day and night care, three hundred and sixty-five days of the year. It's their home.'

'Are they all little like Matilda?' Kate was fascinated, picturing rows and rows of cots and cribs.

'Well they were once! But, no, a mixture of ages; sometimes they come to us as newborns, but more often it's when they get a little older, when things get too tough for Mum or Dad, various circumstances. We get teenagers too, in need of guidance and a place to stay.'

'I think the mission sounds amazing.'

Simon nodded, quietly. Kate felt her cheeks blush, aware that she could have easily substituted 'you' for 'the mission'. It disconcerted her that there were calm, good men like Simon, with such capacity for kindness, whether to a child in need or a stranger on a beach, and yet men like Mark also had a place in the world, men who were the exact opposite.

'Your accent is hard to place, where is it from?'

Simon laughed, a low, deep chortle. This obviously wasn't the first time he had been asked that.

'Ah, therein lays a tale. I shall give you the twenty-second version; are you sitting comfortably?'

Kate nodded.

'I was born in south London, Battersea to be precise, illegitimate, mixed race and in those days, this did *not* bode well. I was put up for adoption as soon as I was born and someone was smiling down on me! I was adopted by a Canadian couple who were living in the UK at the time. We then lived in Canada from when I was eight until my thirties, until I was called home. My birth father is St Lucian and here I have been ever since.'

'That's quite a twenty-second tale!' Kate smiled, thinking that her own could match it in terms of intrigue and adventure. '"Called home", that's a nice phrase. Nice to be needed.'

'Oh yes, and needed I was, although I didn't know quite what my purpose was when I first arrived.'

Kate found his slow speech and warm tone quite hypnotic.

'Did you come back because of your father?'

Simon laughed again loudly and open-mouthed. 'Yes, yes I did, Kate. That is exactly why I came home – because of my Father, but not in the sense that I am sure you intend it. I was called here by God. You can call me Simon, but on the island I am known mostly as Reverend Dubois.'

'Jesus!'

'Exactly. Amen.'

'No, I mean, I would never have guessed. You don't look like a man of God!'

His ready laugh again boomed into the surf.

'I see. And what are we supposed to look like?'

'I don't know really.'

Kate pictured the bald, sober chaplain at Mountbriers and the ancient decrepit vicar of her youth with his faint aroma of formaldehyde, his hand shaking against her mother's best china teacup and the spit gathered at the corner of his mouth. He had elivered each word, sermon or not, as if he was bestowing the gift of insight. Whether the phrase being uttered was, *'Yes, Mrs Gavier, I would indeed like another biscuit,'* or *'You are Peter, and upon this rock I will build my Church, and all the powers of hell will not conquer it,'* his voice and tone had been unchanging.

Kate considered her response. 'In my experience, you tend to be quieter, contemplative, not wearing beautiful beads or walking barefoot on the beach.'

'We do things a little differently on this island.'

'I can see that!'

Matilda teetered backwards and came to a stop, plonking herself bottom first into the sea. She wailed. The temperature was a little cooler than her pioneering toe-dipping had suggested.

'Time to get her back, she wants a nap.'

Simon the man-mountain scooped the little girl up into his arms.

'Tell you what, Kate, you should come and see us. Jump in any taxi, ask for Dennery and you'll find us when you get there.'

He turned without waiting for a reply, carrying the toddler on one arm like she was a bunch of feathers. Kate couldn't decide if the warm glow that had spread through her body was a result of the sun-and-beer combination or something else entirely.

It took two more days of avoiding poolside interactions, kicking her heels and internal debate before she decided that maybe Simon wasn't just being polite but had actually been sincere with his invite. There was only one way to know for sure.

The taxi snaked up steep mountain roads that dropped away in large craters without warning. Kate tried not to picture the vehicle tumbling down the side and bouncing off the giant ferns that would offer little resistance. Deep jungle on either side was spiked by the bright blues and fiery reds of tropical plants. Without the cool breeze that wafted in from the ocean, the air was thick and the heat more intense. It was in this environment that St Lucia felt most foreign. She loved it.

The taxi driver dropped her, as instructed, in Dennery – she hadn't wanted to be more specific about her destination in case she changed her mind. She figured that on this small island, the news would have reached the Reverend Dubois's ears in a matter of hours. From what Kate could see, Dennery had no recognisable centre, but was a sprawling district, houses, farms and slant roofed shops all sat along tiny lanes like tributaries from the main winding road on which she now stood.

It was only once he had left that Kate realised she might still be very far from her destination. She walked along the road looking for a clue, but without really knowing what she was looking for. A small crowd of people were sheltering under an elaborate pyramid-shaped bus shelter with yellow walls and an ocean-blue roof. The hourly rain showers could be quite fierce and as the bus might come along in five minutes or forty-five, depending on the driver's mood, the hazards he encountered en route and how many of his mates stopped him for a chat, these shelters were well used.

'Excuse me?' Kate spoke to no one in particular. 'I'm looking for the Reverend Dubois, Simon and the youth mission. Am I heading in the right direction?'

Two women, one resplendent in a yellow floral headscarf and the other carrying an enormous purple plastic laundry basket, broke away from their conversation.

'Whatya want with the Reverend? He a friend of yours?'

The two winked and laughed.

Kate laughed too; clearly she was not alone in her admiration of his beauty.

'Not exactly, no, but he invited me over and I'm afraid I'm a bit lost.'

'Y'aint lost girl, you need to keep goin' and keep goin' and y'ask again.'

'Right. Thank you.'

Kate carried on up the hill, still none the wiser. She followed the road's twists and turns. Gigantic fern fronds and banana leaves brushed her face and legs. She peered once into the jungle, her stomach jumped at the knotted trunks and hanging vines, imagining each one to harbour faces and the lurking shadows of wild animals. Instead, she kept her eyes firmly on the road ahead, navigating the potholes and cracks, aware that she was climbing higher still. Her T-shirt stuck to her back and her hair lay flat against her head in spiky tendrils. She was beginning to wonder if this had been such a good idea, when a small white sign with black lettering caught her attention on the road ahead. It read 'Prospect Place' and beneath the words a child had painted a sun with a smiley face on it. Next to it was a quote: 'Faith makes things possible, not easy'. This had been written by a more adult hand.

Kate wondered not for the first time if this whole venture was a bit of a mistake.

She turned down the narrow lane and followed the tyre tracks until she reached a clearing. The view was magnificent. There were jungle-covered mountains on either side of the valley, with the azure ocean twinkling in the distance. It was breathtaking.

In the middle of the clearing sat a dilapidated building. It was single storey, wooden and had been painted bright green. The sun, however, had bleached it in places to a paler shade, and where the panels met windows and doors the paint was missing entirely, hanging in thin strips to reveal bare wood and knotty grains.

The main structure had smaller wooden additions tacked on to its sides, forming an irregular shape that from space might have looked like a poorly drawn pentagon. For poor it was. The whole construction seemed to be listing to the right and most of the windows were without glass, but instead had fly screen tacked over the frames. Kate hadn't known what to expect, but would have guessed at something solid, brick, possibly hospital-like. This was very different. Welcoming and bright, but without any of the grandeur or sturdiness that she had hoped to find.

'There you are, Kate. You found us!' Simon clapped his hands together as he appeared from the side of the building.

'Only just, it was more luck than judgement!'

He took both her hands inside his own. 'Welcome. And what perfect timing, you can join us for lunch!'

Kate smiled, that did indeed sound perfect. She noted his lack of surprise at her arrival, as though he had been expecting her at that precise moment.

Inside the main building was a large T-shape of tables covered with a peony-patterned oil cloth and encircled by thirty metal-legged chairs. They were the same chairs that you might find stacked in any English village hall or being scraped along tessellated wooden floors by a Brownie pack on a Thursday night.

The hubbub of conversation stopped rather abruptly as Kate walked into the room. Each seat was occupied by a child. First glance revealed their ages to be between two and fourteen. The girls had ribbons in their plaited hair and the boys were radiant in yellow-and-orange checked shirts.

'Everybody! This is Kate. Would you like to say hello?'

Some waved, others smiled and a couple giggled into their palms at the sight of this strange lady standing in their dining hall.

'Hi, hello everyone.' Kate waved back.

'Mind your backs!'

Simon and Kate swerved to the right as a short, fat man wearing a chef's hat swung around them both to place large platters of chicken patties on each of the tables.

'This is Fabian – the chef, as denoted by the

hat. He is also the driver – he wears a cap for that – and when he's the maintenance man . . .'

Fabian nodded at her as he made a return swoop in the direction of the kitchen.

'A different hat?'

'You got it!'

'And again, folks! Hot food coming through!' This time Fabian was loaded with a large bowl of rice and what smelt like hot bread rolls.

The children sat patiently, hands in laps, waiting. Kate compared the scene to the unruly bun fight that used to ensue each morning at Mountbriers as the pupils clamoured for French toast and bacon. The bigger boys would elbow the smaller ones out of the way and girls of all ages would moan about the lack of fat-free yoghurt and demand blueberries. This was much nicer.

'Kate, please take a seat.'

Simon pulled out a chair between two younger children who found it hilarious that this stranger was to be seated between them and could barely contain their laughter. Kate shook hands with them both. The little boy to her right reached up and stroked the ends of her hair between his thumb and forefinger, before collapsing in giggles onto the table. She smiled, having never before considered her limp, mousy hair that funny.

Simon stood centrally, raising his palms towards the roof and bowing his head with his eyes tightly shut. His big voice filled the space.

'Lord, we thank you for the gift of food that you have bestowed upon us on this day . . .'

There were a few impromptu shouts of 'Praise be to the Lord'. Simon was not finished.

'We give thanks for all your mighty gifts, not least the gift of forgiveness. We are thankful that when we need shelter, when we need escape, we can find refuge under your mighty wing.'

A large chorus of 'Amen' echoed around the ceiling and *then* the bun fight started.

Kate noticed that when Simon opened his eyes he was staring straight at her. It made her feel a little uncomfortable.

Lunch was boisterous and exciting. Kate had difficulty keeping up with the many strands of conversation that flew across the room; the speed of the kids' speech and the heavy patois meant she could only participate with nods of encouragement and smiles of vague understanding. She threw Simon many a furtive glance and was fascinated to watch him engage with the children, clearly interested in their snippets of news and gossip.

When their tummies were full, the children went out to play cricket and Kate was given the top job of dishwashing.

'Is this what they mean by no such thing as a free lunch?'

Simon laughed. 'You got it!'

'The atmosphere here is amazing, Simon. I expected the place to be a bit sad, lots of little children without parents, but this is anything but. It feels hopeful.'

'You are exactly right, it is hopeful. That's why it's called Prospect Place. Most people think "Prospect" refers to the spectacular view, but it's the dictionary definition that best defines us: the "possibility of something happening soon, a chance or the likelihood that something will happen in the near future, especially something desirable". These kids have had enough sadness in their short lives and it stops when they arrive here. Each has his or her own story, but they are not all without parents. Some have one or both still living on the island, but they are maybe not in a position to look after their kids right now.'

'Why?'

'Oh, many reasons. Addiction, poverty – the two are often closely linked, and there are no social services here like there are in the UK. If your parents are living hand to mouth on the street, then so are you.'

Kate pictured her English class at Marlham. Addiction and poverty: she knew how that story ended.

'I feel foolish, Simon. If I think of the Caribbean, I picture yachts, private jets and large cocktails being sipped through straws. I've only ever associated St Lucia and islands like it with luxury and wealth.'

'And you are right; you will find both here in abundance. But sometimes, Kate, this comes at a cost.

130

This afternoon I will take you on a little trip, I want to show you something.'

'How lovely! We could go a lot quicker if you had a dishwasher!'

Simon laughed as they transferred the scrubbed crockery covered in suds to a waiting bucket full of clean water for rinsing.

'Oh, Kate, there are many, many things we need before we have the spare cash for a luxury like that! Regular, reliable hot water, a decent bathroom, computers and a playroom for when it's rainy outside. The list is long and ever growing.'

'How is the place funded, if you don't mind me asking?'

'I don't mind at all. And the simple answer is it isn't, not with any regularity. My adoptive parents back in Canada very generously send us a cheque when they can; they hold fundraisers in their church and at the university where my dad taught, but it's often hard for them, they are not getting any younger. We sell any surplus produce that Fabian "the farmer" grows on our plot. We barter a lot, and people are very kind. The community here is small and when word gets out that we might need another room, a truck with some lumber will show up. It's a small miracle every time!'

'It's a big responsibility for you, Simon. It must be hard with so many people relying on you and no guarantee for the future.'

'I guess that would be difficult for some, but not

for me. My load is light. The kids are my purpose and I feel it was why I was brought here. If I thought about the cost and what we don't have, it would feel like a burden, so I don't dwell on that. I concentrate on what we do have, which is an awful lot.'

'Do you see your father . . . real father – your dad – here at all?'

Kate blushed as she tried to make the distinction between the man that had fathered him, his adoptive dad and Jesus.

'Oh, Kate, that is a very long and complicated story. I did see him for a while and then he died. We were never really reconciled. It was as if when I was in England and Canada I felt quite alien in those environments and longed to be here and when here, the exact opposite. Oddly, the older I get and the less time I have left on the planet the more I gain a sense of belonging right here.'

'I get that. Age crystallises things in a way that's hard to explain to anyone that hasn't experienced it.'

Simon laughed. 'That's because old age is what happens to other people! I know I don't see myself how I used to view people of my age when I was young; goodness no. Anyone over fifty was ANCIENT!'

'I feel old sometimes, Simon. Like I'm slowing down and everything I do takes slightly longer. The speed at which I take the stairs and even chew a biscuit is now sluggish, slightly laboured. I'm worried that one day soon I might come to a complete halt!'

'You don't look like a woman that is coming to a halt, Kate; you look to me like a woman that is on the edge, about to dive in, about to start over.'

'Ooh, I like that. I like the idea of starting over and having new adventures before slipping gently into old age. Much better than suddenly hitting a geriatric wall and having the bricks rush up to meet me with such ferocity that I just want to shout stop!'

'It won't happen like that; you won't have to shout stop!'

'I hope not. What about you, Reverend Dubois, what does your old age hold?'

'Oh that is definitely a topic for another day, over a cold beer.'

'You drink then?'

'Girl, you are so out of touch! I'm a preacher not a martyr! Everything in moderation, Kate, everything in moderation.'

'You are an incredible man, Simon. The children are lucky to have you.'

He ignored the compliment.

'Ah, Matilda!'

Kate turned from the sink to see her little friend hovering in the doorway.

'Hello, Matilda, how are you? It's lovely to see you again. I have put my little shell in a safe, special place and I look at it every day. It's very beautiful.'

The little girl smiled.

'Are you not playing cricket with everyone else? Did someone get you out already? I could tell you a very funny story about an important cricket match and two naughty chickens called Nugget and Kiev, if you have the time?'

Matilda hesitated, shoving the best part of her small, bunched-up fist into her mouth before deciding that no, she did not particularly want to hear that story. Besides, her best friend, Hans, had promised her a go on the tyre swing. She ran outside.

'Is she shy?' Kate was worried that she might have said the wrong thing.

'No, far from it. But she hasn't spoken since she arrived here. That was about nine months ago. She seems happy and settled, but we can't get her to say a word. The doctor says there is no medical reason and so I'm confident that she will start talking when she feels she has something important enough to say.'

'Did she used to speak?'

'Oh yes! A lot! But she had a shock and it's her way of coping. Children are wired quite simply and it's her way of putting things in order, trying to make sense of her world.'

'What happened to her?' Kate whispered, not sure if she wanted to know.

'It's a common enough story, but no less sad because of it. She was with her daddy in a bar when he was stabbed in a knife fight. He died.

Her mummy is not in a good place right now, battling her own demons, and so Matilda is here where she is loved, and when the time is right, God will find a way to heal her.'

'Oh, Matilda . . .' Kate felt an unbearable wave of sadness. *Her daddy was stabbed to death.* The name Matilda had fallen from her lips, but it could just have easily been 'Lydia' or 'Dominic'.

'You miss your children?' It was as if he read her thoughts.

'Yes, yes I do, very much. I ache for them. It's rather complicated, I'm afraid.'

'Can I assume it's not only physical distance that prevents you from being with them?'

She nodded.

'They were going to come here with me, it would have been perfect, but they changed their minds, need more time . . . It's difficult. I don't want to force them into seeing me, but at the same time I find it so hard to let things take their course, it doesn't come naturally to me. I think I can heal them quicker, if they'd just let me.'

'You know, Kate, it will pass, everything does. Your children will come to realise just how much you love them and how much they love you, I am certain. I'm sure they will find the path back to you. My mum is amazing; I know that no matter how much time or distance separates us, she is only ever a heartbeat away from me. It's very comforting and your kids will seek out that comfort when the time is right, when they need you the most.'

'Did you ever meet your birth mother?'

'No. She gave birth and pretty much abandoned me. I don't know if she ever held or fed me. By all accounts she was just relieved that the whole sordid affair was over. I don't know if she ever gave me a second thought. I have prayed for her and I do forgive her lack of interest; I don't judge her, Kate. I'm grateful for the path she set me on. I have been blessed and she did give me life. That's pretty amazing, eh?'

Kate could only nod.

Simon threw the tea towel onto the sideboard. All the dishes and pots were now clean and in the cupboards ready for supper time.

'How about that trip?' he asked. 'Your work here is done!'

'I'd like that very much.' She beamed.

Simon's open-topped jeep bounded along tracks that Kate doubted were wide enough to cope if a similar vehicle should come along in the opposite direction. The thick canopy of leaves dripped with the recent rainfall. Pale crabs the size of dinner plates scurried into the undergrowth and out of the path of the roaring engine. The car stopped abruptly at the edge of a small forest.

'Here we are.'

He smiled at Kate, his beautiful open smile that gave her a glimpse of the man behind it, a good man.

Simon strode with confidence through the copse.

Kate followed in his wake, tripping as her urban feet, more familiar with the grey slabs of English pavements, struggled with the alien terrain. She trod gingerly over tangled roots and fallen branches. She slapped at her skin, trying to squish the mosquitoes who tucked into the all-you-can-eat buffet that was her arms and legs. It was worth it.

One more step forward and she knew how Lucy Pevensie in *The Lion, the Witch and the Wardrobe* felt. Only Kate didn't stumble into a snow-covered kingdom; instead she found herself in paradise.

The bay was horseshoe shaped, on a gentle incline that allowed the crystal-clear blue water to lap its shore. The fine sand was undisturbed. The trees of the wood behind them cast gentle shadows and shady pockets over the beach. Mother Nature had dotted palm trees where the jungle met the sand. It was perfect.

'Oh, Simon! I have never seen anything like it. This is so beautiful.'

He lowered his bulk onto the sand and Kate sat next to him, bunching up her linen trousers to tan her calves. She never wore swimwear, preferring to keep her scars covered. There was no need for a towel or a blanket; this was the way to do beach life. She ran her fingers through the sand and let the gentle wind lift her hair and her spirits.

'Not so very long ago, the whole island was like this. In the last twenty years I have seen many changes and not all of them good, Kate. I wanted to show you this bay—'

'I can see why, it's stunning.' She interrupted him.

'But pretty soon I will not be able to come here and neither will the children.'

'What do you mean? Why?' She thought this was his way of telling her that he was moving away.

'It's been sold, Kate.'

'Sold? How can it be sold? It's a beach, it's part of the island!'

Simon gave a low chortle and shook his head.

'It seems obvious, doesn't it? But sadly it's not that straightforward. This plot and the two either side have been bought by a large corporation and they will build a huge, luxurious hotel. They will use boulders to block access to the land. They will hire local security guards who used to play here with their kids to patrol this strip of sand and discourage me and many like me from coming here.'

'How can they do that? It's not like there are hundreds and hundreds of miles of beach; it's a small island!'

'That's true and yet every year that is exactly what happens all over the Caribbean. Special places and stretches of beach that have been loved and enjoyed for generations are suddenly not ours any more. The island is shrinking and unless you have an awful lot of money there isn't a whole lot you can do about it.'

'That's heartbreaking, terrible! I don't understand how it's allowed to happen.'

'It's a problem, but it's just one small part of a very complicated puzzle. It would be better if more tourist dollars were invested in facilities for those who need them the most, but it doesn't seem to happen like that. We are like every other island: we need the money that tourism brings, but it comes at a very high price.'

'I don't understand it, Simon. I'm trying to imagine a big company coming along and buying up England's green spaces. Can you imagine if Exmoor, the Yorkshire Dales or the Lake District were suddenly no-go areas because they had been *sold*? Or Hyde Park or the Bristol Downs? People simply wouldn't stand for it!'

'They would if they had no voice. Sometimes money is very hard to be heard over; it talks the loudest of all.'

'It makes me feel guilty. I'm staying at one of those flash hotels.'

'It's good that you are aware and I don't want you to feel guilty. We want to share our beautiful home with you. I just wish people knew when enough was enough.'

She nodded. 'All things in moderation, is that right?'

'You got it.'

The two sat in silence for a moment, letting the sun warm their skin.

'What is it you are trying to escape from, Kate?'

So suddenly had the topic been broached that his question caught her off guard.

'Well, I don't really know where to start.' She dug her toes into the sand.

'How about the beginning?' he prompted.

'I wish it was that easy. Actually it's not that I don't where to start so much as how to. I think you may feel differently about being my friend after you know a bit more about me, you being a man of faith.'

Simon smiled. 'Isn't that strange, Kate, that you judge me, decide on my reaction, second-guess my opinion and yet I would do no such thing to you?'

'You don't know what I did.' Kate bit her bottom lip, fighting the nerves that trembled there.

'Try me.'

She exhaled slowly, trying to think of the right phrase, of a way to deliver the information in the least shocking manner.

'I've been in prison for the last five years, serving a sentence for manslaughter. I killed someone. Well, not just someone . . . I killed my husband.'

Kate waited for a reaction or comment. There was none and so she continued.

'I need to start over and find a new life, but I don't really know how to do that. I don't know how to begin. My children, Dominic and Lydia, are angry with me and of course I understand that, but I miss them so badly that some days I can hardly breathe. My husband was a cruel man, the cruellest.'

Kate ran her palm across the underside of her thigh, in an almost subconscious gesture.

'I spent years trembling at the prospect of being alone with him, two decades when I was too afraid to speak up, to ask for help or tell anyone how I lived. Every thought and action had to be contained. I was shrinking inside myself and I knew that one day I would disappear completely. I don't regret what I did, Simon, but I do regret the hurt I have caused others. And then I feel tremendous guilt because I am finally free, but in gaining that freedom I have spoiled things for my kids.'

Simon paused before slowly delivering his words. 'Luke says, "Do not judge, and you will not be judged. Do not condemn, and you will not be condemned. Forgive, and you will be forgiven." This is how I live my life and those like me that follow Jesus shall know forgiveness when they need it the most. It can bring great peace, Kate.'

'Ah, but that's just it. I don't follow Him and I don't believe. I could really have done with a spot of divine intervention over the last few years: where was your God then? I used to pray, asking for help from anyone who was listening; I got nothing. So I stopped asking – at least that was one less disappointment to contend with.'

The two sat in silence for a few minutes. Then Simon stood.

'Come on!'

He took her hand and pulled her towards the shoreline. Without waiting to test the temperature and without the caution of those less comfortable in the ocean, he ploughed on until he and Kate were wading waist-deep in the water. Eventually he stopped and grasped her hand. Her linen trousers clung to her.

He placed his hand on her lower back.

'Stand very still.' His voice was almost a whisper.

Kate did as she was told. The sediment they had disturbed quickly settled around their toes until it was like looking through dappled glass.

'Look!'

Simon pointed downwards. It took a while for Kate's eyes to adjust to their watery filter, but when they did she could see tiny silver fish darting around her feet. A small crab scurried into a hole on the sea bed and a larger fish sniffed at the new obstacle that had appeared in his playground.

'Can you see the tiny fish, Kate?'

She nodded. 'Yes! I saw him!'

'Do you think that the tiny fish is aware of everything going on up here above the surface?'

'I doubt it.' She chuckled.

'You'd be right. He swims along in the warm water, looking for shade, searching for food and interacting with the other little fish that he meets. He is thoroughly preoccupied with the small things that fill his day and has no idea about the beach, the island, countries, buildings, men and their machines, airplanes, currency . . . in fact anything that makes up the world that exists right over his head. But you know what, Kate?

Just because he is unaware of it doesn't mean that it isn't there.'

Kate turned her attention from the water to the man standing next to her who was now holding her hand.

'Are you saying I'm a tiny fish?' She smiled.

'Yes, Kate. That is exactly what I am saying. God is there whether you choose to look for him or not and he is all about forgiveness. I want you to try and remember that hope comes in many forms; sometimes it's an idea or a place and sometimes it's a person.'

Kate threw herself backwards into the warm Caribbean current. It had been a long time since she had swum. The salt water stuck to her eyelashes and stung her sunburnt skin. She felt alive.

'Maybe I like being a tiny fish!' she shouted.

Simon watched her swim underwater deeper and deeper into the ocean.

'Maybe you do.' He smiled and shook his head. 'Maybe you do.'

It had been a long day, but one that Kate would never forget. The jeep purred as it drew up outside the entrance to The Landings.

'I don't feel quite as comfortable about sleeping in my beautiful marble-floored bedroom now I know its true cost,' she mused.

'If not you then someone else, Kate, and at least your head is fully informed as it hits the feather pillow.'

She smiled at him.

'We have a Prospect Place outing tomorrow to Carnival – would you like to come with us?'

I'm not sure. I don't want to burden you with my company.'

'It's a pleasure not a burden and besides, no good comes from refusing an invitation to Carnival.'

'Is that right?'

'Oh yes. Many, many years ago the owner of one of the big plantations was invited to Carnival along with her entire household. She politely refused as she had a royal delegation staying at the house, but that meant she refused on behalf of everyone. A young kitchen maid was so angry and frustrated to be missing the celebrations that she grabbed a handful of nutmeg and shoved it into the cake mix. Too much nutmeg is never a good thing and legend has it that the royal party spent the evening hallucinating and were then violently sick and confined to their beds.'

'Ooh, sounds grim. That's a shame – I love nutmeg!'

'All things in moderation.'

Kate laughed. 'Is this a ruse to get me to wash up again?'

'You got me!'

Kate watched the lights of the jeep disappear into the night. She hadn't wanted the evening to end.

Lying awake and listening to the chirping crickets and croaking frogs, her tummy had a bubble of anticipation that wouldn't allow her to sleep; she couldn't remember the last time she had felt this way. Maybe this was what it felt like to dive in, start over.

Kate was woken by the unfamiliar ringtone of the phone by her bed. It was a full three seconds before she registered where she was. Through the fog of deep sleep she grappled in the half light towards the noise.

'Yes?' She blinked hard and rubbed at her eyes, trying to quickly reach a state of alertness.

'Good morning, Ms Gavier, I have a telephone call for you.'

'Oh, right, thank you.'

Her heart beat a little too fast for comfort. Questions fired in her brain: what had happened, why the need to call at this hour, who was it? She glanced at the red digital clock display on the television. It was four in the morning. She listened to the change in tone, no longer the sharp, tinny sound of hotel reception, but a silence that was softer, further away. Kate could make out the faint sound of irregular breathing.

'Hello?' she ventured, sharper than was usual. The silence unnerved her.

'Mummy?'

'Oh!' The breath caught in her throat. Kate sat upright and shook her head to clear the doubt. Had she heard correctly?

'Mum, are you there?'

145

It was the unmistakable, beautiful voice of her daughter.

'Yes! Yes, Lydi, I'm here. I'm right here.'

She clutched the phone between her palms, pushing it hard against her ear and mouth, trying to get closer.

'Is everything all right, darling?' It was an odd question, given that they hadn't spoken for five years, but Kate's immediate concern was that there was an emergency.

'Yes. I wanted to talk to you.'

'I wanted to talk to you too. I've wanted to talk to you for so long . . .'

She heard Lydia swallow.

'Thank you for the tickets and everything, Mum.'

Mum . . . Mum . . . Mum . . . Was there any word sweeter?

'I really didn't feel like I could come. I'm just not ready, not yet. I hope you understand.'

'It's okay, Lyds, it's all okay. It is wonderful to hear your voice, so wonderful. I can't tell you how much I miss you, every second of every day. I just wanted us to have time to talk.'

Kate wasn't sure how much to suggest, how much to push.

'Thing is, I'm a bit scared about seeing you, Mum.'

'What are you scared of, darling?'

Kate's eyes pooled with tears; the idea of her little girl being afraid of her in any capacity horrified her.

'I'm not scared of you exactly. But I'm worried

146

about seeing you and I'm just as worried about not seeing you. I just don't know what I'm supposed to do.'

'That's understandable, Lyds; there is no rule book for this. We have to find a way through it together. I can only say that by seeing each other we can sort out all the things that are scaring you. One by one we can go through them and figure them out together.'

She was throwing her daughter a rope and when Lydia caught it, Kate would pull her in and never let her go.

'It's kind of hard to explain, Mum. I'm worried that you might have changed, you might be really different now—'

'I'm still your boring old Mum. It's still me, Lyds, I promise.'

'I'm also worried in case how I feel about you has changed. I'm worried that I might not love you the same any more.'

Kate was silent as tears slid down onto lips that mouthed a silent prayer: *Please love me, please don't stop loving me.*

Lydia's voice had dropped to little more than a whisper. 'If I don't see you, Mum, I can pretend. I pretend that you and Dad are away somewhere, you know, like when you both went to Rome and we boarded for a week? I make out things are all just as they were. But if I see you, I'll know that's not really true because Dad won't be with you and you will be different . . .'

Kate could only nod, unable to speak.

'And sometimes, Mum, I pretend that you are both dead, and that makes it easier somehow. I pretend that you were both killed in an accident and then I don't have to think about you doing something so horrible to Dad or about the horrible things that Dad did to you. I don't like to think about it, Mummy.'

Her voice broke off in breathless sobs. Kate ached with the need to put her arms around her little girl and give her comfort. *I'm not dead. I'm here, Lydi, I'm right here waiting.*

'Lydi, Lydi. It's okay. It will all be okay. I promise. We can work through anything. We can take our time and talk things through.' She adopted the tone that she had once used to lull her little girl back to sleep after bad dreams.

'I don't know if it will be okay, Mum. The longer I don't see you, the harder it is for me to imagine seeing you and so it feels easier not to, if that makes sense. I sometimes wonder if it's better just to say goodbye and only think about how we used to be, when we were happy – well, not you, but the rest of us. I thought we were a happy family, but we weren't, were we?'

'No, Lyds, I guess we weren't. But I thought I could hide things, thought I could make it all okay . . .' It was the first time Kate had voiced this admission.

'And that's part of it, Mum. All I have is my memory of my family, but now I know that it was

148

all rubbish. You and Dad were making it up; it was all fake, all of it.'

Her voice faltered.

'And that's tough, knowing that my whole life and the people I trusted, it was all pretend. It's like I've got someone else's memories and not my own.'

She paused.

Kate waited for Lydia to gather her thoughts before interjecting with words of solution and solace.

'I've got to go, Mum, I'm sorry.'

Immediately and without preamble the phone clicked. It came too quickly and without warning, leaving Kate shouting at the whirring drone.

'No, Lydia! Please don't go! Please, darling girl!' she shouted into the disconnected mouthpiece, refusing to hang up, not yet.

'When you change your mind, when you are ready, I'll be waiting. I will always be waiting. You just give me the word and I'll come and find you.'

Kate continued to hold the phone to her face as she sobbed into the dawn.

She watched the sun rise through swollen eyelids raw from crying. She replayed Lydia's words over and over until they were there for perfect recall and would be until her dying day. *My whole life and the people I trusted, it was all pretend.* Kate tried to imagine being robbed of her childhood recollections, the very foundation of the life created by her parents, everything that made her feel safe and secure. Whatever the situation, however bad things got, Kate could mentally escape to a time of laughter and joy. The thought of that being taken away was too horrible to contemplate.

The midday sun was fierce and Kate wasn't sure that going to Carnival was such a good idea. She felt cloaked in desolation and wasn't keen to be around people. But the idea of spending the day pacing her room, no matter how luxurious, was more than she could bear.

Kate shunned the taxi service into town and set out on foot with a determined bounce to her step. The main road to the island's capital, Castries, was closed to traffic. She heard the thrum of music and the tinny echo of steel drums long before she could see anything. As she rounded the last bend in the road, she was greeted by a sight that would stay with her forever. It was as if every colour of the rainbow was dancing before her eyes. The whole island had turned out, and nearly everyone was sporting elaborate costumes adorned with feathers, sequins, ribbons or braiding.

Beautiful girls in sparkling bikinis with matching arm bands swayed in time to the music, taking great care not to dislodge the ornate headdresses that balanced on their heads. Children bounded like kangaroos among the floats, fuelled by excitement and the liberal consumption of sugar; some were dressed in miniature versions of the adult costumes and everyone looked wonderful.

Kate found Simon and the kids on a grass verge. They had spread blankets and were organising their picnic. Each child had made a headband; some were more intricate than others, but each had been handmade. They were clearly proud of their efforts.

'Hey! Here's Kate! Where is your costume?' Simon was pleased to see her.

'I didn't know I needed one! I've never felt more overdressed!' She clutched at her linen shirt and glass beads.

'Matilda and I thought that might be the case, so we made you this.'

He presented Kate with a headdress. It was a stunning plume of pale green feathers, with gold sequins stuck in a row along the base. Kate dug deep, found her fake smile and placed the gift on her head.

'I love it!'

'You look like a green chicken!'

'Good! Green chicken was what I was going for!'

The two shouted alternately to make themselves heard above the deafening music. Simon studied her face.

'Is everything all right, Kate?'

She nodded, not trusting herself to speak.

The atmosphere was electric and Kate did not want to be anywhere else in the world. Carnival was the distraction she needed. Her heart jumped with every drum beat and her body moved to meet the rhythm of the music that ignited her spirit. Floats

151

crawled past with bands and musicians standing on steady platforms. The procession of floats was punctuated with troops of dancers. Men, women and children in identical costumes sparkled like fireworks and moved in time to the thrum of the steel drums.

When the heavens opened, Kate raised her arms high over her head and allowed the warm tropical rain to wash over her head. She laughed, feeling a surge of optimism about her very uncertain future. At that moment in time, everything felt possible. She focussed more on the fact that Lydia had called and less on the actual words spoken, and it lifted her. *'Mum . . . Mummy . . .'* The words twinkled like diamonds in her mind.

With Matilda's hand in hers, the insistence of Simon and the upturned faces of the kids, it hadn't taken much to persuade her to accompany them back home. So towards the end of the afternoon, the weary troupe piled into minibuses and made its way back to the mission. On the road to Dennery, the smaller kids slept on the laps of the larger ones and the eldest recalled the day's highlights in hushed tones, careful not to wake their younger charges.

Simon helped all the children alight, counting them as they went and suggesting that it might be a good idea to change into dry clothes. The kids dutifully dispersed to find pyjamas or clean shorts. Fabian headed straight for the kitchen; Kate was sure he would be happy never to leave that large stove and his cramped workspace, such was his dedication to feeding the children in his care.

'You've got yourself quite a family there, Fabian. You should be very p . . . p . . . proud.' Kate shivered and stammered through her words.

'I am very proud of them all, but look at *you* – you're freezing, drenched through! And as amusing as it is to see, you have green dye all over your face. I think someone got their feathers wet!' Fabian shook his head, with his hands on his hips, as though he was addressing one of the children.

'I did!' Kate laughed, wiping at her forehead and cheeks.

'Why don't you have a hot shower and lay your clothes in the sun; it shouldn't take too long to dry them out. I can fetch you something to put on, how does that sound?'

Kate grinned though chattering teeth and nodded. A hot shower sounded like bliss. The bathroom was larger than she had expected, but contained nothing more than a pipe sticking out of the wall, a small grate in the concrete floor and a plastic shower curtain suspended across the room. Having hung her towel on the hook and lowered the latch on the door, she watched the brown water spurt sporadically from the pipe. Whilst it didn't look too appealing, it was hot and that was all that mattered.

Kate observed her skin turn from goosebumpy

to mottled and felt warm once again. She soaped her face and watched the green dye dribble down the grate. It had been a brilliant day.

She pulled back the curtain and turned the handle to stop the water. Standing with her back to the door, she ran her fingers through her hair, attempting to dry and style it with the tips of her fingers. What with the guttering sound from the pipe as the last of the water hit the concrete floor and her tuneless rendition of 'One Love', Kate didn't hear Simon's knock.

The door creaked as the latch was raised. It was as if time froze for the briefest moment. Neither moved, each uncertain of how to react.

Simon had assumed he could hang clean, dry towels on the hooks and retreat as he often did, ensuring there were enough towels for the kids in the endless cycle of laundry. Kate had forgotten to lock the door.

It wasn't her naked form that drew Simon's stare, but the latticework of scars that crisscrossed her bottom and the back of her thighs. They had the look of deliberate, patterned tracks that could not have occurred by accident.

Simon narrowed his gaze, as though by changing his focus he might alter the sight that greeted him. Kate quickly placed her hands over her breasts, even though they were the only bit of her that was hidden from view. A blush crept along her neck and chest, and the breath stopped in her throat. She was beyond embarrassed; she was mortified.

No one ever saw Kate's scars. Keeping them invisible, she could pretend that she had not suffered all that she had, and avoided having to deal with the judgement and sympathy of others. Her mind flew to the last and only person other than the perpetrator who had seen her body. The police doctor had stuffed his fist into his mouth to stem the urge to vomit. She would never forget it.

Kate did not want to elicit a similar response from Simon. She couldn't decide whether to reach for the towel and hide the evidence of her shameful existence, or to stand still and hope that he would simply disappear. Her indecision rendered her useless; she looked like a rabbit caught in the headlights of an oncoming train and felt just as scared. It was horrible for them both.

There was silence as each wondered how to proceed, how best to salvage some semblance of dignity.

Simon almost rushed forward as he grabbed the towel from the hook and wrapped it around Kate's back, partly covering her modesty. He pulled her backwards against his body, folded his large arms across her chest and held her tight. Kate eventually relaxed in his embrace and, still facing the shower wall, enjoyed the feeling of being held, protected. She closed her eyes and spoke to the strong man whose face she could not see, but whose arms held her fast.

'My husband, Mark, would allocate me points,

each and every night. I would be given points for not doing a chore properly or for not listening well enough; for not asking the right questions or for reading when I should have been working. I was always doing something wrong. Depending on how badly I scored would determine how deeply he would cut me. To cut me he would use a razor blade that he kept wrapped in a small piece of waxed paper in the drawer of his dresser. You can't imagine how scary it was to hear that drawer slide open. When he had finished cutting me, which could take anything from seconds to a few minutes, he would rape me. That's how I lived, for many, many years.'

'I have never heard anything so sad. What sort of man would want to cut you?' Simon's voice rose and quivered.

'Cut me and then rape me. What sort of man would do that?' she repeated slowly, her voice devoid of expression.

'Why did he do this to you?' Simon whispered into her damp hair.

'I don't really know. It was the ultimate way to control me. I'm certain it was an act of madness. I believe he was mad.'

'Why did your family not stop him? Your kids?'

'Oh, I never told a soul. Even now, I don't really discuss it. He never cut me anywhere that would be seen, always on the backs of my thighs and my bottom. I pretended to my children that nothing was wrong and Mark seemed to genuinely believe that nothing was wrong. Between us, we deceived everybody.'

'For very different reasons, though, Kate. One to preserve the charade through goodness, the other through evil.'

'I guess.' She liked his simple logic; it comforted her.

Simon shook his head and squeezed her tighter, as if by doing so he could absorb her pain.

'Can I look at your scars again, Kate?'

She half shrugged, not sure if she was comfortable with the idea.

Simon slowly unfolded his arms and stepped backwards. He stared at the geometric pattern, which reminded him of a burn. Reaching out confidently and starting at the base of her back, still damp from the shower, he ran his smooth palm over her buttocks and the backs of her thighs, feeling the bumps and lines beneath his fingertips. He was the only man ever to have done this. She didn't flinch, but instead felt warmth spread through her body.

'These are your battle scars, Kate. It's a battle that you will win. I promise you. You are beautiful.'

Kate's shoulders shook as a large sob made her body heave. Fat, salty tears snaked down her face. She couldn't remember the last time anyone had told her she was beautiful. She wished she was strong enough to respond to the feelings those words awoke within her.

157

Neither Kate nor Simon heard Matilda creep into the bathroom. The little girl was interested as ever in the whereabouts of her protector, and was still intrigued by the kind lady who'd liked her shell present. Ducking around Simon's legs, Matilda trod with caution until she stood between them, in front of Simon and behind Kate, who was trying to compose herself. Slowly she reached with outstretched hands and ran the pads of her dimpled fingers over the back of Kate's thigh.

'Ouch! Poor Kate.'

Simon smiled and bent forwards, scooping Matilda into his arms. He threw her gently into the steam-filled air before catching her and holding her tight against his chest.

'That's right, Matilda! Ouch indeed.' He grinned widely. 'Did you hear that, Kate? She finally had something important to say and so she said it!'

Kate reached for the dressing gown and wrapped herself toga-like before joining in the celebration. Matilda had broken the spell. The three circled the bathroom, dancing on the concrete floor as Kate and Simon whooped with delight.

'Matilda, your voice is the sweetest gift to my ears!' Simon beamed.

Kate felt intoxicated by the joy that filled the space. She threw her head back and laughed. It was all okay; in fact it was more than okay, it was bloody marvellous.

★   ★   ★

Later, as the sun sank low in the sky and once the supper dishes had been scrubbed and dried and the last of the sequins and face paint washed from sticky hands and faces, Simon and Kate sat on the wooden step. They listened to the competing orchestras of bugs and wildlife, each making a new noise louder than the one before.

'What a day.' She was tired.

'Exhausting but memorable, I hope!'

'Oh, Simon, very memorable. I spoke to my daughter this morning.'

'Well, praise be! That is wonderful news, Kate; a big step.'

'I hope so. It's given me a lot to think about. I tried for so long to protect them, keep the truth from them; I hadn't considered that they would see me as anything other than a victim. I find it hard to shoulder all the blame . . .'

'Kate, you are the only one left to blame. And it shows you have given them a sense of balance, weighing up the rights and wrongs, forming their own judgement; that's healthy.'

'I hadn't thought of it like that. You are very wise, Simon.'

'Oh, I don't know about that.'

'I would have brooded all day had you not taken me out. Thank you.'

'You like Carnival, Kate?'

'Oh yes, I like it very much. It's the most fun I've had in a long while. Exhausting but fun!'

'Well, you are welcome to Carnival anytime.

Should we put your headdress somewhere safe for next year?'

Kate looked into the face of the kind man who had shown her a new and wonderful slice of a different world.

'I don't know, maybe. I do know that whatever happens to me, Simon, I will never forget my time here or any of you, especially Matilda.'

'Today was a big step for her too; I hope it continues. Maybe she will talk more, maybe she won't, but at least we know she can and she did! Wonderful.'

Simon placed his hands flat-palmed together and lifted his eyes skywards, silently offering thanks. Then he turned his attention to Kate.

'She has touched your heart.'

'Yes, she has. She has helped my heart, actually, and she's got me thinking.'

'As I said, hope comes in many forms, sometimes it's a person . . .'

Kate smiled. 'She's got me thinking quite practically about my future and where I might be needed.'

'In what way?'

'Well, I think that the world needs more "Simons", more people who provide a haven for those that need it the most, and I think that I would like to try—'

'You want a job?' He looked fearful and hopeful in equal measure.

'Oh! Goodness no!' Kate laughed. 'I can't exactly

get you a good reference and it's too far for my kids to be able to nip over. But I think maybe I could create a Prospect Place in England. It's a wealthy country, but that doesn't mean that we always know what to do with people who fall through the gaps – the vulnerable, the young and the hurt. I met a lot of them in prison.'

Kate breathed deeply as she remembered the conversation between Kelly and Jojo: *'Did you stay because of the kids? No, I stayed because of the drugs . . . I don't see the kids no more . . .'* She wondered what they were up to now.

'Kate, I think you would be brilliant at that.' Simon brought her back to the present.

'Really?'

'Really.'

'Well, that feels like an endorsement!' She beamed.

They sat in silence for a while. Kate knew that his next choice of topic was inevitable and had subconsciously been waiting for him to raise it.

'Kate, I could never and would never condone the taking of a life, but that doesn't mean that I can't offer you my sympathy and understanding for how you have suffered. What I saw today—'

Kate placed her finger over his mouth.

'No. Please, Simon, I don't want to have that conversation, I really don't. Can we just make out that this afternoon never happened? Can you go back to looking at me quizzically like you have since we met and not with the doleful expression

161

you usually have when talking about one of the kids? I don't want that to be how you see me.'

He nodded. 'If that's what you want.'

'It is.' She looked directly at him. 'I want to thank you, not just for that, but for everything. I feel somehow renewed and ready to face the world!'

'You were brought here for a reason, Kate, and reasons aren't always instantly obvious.'

'Now don't start with that. I'm a tiny fish, remember?'

Simon laughed.

'Also, Reverend Dubois, I don't intend to do the washing-up here ever again. If I do manage to come back, then I want to use a dishwasher.'

Kate unfurled a small square of paper from her pocket.

'With that in mind, Simon, my lovely friend, I want to give you this. It's something I want to do and it will bring me a great deal of happiness.'

Simon opened the cheque and gazed at the sum. It was enough not only for a dishwasher but also to rebuild the whole structure of Prospect Place with proper plumbing, playrooms and all the things that he could only ever have dreamed of.

'Kate, I—'

'No. Don't say another word. It's for Matilda and all the Matildas that might come after her.'

Simon placed his hands on either side of her head and kissed her gently on the mouth. Kate had forgotten that there was this kind of kiss. It was very different to the kiss that you gave a child or a friend and wasn't a kiss that scared or controlled you. It was a kiss that brought warmth to your core. It was the way a lover might kiss a lover. Simon pulled away slowly and, for the briefest of moments, the two pondered the possibility of more kissing in a different place, at a different time.

'Kate Gavier, you are a big fish, never doubt it. You are a very big fish, my lovely friend.'

TEN YEARS AGO

It was nearly time for the school bell to ring, announcing the end of the last period. Kathryn stood with her back to the door, twisting a tea towel inside a coffee mug, soaking up any drips, filling her time.

'I must remember to chill the dips and give the glasses a good wipe . . .'

'Who are you talking to?'

His voice surprised her; she spun around, tea towel in hand and looked at her son as he delved into the bread bin in his relentless search for carbohydrates. He was a handsome boy, tall with a laid-back demeanour and appealing voice that was just on the right side of posh. It still took Kathryn slightly by surprise, how her baby had grown into this teenage life force. It staggered her how quickly the years had flown by, staggered and frightened her. For every year that sped by, allowing her child to stride towards adulthood, was also a year of her life that she had spent tethered to Mark.

'Hello, my darling! I didn't hear you come in. How was your day?'

'My day was complete and total shit.'

'Oh right, I shan't ask then.' She attempted to win him over with humour.

'Well you can ask as much as you like, but I won't tell you.'

She swallowed his sneer and let it settle in her stomach. It was easier to ignore his comments than allow them to escalate. He was probably just tired.

'Are you here for supper, Dom?'

'Depends.' He had turned his attention to the cupboard and was now addressing her from behind the open door.

'Depends on what?'

'On what supper is.'

She chewed her bottom lip, containing it all, swallowing the latent aggression, the indifference, the mild hostility, the unspoken irritation. These behavioural traits were typical of boys his age. He was a child-man trying to find his place in the world and not quite sure how to fire off the steam that built up inside him. He had also adopted some of his father's views and attitudes, albeit subconsciously.

'It's coq au vin with steamed fresh green beans and purple sprouting broccoli.'

'I really, really hate the way you do that.'

'The way I do what?'

He closed the cupboard door and looked at his mother.

'The way you try and entice me to stay for supper

by delivering the menu as though it was a fancy restaurant. Why can't you just say "We're having chicken"?'

She would play along, she would humour him; she didn't want to argue – she hadn't seen him for a day or so.

'Fine. I shall no longer try to entice you to allow me to cook for you. Tonight, Dominic, we are having chicken. Are you here for supper?'

'No, I've already eaten.'

She looked into his eyes. 'So can I assume that you've already eaten whether we are having coq au vin or just chicken?'

'Yeah.' He scowled.

She bent forward and rested her arms on the counter top. Her hands joined together, subconsciously simulating prayer. She brought them up to her forehead and exhaled deeply. Closing her eyes, she spoke to the presence that she could still feel but could no longer see. It was sometimes easier that way.

'Dominic, is there something going on with you that you want to talk about? Anything upsetting you?'

'No.'

'Because you can always talk to me, you know. That's my job!'

'There is nothing I have to say that I think you will want to hear.'

'Well in that case, I really need you to think about the way that you treat people; more specifically, the way that you treat me. I am not your enemy, or the hired help for that matter. I am your mum and I don't know why you think that it is okay to talk to me like that, but it is not. I know that life is not always perfect for you, but let me tell you, mister, that your life is a lot more perfect than most people's. I understand that you have the pressures of school work, the distraction of girls and having Dad work here . . . I know that it's not always easy, but please, please don't shut me out. I love you, Dominic, I love you very much.'

Dominic stared at his mother's back, bent over the kitchen counter, and studied the knobbles at the top of her spine, which were visible through the thin fabric of her shirt.

'If you must know, Mum, it's nothing to do with Dad. It's you.'

'Me?' She tried to keep the surprise from her voice, tried to mask the sadness and resignation at his comment. 'How is it me?'

'You are just so . . .' He fought to find the words as he breathed out from inflated cheeks.

'So *what* exactly, Dominic?'

She stood straight now, with her hands on her hips, and he faced her.

'You're weird.'

She laughed. It was a quick, loud laugh to hide her nerves, and something else – relief?

'I'm weird?'

She posed the question and yet did not want to hear the answer.

'Yes, Mum, you are weird and it is so not funny so I don't know why you are laughing.'

She noticed that he emphasised the 'so'. He wasn't finished.

'You talk to yourself and people in school notice, my friends notice. You float around the place as though you are only half aware of what you're doing; it's like you're completely bonkers or on drugs or something. You smile even though you are clearly unhappy. It's like living with someone that's got a secret; it's like you know something that no one else does and it sets you apart from us, from me, Dad and Lyds. I feel sometimes like you're not part of this family and all my mates joke about how bloody strange you are with your clean sheet obsession and it's shit because it's true and worst of all it makes me weird by association. It's just complete shit.'

She looked at her son.

'I understand, Dominic. It's shit.'

'No. No, Mum, you don't understand and that's just it.'

He turned and left the room. She was once again alone with her tea towel.

The ghost of his words swirled and spiralled around her form and settled over her like a fine mist. *'It's like living with someone that's got a secret; it's like you know something that no one else does and it sets you apart from us . . .'*

Clever, clever Dominic. My clever, beautiful boy. He was right, that was exactly what it was like.

Kathryn gathered her thoughts and tried to focus on something, anything other than the ache of her son's words and the manner in which he had felt it appropriate to deliver them. She was sifting through the encounter, trying to pick out any tiny positives, when in walked Lydia with an oversized sketch pad shoved under her arm.

'What's for tea?'

'Hi, Lydia, yes I'm fine, thank you, my day was fairly good and how are you?'

'What?'

'Never mind. It's chicken.'

'Just chicken? Yuk. That is so totally boring.'

'Well it's coq au vin actually with steamed fresh green beans and purple sprouting broccoli.'

'Oh, well why didn't you say that? God, Mum, sometimes you can be so—'

Kathryn held up her hand, interrupting her daughter's flow before she had the chance to throw any fuel on her already broken spirit.

'Yes, Lydia, I know. I have an inability to accurately describe supper. Forgive me. I am weird beyond belief. I'm an embarrassment to you, life is shit and it's all my fault, everything from world famine to the war in the Middle East, global warming, the current economic crisis and of course the fact that Luca Petronatti won't go out with you. It is all my fault, all of it. You can quite legitimately blame me for everything.'

Lydia was speedy with her retort.

'Are you menopausal? Is that what this is all about?'

'Probably, Lydia.'

'I'll eat in my room.'

Lydia marched back into the hallway and up the stairs. That was it, end of discussion. Kathryn tried to imagine a similar conversation with her own mother. She tried to imagine first of all enquiring about the state of her mother's biological cycle, commenting on it and then demanding in so many words that her supper be waitressed up to her room. She could of course imagine neither, for she wouldn't have dared or wanted to. Things had been different.

Opening the cupboard door, she turned the tin of peas to face the 'right way'. For the first few years of their marriage, the tasks that Kathryn performed which required detailed and careful instruction were varied and numerous. Up until then she had inadvertently been executing many tasks wrongly. Who knew? Not she. She had been blissfully unaware that there was a right way to put honey on toast, a right way to make coffee in a cafetière. Luckily, Mark was on hand to help her realise the error of her ways.

The list was long and meticulous. Tins had to be stacked no more than three high and with all the labels facing outwards; when opened with a tin opener, their lids had to be removed entirely – never, ever left jagged and hanging by a thin hinge of metal – and placed inside the empty tin for disposal.

A carpet had always to be vacuumed in straight horizontal lines, allowing you to follow the previous edge – haphazardly roaming around a room until you were sure that you had covered each area at least once was out of the question. There was a right way to store socks (balled together with its opposite number and placed in colour-coordinated order in the drawer); a right way to stack a dishwasher, fold a towel, tie and dispose of a bin bag, brush your teeth, park the car, drive the car, feed the children, comb and cut your hair, make the bed, polish the floor, address the neighbours, write Christmas cards, answer the phone, dress, walk, talk, think . . .

Mark Brooker always entered a room loudly, even if he didn't say a word. He never simply arrived anywhere. It was as if he always had to announce his presence, like an actor walking onto the set of an American sitcom. As his head appeared around the door, Kathryn always half expected to hear clapping and canned laughter, merely at the fact of his arrival.

He came to where she stood and eclipsed her with his form.

'Good evening, Kathryn.'

'Hello, Mark.'

'You look neat and pretty.'

She smiled weakly up at him. 'Thank you.'

'Something smells good. What's for supper?'

'It's . . . err . . . it's . . .'

'It's . . . err . . . it's . . . what?' His tone was clipped, through his smiling mouth.

'It's chicken . . . It's coq au vin . . . Chicken.'

'Chicken coq au vin chicken. Splendid.'

He pulled her face into his hands and kissed her hard and full on the mouth before turning on his heel and retiring to his study. She waited until the door clicked in its frame before raising the checked tea towel to her mouth and wiping away the moist evidence of his presence.

She set the table for the two of them; her lips ached and swelled slightly from his aggressive contact. Her mind flitted to an evening during their courtship. They had been in the bar at University College, London, among a small group of fellow students, when the conversation shifted to the subject of working women. There was the usual banter about chaining wives to sinks and the old jokes about why were women married in white? To match the rest of the household appliances – boom boom! How they all laughed.

After walking her home, Mark had turned to her as they stood in her parents' doorway.

'You will stay at home, won't you, gorgeous? You'll stay at home and grow our babies and I will look after you so that you never have to worry about a thing, not one single thing.'

She smiled up at him.

'Well, Mark, I will stay at home eventually, when I do have babies, but up until then, I definitely want to teach. I want to use my degree. I think

I'll be really good! I certainly love my subject and I'm very patient – unlike a certain someone I could name!'

'Impatient, *moi*? It's not my fault if most of the kids that get shoved in front of me are retards. I need a better calibre of child, one without the IQ of a pot plant!'

'Ah, what is it they say? "A bad workman blames his tools." Is it the same for bad teachers?'

Suddenly and without any warning, Mark grabbed her right wrist, lifted her hand up to her own face, and laughed.

'Stop slapping yourself, you silly girl!'

He was laughing and smiling as he slapped her hand across her own face, hard. For a moment, she was too shocked to react. Then realisation dawned and she clenched her muscles and splayed her fingers taut. But he was much stronger and simply carried on making her hit herself in the face.

'Stop it! Stop it, Kathryn! You silly girl!'

She cried and gulped air in surprise. It was some seconds before he stopped abruptly.

'Oh my darling! Why are you crying?'

She looked into his beautiful pale blue eyes as her own pooled with tears.

'Because you hurt me, Mark.'

He crushed her to him, folded his duffel coat around her and spoke softly into her scalp.

'Baby, baby, it was just a joke! I love you and I would never hurt you intentionally. I would rather die than hurt you.'

She had been shaken when the mirror revealed an angry red mark across the side of her face.

As Kathryn positioned the table mats, coasters and the salt and pepper centrally on the table, she reflected that this, among many other things that Mark did and said, was a lie. He would not rather die than hurt her. This she knew for a fact.

At eight o'clock, with supper finished, the various masters began trickling in and making themselves comfortable in the kitchen. She circled the room, dispensing wine and mineral water into sparklingly clean glasses whilst nodding, smiling and commenting where appropriate or necessary.

'Yes, it is unusually mild.'

'Thank you, yes, I am well, very well.'

'Dominic? Oh, you know, studying hard.'

'The first eleven? Oh, it's against Taunton School, I think.'

'For aphides, I trust a mixture of vinegar and water, liberally sprayed.'

Kathryn looked at the rag-taggle group of old men clad in their fusty corduroy garments. Collectively they gave off the faintest whiff of decay. Thick tufts of hair sprouted from ears and noses – the kind of thing that an attentive wife would have taken care of. Their teeth were also neglected. She imagined them as a group of ageing penguins, squawking and jostling for position even though no one else in the world was the tiniest bit interested in anything they did or said.

At approximately ten past eight Mark made his grand entrance.

'Good evening one and all!'

He stood by the opened door and Kathryn noticed a flicker of hesitation, correctly guessing that he considered bowing before deciding against it.

The assembled crowd nodded their heads and muttered incomprehensibly, honoured to be in the presence of their esteemed head, waiting to hear what wisdom would follow that dazzling smile and its flash of whitened, straightened teeth.

'Right, gentlemen, shall we get started?'

Mark rubbed his palms together with Faginesque enthusiasm.

The masters took their positions around the kitchen table, each man's status apparent by how close he sat to Mark.

'Agenda item number one: the Excellence in Education Awards, which I may or may not have had a tip-off about today—'

Before he even finished the sentence there was a chorus of comment from around the table.

'Oh well done, Headmaster!'

'Bloody marvellous news, Mark!'

'Much deserved, old chap, really much deserved!'

Kathryn, having heard enough, slipped into the sitting room and closed the door behind her. She crept silently over to the telephone table, opened the drawer and carefully removed the copy of *Tom*

Jones that she had placed at the back, secreted away for just such an occasion. She picked up the novel and ran her fingers over its cover, feeling a small yet familiar surge of happiness, knowing that she could snatch a few minutes of reading until her services were required again. She knew the drill: fifteen minutes to allow proceedings to get underway, then back into the kitchen to serve canapés and dips.

Kathryn sat in the comfy chair in front of the window and dived in.

> *The reader will be pleased, I believe, to return with me to Sophia. She passed the night, after we saw her last, in no very agreeable manner. Sleep befriended her but little, and dreams less. In the morning, when Mrs Honour, her maid, attended her, at the usual hour, she was found already up and drest.*

She fell into the pages happily and allowed herself to slip into the world created by Henry Fielding.

Reading was Kathryn's greatest passion and her only escape. She had always known that it was a very dangerous thing; if a book was good enough, it could rob her of time and awareness, and would entirely consume her, forcing her to take every step with the characters, unable to pull away for fear of leaving them in limbo. This was how it was for Kathryn that night. And when she heard the sitting room door bang loudly against the wall, eighteen minutes had passed – not the agreed fifteen.

She dropped the book without regard for its welfare, caring not that the lovely Sophia would be tumbling downwards unprotected to land with a thump in darkness. Her husband remained by the opened door, saying and doing nothing, his expression blank. She tried not to catch his eye as she sidled past him and into the kitchen. Not one word was spoken between them.

Offering a muted apology to the guests, Kathryn quickly removed the cling film from her canapés and uncorked another bottle of chilled medium white. She waltzed around the kitchen distributing plates and napkins before circulating again with platters of goodies; all were eagerly received and consumed with the appropriate appreciation and thanks. Crumbs littered grey-streaked beards, and sauces and dips were dripped onto ties and lapels. A job well done.

It was gone eleven o'clock by the time all the guests had left. The dishwasher whirred away, the table had been wiped clean, mats and coasters were restored to their drawers and the chairs pushed in just so.

Kathryn climbed the stairs and entered their bedroom. She walked with a measured pace, not over eager to reach her destination, but aware that any delay would only put off the inevitable.

It was a beautiful room. The high ceiling and

177

ornate period coving complemented the magnificent wallpaper design of peonies and cabbage roses whose many shades of aubergine and purple petals looked so real you wanted their scent to invade you. Two large sash windows overlooked the sports field, although at this time of night the roman blinds obscured the view. The carpet was cream and topped with bottle-green rugs to give just the right amount of underfoot snugness. The antique bed was large and grand, with deep floral carvings in the mahogany headboard. It had belonged to Mark's grandmother and was much admired, but Kathryn hated it intensely. She often dreamed of it being consumed by woodworm until nothing remained but a tiny pile of dust and a very fat worm.

For all its beauty, the room held fearsome associations for Kathryn. She was always taken aback when visitors made approving, envious comments: she fully expected them to inhale the misery that lodged in every nook and cranny and would not have been surprised to see the oceans of tears she had cried seeping from the walls and the mattress, forming pools on the floor.

Kathryn removed her shoes and skirt. She paired her tan leather loafers with their heels together under the old, overstuffed, chintz-covered chair that sat in the corner of the room. Her skirt she rezipped and folded in half before hanging over the back of the same chair. Her shirt she rolled into a ball and placed in the wicker laundry basket along with her discarded pants and bra. She undid her earrings and pearl necklace, carefully placing them in the jewellery box on the dressing table. She brushed and flossed her teeth and combed her hair, removing all traces of make-up. Finally she slipped into one of five identical white cotton nightdresses that she owned. They were rather long, plain and Shaker in style, each with a Peter Pan collar and small ivory buttons at the base of pin-tuck pleats on the cuff and neck.

Kathryn then knelt at the foot of the bed, bowed her head and waited. Just as she had done every single night for the last seventeen years and five months.

She heard the creak of the top stair, followed by the tell-tale tap of wedding ring against wooden banister rail. Her muscles tensed as they always did at the familiar sounds; it made no difference how many times she had heard them. Finally she heard the bedroom door snap shut into the frame and the scraping of the old brass key in its lock.

The creep of fear plucked at her muscles, invaded her bones and pricked at her skin. Closing her eyes briefly, she shuddered involuntarily as her heart performed its customary jump.

Mark walked towards her kneeling form and stood behind her in his usual position, with his hands behind his back. His thighs almost grazed the back of her head. She could feel an almost incandescent heat coming off him in waves. His voice, as usual, was calm, lilting, almost soft.

'Well?' he asked.

Her mouth twitched and she swallowed as she tried to form the words. Experience had taught her that it was better to speak concisely, honestly and audibly . . . Much better.

'I think four points.'

'You *think* four points?'

'Yes.' She swallowed again.

'Well you would be wrong. It is seven points.'

'Seven?'

'Did I ask you to repeat that figure? Did I tell you to speak?'

She shook her head. No, no, he hadn't. *Don't look and don't speak.*

'Four points indeed!'

He gave a small laugh before tutting as though admonishing an amusing child.

'I shall now tell you why seven points.'

He cleared his throat with a small cough and began.

'Firstly, I would ask you to cast your mind back to this morning. When I gave you a flower, you did not raise your face to me with thanks, preferring instead to stare at the floor like an insolent teenager. Two points. You had also been chatting in an overfamiliar way with two of the pupils. Two points. When I asked you what was for supper you gave me some hesitant, irritating comment, "Chicken, blah blah, chicken". One point. And finally, after being given specific instructions, you forced me to leave my masters' meeting to call you to serve the appropriate refreshments, which were not only late but were rather average. This, Kathryn, embarrassed us both. Two points. Which makes a grand total of . . .?'

'Seven points,' she replied, in a small voice.

'That is correct.'

He ran his fingers through her hair, gently stroking the nape of her neck. Bending low, he kissed the top of her spine and she felt the air blow cold against the wet imprint from his mouth.

Mark went into the en-suite bathroom to take his nightly shower, leaving his wife kneeling on the floor to contemplate the error of her ways.

Her legs went numb and, as usual, pins and needles consumed her feet and toes.

Fifteen minutes later Mark emerged, damp and lemon-scented. He sauntered over to the bedside table and flicked the button on his alarm clock. All set. He then walked to the wardrobe and selected a tie for the following day: cornflower blue silk with a yellow spot, very dapper. From the drawer of his tallboy he chose some cufflinks, silk knots of course, in a corresponding blue and yellow. He reached for his cologne, Floris No. 89, and daubed the citrusy top notes behind his ears and across his chin. Next, he slid open the lower drawer and removed the small square of waxy paper, which he unfolded to reveal the shiny steel razor blade. He pinched the blade between his thumb and forefinger and examined it in the lamplight.

'Come.'

His outstretched palm pointed towards the bed as if calling a dog to heel.

Kathryn stood on wobbly legs. She knew what to do, she knew the drill; she had done it more than six and a half thousand times. *Six and a half thousand! Unbelievable. Unthinkable, but true.*

She lay face down in the middle of the bed with her nightdress raised to just above her bottom. At this point he always asked, 'Are you comfortable?' and she would either murmur or nod into the creamy silk comforter that yes, she was comfortable. She had learned through experience that there was no point in saying or indicating anything different.

Over the years, Kathryn had come to view Mark's behaviour as 'normal', in so far as 'normal' meant something that occurred commonly, regularly, as standard, something that was routine, predictable, a benchmark; something that happened every day.

Mark had a method and rhythm to his cutting. He would never sever an incision that had not properly healed and he would cut in a pattern of lines, only millimetres apart, always with precision, on a slight diagonal and always working from the outside in. The backs of Kathryn's thighs were a dense matrix of lines and tracks, over six and a half thousand of them, in varying states of healing and recuperation.

Mark only ever made one cut per night – a single line – regardless of the number of points he had dished out. The points were not about quantity: they were a measurement of depth.

The points allocated ranged from zero to twelve. In all their married life Kathryn had never scored a zero and did not believe she ever would. Twelve points meant she would lose consciousness, but this was sometimes preferable to the lingering pain of a nine or ten.

She found it morbidly fascinating that her blood continued to flow. A thick, sticky trickle, night after night. Would she never run out? Would the day come when he would make his incision and there would be nothing? A barren source: used up, finished, gone, enough.

The cutting could take anything from three minutes to ten. Her blood would meander, warm and viscous, down between her legs and onto the white linen sheets. There it would form lake-shaped patterns; on a good day it might be Placid, on a bad day, Geneva. When he had done cutting, Mark would rape her.

Kathryn was not allowed to wash following this nightly ritual. In fact she wasn't even allowed to move until her husband had fallen asleep. She would then wince as she shuffled across to her side of the bed; sleep would come to her eventually when the throb of pain subsided slightly. Sometimes she would cry hot, silent tears into her pillow, but mostly she did not, not any more. This too, experience had shown her, was futile; there was no one to see or hear those tears.

The alarm pip-pipped its irritating echo around the room; it was 6 a.m. Kathryn reluctantly opened her eyes. Mark was already awake and standing by the side of the bed, watching her come to. He reached out and tenderly took her hand as she slid off the mattress, still foggy with sleep. Her nightdress, as was customary, had dried and stuck to the bloody cuts on her thighs. She stood still and upright as he gently gathered the fabric in his free hand and, pulling it taut, yanked it from its plasma tethers. It woke her up.

He took her hand and led her into the bathroom. She watched as he turned the nozzle and allowed the shower to run into the tray.

'Today, Kathryn, you have two minutes.'

He smiled and bent forward, grazing her forehead with a kiss. She raised her bloodied gown over her head and let it fall into a cotton heap on the tiled floor. Stepping into the current, it took a few seconds for her body to adjust to the temperature, which was as usual slightly too hot. But there was no point raising an objection. The fresh cuts always stung in protest, but that too would settle down to almost bearable.

She closed her eyes and let the water run over her face, washing away another night and heralding a new day much like any other. Reaching for the bottle, she squeezed out a blob of apple-scented shampoo, a little larger than the size of a fifty pence piece, just as her mother had taught her all those years ago. Now that the fifty pence piece had become considerably smaller, should she apply a little bit extra to compensate? Kathryn's mind flitted to other things that had diminished in size since she was a little girl: Wagon Wheel biscuits, telephones, journey times to Cornwall . . .

Kathryn applied the shampoo to her hair and scalp, feeling it grow into a mound of froth. Mark stood on the other side of the glass screen, watching her every action. She closed her eyes and scoured her scalp and hair, enjoying the sensation. Suddenly the water stopped running. She yelped slightly in surprise, the suds still in her hands and eyes.

Mark opened the door and she stood there dishevelled, slightly disorientated and covered in sweet-scented foam. Her hair looked like an uncooked meringue.

'I said two minutes.'

She knew that protest would be pointless, even if she were able to find the courage. It was her own stupid fault, daydreaming about rubbish from her childhood. She wouldn't say anything; she didn't want to start the day any more points down than was absolutely necessary. Shivering, she stepped from the steamy cubicle into the cool air. Mark placed a large towel around her body and with one free end he wiped the foam from her eyes and face.

'There now,' he cooed, 'that's better.'

She padded into the bedroom and got dressed while her husband showered. Despite using the towel to remove as many of the suds as was possible, her hair was still a sticky mess. She ran a comb through it as best she could. Looking into the mirrors on her dressing table, she practised her smile. Was it her imagination or was it becoming more and more difficult to get it right?

Kathryn stripped the bedclothes as she did every morning and tried not to look at the scarlet pond of misery that spoilt the white perfection on which it sat. She added her nightdress to the middle of the bundle of linen. As ever, she would have this on a hot wash before the children surfaced, and they would never know. They would never know.

By the time Lydia made her way into the kitchen nearly an hour later, the laundry was ready to be pegged out, the table was set for breakfast, bacon was crisping under the grill and Kathryn was standing at the sink, ready to face the day.

The first she knew of her daughter's arrival was when the chair legs scraped on the wooden floor.

'Good morning, Lydi! Did you have sweet dreams?'

There was no response from her daughter, whose head lay on her arms which formed a triangular cradle on the table.

'Lydia, I said did you have sweet dreams?'

Kathryn approached her slowly and stroked her hair away from her shoulder.

'What?' Lydia shouted, yanking the two tiny white headphones from her ears.

'Sorry, darling, I didn't realise you were plugged in, I was just asking if you—'

'Oh my God! What on earth have you done to your hair? It looks awful! Really awful!'

Kathryn chose to ignore the comments, as she had no adequate response.

'Would you like some bacon?'

'*Would I like some bacon*?' Lydia's voice climbed in incomprehension. Why had the subject been changed? Had her mother finally flipped?

'What are you two shouting about?' Dominic was an unwelcome addition to the already uncomfortable conversation.

'I wasn't shouting.' Kathryn corrected him.

'Jesus Christ, Mother, what's with the wet look? You look like a mental patient. Seriously, like a real total freak! For God's sake, sort it out. My friends might see you!'

'Would you like some bacon, Dominic?'

'*Would I like some bacon*?'

'That's where you came in, Dom.' Lydia rolled her eyes. 'I was telling her how totally weird she looks with whatever you call that thing going on with her hair and she replied with "Would you like some bacon?" I think she's finally lost the plot or, as I've been saying recently, not that anyone listens to me, she is seriously menopausal—'

'Can you two please stop talking about me as though I am not here; it is really very rude and

187

hurtful. What does it matter what my hair looks like? It's only hair! Now, more importantly, can I get anyone some bacon?'

For some reason this was hilarious to her teenage children, who chortled and slapped the table until tears began to gather, among wheezes of '*Bacon!*' And then back to laughing.

'Good morning, family Brooker! My goodness, what is all this jollity for, first thing in the morning? What have I missed?'

'Mum . . .' Dominic managed before pointing and collapsing again.

Mark ruffled his son's long hair and smiled at the twosome.

'Come on, you two, nothing can be that funny.'

'It is!' Lydia squawked.

He shook his head.

'Kathryn, is there any chance of some bacon?'

This sent the two into hysterical convulsions and their dad had little option but to join in, the laughter being impossibly infectious. The three sat at the table and laughed and prodded each other and laughed some more and occasionally pointed at Kathryn's head. It was all very, very funny.

Kathryn picked up the wicker basket and loaded the wet bed linen into it. She wandered out to the clothes line with her floral bag of dolly pegs.

'Come on, Peggy, time to go to work.' She ran her thumb over the little smiling face as it took up its position.

As she stretched the sheet taut on the line and

watched it billow in the breeze, she thought of something else that had diminished: she had. She was getting smaller and smaller and of less and less consequence. She was quite certain that one day she would simply disappear, and absolutely no one would notice. She shivered as she pegged her nightdress next to the sheet.

'Morning, Mrs Brooker!'

'Morning, Mrs Bedmaker!'

Again the two spoke simultaneously, suspecting that she would miss the cruel moniker. They were right, she didn't notice a thing.

'Morning, Luca! Good morning, Emily! How are you both today?'

'Good, thanks. Is Dom ready?' Luca spoke for them both. Emily had the guilty and furtive air of someone who was sleeping with her son.

'I think so. Feel free to go in. There is breakfast ready if you are hungry.' She smiled at the two of them.

Mrs Bedmaker, Mrs Bedmaker, Mrs Bedmaker . . . the words spun around inside her head, a silent taunt.

Clearly they were in too much of a hurry for breakfast as within a minute the four children were making their way back down the path and off to morning lessons.

'See you later!' Dom shouted over his shoulder. Lydia was once again plugged in and oblivious to the rest of the planet.

'Bye, love! Have a good day!'

Kathryn hated the false brightness of her tone and the smile that she knew was an inadequate veil to her silent misery. She watched them disappear behind the hedgerow and seconds later heard a roar of laughter. She knew instinctively that they were laughing at her – about her, at her, it made little difference which. It hurt just the same.

As she walked into the kitchen Mark pushed his breakfast plate into the middle of the table, ready to be tidied away by his wife.

'Kathryn . . .'

He always said her name when starting a conversation, to make sure that he had all of her attention, so that she wouldn't miss a detail or even a nuance.

'Kathryn, I think fish for supper would be good.'

'Fish. Yes of course.'

'Good.'

He rose from the table and pulled his double cuffs to the desired length below his suit jacket.

'I don't know if you have heard on the rumour mill, but I, and as a result the school, are being honoured. I have had it on good authority that the National Excellence in Education Awards are naming me Head Teacher of the Year. How about that?'

She blinked at him. *Speak now, make it something nice.*

'That is very well done, wonderful.' She tried hard not to make it sound stilted or mechanical.

'You are right, it is very well done and wonderful.

You know why I am being honoured in this way, don't you?'

'No, well, yes, I'm not really sure . . .' She didn't know what the correct or expected response was.

'Fret not, Kathryn, I will tell you why. It is because I am quite brilliant. Why did I get it?'

'Because you are brilliant, Mark.'

'That is very kind of you to say so, my sweet wife.'

Pulling her forward by the tops of her arms, he kissed her full and hard on the mouth just as Judith opened the back door.

'Only me!'

Seeing that she had interrupted an apparent moment of tenderness, Judith felt the scarlet stain of embarrassment creep up her chubby neck.

'Oh, Headmaster! Kathryn! I am so dreadfully sorry to impose! I'm obviously interrupting at a delicate moment.'

She was flustered, jealous and intrigued all at the same moment.

'Not at all. My wonderful wife was just telling me that I am brilliant!'

Judith pushed her glasses back up onto her nose. 'Oh, but you are, Headmaster, quite brilliant.'

She stared slack-mouthed at Mark, as if she had forgotten that Kathryn was there. Kathryn could imagine her salacious, lewd thoughts.

'That is very kind of you to say so, Judith. Have you come to escort me to the office?'

'Well, yes and no! I mean, I will obviously escort

you, but also I wanted to pick your brains about speech day refreshments and the siting of the marquee; we must prepare for the possibility of light showers!'

'Ah yes, indeed we must. And there was me looking forward to a leisurely stroll to my office. Never mind. No rest for the wicked, isn't that what they say?'

He turned and winked at his wife as the two of them left the kitchen, neglecting to shut the back door. Wicked indeed.

While stacking the dishwasher, Kathryn smiled to herself. Judith's entrances always made her think of Natasha and how much she missed her friend's visits. Natasha used to imitate Judith by entering with a much exaggerated 'Only me!', which would render Kathryn helpless with laughter. She thought back to one particular rainy Tuesday, when the two had been chatting in the school shop. Natasha was stocking up with pencils and Kathryn was putting up a notice about a fund-raising event for the rugby first fifteen's trip to South Africa.

Natasha had turned to her friend and asked, 'Notice anything different about me today?'

Kathryn cast her eye over her friend's striped tights, flared mini-skirt and pale pink ballet cardigan. 'Not really. Should I?'

'Yes! I am rosy and glowing with love! Well, lust actually, but in my cynical book they are one and the same.'

Kathryn felt her cheeks colour. She routinely avoided conversations around this topic, especially with Natasha, so as to evade any reciprocal questioning about the state of play in her own love life. Kathryn felt out of her depth and slightly uncomfortable with the whole subject.

'Oh? Anyone I know?' She prayed that it wasn't anyone that she knew, not wanting the mental pictures that were threatening to form in her mind.

'Actually you well might. Do you know Jacob Whittington, sixth former?'

'Yes, nice-looking boy, off to Oxbridge . . .' Kathryn wasn't sure where this was heading.

'Well, if you think he is a nice-looking boy, you should see his dad. He is hot! I mean, seriously hot! And a surgeon and divorced and shagging me! Aren't I the lucky one!'

Kathryn stared at her friend and felt her jaw drop, quite literally.

'Really? Dr Whittington?'

'Yes, really! Dr Whittington – or Max, to those of us that get to see him butt-naked and making me cups of tea at three in the morning! God, don't look at me like that, Kate. It's like I've just told you that I've committed a heinous crime, you look so disapproving. Why are you looking like that? Is it because he's so out of my league? You're right, of course, he is and I know we are not supposed to fraternise with pupils' parents, but he is really scrummy and I am rather keen, in fact super keen. I can almost guarantee that young Jacob will be getting the A star that he is so desperately seeking if it means I get to keep seeing Daddy! Kate, say something, anything . . .'

'Are you not a lesbian?' Kathryn blurted.

The question caught Natasha off guard and left her momentarily lost for a response, until eventually she screeched with laughter, her head thrown back, loud and unrestrained.

'Am I not *what*?'

'A lesbian,' Kathryn repeated, feeling embarrassed at even using the word on school premises.

'A lesbian? Oh my God! Why did you think that? Because I have short hair and wear men's shoes?'

'No! No, Natasha, not at all. It's just that Mark said—'

'Oh well, that figures. Mark wouldn't know a lesbian if one came up and bit his arse! He is so keen to pigeon-hole everyone with his nasty clichés. Grrr, that bloody man! It's not that I give a shit what he thinks about me, but he could really cause some damage with his mean little rumours and nicknames.'

She remembered suddenly that she was talking to not only her newest best friend, but also to Mark's wife.

'Sorry, Kate, no offence intended, but you know what I mean.'

'None taken, and I'm sorry, I should never have supposed that his assumption was correct. I should have known better. And there was me feeling terribly cosmopolitan with my first ever lesbian friend.'

'Ah, honey, I have really disappointed you, haven't I? I'm sorry if I've let you down with my boring heterosexual practices, all that deviant sleeping with men.'

They both laughed and strolled off arm in arm. The shop staff watched them walk from the store and no one commented as Natasha playfully squeezed Kathryn's bottom as they were about to round the corner.

'Well, Kate, if they are going to talk, we may as well give them something to talk about.'

Kathryn had jumped and shuddered, not at the playful act of her friend, or even with embarrassment at the gossip it would create, but because Natasha had inadvertently pulled apart a cut that was trying to heal, breaking the skin and causing her to bleed.

Kathryn smiled at the memory. She closed the dishwasher door and focussed her attention on the task in hand. Tuesday, Tuesday . . . Think, what are the chores for Tuesday? She had had years to memorise the weekly calendar of chores, and yet increasingly she found herself forgetting. It must be her age. Ah yes, it was coming back to her now. Tuesday's chores included removing all of Mark's textbooks from the shelves in the study, dusting the shelves as well as each individual book and replacing them just so; stripping the children's beds and washing and ironing their bed linen; weeding the flower bed at the back of the kitchen door; and cleaning both the family bathroom and the en suite thoroughly, ensuring that baths, taps, sinks and loos were all shiny. Finally, before going into the village to collect eight organic salmon fillets and the accompanying veg, she had to wax and polish the parquet flooring in the hallway. It was a day like any other, but a busy day nonetheless.

Kathryn clicked the kettle on to boil. The salmon fillets were herb encrusted and roasting nicely, the asparagus and ribboned courgettes sat in their steamer and there was ten minutes before she had to make herself 'neat and pretty'. She extracted the thin book from its hiding place between two cookery books. She knew no one would consider looking between *Jamie's Italy* and *Jamie Does* . . .. Kathryn thumbed open R. K. Narayan's *Tales from Malgudi*.

> *When he came to be named the oldest man in town, Rao's age was estimated anywhere between ninety and one hundred and five. He had, however, lost count long ago and abominated birthdays; especially after his eightieth, when his kinsmen from everywhere came down in a swarm and involved him in elaborate rituals and with blaring pipes and drums made a public show of his attaining eighty. The*

religious part of it was so strenuous that he
was laid up for fifteen days thereafter with
fever.

The snippets of books that she managed to
devour were enough to transport her, to give her
the means of escape in the spare minutes of her
day. The time constraints allowed her little more
than eighty words at any one reading, but those
eighty words were her salvation. For the next few
hours, her mind would be full of questions. How
old was Rao? Where did he live? How did he die
and at what age?

Kathryn took her cup of tea upstairs to the
dressing table and sat in front of its triple mirrors,
angled to show her whichever way she glanced.
There was no escape.

She placed her finger against the cool glass of the
mirror and traced the reflection of her nose, eyes
and mouth. She stared at the image in front of her,
the face of a sad lady trapped inside the mirror who
needed to practise her smile. Kathryn was unable
to decide which the real image was. Was it the flat,
cool face that stared back at her or the bewildered,
lonely mask from behind which she viewed the
world? Withdrawing her hand, she realised that it
didn't matter. The flat-featured woman that stared
blankly from the glass and the veiled lids through
which she saw were one and the same.

At such moments Kathryn felt she was living in
a state close to madness. She figured that as long

197

as she recognised how she lived was indeed 'mad' then there was always hope.

She combed her sticky hair and placed a marcasite clip in the side, to try and distract from the texture. What had Dominic said that morning? *'You look like a mental patient.'* Any nasty statement hurt, but its impact was doubled if not trebled when it came from someone you loved.

She applied a little rouge to her cheeks and sprayed scent along her décolletage. As usual, the words of the song entered her head and spun around until she listened and gave them an audience:

> *For wives should always be lovers too.*
> *Run to his arms the moment he comes home*
> *to you.*
> *I'm warning you.*

FOUR YEARS AGO

The house on the Cornish cliff could best be described as 'rambling'. It had been constructed at the beginning of the twentieth century when there had been no shortage of local building materials and was a collaboration between an extravagant and whimsical architect who had a fancy for New England, and a wealthy tin baron who wanted a home befitting his station. The result was corridors that led nowhere in particular and a property that boasted not one but three Gothic-style turrets and innumerable church-style windows that let little light into the small square rooms that they graced. A decked terrace ran along the front of the property, held up with thick porch posts and gabled arches that gave the whole place a feeling of New Hampshire.

A wooden swing-seat just big enough for two adults of close acquaintance had been suspended from a length of industrial rope and hung in pride of place to the left of the front door. In the summer it would be padded with comfortable striped cushions, making it the perfect place to while away the warm evenings. Kate pictured herself with a glass of wine in hand and her toes rocking back and forth on the deck; it would transport her back to those hot Caribbean evenings, with the sound of the waves and chirping crickets confirming that she was in paradise. The only thing missing would be the dulcet tones of a certain reverend, whom she would happily have budged up for.

The front of the house was half timbered and one of Kate's first jobs had been to restore the wood and paint it a pale duck egg blue. This ensured that Prospect House blended perfectly with the sea and sky against which it sat.

The phone rang on the desk in the study. It was perched on a stack of papers, all awaiting her attention with varying degrees of urgency. Kate hadn't realised there would be quite so many administrative hoops to jump through before she could make her dreams a reality. She figured that if the demands were that pressing, the topic would come to light again, a bit like cream rising to the top or a bobbing apple in a busy Halloween bucket.

'Prospect House.' Kate still felt a certain thrill at saying the name. She balanced the phone between her head and her shoulder, crooked to one side.

Kate loved the place in which she now lived. When she had sat in the car park on the harbourside five months earlier with the windows rolled down and the unforgiving Cornish wind buffeting her car, it had been the name that had initially drawn her. She had looked out across the harbour wall and thought of Simon as she sometimes did, wondering how his construction project was coming along. He was often never more than a small reminder away.

The estate agent's details had fluttered in her palm, the third or fourth set that she had flicked through; the name made her do a double-take, immediately pushing it higher up the list than 'Jasmine Cottage' and 'The Lodge'.

Her pulse had quickened. 'Surely not!'

But there it was in black and white: 'Prospect House', on the market and, miraculously, excitingly within budget.

It had turned into a momentous day: not only did the property match the one that had existed in her head for a while, but she immediately realised that it was not meant to be just a holiday house. Penmarin could actually become the place she called home.

The house had been named for the amazing sea view from its prime cliff-top position. For Kate, however, it was the dictionary definition of 'prospect' that most inspired her: *Possibility of something happening soon, a chance or the likelihood that something will happen in the near future, especially something desirable.*

This was the definition she shared with all newcomers to the house, in the hope that they might believe in the possibility of a better future, for Prospect House was all about hope.

Kate tried to concentrate on the voice on the end of the phone while she prodded at the pile of paper with her pen, hoping it might topple into the bin and disappear for good. No such luck.

A workman's drill stuttered to life in the old stable. She plugged her ear to try and block out its drone. The staff would have their own quarters in the converted buildings to the side of the property, across a courtyard; far enough away to give the girls their independence, but close enough to be on site in a matter of seconds. As yet, though, no staff had been hired. Kate wasn't sure how to find exactly what she was looking for. It was one more thing waiting to be crossed off her ever growing list.

She turned her attention back to voice on the end of the phone.

'Yes, I understand completely. I think we've complied one hundred per cent: fire doors, new escapes and so forth. All work was recommended and approved by the Cornish fire service . . . My certificate?' Kate stared at the pile of papers; it had to be hidden somewhere. 'Yes, I have it right here!' she lied. 'I'll pop a copy in the post immediately!'

She added it to her list and replaced the handset in its cradle.

'I need some fresh air!' Kate threw her hands in the air and shouted into the empty house.

It was one of the first glorious days of summer and Kate was relishing the novelty of living on the coast, bringing new adventures every day. The sun warmed her through the window as she dawdled in the post office, browsing the jars of homemade preserves. She wondered if it would be undiplomatic to ask who made them, so that she could go direct to the source and save a few bob. As far as possible, she wanted organic, homemade produce for every meal. It was all part of establishing Prospect House as completely distinct from her residents' previous lives, in which Kate could almost guarantee that most of the food they ate came fast or shrink-wrapped. She had hated the plastic trays on which the prison food was served. An indentation for stew and another for custard meant that one slip and the courses would slop and merge together like the contents of a toddler's pelican bib; it was disgusting.

'You just bought the big house on the top.'

It wasn't a question, so she didn't answer, but instead stared at the young man who stood to her right, clutching his pot noodle and a packet of chocolate bourbons. She estimated him to be about thirty, with the high tan and weathered face of someone who had grown up and worked his whole life in the outdoors.

'We're not 'appy about your plans.'

This also did not merit a response, causing him to redden slightly under her silent scrutiny, but not enough to deter him from repeating his phrase.

'I said we're—'

'Yes, yes, I heard you the first time. I am just

trying to figure out two things before I answer you. Firstly, who is the "we" in question, and secondly, what do you or anyone else know about my plans?'

He shifted his weight onto his other foot. Kate noticed one of his legs was considerably shorter than the other, the deficit made up by an unwieldy built-up boot.

'We is the whole village, all of Penmarin really.'

Her eyes widened. She placed her hand on the cameo brooch at her neck, feigning shock.

'Is that right? The whole village? Goodness, I don't think I have spoken to more than four people since I arrived and yet the *whole* village is unhappy with me? That's quite an achievement.'

'It's not you personally; it's what you are going to do up there, bringing all sorts of undesirables into this little place. Most of us have lived here our whole lives and there are kids and old people to think about . . .'

'Where is it exactly that I am communally discussed?'

'You what?'

Kate shifted her shopping basket on her arm and repeated her enquiry.

'Where is it that everybody talks about me and my degenerate plans to corrupt your children, destroy your community and life as you know it?'

His nervous stutter told her all that she needed to know.

'In . . . In the pub mainly . . .' He looked at his feet. Had he divulged a secret?

'Great! Well, you can tell the great "we" that I will be in the pub tonight at seven thirty, to discuss my plans and I'll be happy to answer any questions that anyone might have. I'm Kate by the way.'

She held out her hand. He took it and smiled.

'Tom, Tom Heath.'

'Lovely to meet you, Tom. I'm sure I will see you later.'

With that she swept past him and the counter where the postmistress was listening and watching, mouth agape. Kate's appetite for preserves had suddenly abated.

She marched the two miles home; the winding lane with its steep incline was no challenge for her determined stride, she was a woman on a mission. Despite her strong resolve, hot tears pricked her eyes. Why did everything have to be a bloody battle? The warm, salt-tinged breeze irritated rather than soothed. Kate cared little for the sprouting cow parsley and red campion as she kicked at the hedgerows, sending the heads scattering onto the scorched tarmac. Slamming the kitchen door behind her, she plonked her basket in the middle of the kitchen table and gave a guttural yell.

'UUUrrgghhh!'

'Why don't you just swear? It is so much more satisfying,' said the voice from the breakfast bar.

Kate laughed, but chose not to take up the suggestion.

'I didn't know you were back. How was Truro?'

'Good, thanks, but stop changing the subject. It's true you know, Kate, a good swear can be most therapeutic. Do you know that in all the years I've known you, I have never, ever heard you properly swear apart from the odd "bloody" and a couple of "shits", which frankly don't really count, and I honestly think that sometimes you would find it of great benefit. I love a good swear, especially in the car, and I can tell that right now is one of those times. Come on, Kate, repeat after me. Boll—'

'I don't think so.' Kate raised her hand and cut her friend short.

'I have never sworn habitually and I'm not going to start now in my forties!'

'You are such a goody-goody.'

'That's me!'

'Anyway, what's up? Why the need for an almost-nearly swear?'

Kate looked at her friend sitting astride a high stool and sighed.

'Oh, Natasha, I've had a pants day. People are coming out of the woodwork and demanding certificates and insurance policies and goodness knows what else before we can open properly and as if that isn't enough, I'm afraid we've got a bit of a situation on our hands.'

'Ooh, that sounds dramatic. Tell all!'

Natasha placed her paintbrush into its pot of water, swirling it to create the most vivid shade of blue.

She bunched her voluminous skirt into her hand and gave Kate her full attention.

'I ran into a young chap in the post office who told me that the locals are not happy about what we are doing up here.'

'Oh my God! It's out, isn't it! The fact that we have been drinking Chablis and eating crisps while watching *Mamma Mia* into the early hours. Oh my God, the shame! I confess all; I have a weakness for Pierce Brosnan!'

'This is serious, Natasha, and worse still, I have agreed to go and face the masses at the pub tonight for a bit of a question and answer session. I don't know what I was thinking, I was just so incensed! I felt a lot braver then than I do now.'

'I think it's a great idea. We should be open and up front, not hide here as though we have a guilty secret. It will be okay once we have actually met the locals. They probably think we are a couple of lesbians living a life of debauchery all alone and thoroughly enjoying ourselves!'

'Goodness, Natasha, not the whole lesbian thing again, please!'

They both laughed.

Half-past seven came round very quickly. Kate quietly closed the front door and felt a wave of anxiety. The next time she stepped through its frame she would either be accepted or alienated – quite a daunting thought.

The two sauntered along the lane in the dying

207

warmth of the summer's day. Kate had dressed with care in a pair of tailored jeans, a floral poplin shirt and the faintest smidge of make-up. The novelty of being able to wear jeans after two decades of Mark's sartorial restrictions had not worn off; she doubted that it ever would. In her deck shoes and with a cotton jersey over her shoulders, she looked somewhere between a local and a visiting yachtie.

Natasha looked magnificent in a turquoise linen shift with an array of lapis lazuli at her throat and wrists. No understated dressing for her – Kate wouldn't have expected anything different.

'It'll be all right you know, Kate. What's the worst that they can do? Hound us out of town?'

Kate smiled weakly and thought that yes, that was exactly what they could do.

The Lobster Pot pub radiated light against the natural landscape, throwing out its shadowy beams across the tarmac car park and grass beyond. It was the same glow that drew teenage adventurers, with the lure of all that it held within, but for Kate Gavier it looked like the Admiral Benbow from *Treasure Island*, and tonight held as much menace.

The two women stepped through the door and were greeted by at least forty pairs of eyes and a curtain of silence that descended with alarming speed. The place was packed to the rafters with the old and the young; denim-clad bottoms were balanced on stools and filled the shabby booths; women were perched on the knees of their menfolk.

The air was thick with the sweat and alcohol-breath of the crowd. The windows had steamed up and the place pulsed with the anticipation of forty expectant souls whose tongues and wits were being lubricated by the local real ale.

Kate hesitated for a fraction of a second, loitering in the doorway. To flee or fight, that was her dilemma. A loud voice roused her from her stupor.

'Ah! Here she is, our guest of honour!'

A large man in his mid fifties stepped forward from the crowd, a generous measure of whisky swirling in his hand. His mustard cords, checked shirt and floppy hair identified him as the wealthy restaurant owner from the harbour. He was a minor celebrity in these parts, with a stake in nearly all the local businesses, including the pub. His shiny yacht, which was permanently moored alongside the shabby fishing boats, made a bold statement.

Kate and Natasha had seen him from afar at least twice. He was a man for whom ageing was not only a problem but also a preoccupation. Tooth veneers and a regular root touch-up to keep the grey at bay both helped. Little, however, could be done to disguise his elderly hands, aged with liver spots and reminding Kate of prime pork sausages: meaty, bloated and growing more inept month on month. He dressed as he always had, paying no heed to his expanding waistline or the swell of his neck that strained beneath his collar. Kate and Natasha could see that two or three decades earlier he might have been attractive in a rather caddish, country gentleman type way. But not now, now he was past his prime. They had snickered, knowing that to be similarly assessed would be devastating.

He reached out his chubby hand and Kate shook it firmly, noting the heavy gold signet ring on his little finger.

'Rodney Morris. Delighted to meet you.' His voice boomed with the confidence of a man who wanted to be heard.

'Kathryn Br— Gavier, I'm Kate Gavier.'

Damn! She didn't know why she did that, but whenever nerves got the better of her, she almost always referred to herself by her married name. Any high-anxiety situation had the potential to kick her back into that state of terror she'd permanently endured during her marriage, all but flipping her brain into assuming the role of Kathryn Brooker, tortured wife.

'Well, Kate, I have been nominated "unofficial spokesman", if you like, to try and add a semblance of order to proceedings.'

Kate was pleased that Natasha, who was now standing to her right, did not correct his use of 'spokesman' to 'spokesperson', although she knew that her desire to do so would be strong. She herself fought the need to giggle, accurately surmising that far from being put out at his role, Rodney Morris would have volunteered to take centre stage.

The whole charade was quite hilarious. The rag-taggle brigade in front of her, ranging from the estate agent who had sold her the house to the milkman who delivered to her daily, were there to decide whether they would accept her or not. Who the bloody hell did they think they were? Kate was suddenly invigorated with strength and confidence. She had faced worse than this motley collection over the last few years, was she going to fall at the first hurdle? No, no she wasn't. She stepped into middle of the room and very quietly and calmly took control.

'Excellent. It's great to finally meet you, Rodney, in fact to meet all of you, whose paths we have crossed anonymously for the past few weeks. This is my friend and colleague, Natasha Mortensen.'

Natasha waved to anyone whose eye she could catch.

'It's great to see so many of our new neighbours here tonight and I am very grateful for the opportunity to tell you all about our new venture. So I guess it's best if I start by giving you a brief summary of what it is that we are planning to do at Prospect House and then take any questions. How does that sound?'

There were several loud, inarticulate mutterings, but the general consensus was 'Yes', 'Fine' and 'Let's get on with it'.

Rodney Morris nodded and twisted the chunky ring on his pinkie, feeling that his role as unofficial spokesman had rather been usurped. He took two steps backwards in a physical gesture of redundancy.

Kate turned to face the crowd. They were silent, drinks held aloft, awaiting the sermon.

'I would firstly like to say how very fortunate I feel to now be living in such a beautiful, tranquil place as Penmarin and I am sure that I don't need to tell you people how lucky you are to live and work in somewhere so blessed.'

Natasha was stunned by her friend's commanding, steady voice. *You go, girl!* This too she managed to refrain from shouting.

'I intend to open Prospect House as a residential home for people who have not always been so blessed in their environment or their lives—'

'Yeah, we heard it was going to be full of paedophiles, rapists, druggies and whatnot. Truth is, we don't want them here, we really don't!'

The voice of dissent belonged to a fisherman, who was still wearing his padded wading trousers. His angry words had been battering the inside of his lips ever since Kate had entered the pub. Several shouts of agreement came from the crowd and there were some nods as well.

'Paedophiles and rapists? Goodness me! Who would want that?'

Her smile was for Natasha alone. They both knew that Kate had lived amongst those types and worse for the last few years and that a good few of the people in the pub would likely be either or both, such was life. A small ripple of comment and laughter spread among the crowd; they were clearly divided. She continued.

'I can assure you that the last thing I would do is to place you or anyone in this community in danger. The people that I will be taking in may have criminal records, but I am talking about a maximum of six residents at any one time and they will be females, girls between the ages of sixteen and twenty-three. They will probably have had horrid childhoods and as troubled teens most will have never been given a chance or shown kindness. They certainly will never have experienced the beauty of living in a place like this.'

'Well that all sounds lovely, but the big question for me is how will you control them?' Rodney Morris looked around the bar to garner support for his crass question.

'Control them? They're not animals, Mr Morris! They are just kids who deserve a break and a better life. We will help them heal through various means, through therapy and coaching. We want to send them on their way with a sense of worth so that they can become valid members of society and make decent lives for themselves.'

'Therapy? What's that? Do you mean aromatherapy and the like?' The postmistress's question hadn't intended to amuse, but people tittered nonetheless.

Natasha stepped forward. 'This is probably where I come in. I was an art teacher for a number of years and a couple of years ago I retrained as an art therapist. I'll work very closely with our residential counsellor—'

Rodney Morris couldn't help himself. His voice boomed.

'Ah, I see. The old "let's stop them reoffending by letting them paint a pretty picture" strategy. Marvellous! But does it work? Why don't we just send them to Disneyland? In my day we believed in proper punishment, not all this leftie pandering.'

He sniggered into his knuckles. His cronies at the bar raised their glasses in his direction, a gesture that screamed *'Well said, that man!'*

'Punishment?' Natasha fought to control her rage at his ignorant, outdated views. 'You have a point, Rodney, but in the case of these children and young adults, we are not talking about punishment. Our residents will have already been "punished", as you put it. What we are interested in doing is helping them come to terms with the traumas they have experienced in their young lives. Youngsters like them are not always able to verbalise what has happened to them or how they feel about it. Often they block out feelings and thoughts which need expression. Quite literally, I give them a blank piece of paper in a safe environment. The art therapy provides a safe, non-threatening space and invites the individual to explore their issues. It is often the first time that these kids have been able to communicate what they have been through and once we understand that, we can look at how best to help them.'

'I think it sounds wonderful and if you need any help or materials, I would love to be involved.'

Natasha looked across at the elderly lady sitting at the bar in her artist's smock. Natasha had seen her small studio and gallery on the harbour.

'Thank you, yes! That would be wonderful.'

Rodney Morris did not like the way that events were unfolding. He felt his position as self-appointed village elder was being undermined.

'I think I have heard enough. What next? Free beach barbecues for all the local benefit scroungers? Oh, I know, why don't I just give all the food in my restaurants away to anyone that didn't get enough hugs as a child?' He snorted and turned towards the bar. 'I need to top up this drink!'

A couple of Rodney's chums chortled obligingly. There was the briefest moment of awkwardness before Kate once again took the floor.

'I guess what we are saying is that these girls are coming here voluntarily because they want to make something of their lives, but it will only really work if they have the support of the community they live in. They have been shunned and treated like dirt everywhere they have ever been and I want their experience here to be different. I want to give them that chance; I want to show them that there is a nice side to life. I want to give them hope.'

No one heard the door creak open. In the midst of the debate, a girl carrying all she possessed in a heavy grey bin liner entered and stood in the shadows. She listened intently to Kate's words. Without any pre-planning, she stepped forward and took her place centre stage. Her large frame dominated the low-timbered room. She deposited her bin liner on the floor.

'Kate's right. I've been shunned and treated like dirt since I was little. And let's face it, it was just bad luck. Some of you got lucky and were born here to parents that loved you, and I got the exact opposite. But I have decided to change my luck. I shall be studying at Plymouth University. I'm going to study psychotherapy. It's something I could never have imagined doing a few years ago, but someone gave me a chance and showed me that there is a nice side to life.' She smiled meaningfully in Kate's direction and Kate beamed back, astonished and thrilled at the surprise arrival of her old friend. 'If I hadn't been given that chance,' the girl continued, 'my life would be very different, believe me. Now I want to give other people a taste of that hope, and when I finish my course I would like to work at Prospect House to help people like me, people who need better luck. My name is Janeece, by the way.'

The bar was silent for a moment, then the regulars started mumbling among themselves, casting mental votes, seeing what their neighbours thought before throwing in their support. Tom Heath stepped forward.

'I think it sounds like a wicked project, Kate, and maybe if I'd had a bit more support when I was younger, I might of made something of myself. I could have done with a bit better luck. I will help you in any way that I can.'

The locals stared at Tom, who had been one of the loudest objectors to Prospect House only minutes before Kate and Natasha's arrival.

'Thank you, Tom. Actually I do need help; we are looking for a cook and a housekeeper, and there are other roles that need filling.'

I can definitely help you there; that's my trade, the hotel game . . .'

The volume in the room rose by an octave. Jobs? They hadn't thought of that.

The fisherman spoke again. 'So I guess we won't be overrun with muggers and murderers!' He laughed and his friends laughed too. The lion had been tamed, for now.

'No, I can almost guarantee that there will only ever be one killer living at Prospect House.'

Rodney Morris seized on Kate's statement.

'A murderer? You are telling us that there will be a murderer living among us, interacting with our kids, roaming our paths? Good God, I don't like the sound of that one bit! How can you guarantee that we'll be safe?'

Kate smiled at his flustered rhetoric.

'I personally guarantee that you will be safe from the killer, Rodney.'

'How? How can *you* guarantee it?'

Kate turned to face him and spoke loudly enough for them all to hear.

'Because, Rodney, the killer is me. I have, however, served my sentence for manslaughter, done my time, as they say, and don't expect to be tried again by you or anyone else. And incidentally I am not planning on bumping off anyone else any time soon.'

The pub was once again silent. Everyone stared at her, each drinker digesting the words and deciding whether they had been spoken in jest.

Tom stepped forward and placed a pint of real ale into Kate's hand.

'Cheers.'

'Cheers, Tom.'

Kate raised her glass at the crowd, then glugged the beer. Impromptu clapping broke out, and she got the feeling that they were clapping for much more than the fact that she was downing a pint. She was right about that.

The unlikely trio made their way down to the beach below Prospect House. As they spread picnic blankets on the sand and unpacked a cold roast chicken, a large bowl of Greek salad and slices of vanilla cheesecake, they all felt a giddy sense of excitement.

Natasha produced cold cans of Pimm's and dished them out. She held hers aloft.

'Here's to our success and may I say well done to you both for your outstanding performances last night!'

The three knocked cans together and each took a long swig.

'I was scared,' Kate confessed.

'*You* were scared?' Janeece laughed. 'Did you see their faces when I pitched up? Half of them were eyeing me bin bag, wondering if I had a sawn-off shot gun in there!'

The three howled with laughter.

'It is so lovely to see you, Jan, how did you know where to find me?'

'I knew you were in Penmarin from your last letter, and the rest was down to luck. I decided to ask in the pub if they knew where you lived; I mean how many reclusive jailbirds could there be shacked up in a place like this?'

'Well I'm jolly glad you did, do you know I really feel like this could happen!' Kate felt her stomach jump with excitement and nerves.

'You'd better believe it, Kate. This is it! Prospect House is nearly open for business! Woohoo!'

Whether down to the Pimm's or high spirits, the three danced and laughed for most of the morning. Natasha's impression of the po-faced Rodney was the highlight.

The three dozed off the effects of the Pimm's in the midday sun. Janeece lay propped on her elbow, wondering what other beautiful places like this existed in the world and whether she would ever get to see them.

'Have you heard from your kids?' It was an innocent question asked out of concern. She knew what they meant to Kate.

Kate exhaled slowly and opened her eyes. 'No.

No, I haven't, more's the pity. I'm hoping that once we've settled in here, they may want to come and visit. I've told Francesca all about it, so it will all be passed on.' Kate sat up and rested her chin on her knees. *Please, please come soon.* 'The trouble is it's a very long way—'

Whether it was Natasha's tongue or her confidence the Pimm's had lubricated, Kate wasn't sure; the effect, however, was the same.

'I don't know how you put up with them, Kate, I really don't. I think it's a bloody disgrace. Yes, we know it's tough for them; yes, we know it's a long way to travel, but enough already! They're not babies. How long are they going to punish you for? And how is it their job to punish you after all you have done for them, after the life you led for years just to create a happy family for them?'

Kate was taken aback, angry and defensive in equal measure. 'It's not that straightforward, Tash—'

Her friend was not done, interrupting Kate for the second time in as many minutes. 'Actually, Kate, it *is* that straightforward. Their dad was a prize knob, a nasty piece of work, and you did your best to hide it from them, suffered for the sake of their convenience and this is how they repay you? Dominic travels the length and breadth of the country to go to a bloody party and yet can't tootle to Cornwall to see how you are at a time when you need him more than ever? You let them get away with it, Kate, but you should get tough with them. I know I bloody would.'

Kate was incandescent. 'Then let's hope for everyone's sake that you never actually become a mother because God help your kids!'

'I wouldn't let them walk all over me, Kate, that's for sure. You need to set them a boundary, set them an example!'

Kate stood up. Her voice shook with barely controlled anger. 'Set them an example? I've spent my whole life setting them an example! My whole life trying to show them how to be decent human beings by being kind and attentive—'

'Yes! And look how that's worked out. How kind and attentive are they exactly, Kate?'

Kate ran from the beach towards the path. The sound of her sobbing drifted back on the breeze.

Janeece looked at Natasha. 'I'm glad I asked . . .'

Natasha buried her hands in her face. 'Shit!' She knew she had gone too far.

Natasha knocked on Kate's bedroom door and entered without waiting for an invite.

'I'm sorry, Kate.'

Kate stared at her through swollen lids. 'For which bit?'

'All of it. I shouldn't have said it.'

'I know you didn't mean it, Tash.'

Natasha held her friend's hand. 'Oh but I did mean it, Kate! I just shouldn't have said it.'

'But you know my kids; you love them!'

'Yes, I do. But I love you more. I will always do and say what I think is best for you and right now I don't like the way they are behaving.'

'You're right, Tash; it is my fault, the way I brought them up. I thought that hiding things from them was the best course of action, but it wasn't. They are young adults who don't know how to trust because what they trusted was a mirage and that's all my fault.'

'But that's just it, Kate. It's not all your fault, it's all Mark's fault actually, and I wish they would realise that. I try to do everything in my power to support you, Kate, and make you happy. You're my best friend in the whole world and it kills me to see how much you suffer when the solution is so simple. Just one visit, that's all it would take. I don't think they're being fair.'

Kate hugged her mate. 'You are my best friend too. They will come eventually, Tash. I know it.'

Kate bit her bottom lip. She had to believe that was true.

'I'm sure you're right. I forget sometimes what you have been through, that while I've been working away you've been in prison. It's because you seem to cope so well and are so resilient, I just forget.'

'I forget too sometimes. It's like I've blanked out large chunks of my life. The time in jail neither flew by nor dragged particularly; it was a bit like a pregnancy or a long school holiday – felt like an eternity at the beginning, but now it's over seems to have passed doubly quick. I find it hard to remember the detail of my life in there; I can only recall how much I missed the kids.' Tash squeezed her friend's hand. 'It was also a haven of sorts, a relief not to be gut-wrenchingly terrified all the time. I could watch the clock hands whizz towards bedtime without feeling petrified. And life inside was actually quite easy, not what you might think. There was no scrubbing concrete steps with a toothbrush or having to peel a never-ending mountain of potatoes whilst sat on a cold, concrete floor . . .'

There was a silence while both women considered how to continue.

'Do you really hope I never become a mother?'

'Yes, but only because of your horrendous dress sense and non-conformist ideas. The poor kid would be a weirdo!'

The two laughed. They were back on track.

'I've thought of names for if I ever do have kids . . .'

'Oh you have to tell me!'

'Well, for a boy I like Radar and a girl, Philadelphia.'

'Philadelphia, like the cheese?' Kate roared.

'No, like the city!'

'Radar and Philadelphia? I rest my case, poor little weirdos.'

Janeece poked her head round the door and was relieved to find the two of them laughing.

'Sorry to interrupt, but Tom from the pub is downstairs.'

★　　★　　★

Kate noticed that Tom had spruced himself up, shaved his stubble and flattened his unruly hair. Her feet had barely touched the bottom stair when he fired his question at her.

'Were you serious about a job, Kate?'

'Depends, what did you have in mind?' Kate wondered what his skills were.

'I'm a trained chef and I've worked in the local hotels since I left school, doing every job you can think of. For the last couple of years I've mainly been mending fences, building walls and painting, but I prefer working inside. I'd like to be your cook and housekeeper. I reckon I can keep a few bedrooms shipshape and rustle up good breakfasts and meals for all your guests.'

Kate looked him in the eye. 'Can you promise me, Tom, that I will never, ever, ever have to wash a sheet or make a bed for the rest of my life?'

'Yes, I can do that, no problem.'

Kate held out her hand. 'Then welcome aboard, Tom!'

'When shall I start?'

'You just did. Four coffees and a plate of biccies please, and then the four of us can figure out how this place is going to work.'

Tom beamed and limped off to find the kitchen.

TEN YEARS AGO

Mark spooned the asparagus onto his plate and proffered the bowl to Lydia, who was sitting to his right.

'So, Lyds, how's the revision going?'

'Not too bad. Struggling with Latin and Chemistry, but getting A stars in Art.'

'That's great, but art isn't exactly a career choice, is it? I'm sure your brother could give you a hand, eh, Dom? There's no point in having a good academic brain and not sharing it!'

Dominic glared at his father and gritted his teeth. 'Sure.'

His smile was fleeting and forced and for a split second Kathryn thought he looked a bit like her. For some reason this gave her a jolt of joy.

Lydia was incensed. 'That's a crap thing to say, Dad. There are plenty of careers that involve art! I could work in graphic design, illustration, fashion and a gazillion others – what you mean is it's not a career that you would like me to go into!'

'I never said that, Lyds.'

Mark flung his hand to his breast, feigning hurt.

'Darling, I honestly don't mind what you do as long as it makes you happy – and makes you money! And I don't want you to feel pressurised by the fact that you are being given an education that most people would kill for. It's perfectly okay to take that expensive tutoring and put it to best use by colouring in pictures all day.'

'God, I knew it!'

Lydia threw down her fork in protest.

'Lydi, I'm joking, kind of. If art becomes your thing then you must follow your dream, but you can't neglect other subjects that might help you achieve that dream, that is all I am saying. For example, if you want to run an art gallery, you will need an understanding of commerce and marketing. Graphic designers still have to work to a budget and be aware of material constraints and so forth.'

He ruffled his daughter's hair.

Lydia grinned at her smart dad.

Mark changed tack and kept the teenage duo amused with his impersonations and stories of his colleagues, their tutors. Kathryn thought this was most inappropriate. It was not the way to teach the kids respect for other people, but she was not about to raise that at the dinner table.

'So, I expect everyone has been nattering about the big award, have they?'

Dominic looked blankly at his father.

'What award?' Slivers of salmon fell from his lips and back onto his plate.

'Please do not talk with your mouth full, Dom, it's disgusting.'

Everyone ignored Kathryn's comment.

'The Excellence in Education awards. I am to be named Headmaster of the Year. Ta da! There'll be a swanky all-expenses-paid do at a posh hotel in London, which will be very good publicity for the school. Governors are over the moon. It'll be in all the Sundays . . .'

Dominic snorted through his nose.

'Actually, Dad, no, I haven't heard it mentioned. Have you, Lyd?'

She shook her head. 'Nup.'

Kathryn tucked her lips inward and bit down to stop herself interjecting, but she was dying to know what 'nup' meant and where it had come from. However, having already commented on Dominic's eating habits, she didn't want to wade into Lydia about her speech, didn't want to give them any more ammunition, didn't want to be continually branded as the baddy. There were lots of things that she didn't want.

Dominic was still snorting.

'So, Dad, if you're going to a swanky do, are you going to take a swanky bird with you? I mean, you can't turn up with Mum!'

'Once again, Dominic, I feel I should point out that I am actually here, sitting at this table in the room and not absent. I am also not deaf, so please refrain from talking about me as if I am either or both.'

227

Everyone ignored her and a curious thought struck her: maybe she was invisible.

Dominic's statement caused her husband to roar with laughter whilst shaking his head in mock disapproval.

'You might have a point, Dom, but who would you suggest I take?'

He winked at his daughter, reassuring her that it was all just a bit of banter, good fun, no harm intended.

'Dunno, you could always dust Judith off and give her an airing.'

This made Mark roar even louder.

'Oh my God, please! Judith!'

He pushed his plate away and feigned being sick.

'That has really made me lose my appetite!'

Dominic then piped up.

'It's a shame Natasha Mortensen has left. She would have done you proud, Dad! I can just see her frock now, Oxfam meets Tinkerbell.'

Mark gave an exaggerated shudder of revulsion.

'Oh please, Dominic, I will have no mention of that grotesque lesbian.'

'Actually, she is not a lesbian. In fact she was sleeping with Dr Whittington the whole time that she was here; may in fact still be seeing him for all we know.'

Kathryn didn't know where the idea to say this aloud had come from, or the actual voice, but one thing was sure: she now knew that she wasn't invisible as all three members of her family stared at her in surprise.

'No way!' was her son's response.

'Lucky Ms Mortensen, he's a total dish.'

It was Lydia's retort that caused Mark's eyebrows to rise the highest. He said nothing.

For the second time that evening Kathryn turned her lips inward and bit down. She hated them being so mean and openly mocking of her friend, and Natasha had also been very kind to each of them in different ways. It felt nasty and she hated nasty.

'How was your day, darling?'

It took a split second for Kathryn to realise that she was being spoken to.

'Oh! Sorry, I was miles away. Fine. Good, thanks. Fine.'

'*Fine. Good, thanks. Fine!* There we have it, kids, the engaging description of how your mother spent eight hours while the rest of us toiled over dog-eared pages.'

Mark's comment was clever. Not only did Kathryn recognise it as a cruel and pointed reference to her love of reading and the fact that while every other individual in the school had access to hundreds of books, her passion was denied her, but it also told her children that her life was pointless, wasted. Instead of retorting, she busied herself with clearing the table. The scraping of plates was always a good diversion.

★   ★   ★

Dominic and Mark had taken a cricket ball to the nets. Lydia, however, remained slumped in her chair, observing her mum with a furrowed brow.

'Why do you do that, Mum?'

'Do what, Lydia?'

'I can't really describe it, but it's like you don't listen to what's going on around you. You should try to join in more; it would make everything so much easier.'

'Easier for who, Lyds?'

'Well, all of us actually. You never find Dad's jokes funny and he really tries. I know he can be a bit of a chauvinist, but he doesn't mean it. He's just being Dad.'

Kathryn sat down opposite her daughter; the plates could wait. She swallowed her automatic response, *'Oh, he means it, darling. He means it more than you could ever know.'*

Her daughter wasn't done.

'And like when we are on holiday, it would be so much better if you did what we did, if you joined in more. I hate it when we are all in the sea just mucking about and I look up and you're sitting on the beach on your own looking fed up. You have never, ever come swimming or even for a dip! You shouldn't be so self-conscious, Mum. No one cares if you've got cellulite or whatever, lots of old people have it. We would rather see your cellulite than have you sitting on the beach in your linen skirt every day. It's like you're Victorian and can't show off your body!

You make yourself more obvious by never getting undressed.'

Lydia let out a long sigh.

Kathryn looked at her daughter in earnest.

'What do you think of me, Lydia?'

'What d'you mean?'

'I mean, when you look at me, what do you think?'

'What do I think?'

Lydia poked her tongue out of the side of her mouth; it was her thinking face. Kathryn watched her strike a similar pose whenever there was a paintbrush in her hand.

'Well, I don't think much . . .'

'Charming!' Kathryn swatted at her girl with the end of a dish cloth.

'No, I don't mean it in that way. I mean, it's never a shock or surprise to see you because you are always there and you have always been there, obviously.'

'I'm not sure if that's a compliment or not, Lyds!'

'When I look at you, I see my mum and so I don't think much beyond that. You are just Mum, always there and always doing . . . something. You are like background noise or my favourite pillow. I don't have to look for you or think about you much because you are always there, but in a good way.'

'Background noise, but in a good way?' Kathryn was struggling to find the positive.

'Yeah. It's like, you could be really bad background noise – like, say, one of those naff boy bands, or classical music, which I really hate. But you're not; you are background noise like something soothing or a lovely smell, baked cookies or jam. Which is really cool.'

'So I am cool?'

Lydia snorted her laughter through her nose and rolled her eyes.

'God! No! Mum, you are so not cool. Even hearing you say that is funny!'

'Right.'

Kathryn rubbed at her eyes and tucked her hair behind her ears. She didn't like the verbal cul de sac into which they had talked themselves; it was three-point-turn time.

'Okay, Lydia, let's move away from jammy-scented background noise and let me put it another way. When I say what do you think of me, I mean more explicitly, would you like to live my life?'

Lydia was silent, thinking. Her mother prompted her further still.

'A good example would be that when I was your age, I was sure that I would teach English. That was always my ambition. I've always loved books and I always thought I'd be a really good teacher. I got a first in English and I sometimes think it's a shame that I've never put it to good use.'

'Why haven't you?'

How to answer that? What to say? Neutral, watered down, diluted, agreeable: she had to find the words that fitted the formula.

'I don't really know, Lyds. I guess life just got in the way.'

It would have to suffice as an explanation; it would have to suffice, for now. Kathryn again tried to steer the conversation.

'Want I want you to do, Lydia, is to picture yourself in your forties. What does your life look like?'

Her daughter let out a deep sigh and lowered her voice in pitch and volume. Imagined or otherwise, it made the whole conversation smack of conspiracy. She looked at her mother through lowered lashes.

'It's hard because that is like *so* old, but I know I want to be in great shape. I'd like to look like Luca and Guido's mum.'

Kathryn resisted the temptation to point out that with the same surgeon and if she didn't touch a carb for twenty-five years, she could.

'Plus, I guess, Mum, that I wouldn't want my life to be quite as ordered as yours, you know, not quite so predictable. I think that I would like more variety. I know that I will always paint, but apart from that one constant, I'll probably move around a bit, meet new people, go to different countries, have new experiences and fall in love a lot. I guess I think that unless you try everything, you might settle for the wrong thing and then you might be stuck. I don't want to get stuck, Mum. I like the idea of not really knowing what I might be doing one year to the next. That would make it feel as if my life was an adventure and not just happening around me, if that makes any sense. I don't think that I want to be married and having to look after people in the way that you look after us and Dad. No offence or anything, I mean, you are really good at it!'

Kathryn could only nod and swallow the internal tears that slid from her nose down the back of her throat, rendering speech impossible. In her head she was saying, *'None taken, my darling, clever girl. You're right, try everything! Go everywhere, never settle for anything that isn't the best possible thing for you! Make good choices! Make the right choices! Have an adventure! Don't get stuck . . .'*

It was a massive relief to hear her daughter's words. Kathryn knew that her little girl would be just fine, no matter what happened.

It was nearly bedtime, an hour that always seemed to come round much too quickly. In earlier years she would try and delay going up to bed, but this only postponed the inevitable and angered her husband more.

Kathryn trod the stairs, changed into her familiar white cotton garb and waited.

Mark bent down as he walked past the end of the bed and inhaled her scent.

'Your hair smells of fish.'

She winced, remembering running her fingers through her hair after touching the salmon and knowing what that might mean. She was embarrassed. No matter how routine, it was still humiliating to receive negative and nasty comments.

'That was an interesting revelation about Miss Mortensen earlier and I am surprised that you found it appropriate to raise it not only at the supper table, but also in front of the children.'

Kathryn knew that it was better to say nothing, although the temptation to point out that he frequently raised far more inappropriate topics at the dinner table and in front of the 'children', one of which she knew for a fact was sexually active and smoked like a chimney.

'Tonight you will read to me. I know how much you like reading.'

He smiled briefly at his wife, who was kneeling and waiting in her regular pose.

While Mark showered, her heart lifted slightly at the prospect of reading, albeit aloud. She was unsure how she should react. If she showed any joy at the task, he would surely be angry, yet indifference could provoke the same reaction. She needn't have worried. There was to be no joy in the task, none at all.

She rose shakily from her kneeling position as Mark handed her the book. He unfastened his dressing gown and indicated the ladder-backed chair that he had placed by his side of the bed. Kathryn handled the weighty tome and read the title: *The*

Iliad. Her fatigue and desolation felt overwhelming. She was tired and the idea of having to plough through that particular text at that time of night felt like she had a mountain to climb.

Mark positioned himself centrally on the bed, lying face down with this head on his raised forearms, his face averted. She opened the first page and tried not to look at the plump pillow next to her husband's head, to which her eyes were powerfully drawn.

She started to read, struggling to find a rhythm as the unfamiliar words formed on her tongue.

Sing, Goddess, sing of the rage of Achilles, son of Peleus – that murderous anger which condemned Achaeans to countless agonies and threw many warrior souls deep into Hades, leaving their dead bodies carrion food for dogs and birds – all in fulfilment of the will of Zeus.

Kathryn was not sure how long had passed. It felt like hours, but was in reality just one hour, singular. She shivered as the chilly breeze swept along the floor, rushed under the door and gathered in a swirling current around her feet and calves, causing her whole body to jerk and twitch with cold.

The raffia chair seat had started to bite into her thighs through the thin white cotton of her nightgown and was stinging her cuts. The desire to stand, to change position and ease her suffering was strong. The words started to blur. Each letter became a blackened mote on the pale page: no longer distinguishable as words, they were merely smudges and shapes that swam before her eyes, making the deciphering of each syllable and stanza almost impossible. Her head sat heavy on her neck, like a meatball supported by spaghetti; it wobbled and sought refuge by sinking to her chest. Her throat was parched, each word a dry husk. She wanted to drink, but mostly she wanted to sleep.

Her eyes were itchy and sore, and cramp crept along her forearms as they protested at holding the heavy book unsupported for that length of time. She had endured a long day, a busy day, like every day. She wanted to close her eyes, just for a second . . .

Bang! The two noises woke her simultaneously, followed by a sharp pain. The first sound had been the smack of her skull against the back rung of the chair and the second was the scream of surprise and fear that had jumped from her throat as she was unexpectedly wrenched from her dream. The pain was her head, protesting from being smacked with force against the wooden bar. Her breath came in shallow pants; she must have fallen asleep, just for a second.

'Everything all right, Dad?' Dominic shouted through the closed door, alerted by the scream.

'Yes, son, go back to sleep. I think Mummy had a bad dream.'

The creak of the floorboards signalled Dominic's return to bed.

I'm living a bad dream . . . Kathryn pursed her lips, resisting the temptation to either utter this or, worse still, scream again, scream for help, for escape.

The book had fallen shut on her lap. Mark stood over her and was holding her by the hair, keeping her head upright. He spoke softly, his face invisible, above her, slightly behind her.

'It would not be advisable to wake the children again, Kathryn. When I said tonight you will read to me, I meant tonight you will read to me, not some of the night but all of the night, is that clear, darling?'

'Yes.' Her voice sounded croaky.

'Good.' He bent low and kissed her mouth.

'That's my good girl. I think maybe we should go over the last few pages, who knows how much you have missed.'

He let go of her hair and walked over to his chest of drawers. After rummaging among his underwear, he produced a silk scarf with a tasselled fringe. She stared at it, dreading what might come next.

'Sit back, sweetie.'

She sat bolt upright.

Mark took the scarf and wound it around her forehead and under her chin. Taking the ends, he tied them to the frame of the chair. She was anchored and fast, unable to turn her head.

'You may start reading again now, Kathryn.'

For the second time that night he lay face down on the mattress and made himself comfortable, again with his face averted. The instant rise and fall of his back hinted that he might be sleeping; this was probably the case, but she couldn't take the risk. The only way to see the text was to lift the book up to eye level, with her arms at right angles. The cramp came quickly, but she had no option other than to try and ignore it.

Achilles, interrupting Agamemnon, shouted:
'I'd be called a coward, a nobody,
if I held back from any action
because of something you might say.
Order other men about. Don't tell me
what I should do. I'll not obey you any more.
But I will tell you this – remember it well –
I'll not raise my hand to fight about that girl,
no, not against you or any other man.
You Achaeans gave her to me, and now,
you seize her back again. But you'll not take
another thing from my swift black ship –
you'll get nothing else with my consent.
If you'd like to see what happens, just try.
My spear will quickly drip with your dark blood.'

Kathryn fought to maintain the unnatural position, struggling against the desire to wrench herself free from the silk binds. She was grateful for one thing: with his face averted, she could cry silent tears as she sounded aloud the words into the dawn.

The alarm as usual heralded the start of another day. Her eyes, red and aching, were running; she was no longer consciously crying, but it was as if her very soul was shedding tears. Her speech was slurred with the confusion of a drunkard. Her cramped muscles and painful limbs had simply numbed themselves, and to move even slightly was agony.

Her husband almost sprang from the bed and performed an elaborate stretch whilst yawning to indicate a sleep well had. He walked slowly over to the chair and untied the silk scarf. Her head fell forward involuntarily and felt surprisingly light and unstable, as if her neck had forgotten how to support its weight unaided.

Mark reached for her hand and helped her stand. As her legs became separated from the raffia, the pain was intense, as though her skin and the chair base had become fused and to remove one from the other meant undergoing the agony of dissection.

'Come.'

He gave the usual command, the one word with which he could summon or direct. She followed his lead, too weak in every sense to protest or resist. He laid her face down on the bed and took his pleasure in his usual violent way. With her body prostrate against the mattress, her face felt the softness of the pillow and she fell into a deep sleep that rendered her immobile and removed from what was occurring.

He tapped her cheek with his palm, rousing her into consciousness.

'Shower time for me and you must get breakfast for the children. We are running a couple of minutes behind schedule and so no shower for you today, Mrs Sleepyhead.'

Kathryn stripped the bed and stepped into her clothes, exhaustion rendering her weak and unsteady. She teetered on the stairs and had to clasp the banister rail to ensure she didn't fall. She put the bedclothes into the washing machine and started to lay the table, fishing around in the cupboard like a blind woman groping for cereal boxes, bread, honey and anything else that she considered necessary for a good start to the day.

Dominic was the first to appear. She looked at him and waited for his comment. She searched for her happy voice, for that false brightness that dispatched her children each morning with a sense that all was right with the world. But try as she might, she couldn't find it.

'Oh my God! You look like total shit.'

She nodded and fought to swallow the tears that had gathered behind her swollen eyes. Still no words came. She implored him with her eyes: *Please, Dominic, please be kind to me today.*

'What's going on, are you ill, Mum? Is that what this is?'

'Yes, probable.'

She had meant to say more, she had meant to say 'probably', but the exhausted state in which she was trying to function made even the smallest of tasks impossible.

Her son took a seat at the table. Kathryn reached for the teapot and poured clear hot water into his mug.

'You forgot to put the tea bags in.'

Dominic stared at her with a lack of understanding and something bordering concern.

'It's okay, Mum, I'll do it.'

He stood and emptied the water into the sink and filled the kettle, ready to start the process again.

'Is this anything to do with last night?'

She stared at him, mouthing silently, not knowing how to respond or where to start.

He continued. 'You know, the bad dream you had?'

There was something about the flicker of his pupils, the irregular rhythm to his breath that told her he hadn't bought the bad dream story.

'Yes, Dom, just a bad dream.' She smiled at him.

'It will all be okay, Mum. Don't worry.'

'Will it, Dominic?'

'I hope so, Mum, I really do. I hate to see you like this. Sometimes I wish I could make things better for you. I just don't know how.'

Her sweet boy. She nodded her thanks and wandered over to the washing machine.

*   *   *

With her wicker basket under her arm, Kathryn stood in the garden in front of the washing line and allowed the start of the working day to wash over her. It went some way to restoring her mind, the feel of the early morning sun against her skin and the slight breeze that lifted her hair and let it settle again. She breathed in deeply and tried to heal herself from the inside out.

Kathryn reached into the basket and caressed the wooden pegs that had spilled from their bag and now sat on top of the linen. A picture of her mother swam in front of her eyes; she looked concerned. Kathryn shook her head and blinked her mother away.

The pegs sat in her palm, they knew what came next. She placed three of them in her mouth and with Peggy in her hand, pulled the large white sheet taut, anchoring it with the precious wooden splints, removing them from their floral holding pen, one by one.

'Good morning, Mrs Brooker!'

'Good morning, Mrs Bedmaker!'

For some reason, call it hysteria or despair, today this made her laugh. Not just the subtle chuckle or smirk of an adult in the know, oh no, it was a full chortle that was almost a combination of crying and laughing. She didn't really know where it came from.

'Morning, George! Morning, Piers!'

She dissolved once again into laughter, shaking her head to try and regain composure as her tears continued to fall.

'Are you all right, Mrs Brooker?'

'Yes, thank you for asking, quite all right.'

She mopped at her eyes with her sleeve.

'Have you had a good night, Mrs Brooker?'

She looked at the daring George Nicholls, whose bravado would be common-room gossip by break time. She could hear the whisper now: *'And then she said, "Quite all right," and then he said, "Did you have a good night?" I swear to God he did, because Piers was there and he heard him and my best friend's sister is going out with his brother and he told her and she told me! Can you believe that he said that? And what did she say?'*

Kathryn thought long and hard. What should she say? *Come on, Kathryn, think! You're becoming folklore. Think smart, say something, for goodness' sake. Speak, Mrs Bedmaker!*

'Oh, you know, George, the usual – up all night.'

She gathered her basket and winked at him briefly before turning on her heel and treading the path back towards the kitchen and her breakfasting family.

George and Piers stared at each other. This was bloody gold dust!

She opened the door and the three members of her family paused from their cereal munching and conversing to stare at her.

'Morning, everyone!'

She had found her happy voice, just in time.

Lydia abandoned her spoon in its murky bowl.

'Blimey, Mum, you look like total—'

244

'Yes, I know.' She cut her daughter short. 'I really don't need an unfavourable analysis from you on how awful I look this morning, thank you, Lydia. I would like to propose that if we can't say kind and nice things in the mornings then we say nothing at all, how about that?'

Kathryn restored the wicker basket to its usual position. The family were unnaturally quiet behind her. She glanced at them all as she returned to the table and reached for the teapot.

'Well,' she commented as she filled her cup, 'that was easy.'

Both children seemed to lose their appetite in the strange, edgy atmosphere. In silence they scraped their chairs on the wooden floor, pushed bowls of half-eaten cereal to the middle of the table for collection by their waitress mother later, and sloped out of the door. Heavy bags were carelessly slung onto backs, weighing down fragile shoulders and banging against bony spines.

'Did someone get out of bed the wrong side this morning?' Mark's tone was almost sing-song.

Her smile was thin as she acknowledged her husband's comment.

'Yes.' She nodded.

She looked at his eyes, which were bright and animated. She had so many questions for him, so much that she wished she had the courage to say. Her very first question, the one that hovered at the front of her mind, would be: *'Are you mad,*

Mark? Is this where this comes from? Are you insane? Do you know that you are mad, or do you think that you are not? It surely has to be madness that drives you. It has to be an unsound mind, a cruel and mad disposition that drives you to do those unspeakable things to me. Where does it come from, Mark? Did someone do bad things to you? Where do these ideas germinate? Does your behaviour bring you joy or sadness? It brings me sadness, Mark; it brings me great sadness. You have taken the person that I was and you have slowly dismantled me over the years until this is all that is left, this shell, this casing, that used to house a person. It used to house me, but me is gone and the husk is all that is left. I am gone and you have done that to me. Why me, Mark? Why did you pick me? I had so much to offer, I had so much to give. I had a life . . .'

Her husband continued. 'Well, an early night for you tonight, my darling.'

She nodded at the comment, which was heavy with connotation. She felt an overwhelming urge to cry; it was tiredness, she knew. She found it so much harder to cope when she was exhausted.

Kathryn downed two cups of very strong coffee, knowing that she would need it as fuel to get through the day's chores. Failing to complete the requisite chores meant a dire end to the week. On Sunday nights Mark would sit with a checklist that he would print off from the computer. If a tick could not be applied to each chore that was listed, alphabetically, then each chore without a tick would earn her one point. That could mean as many as six or seven extra points.

Chores for Wednesday began with the polishing of all 'best shoes', or 'chapel shoes' as they were also known. This meant a good coat of wax polish and then a stiff brush followed by a shine with a soft cloth, for four pairs of shoes, one per family member. She then had to change the water in all the vases of fresh flowers, to avoid that nasty rotting smell; plump all cushions; remove all the objects and detritus from the kitchen dresser, wash and dust each item as appropriate, and return them to their correct positions after dusting the shelves and wiping out the cupboards; polish all the mirrors until they were smear-free and shiny; and rake the shingle on the front driveway to ensure that it was as evenly dispersed as possible, removing any litter or other objects that might be lurking under those tiny stones.

Kathryn had in the past tried lying about the chores. She recalled one particular Sunday night when Mark had been reading from his checklist. His modus operandi was to read out the chore and the day and wait for her to reply 'Done' or 'Fail'. That night he was standing behind her as she knelt, and read, 'Cleaning on top and inside of medicine cabinets, Friday'. She knew that she hadn't done it; she had been distracted and had simply forgotten. So she lied. To avoid being cut, she lied and said, 'Done'.

He had swiftly and accurately swiped her around

the side of the head with the clipboard, the plastic corner of which cut her just below her left eye. A single drop of blood ran down her cheek and dripped onto the shoulder of her nightgown. Mark had broken one of his own cardinal rules: never to hurt her where it would show or require explanation.

'Look what you made me do!' He was furious. 'Do not ever lie to me.'

He pulled her face towards him by gripping her chin in his fist.

'What is this?'

In his hand was a small ball of rolled-up newspaper, no bigger than a large grape.

'It . . . it's newspaper,' she stammered.

'Correct. And do you know where I hid it?'

She shook her head, although she could have made an educated guess.

'I placed it on top of the medicine cabinet, and in the dust that sits there I wrote the word 'filthy' with the tip of my finger. And do you know what I saw when I went there earlier today?'

Again she shook her head, knowing that despite asking her questions, he didn't really want her to give him the answers, it was all part of the game.

'This ball of paper was still there and so was my word, "filthy". Not only do you expect this family to live in total squalor but you are also a liar. That is very bad indeed.'

Kathryn for some reason could see the humour in the fact that Mark's definition of total squalor

248

was that there was a film of dust on top of the medicine cabinet.

Ten minutes later, however, she found very little humour in anything as his punishment had been exacting and deliberate.

ONE YEAR AGO

It was a full day, but no busier than any other. Kate was preparing for a new arrival. The first few hours of interacting with a resident always told her everything she needed to know. In the four years that she had been running the house, she had honed this skill and knew what to look for, what to glean from inadvertently offered clues. The flinch at a handshake, the lack of eye contact or the false bright smile and counterfeit confidence – she had discovered that these were all ciphers. She was slowly learning how to crack the codes and read the truth that lay behind them.

It was inevitable that Kate would draw comparisons between the life that she used to live and the life that she had now, but it wasn't always the obvious things that made her look for similarities and differences; quite the opposite in fact. When a girl trod the path to the front door, often either undernourished or overweight and malnourished, clutching all that she owned and was precious to her in a tatty carrier bag, it would make Kate think of the arrival of new boarders at Mountbriers. Eager and anxious parents would alight from shiny convertibles. Beautiful, surgically enhanced mothers and smartly suited fathers would help unload the trunk, the case, the bag, the valuables, the electronic wizardry, the designer labels, the rucksack bursting with tuck and the child's allowance. It fascinated her how some had so much and others so very little. She had learned in the last four years – actually in the last nine years – that life was very unfair.

The sudden ring of the telephone made her jump; she had been miles away.

'Yes, this is Kate Gavier speaking. Ah great, so all on time. Yes, yes, someone will meet her from the station. I'll call you when she's settled, many thanks.'

She ran her fingers over the foolscap file in front of her; a white sticky label told her that it was Tanya Wilson who was arriving on the 2.30 train. She opened the cover and scanned the front sheet, taking in only the most basic information. She hated these formulaic reports. One of her biggest frustrations was that these girls had had reports written about them and judgements passed on them from when they were tiny.

Before the first wave of adolescence hit, they were described, assessed and stamped, and their fate was sealed. There were only so many permutations of character that 'the system' could identify and none were particularly positive. According to the typed sheets in triplicate that Kate handled daily, these girls were nearly always helpless and hopeless.

That was where Kate and her team came in. From the first glance at Tanya's file, she could see that she was a standard case, sadly. Tanya had been removed from her mother's care when she was six, following sustained physical abuse. Twelve different foster homes and two residential care homes later, she found herself in a juvenile correction centre and then graduated to prison for assisting in a burglary and carrying a weapon.

Kate was certain that there would also be prostitution, drug addiction and a whole host of psychological problems. She snapped the file shut and placed it in an already cramped drawer. She would make her assessment by looking Tanya in the eye and talking to her. She no longer paid much heed to what she read, knowing that these white sticky labels were interchangeable for every girl under her roof. They had all had the same life; they were all the same person. Only they weren't, not to her, and her job was to help them realise that.

She considered what her own white sticky label might read: 'A cool unrepentant killer that has seemingly abandoned her children and lives with a certain indifference to the establishment.' And she recalled what she had said a while ago: *I can see that some people will only ever see what they want to see.*

Kate was on hand at all hours of the day and night for the many and varied emergencies that seemed to occur weekly at Prospect House. In her four-year tenure she had dealt with everything from attempted suicide (twice), fire (once), flooding (once), fights (sixty-three) and the unexpected birth of a baby on the loo floor, Jayden Lee, who had weighed in at a respectable 7lb 3oz and now lived with his mother and her new partner in Truro. Of all the words you could use to describe existence at Prospect House, dull was not one of them.

Kate knew the residents were ready to leave when the journey from hopeless to hopeful was complete. For each of her guests – seven so far – the timing of that journey varied enormously. Arriving without optimism or any reason to feel positive meant the process of healing was often long and arduous. Only the brave attempted such a feat and not all would succeed. For some, to turn over the boulders that represented their lives and rake through what lurked beneath was not a good experience, and for a few it would end in disappointment.

This had been a bitter lesson for Kate to learn: that sometimes people were too far gone and for those individuals it felt better to leave the lid on their troubles. Prospect House could only help them so far, but each left with the words that if they wanted to try again, the door would always be open. For many, this was hope in itself.

Tom walked past the open door of the study with a stack of clean towels balanced on his forearm.

'Oh, Tom!'

He retraced his steps, careful not to let his towel tower topple.

'Yes, boss?'

'Don't forget Tanya's arriving today. Her train gets in at two thirty. Can we get her something ready in case she's famished?'

He nodded. It was pointless telling her that he had already considered this and would prepare sandwiches after he'd finished lunch. It wasn't that she was a tyrant, far from it; the whole staff loved working for and with Kate. But sometimes her meticulous need for every detail to be right for these girls meant she worried needlessly about things they were capable of executing perfectly without her comments or suggestions.

'I'm on it.'

She smiled at his back as he resumed his journey to the stairs. Of course he was, dear Tom.

Tom was a vocal advocate for Prospect House within the local community, extolling all that was good about it to anyone that would listen. The support they had received had been incredible; they had many regular visitors, all wanting to be involved. The first visit would be for no other reason than to satisfy a curiosity, but the second and third would be because they liked the atmosphere and the sense of hope that pervaded there. The odd few who were vehemently opposed remained so. Thankfully Penmarin was just big enough for their paths not to cross with any regularity.

Natalie, who had only recently left and had been with them for eight months, was currently working

254

in the local delicatessen with a bedsit above and a regular boyfriend. Many of the girls had enjoyed comparable employment and acceptance; these were her success stories. She sincerely hoped that Tanya would be similarly and fittingly dispatched when the time was right.

Kate sat on the slatted wooden bench and listened to the loud tick of the clock on the platform. The white-painted wooden canopy held well-tended hanging baskets and there was not a speck of litter anywhere. As for graffiti, she doubted that the maintenance team had ever seen it. It was the station of a bygone age; even the station master stood rocking on his polished heels with a pocket watch in place and a flag furled in his hand. She half expected to see Miss Marple alight, with her cloche slightly askew, from a coach full of steam.

The train when it arrived brought the twenty-first century with it, a shiny red-and-yellow bullet streaked with the filth of cities only briefly visited. Kate spotted Tanya immediately. Among the groups, couples, and parents clutching the hands of children stood a teenage girl who looked around her and stood out by the fact of her sheer alone-ness. Her confusion was exacerbated when she realised that she didn't know who or what she was looking for.

Kate dashed over to her, holding her arm aloft, waving and trying to spare her the fear of the unknown as quickly as she could. The girl's thin legs were clad in tight black jeans; her sneakers were worn and grubby and her skeletal arms dangled from the gaping sleeves of a T-shirt. Her red hair hung in two thin strips either side of her wan face, but her most outstanding features were her lips – blood red and full, a perfect ox bow. She reminded Kate of a delicate china doll.

'Tanya! Hello!'

'Hello.'

Tanya's voice was small and came from a throat dry with either dehydration or nerves. Her eyes darted from Kate to the crowds around her, to the clear blue sky above her head, all too much to take in.

'You made it okay. How was your journey?'

'Long.' She flashed a brief smile.

'Yes, I'm sure. I'm Kate and you are very welcome here, Tanya.'

Then came the sideways glance from beneath the fringe, what was the catch? Why was this complete stranger being nice to her? What did she want?

'Do you have any luggage?'

Tanya bent and retrieved the small sports bag at her feet. It was approximately thirty centimetres in length, yet big enough to hold everything she owned.

The two strangers walked together from the platform to the car park. Kate was careful not to overdo the friendly welcome, having learned that this could be just as off-putting as being unfriendly.

Tanya wondered what she was doing in this place without buildings, cars, shops or grime and all the other things that made her usual surroundings familiar and safe.

'You are arriving at the best possible time of year. The weather has been glorious and when the sun is out there is no place that you would rather be than the beach. We take little picnics down and sit on the sand and have great gossips, it's lovely!'

Kate watched the girl glance at her from behind her fringe, trying to fathom her tone and energy, waiting for the catch. They drove the short distance in silence. Kate negotiated the lanes and the holiday traffic. Tanya stared at the hedgerows.

Pulling the car up onto the driveway, Kate killed the ignition and allowed the full splendour of Tanya's new home to sink in.

'Welcome to Prospect House. You are welcome here for as long as you want to stay, Tanya.'

The girl nodded.

'What do you think? First impressions?'

'Of you or the house?'

Kate liked the girl's intelligence. 'Both.'

'The house looks like something out of an American film . . .'

Kate smiled and nodded. Yes, yes it did.

'And I'm not sure about you. Are you a . . .? I mean, do you . . .?'

'Yes?' Kate wanted questioning.

'Is this a Christian thingy or some religious sect? I'm just hoping you're not a bunch of nut-job

Jesus lovers, cos if you are I'm getting straight back on that train.' She thumbed the direction over her head. 'I think I'd prefer the nick to living with that.'

Kate's laugh came loud and suddenly, making her eyes water.

'Oh, Tanya! No wonder you look so worried! Is that what you thought?'

Tanya flicked away her fringe and tried making a hesitant smile in Kate's direction.

Kate considered giving Tanya a speech about being a little fish, but decided against it.

'No. No, love, nothing like that. I myself was released from prison just over four years ago; I served five years for manslaughter. Janeece, our counsellor, was a fellow inmate of mine, a wonderful girl who will tell you her story if and when it's appropriate. Natasha is our art therapist—'

'Art?' Tanya interrupted.

'Yes, art therapy. It's where—'

'You don't have to tell me about that. I know how it works. I love paint and I love painting.'

Kate looked at the girl and noticed the widening of her eyes and the flush of colour to her alabaster cheeks.

'Well then, it looks as if you are going to get along just fine.'

Tanya exhaled loudly and they both realised that she had been holding her breath for most of the journey.

'Come on, let's get you inside.'

Tanya trod the wooden steps to the terrace with her bag clutched to her chest, a bodily shield against the physical and mental blows that she always expected and often received. Best to be prepared.

The house was silent; everyone had scattered after lunch. Tom would no doubt be on one of his 'trips for supplies' – although what he thought he could purchase from inside the van with the seat reclined in siesta position was beyond Kate. Stacey Hill, the only other resident, was probably on the beach, trying to clear her head; this too was a daily exercise and would one day, hopefully, enable her to sort the muddled thoughts that plagued her.

'Are you hungry, Tanya?'

The girl shrugged. Her confusion was not over whether she was hungry or not – she was starving – but whether or not she was comfortable in saying so.

Kate read her reaction.

'Tell you what, why don't I pop some sandwiches up to your room while you are getting settled?'

'Thanks.'

A deal had been struck.

As they climbed the staircase, Kate pointed out the sitting room with its oversized sofas, the dining room, where all meals were taken, and the kitchen with its central table, perfect for catch-ups over coffee or the issue of tissues as and when required.

They stopped at a door with a sign on it that read 'Dream'.

'All the rooms have different names. We have "Wish" and "Faith" and "Free", but "Dream" has the best views and I want you to have sweet dreams.'

She turned the handle and let Tanya walk in first. The girl walked straight to the sash window and stared at the expanse of ocean.

'Where does it go? I mean, what's the other side of the sea?'

'That's a good question. Geography was never my strong point and I had to look it up when I first arrived, but I have been reliably informed that if you swam as far as you could, the first country you would hit would be Canada.'

'Canada near America? You're shitting me?'

'No, it's true – if you swam until you hit a beach, you'd probably be handed a towel by a Mountie! Imagine that.'

'I can't swim.'

'Would you like to learn?'

'No.'

She shook her head. Her answer was loud, emphatic, as she placed her forehead on the cool glass. Kate could not have guessed at her thoughts, the flash of an image, her mother's boyfriend, angry, pushing her face under the water, a deep, cold bath, don't breathe, don't breathe . . .

'I'll go and fetch your sandwiches and leave you to it. Your bathroom is through that door and the wardrobe's here – it's all pretty self-explanatory. I'll let you get settled and I'll be straight back.'

Tanya didn't lift her head from the glass. Instead, she stared at the ocean, vast and black and going all the way to another country, another world, Canada . . . She had never seen the sea before, only pictures of the ocean or in movies. The way the water constantly flexed and jumped leaving tiny white crests wherever she looked was fascinating; it was alive. She hadn't been prepared for its size, all consuming and limitless.

When the door clicked shut, she looked for the first time at her surroundings. The room was beautiful, with pale blue walls, a stripped wooden floor and a pretty rug. There was a small Victorian fireplace with two comfy chairs in front of it and a little table. The chairs and bed were covered in white cotton with the tiniest sprigs of green flowers sewn onto it, like something out of a magazine. Tanya had never seen anything like it. It was lovely.

The bathroom was similarly perfect, with large white fluffy towels and a thick towelling dressing gown hanging on the back of the door. Tanya could not help but compare it to the bathroom of her childhood. When she blinked she could see the image tattooed on the inside of her eyelids, a constant reminder. It was the room that most symbolised the deprivation in which she had lived and it would stay with her forever. The tiny, cramped room, maybe six foot by eleven. It had a plastic bath with a jagged crack along the side panel and two greenish white streaks like the residue from tiny waterfalls snaking from the tap down to the rusted plug hole. The frosted window was small and high up on the wall, too high to reach and open with ease. In lieu of a curtain, her mum had tacked up a child's striped pyjama top. Tanya didn't know where it came from, it wasn't one of hers. It hung like washing trying to dry, suspended with drawing pins and sagging forlornly in the middle. The loo was filthy and the whole room stank of urine and damp.

The exposed concrete floor was curiously daubed with blobs of yellow and lilac paint, though Tanya had no recollection of any decorating ever having been done, and there was certainly no evidence of it anywhere in the flat. Looking back, Tanya decided that if yellow and lilac were the chosen colours, it was a good job they hadn't been used. In every corner of the bathroom, gathered behind the pipes and along the side of the bath, were piles of short black curly hair, matted with a curious grey fluff that seemed only to gather in this one room. The wall next to the loo was streaked with long brown tears, sticky droplets of old urine where a drunken cock had misfired. A medicine cupboard that had long ago lost its door hung above the sink, crammed with objects that made her tummy flip, adult things, forbidden things. Tampons, condoms, gels and potions, items that when she glimpsed them made her feel vulnerable and inexplicably queasy. The taps of the sink were relics of the 1970s and dripped constantly, adding to the brown pool that stained the bowl.

Tanya decided that she would like taking a bath in her beautiful new bathroom with its shiny taps and she looked forward to feeling the soft fabric of the dressing gown against her skin and the woolly rug beneath her feet. In prison, everything had been thin: the hard carpet tiles, the watery food, the bars of soap, the worn sheets, the napless towels and communal clothes. All thin, barely grippable between her fingers; frail and insubstantial. She had been cold when clothed, and wet long after her bath as the towels didn't dry her skin. The bed sheets had been so shabby that she would feel the stitching of the mattress against her cold, goose-prickled skin as she tried to sleep.

Here it was different; things were luxurious and voluminous, downy, soft and inviting. She had never slept in an environment like this, had never even been in a room like this. A bubble of excitement snuffed out the wariness and nerves that had dogged her since she had stepped from the train. Was she really going to sleep in here? Was this really *her* room to live and spend time in as she pleased?

Her thoughts were interrupted by a knock at the door. Fear leapt in her throat. She didn't move and said nothing.

'Tanya, can I come in?'

'Yeah,' she managed, after a pause.

Kate entered slowly, balancing a tray with sandwiches, a large slice of Victoria sponge and a pot of tea with just the one cup. She knew that Tanya would need to acclimatise alone.

'Here we go. Room service!' Kate joked. Looking up, she was dismayed by Tanya's tears that fell thick and fast.

'Oh, lovey, please don't cry. Here, let me get you a tissue.'

Kate deposited the tray on the table by the fire and walked over to the bedside table, where a box of scented tissues had been placed.

'I'm sure that it's all a bit strange, but I promise that you will get used to it here and you'll love it! We are so glad to have you here, Tanya, really I—'

'It's not that.' Tanya interrupted her.

'Oh.' Kate was trying to think of what might be ailing her. Missing someone? Feeling lonely? Something else? She didn't have to guess much longer.

'No one has ever knocked on a door and asked if they could come in, never, ever, anywhere. Not in my whole life. It's been as if I was invisible, as if I didn't count.'

Her tears once again fell unchecked. Kate put her arm round the girl's shoulders. She knew what it felt like to be invisible.

'Well, Tanya, that is house rule number one: to treat everyone with respect and to give them privacy when they want it. Your room is your sanctuary, your own private space.'

'My own private space.'

Tanya repeated the words out loud, trying to

comprehend what they meant and thinking that if she said them aloud, it might just make them true.

The study door was closed, a sign to all not to disturb the occupants.

Stacey pushed stray strands of hair behind her ears; her ponytail was pulled back tightly to reveal her forehead, which was peppered with tiny spots. Her fingers gently touched the four gold hoops of differing sizes that hung from each earlobe, before yanking her jersey sleeves over her hands. She pulled her knees up under her chin and curled her frame more snugly into the wing-back chair facing the desk.

Kate was extremely fond of Stacey, who was fighting her way back to strength after a violent rape. Prospect House was giving her the breathing space to get back on track, in a place where memories of her assault weren't lurking around every corner.

'How you doing, missus?'

'Okay, I think. Bit better.' Stacey's voice was quiet as usual.

'Good! Are you okay to talk, Stace?'

The girl shrugged her shoulders; on some days, even the most basic decision was too tough.

'I've been thinking about going home . . .' This she delivered with her eyes averted, as though it were in some way disloyal, rude.

'Well, that's a good thing. Only you will know

when you are ready. You can of course stay as long as you want to.'

'I know.' Stacey gave a small smile of gratitude.

'Sometimes it's a good idea to write down your thoughts: reasons to stay a while and why you want to go home. It might help.'

'I don't have to write it down, Kate. I know I have to go back to my mum's at some point, but East Ham's not that big. Everyone knows . . .'

'Stacey, you didn't do anything wrong. You were the victim, don't ever forget that.'

'Yeah, I know that too, but it doesn't really matter how or why when people are pointing at me. It still feels really shit.'

'I can imagine, love. It will take enormous courage.' Kate swallowed the hypocrisy, knowing it was courage she herself didn't possess. She would never return to Mountbriers Academy. 'And you do have a lot of support. You've got your mum and your brother, and from what you've told me you and Nathan are very close.'

'Yeah, we are; he's brilliant. We were on our own a lot when we were little, my mum always worked and he was more like my mum in some ways, looking after me and stuff. But it's not been the same since this happened to me. Mum doesn't know what to say to make it better, so we just avoid the subject, both making out everything is okay. And Nathan's life hasn't really changed, he's still working at the care home, getting too involved with the old dears that he looks after and trying to find a new boyfriend. It's not like it was when we were little, when we were always together and he could make things better for me just by making me laugh. He's still my very best friend, but things are different.'

'What you've been through won't change how he feels about you, Stacey.'

'I know, and I know Nathan loves me, but he's busy. He copes with bad things by distracting himself. None of us are very good at talking about anything that matters. One of his old ladies that he really loved died – Dorothea, I think she was called – and he was gutted, but I only found out by accident. We hide things in our house, make out everything's all right. It's like we can't cope if we're not laughing, but it makes me feel panicky to think of being at home and having to laugh and joke when I'm broken inside.'

Kate nodded, understanding this too well.

'I know your mum wants you back and that is only natural, but you are the one who must decide when the time is right to go home, and there is no rush, Stacey.'

'I guess so.'

Stacey's mouth moved to form words that were a struggle to sound. She dug deep, found her courage.

'It's not really about my mum or Nathan, though; it's more about people I haven't met yet . . .'

Kate tried to anticipate her concern.

'You don't have to tell anyone unless you are comfortable doing so, Stacey. What you went through doesn't define you; it's just a small part of you that feels like a big part right now. But its hold on you and its domination of your thoughts and actions will diminish with time. I promise you.'

'I . . .' Stacey tried and failed to reveal her thoughts.

'What is it, love?'

'I don't know how anyone will love me and I don't think I will be able to love anyone, not now I know how bloody awful people can be, and that makes me so sad. It's like my life has finished before it's started. I'm glad for my mates whose lives are moving on, they're having babies and stuff, but I feel a little bit jealous sometimes, that that will never be me. I can't see me ever getting married, being someone's wife, not now.'

Stacey snatched at the buttons on her cardigan.

Kate reached across the desk and took the girl's hand inside her own.

'Love, Stacey, is a weird and wonderful thing. I thought I had found love when I was not much older than you and it turned out to be the exact opposite of love, because love means freedom and acceptance and I had neither of those things. Then I felt more love than I ever knew possible when I became a mum and this too is now tested to the limit; to have that love taken away from you is another form of torture. But one thing I do know is that when love comes along, it doesn't judge and it doesn't condemn, it simply accepts you for who you are, all of you.' For some reason, Kate saw an image of Simon, his open smile, his beautiful skin, slicked with seawater. 'And this will be what it's like for you, Stacey, I promise. Just you wait and see.'

'I guess so.' Stacey tried out a small smile.

'I know so,' Kate replied. 'And when the time comes for you to go home and rebuild your life, I'll put you in touch with people who can support you at home. Janeece would come and see you, I'm sure.'

'I'd like that, Kate. I just want to go back to how I was before. I want the old me back. I used to laugh all the time, I used to sing a lot and I thought everything was funny. I enjoyed every single day. I never had much, always skint, but always happy.'

'You will be like that again.'

'I hope so, cos I'm sick of feeling this low, this scared.'

Kate squeezed the girl's hand inside her own.

'You won't always feel this way. With each day that passes you will get a little bit stronger until eventually you'll rediscover the person that you used to be. Look at how far you've come in the eight months since you arrived! You didn't want to leave your room at first, remember? And now look at you, out and about on the beach, talking. It's wonderful; you are doing so well.'

Stacey nodded, not daring to believe that it was

true because the disappointment of discovering otherwise would be too much to bear.

'How are you getting on with Tanya?' It mattered to Kate that there was harmony.

'All right, yeah. She's from North London though, a different world, Kate. I never thought I'd be living with an Arsenal fan!'

They both laughed.

Kate considered the importance Stacey placed on being married. It was touchingly old-fashioned and echoed how her own generation had felt at that age. She wondered if Lydia had a boyfriend. The thought of Lydia marrying without her being present was something Kate just couldn't contemplate. The very idea of her little girl taking her last steps as a single woman and betrothing her love to another without her mum there to witness the momentous act of transition was incomprehensible. She wanted to be there to support her, hand her over, add in any way possible to her special day. She wanted to fluff her train, blot her lipstick and arrange her posy just so.

Kate had pictured it over and over since Lydia had appeared one day, at the age of seven, clad in an old net curtain and carrying a plant pot up and down the hallway whilst humming the tune of 'Here comes the bride', trying not to wobble off the sparkly heels that she had found in her mother's wardrobe.

Kate thought of her own wedding. In recent years she had many a time replayed the day in her head, rewriting history at the bit when the vicar spoke. In her new, rewritten version of events, she would run from the altar as fast as her white stockinged legs would carry her, holding her bouquet aloft as she wrenched the antique veil from her head and disappeared down the steps into a waiting car being driven by Pierce Brosnan. Well, why not? It was her fantasy after all.

Her actual wedding had not been nearly so dramatic, although there was a moment when it threatened something similar. She and Mark were standing inches apart, facing the vicar, whose arms were spread wide. As the familiar words were cast around the rafters, there was the faintest hesitation on her part. She knew the lines, had unwittingly been rehearsing them in a deep crevice of her mind since she was a little girl, and yet at that exact moment, with friends and family stood in their finery, waiting, she nearly failed. It had been a simple enough question, not a complicated maths equation or something equally taxing that would have sent her into a nervous spluttering of mumbo-jumbo; it had been clear and concise.

'Do you, Kathryn Gavier, take Mark Brooker to be your lawful wedded husband?'

With breath drawn, tongue poised and words ready, it was as if an unseen force had placed magic on her lips. She had to fight to say it, struggle to get the response out that the vicar, Mark and the assembled congregation had waited her whole life to hear . . . If only she had let the magic do its work and not fought so strongly to utter the two syllables that would alter the course of her life forever.

Stacey left for her daily stroll on the beach and Kate sauntered into the kitchen.

'Coffee?' Natasha stood at the countertop and raised the cafetière in the direction of her friend.

'Mmmn . . . Please.'

'How's she doing?'

'Worrying about the future and starting to think about going home.'

'Well, those are good signs, aren't they?'

'Yes. When she's ready. I don't want her to rush into anything.'

'You'll miss her, won't you?'

Kate nodded. Yes she would, she would miss her greatly. She smiled at her mate, acknowledging the unspoken words, the dangers of getting too close.

Kate understood the bond between Stacey and Nathan as those who are fortunate to know the love of a trusted sibling or best friend do. Kate knew that no matter how much time passed, she would always dearly love *her* best friend. The day Natasha had turned up unannounced at the prison was one she would never forget. The memory would, however, always be tinged with the bitter disappointment that her unexpected visitor hadn't been one of the kids . . .

'Oi! Daydreamer!'

Natasha's shout pulled her back into the present.

'I was saying that I'm struggling a bit with Tanya. A great girl, really open to my suggestions and seems happy enough, but I kind of get the feeling that she is going through the motions and saying what she thinks will please me, but not truly opening up. Classic closed-in state of the abused.'

'What can I do to help?'

Kate was as usual looking for a way to ease the path of her latest charge.

'Oh, nothing different. She'll open up when she's ready. I mean, look at Stacey. It took her months. And of course she's a different kettle of fish, a victim and not a perpetrator, plus she has a brilliant network of support, which means in the long term her prospects of full recovery are good. With Tanya it's different; we have to be careful. She's fragile, Kate, more than most. I'm not fooled for one second by that sunny smile or the indifferent shrug; there's a lot going on in that pretty head.'

'I know what you mean, Tash. We should pick it up with Janeece.'

'Good idea.' Tash nodded.

'Does she ever mention her mother?'

'Couple of times, but no real revelation. She occasionally drops her name in passing, usually associated with a memory. I find she wants to talk more about the sea; she's fascinated by it. Her pictures are quite dark and nearly always with some water theme – the sea or just blocks of black and blue.'

Both noted the bruise analogy.

'I can't work out if it's just because the ocean is new and exciting or whether she is subconsciously looking for a way to escape, sail off into the sunset, quite literally. There's a piece she is working on that I find a little unsettling . . .'

'What is it?'

'It's the sea again, but with a skeleton arm coming up and breaking the surface. Lots of black as is usual in her work but it's almost Gothic, with horror undertones. I don't think her memories or associations with water are good.'

'Doesn't sound like it. What will you do?'

'I'll see how it progresses; get her to interpret it for me, a number of things. Sometimes it's enough that it's been put down on paper, almost like exorcising the bad thoughts. It's similar to having someone to talk to, getting all that dark stuff out into the open so that you don't carry it around.'

'Has she told you about the ex-boyfriend?' Kate was curious.

'A bit. He sounds like a total shit, *comme toujours*. She mentioned he was a dealer, but quickly checked herself, she's still not confident in how much she should reveal. It amazes me how these bastards seem to have some kind of sixth sense that enables them to seek out girls that are needy, vulnerable, and they know exactly how to exploit it. How do men do that?'

Kate hunched her shoulders inward.

'I guess because some girls let them . . .'

'Oh God, Kate, I didn't mean you!'

Natasha slapped her own forehead in mock reprimand.

'It's fine, Tash. It's fine, really. And you are right, it's important for girls like Tanya to know that they are not alone. It can happen to any woman, even one like me!'

'Top up?' Natasha once again lifted the coffee pot.

Kate raised her mug before dropping it loudly on the table. Coffee drops scattered rain-like as the china crashed and split into pieces.

'God, that made me jump! What was that?'

A motorbike roared into view, its deafening engine powering it up the drive.

'I can't say exactly, but I can predict that it's a new Mr Someone in whose arms Tanya can forget – and he has a *very* large motorbike!'

Kate placed her head in her hands.

'Oh that's great, just what we need, a rebel without a cause.'

'Kate, you worry too much. It might be good for her, a little diversion. Mind, you have to give it to the girl, she's a fast worker. How long has she been here?'

'Nearly three weeks.'

'Blimey, we've been here years and not so much as a sniff!'

'Speak for yourself. I got propositioned at the fish market a couple of weeks ago, by an octogenarian with a customised scooter and a fancy for gurnard!'

'Bloody hell, you dark horse. What did you say?' Natasha squealed, reminding Kate of her sister in their teens.

'I said no.'

'You're kidding me! Are you mad? Customised-scooter-driving, gurnard-wielding octogenarians are fairly thin on the ground in these parts.'

'I know. I did, however, manage to resist. Although to be honest, Tash, even if it had been Mr Clooney himself with whitebait for two I'd have said no. I've got enough to think about.'

'Did you get his number?'

'NO! I've told you, not interested.'

'Not for you, you dozy cow, for me!'

The two laughed as they mopped coffee into paper towels and retrieved the scattered slivers of china. Kate thought how lovely it was to break a mug without breaking sweat, knowing that she would not be 'punished' later for this accidental misdemeanour.

The kitchen door opened to reveal Tanya with a flush to her cheeks and her hair perfectly tousled. She looked beautiful.

'Hello you, what was that mighty roar? Have you been on a motorbike? If yes, I hope you wore a proper hat thing.'

Kate was aware that her tone was a little too censorial, but it was difficult. She wanted Tanya to hook up with a boy who would do the right thing, treat her properly. Anyone who would roar off without seeing her safely through the door or introducing himself was already falling short of Kate's exacting standards. It was difficult for her not to apply Mountbriers etiquette.

Kate felt a huge sense of responsibility towards all the residents who had come under her care; her biggest battle was to remain objective. She could only look at Tanya's new beau in clichéd terms: an unsuitable boy, a member of the wrong crowd, trouble waiting to happen.

'Thanks, but I'm a big girl, Kate. I've told him to get me a helmet.' She rolled her eyes skywards.

'Oh good. It's just that apart from being illegal not to wear a helmet, the roads around here are winding and unpredictable. I want you to be safe.'

'Yes. Winding and unpredictable, understood. Can I go now?'

'Of course you can go, Tanya. I'm only trying to show you how dangerous it is and to take an interest in your new friend. It would be good if he came in to say hello next time he collected or dropped you off.'

'Err . . . don't think so, that would be too weird!'

'I worry about you, Tanya. This is all new for you and I want you to take things slowly.'

'No, that's not what you mean at all, Kate. You don't want me to be happy. You want me to sit around feeing miserable and still broken like Tracey or whatever her bloody name is, so that you can be the great fixer and feel slightly better about your shitty life. That's why you do this, isn't it?'

Kate's response was measured.

'Oh, Tanya, I wish that were true. I wish that by helping you and the others I could heal myself, but sadly, no, it doesn't quite work like that.'

Tanya covered her face with her palms, speaking through the gaps in her slender fingers.

'Oh God, Kate, I'm sorry. I don't know why I said that. I didn't mean it!'

'Tanya, it's okay. I am really rather chuffed that you can say exactly what you think. Goodness me, when you arrived a few weeks ago, you would have nodded and agreed to just about anything. You've come a long way in a very short space of time.'

'It's just that I'm not used to anyone being nice to me and I think any comment is going to lead to a fight, so I tend to get my side in first.'

'I understand, Tanya. Don't worry. I don't want it mentioned again.'

Tanya looked thoughtful and a little sheepish as she trod the stairs to her room.

Natasha had been silently observing from behind the breakfast bar.

'You are remarkable, do you know that?'

Kate raised an eyebrow by way of reply, wishing beyond wish that it was Lydia she had been reprimanding.

It was Kate's turn to cook while Tom held court in the Lobster Pot, as he did every Tuesday evening, the open mic night providing an excuse for him to play to an unpaying crowd. Natasha had gone to a fine art and sculpture seminar in Truro and Kate served dinner to the girls. She dug the spoon deep into the fish pie. Steam rose from the fractured brown crust of buttery mashed potatoes.

Tanya wrinkled her nose.

'You don't know that you don't like it until you try it, Tanya.'

'I didn't say a bloody word!'

'You didn't have to.' Kate laughed. 'You did your nose-wrinkling thing.'

'Well I think it looks lovely, Kate,' Stacey piped up.

Kate smiled at her, always sweet, gracious and positive.

'Okay, Mrs Suck-Up! God, you'd eat poop pie if Kate made it!'

Tanya's retort was biting and predictable.

Kate didn't comment. She had enough experience to know that interrupting warring youths was never a good idea. A pang of grief scraped at her chest and spread throughout her body. She used to think you could only grieve for people long gone, but she now knew that it was possible to grieve for a time long gone, more specifically a moment in time, when her own children had been under her wing, squabbling at her table.

She missed cooking for the kids; there was something quite primal in the preparing and cooking of food for your offspring. It was one of a thousand comforting daily rituals that had marked her life for so many years. Sometimes she would recall a chubby hand resting in her palm, a sticky face lifted skywards awaiting a kiss, or the smell of a fragrant bay-scented scalp, and her tears would pool. Her babies, long gone. The role she fulfilled for these girls was multi-faceted: she was counsellor, protector and guardian, but never mother, even when the barriers were down and hope was at its strongest. Having never had children, Natasha would smile across the table when these tense exchanges occurred; it was the closest she came to living in a challenging family environment.

Tanya forked a mouthful of the pie into her mouth and now felt fully qualified to talk with authority.

'I don't like fish pie.'

She folded her arms across her chest like a petulant toddler.

Kate looked at her stern face.

'Well that's fine, Tanya,' she sang, as she removed Tanya's plate from in front of her and deposited the contents into the pedal bin. 'You can jolly well starve.'

Kate was happy to wave the girls off for the evening, Stacey to a movie in the village hall and Tanya to the pub, to mock Tom's vocal efforts no doubt. It was a luxury to have the house to herself. She poured a large glass of plonk and turned on the sitting room lamps. Cosy. She was alone and happy with the idea of an uninterrupted few hours, a chance to gather her thoughts. When Mark was alive, evenings had been the worst part of the day as the threat of bedtime loomed ever closer. Now, however, it was her time, and the thrill of knowing that a peaceful night lay ahead had not lessened over the years.

Down at the pub, at the clanging of the bell and the gathering of swilled glasses, the bar had gone from crowded to empty in a matter of minutes. Drunken revellers had been cast into the real world, where the air still carried the lingering warmth of a blissful summer day. It was one of those days when night would never truly fall. A light glow persisted, offering a peek at the morning that hovered in the distance.

Tom had been in full flow, his mouth organ twittering out shanties and tunes. Even those not native to Penmarin, who didn't know the ancient rhymes and lyrics, had participated through foot stomping and clapping. It had been a golden night, one to remember.

Tanya loitered at the end of the bar. Her red hair fell over her shoulder as her head lolled to one side. She gripped the motorbike helmet under her arm, the biker's first and last present to her. She was ready for her ride home.

Rodney grinned at her as he gulped the remains of his single malt. She was gorgeous and for once it wasn't his beer goggles that gave her that irresistible edge; she had been drawing his gaze since he first saw her. If he was being honest, he liked

281

the idea of the rough diamond that wouldn't be looking for romance and whispered exchanges. He would take a guess that her usual beau was sparing with the chocolates, corsages and Moët. This would be easy.

'A good night?'

'I've had better.' She smiled.

He liked her confident banter, not like some of the dozy tarts who hung around, laughing at his every word, dreaming of living in the big house or at the very least hoping for a day trip on his yacht. Her cutting repartee told him all he needed to know: this was no-strings fun. He had let the pot boy and barmaid go early, almost as if clearing the stage for this long awaited performance. Perfect.

'Where you going with that?' He grinned and pointed at the helmet.

'Dunno, any suggestions?'

Her retort might have been sexy were it not for the sad familiarity with which the words dripped from her glossed lips, and the Lolita-like pose that she had been perfecting for a while. It was how she got things done, reeled them in, gave them what they wanted, felt loved.

Rodney sauntered across to where she stood and slowly pulled her behind the bar. She giggled, but didn't find any of it funny. It was a laugh that they expected, a laugh that gave them permission: *it's okay to carry on, just a bit of harmless fun.*

Gripping her from behind, he breathed into the

back of her neck, inhaling the scent of her young body. Slipping his hand under the thin material of her T-Shirt, flat-palmed against white skin, he drew small circles that warmed the space they touched. Tanya turned around slowly until she faced the man that would seduce her. He was old. She studied the creases and lines that traversed his sagging face and noted the coarse hair that sprouted in trimmed clumps.

She smirked at his inexpert kissing. She'd assumed that an older lover would have mastered the art, but apparently not. He felt huge against her tiny frame, a giant that she would fell. His impatience amused her; fumbling at belts and snatching at buttons, he grabbed and pawed, his need urgent. She smirked in recognition of the fact that they were all the same when it came right down to it, aged twenty, thirty, forty or fifty . . . At this point, it was all about a need, a longing and an ache that she could satisfy. With her eyes closed, all her lovers past and present were remarkably similar.

The mismatched pair slid down onto the sticky red linoleum behind the bar. The smell of beer and the sugary scent of spilt wine was overwhelming. There were no words of seduction, no affection or intimacies of love. This was an act of pure physicality, animalistic, verging on aggressive.

Tanya laughed into his plaid-clad, middle-aged shoulder, which had long since lost its definition.

She enjoyed the brief power, it was always this way. This was the moment when she felt supreme. She radiated at the thrall in which she held the local big-wig, he of powerful car and fat cigar, a connoisseur of life's finer things. For a few seconds this union would make her too feel like a finer thing.

She wanted the pace to be slow; she hoped for a few words of tenderness. She got neither.

Her spike of elation was not to last. All too quickly the pair were restoring clothing, tucking in hems and patting down wilful hair. This aftermath was conducted in silence, not the awkward variety, but, judging by Rodney's expression, a hush born of disgust.

Tanya's sense of omnipotence was immediately and forcibly replaced with a deep self-loathing, a feeling that was more comfortable, familiar.

Rodney jangled the keys in her direction, informing her it was home time. Her humiliation was complete; he wasn't wasting any words on her. The best he could manage was an action, the rattling of chunks of metal to coerce her, in the way one might distract a baby or quiet a rowdy pet. As he reached over, she hoped to feel the caress of his palm against her face; it would have helped. Instead, he pinched her cheek, in the way one might a naughty nephew, or as if he were a cane-wielding schoolmaster.

He dropped her off at the bottom of the driveway. She had barely placed her feet on the ground when the Kawasaki roared off into the night. The honey glow of Kate's carefully positioned lamps shone through the windows of Prospect House. Tanya eased her key into the lock.

Kate was on the sofa, blanket bound and reading.

'Hello, love. Good evening?'

'Yeah, not bad. If shagging on the bar floor is your idea of a good evening.'

She wanted to shock, transfer some of the tension to this woman who was easy prey.

Kate sat up, *The Time Traveler's Wife* suddenly of less interest than the topic in hand.

'Actually, no, it isn't. I'm a bit old-fashioned like that, preferring at least a mattress, a decent courtship or a bag of chips first, but that's just me.'

Kate refused to take the bait. She'd seen it all before, heard it all before. She suppressed the many questions that danced on her tongue. Who is he? Why are you doing this? Are you okay? Hurt? Happy?

Kate unwrapped the blanket from her legs and closed her book. Henry DeTamble would just have to stay missing somewhere in time until she could pick up his trail again. She knew he would understand, given that he was always having to suffer the inconvenience of disappearing at the most crucial moments.

'Well, as long as you are home safe and sound, I think I'll turn my toes in.'

Tanya stumbled forward and sat down on the sofa next to Kate. Her tears fell quietly, snaking their way into her open mouth. She was not usually given to mournful reflection, but it was as if by being in this wonderful place, she expected her life to be different, *she* expected to be different. But it wasn't. She wasn't. Whether with the old gang trying to score a hit or here in this picture-postcard village by the sea, it would always be her that gave the boys what they wanted, her that only knew how to seduce, but not how to love.

'Oh Kate, Kate . . .'

'It's okay, lovey, you are home and you are safe.'

She cradled the girl's slight frame against her own and spoke into her scalp.

'It will all feel a bit better in the morning, you wait and see. It'll pass, everything does.'

Kate smiled as she regurgitated the advice a good friend had once given her.

The two sat until Tanya drifted into sleep. Kate extricated herself, taking care not to wake her. She needed the escape that sleep offered. Kate tucked the pale pink lambswool blanket around her charge's slender shoulders and pushed a cushion under her cheek. Tanya was calm, for now.

'Morning all!'

Tom was in good spirits.

'Just seen Rodney on the deck of his boat looking like a right plonker! God, if he's not racing around on that ridiculous bloody motorbike, he's poncing about on that boat!'

Kate seized the moment. She popped on her

trainers, snuck out of the back door and trotted off down the lane. She tried to calm her rising pulse, tried not to jump to any conclusions. It wasn't often she knew where to find Rodney, and this was just the opportunity she'd been looking for.

She found him on the deck of *Lady of Penmarin*, his rather ostentatious yacht, wearing a naff sailing hat with gold braiding and a large anchor embroidered on the front, the kind of cap you could pick up at any of the local gift shops for a few quid. He was busy coiling rope, which even though she was a novice sailor, Kate could tell was a futile chore, designed so that he could show off in full view on the deck. Tom had phrased it perfectly: a right plonker.

'Rodney, hi!'

Kate waved from the pontoon.

'It's Cap'n Rodney when I am on my seafaring maiden!'

'Righto. I was wondering if I might have a word?'

Kate ignored his joviality; she was in no mood for high jinks.

'Yes of course, come aboard!'

'Urgh, I was afraid you'd say that.'

Kate groaned. She was an ungainly yachtswoman, clinging to rigging and placing each foot hesitantly for fear of ending up in the drink.

'What a lovely surprise, Kate! Come into my lair . . .'

Rodney indicated the cabin steps and twitched

his rather unkempt eyebrows like the classic caricature lech.

'I'd rather not. I'd prefer to just say my piece and then go.'

'Oh, that sounds ominous.'

'I want to talk to you about Tanya.'

'Ah, the delightful Tanya – talk away!'

'This isn't funny, Rodney, far from it. In fact I've come to ask you to stay away from her.'

Rodney laughed and shook his head slightly as though in disbelief.

'I don't know what tales of wrongdoing she's been running up the hill with, but let me assure you that she was more than—'

'She hasn't mentioned you, not once.' Kate interrupted him. 'It's me that has the problem, not her. Any relationship you might envisage having with her can only do her harm in the long run and I care enormously about Tanya, about all the girls.'

'Relationship? Good God! I think you are rather jumping the gun there.'

Rodney laughed loudly at the very idea.

'I see. Well, that says it all really. Do you know, Rodney, you are an arsehole and a bastard and an arsehole!'

'You already said arsehole.'

'I know, but I'm not very good at swearing in public and it's all I could think of twice.'

'Is there something else going on here, Kate, old girl? Is that a little bit of the green-eyed monster

I detect? Maybe it's not fair because Kate is a lonely girl?'

He winked at her.

'Oh, please! You make me sick, Rodney. Let me ask you a question: how did you become the person you are? How did your unfortunate personality take shape?'

He stared at her, unsure whether she was expecting an answer or not. She wasn't.

Kate continued.

'I bet if you were anything like me, it was because of the people you met, places you went, your education, holidays you took, foreign travel, chatting to people from different backgrounds, races, religions.'

'I guess.'

He shrugged and scratched at his scalp under his hat. His grip on the topic was somewhat loose; he wished she would get to the point.

'Well, Tanya has had none of those opportunities, not yet. She may look like a grown-up and even sound like one at times, but she is anything but. I want you to leave her alone and give her the chance to experience life without being lassoed by someone old enough to be her father, if not grandfather! I am asking you to stay away from her because she is fragile and I am not about to look the other way and watch her get damaged further by your little dalliance.'

'Oh please, Kate. Dalliance? That is a very sweet term applied to what was nothing more than a drunken fumble between two willing parties. I think you are overdramatising and for your information, I have no intention of repeating the event. Where Tanya is concerned, my curiosity is more than satisfied.'

He stood tall, using his physicality to make the point.

Kate saw the smirk on his florid face, watched the sneer to his mouth as he said Tanya's name and she saw red. How dare he use this little girl to 'satisfy' a whim, how dare he do that to Tanya?

'You are a fucking shit, Rodney, a disgusting excuse of a man and a joke. You strut around Penmarin because you put a few shekels into a few restaurants and you think you own the bloody place. You are widely disliked by those who allow you to buy them drinks, did you know that? You are a creep and a tosser. You are a very small fish in a very small pond and that makes you nothing. Arsehole.'

Rodney was speechless.

Kate turned on her heel and with confidence made her way off the deck and onto the pontoon. Natasha was right; having a good old rant with a few choice swearwords thrown in for good measure was really quite cathartic.

Kate swallowed hard as waves of sickness swept her body. Her hands shook and her stomach flipped itself into knots. Her exchange with Rodney had physically shaken her. It had been a while since aggression had featured in her daily routine and its reintroduction left her reeling.

She took a deep breath before entering the kitchen; she didn't want anyone to see her this agitated.

'Everything all right, boss?'

Tom was elbow deep in washing-up suds.

'Yes, Tom, fine.'

Her smile lasted no longer than a second.

Tom nodded at the deep window sill.

'Tanya's left you a note.'

'A note? Why?'

Tom shrugged and pursed his lips. How should he know?

Kate read the hastily scrawled text and dropped her forehead into her hands.

'Oh shoot!'

'Would a cup of tea help?'

Tom wiped his arms on a tea towel and reached for the kettle.

Kate nodded.

'She's gone back to London.'

'For good?'

'No. She says for "a bit", although what that means I'm not sure. Ooh I could kick myself, she needs to be here!'

Kate thumped the table top. It was hard for her to accept the lack of control she had over those she most wanted to help. *Dominic, Lydia, Tanya...*

'She'll be back, boss. Doesn't sound like she's got much up there.'

Kate nodded, hoping desperately that he was right, and headed for the door. She would go down to the beach to gather her thoughts.

The beeping of a horn heralded Janeece's arrival and jolted Kate from her morose reflections. Tom had obviously directed her to the beach.

'Hello! Hello!'

'Oi! You is in my seat!'

Their old comedy routine still made them both laugh.

Kate waved from her blanket and practised her smile.

'I think you'll find it's anyone's seat actually!'

'Jesus, Kate! I swear to God Penmarin moves half an hour further away every time I come!'

Janeece plonked herself down on the damp sand, enveloping Kate in a large hug, releasing her when she was good and ready.

'Oh bloody hell, now I've creased me linen!'

'You look lovely.'

Kate meant it. Today Janeece had chosen a grass-green linen shift with a dazzling array of buttons and beads sewn around the neck and cuffs, over hot pink, cropped jeans with the same design around the hem. Janeece knew how to flatter her Amazonian frame with bold prints and bright colours that more diminutive characters would shirk from.

'And we don't move further away; it's that rubbishy car of yours. I keep saying, take the jeep, we can swap. Mine's more robust for longer journeys and your Deux Chevaux will do me fine for pottering to the station or the shops.'

'Sssshhh, she might hear you. Cars have feelings too, you know, and I would never trade my Bessie in. She's the first big thing I ever bought and I love her!'

'You get more sentimental with age, Jan.'

'Mental yes, not sure about the "senti" bit!'

'How're the kids?'

'Well, I know that all mothers think it, but I *know* that mine are the most beautiful creatures ever created. Jared is walking, although he's very wobbly, got the legs of a drunk; and Eliza is talking nineteen to the dozen – can't get her to shut up.'

'Must take after her father.'

'Ha! Funny girl. She says she wants to be a spaceman when she grows up. I asked if she meant spacewoman, but she was adamant. So she either becomes more gender aware as she gets older or I'm hooking up with Cher to see if she can recommend a good surgeon!'

The two laughed, simultaneously appraising each other. Now that Janeece had started a family and moved to Bristol, they only saw each other once a month, when Janeece returned to lead counselling sessions with the girls. But both women were still quick to notice any changes in the other's mood or demeanour.

'How you doing, Kate, really?'

Janeece knew better than to accept Kate's smile at face value.

Kate looked at the sand, trying to divert her sadness.

'Well, I'm good most of the time. Sometimes, though, I miss Lyd and Dom so much it's painful. I mean literally I feel pain in my heart.'

'I wish I could make it all better for you.'

Kate gripped her friend's hand. 'You do, Jan, you do.'

'I've got something to show you. I was going to wait until I left, but now seems as good a time as any.'

'What is it?' Kate was intrigued.

Janeece delved into her large patchwork book bag and produced a glossy booklet. She placed it in Kate's upturned palm.

'It's a programme of West Country events for the year. Turn to page twelve and see what's coming up in a few months.'

Kate did as instructed and her eyes were immediately drawn to the small black-and-white photo in the top right-hand corner. It was Lydia.

'Oh, Jan! She's so beautiful and grown-up! Look!'

She did her best to dash away the big fat tears that dripped from her chin.

Janeece could only nod sympathetically. Having never met Lydia or seen any other picture of her, it was impossible for her to draw a comparison.

Kate read further. 'She is holding an exhibition, oh my goodness, her very own art exhibition at the RWA in Bristol. Oh, Jan, isn't that amazing!

She must be very good, mustn't she; I mean, they don't let any old person hold an exhibition!'

Her excitement bubbled through her tears. Her little girl, her baby . . . Kate pictured Lydia's fat toddler fingers gripping crayons and producing masterpieces that she had then pinned up around their kitchen walls. It was a lifetime ago.

'It's called "Pictures From Behind the Flint Walls". What do you think that means?'

Kate considered the title and then answered her own question. 'We had flint walls at Mountbriers; it must be that.'

Janeece nodded. 'I didn't know if I should show it to you, but it plopped through the letterbox yesterday and is being advertised a lot locally. I didn't want you hearing about it from someone else.'

'Thank you. It's lovely to see. I can't believe how grown-up she looks, and so self-assured. She looks a lot like her dad too. He was a very good-looking man; that's the one nice thing I can say about him.'

'Are you going to go?' Janeece nodded at the booklet.

'Oh! I hadn't thought. I wouldn't want to upset her big night. I would dearly love to of course. I would love to.'

Kate beamed as though her attendance was a possibility.

'Why don't you ask Francesca what she thinks?'

'Well, it's tricky. I don't phone there any more

– the kids asked me not to and I have to respect that. So she calls me once a month, and emails of course. I think it would be too public a place for our first precious meeting, but you have no idea how much I would love to get a glimpse of her and Dom. He'll be there; he wouldn't miss this for the world!'

'There's no reason why you can't go to the exhibition, Kate. I could go ahead, see who was around and if the coast was clear, then you could come and have a gander. Then I'd whisk you away afterwards. It's on for over a week. What do you say?'

'I don't know . . .'

'Well, think about it. You don't have to decide now.'

'I love you, Jan. I love you to bits.'

Kate gripped her young friend's hand.

'The feeling, madam, is entirely mutual.'

'Are you sure this isn't too much for you, coming up every month, Jan? I hate to think of you doing the journey so often.'

'We're only in Bristol, it's nothing. Anyway, it's good to keep my hand in with the counselling, and to have a "me day", let Nick and the kids have time together. I think they all enjoy being able to eat rubbish and watch their monthly TV allowance in one afternoon. When I get back, they're always bug eyed and bouncing off the walls from sugar overload!'

Their chuckles brought them back on track.

'How's Tanya getting on?'

Kate exhaled. 'Oh God, Jan, bit of a mess really. We had a development last night, I'm afraid. She's a fabulous kid, but a trouble magnet. She's been sleeping with someone and I'm afraid to say it's . . . Well, have a guess: old, slimy—'

'Not Rodney Big-Shot-Have-You-Seen-My-Boat?'

'The very same. I've had serious words with him and I am absolutely furious. But realistically what can I do? She's not a baby and she's not a prisoner.'

The two women smiled at each other. Both knew very well the difference between life behind bars and in front of them.

'What the hell is he thinking, Kate?'

'I suspect he's not, not with his head anyway.'

'Do you want me to sort him out?'

Janeece balled her right hand into a fist and pulled her arm back at head height as if about to land a punch.

Kate laughed again.

'No! Although that's very tempting. Tanya has probably been encouraging him slightly, possibly even a bit more than slightly, so I have to tread carefully to avoid alienating her. Although it's a bit of a moot point right now because she's gone off to London, apparently. Left me a note saying she had to go back there for a bit.'

'How long is a bit?' Janeece echoed Kate's earlier question.

Kate shrugged as she pulled her knees up to her

chin and hung her head forward. 'Oh, why can't it ever be easy?'

'Nothing worth having ever is. Someone brilliant told me that once.' She smiled at Kate. 'It'll work out, mate.'

'Oh, Jan, I hope so. I'm getting tired.'

'No, you're not getting tired, you're getting old!'

'Thanks a million! You're supposed to be making me feel better!'

'Oh yeah? That was never in our contract! Maybe your old age is giving you selective memory as well as fatigue!'

Janeece jumped up to pat the sand and creases from her clothes.

'Right, this isn't what I came here for. I can gossip to you anytime, but today I've got work to do. I'll go find Tash and see what she's unearthed and we'll take it from there. Then how about a rendezvous at the kitchen table for a cup of coffee and a slice of whatever Tom has managed to create in my honour?'

'That sounds lovely.'

'Right, missus, I shall see you after I've had my session with Stacey. Don't worry, Kate, you are doing your best. You know that, right?'

'Mmmn . . . But what if my best isn't good enough?'

'Then it's out of your hands, mate.'

Janeece kissed her dear friend on the cheek before leaving her alone.

Kate watched the girl that had become a woman

tread the wet sand towards the path. She was so proud of all Janeece had achieved, a gifted counsellor and a wonderful mum. Sometimes it was hard for Kate to reconcile the confident woman that Janeece had become with the aggressive teenager she had first met.

As she turned back to stare at the sea, Kate heard the postman's van reverse into the driveway and her heart skipped a beat. She didn't receive letters from Lydia any more but prayed that they would start again – a note, a scribble, anything. This time of day meant a quickening of her pulse, just in case there was a response to her monthly communiqué, an olive branch. There never was, but she would wait.

She pulled her ballet wrap cardigan around her slender frame. These days, her figure was svelte as a result of healthy living and not because she was so scared all the time that she was unable to eat. Stretching her bare calves in the mid-morning sun, she flexed her toes against the edge of the soft tartan blanket. The damp sand clung where it touched. An empty crisp packet cartwheeled along, propelled by the intermittent breeze. Her surroundings were perfect yet the hole inside her could not and would not be filled until her children were once again in her life.

TEN YEARS AGO

Saturday was a day of rest for some members of the school community. The younger years and those that weren't in sports teams were free to idle outside or indulge in a hobby in their boarding house. If the kids had match fixtures, however, it was a school day like any other.

Kathryn folded her son's cricket whites and brushed his school cricket cap. He was at best a keen amateur, but as per school rules could not be seen in anything less than full games kit. She correctly assumed that part of the allure of school sports for Dom was the paraphernalia that accompanied each activity. He was convinced that if he looked the part, he could play the part, hoping that wearing top-of-the-range kit might make up for his lack of natural ability.

Saturday or not, Kathryn had chores to do. Today she would polish the canteen of silver cutlery – it was seldom used, but best to be prepared; empty and clean the two wheelie bins; strip the oven down to its bare components and thoroughly scrub all parts thereof; sweep the garden path and patio; clean and polish all the windows on the landings and hallway including the glass of the front and back doors; and visit the supermarket for a 'big shop', ensuring that the larder, cupboards, freezer and fridge were adequately stocked for any eventuality.

It was a gloriously hot day. Kathryn had enjoyed her trip into town, stopping several times to debate the temperature with the various staff and parents she bumped into, and once to admire a collection of bugs that some pre-prep students had stuffed into a leaf-filled ice-cream carton. It felt like summer had arrived. After donning her sandals and spritzing her cologne she was ready for her next batch of chores.

She glanced at the kitchen clock and was happy to see she was ahead of schedule. This meant she could start preparation for supper and find a few spare minutes later in the day for illicit reading.

'Kathryn?'

She abandoned the bowl of sugar snap peas that she had been prepping, dropping the sharp paring knife into the pocket of her apron as she wiped her hands on its floral fabric. The children regularly laughed at her choice of domestic cover-up, but she cared little; it felt homely and reminded her of her own mother's apron, which she remembered as being constantly spattered with flour.

She followed Mark's voice out into the garden, walking quickly to where she had been summoned.

'Yes, Mark?'

She hovered, waiting to find out the exact nature

of his request, which might be anything from a demand for iced tea to the name of a past pupil that had temporarily escaped him.

'Gardening gloves? Any clues, my sweet? Can't seem to find them!'

'Yes, I'll fetch them.'

Kathryn returned to the kitchen and rummaged in her bits and bobs drawer in the larder. There they were. She heard Mark's loud chuckle before she ventured back outside.

'There she is! Keeping me hard at it as usual, Roland.'

'That I can see. Nice to see you, Kathryn!'

Sophie's dad raised his hand in greeting from beside the rose bed. Kathryn waved as she approached, noting his tailored navy blazer, which he had teamed with white Bermuda shorts and deck shoes. He always looked so dapper, effeminate even, in his immaculate outfits and considered accessories. Dominic referred to him as an 'old poof'. Kathryn would have to disagree; he certainly wasn't old.

'Hello, Roland. Sophie got a match?'

'Yes, tennis. Thought I'd come and offer a bit of moral support!'

'Well you've got a lovely afternoon for it.'

Kathryn swept her arm over her head, to indicate the sunshine.

Mark interjected. 'I wouldn't know about that. Some of us are slaves to the garden and our wives, sunshine or not! I can assure you I'd rather be sinking a pint and having a gander at the paper. Quite keen to know how England are getting on in the Test.'

Mark laughed and Roland laughed too. Kathryn marvelled at how her husband always knew the right thing to say to endear himself – she could swear that he had no interest in cricket whatsoever.

'Now you're talking,' Roland concurred. 'Go easy on him, Kathryn, the man works too hard!'

She smiled and nodded. Her heart thudded and her lips trembled with the temptation to scream.

With supper prepared, Kathryn decided to wander over to the playing fields, hoping to catch a bit of Dominic's cricket match. She packed up a basket with some cold fruit juice and a homemade lemon cake. She would give the boys a treat; they were probably famished.

She had never grasped the rules or finer points of cricket but had to admit that there was something very soothing about the sound of leather on willow and the dainty ripple of applause at a job well done. It all felt very English and reminded her of days in the park with her dad when she was little.

Boys and parents alike lounged around the field, some engrossed in newspapers, some dozing in deckchairs and one or two even watching the match.

She spied a group of kids at the far side of the

pitch and determined by their stance and number that her son would be among them. It took a while to navigate the edge of the field. She stepped over open novels, textbooks and crawling babies. She trotted between picnic blankets and folding chairs and stumbled over discarded shoes and cricket pads whilst nodding hello or acknowledgements to several staff and visitors. As she approached the group, she could see that her assumption had been correct.

Dominic lay face down, prostrate on the grass along with several of his peers. Kathryn averted her eyes as an empty bottle of champagne was hastily thrust under a school sweatshirt. The boys and girls alike were in various states of undress, as was fitting for the weather. One of them was Emily Grant, whose shirt was tied up under her bust, revealing the slight paunch of a tanned tummy. Her hair hung down over her face and her eyes were heavily kohled. She lay inches from Dominic, her head propped up on her angled wrist as she raked his back with painted nails.

Kathryn felt an instant ache of regret at having come; she was intruding and wished that she had stayed at home. This was no place for parents or teachers; she was an outsider. Intuition told her she was unwanted before she had uttered a single syllable. If she could have reversed unseen and slunk back into the shadows, she would have.

She looked back to examine the route that she had taken, trying to plot a quick escape. So many obstacles and people littered her view, she couldn't easily decipher a path. There was a split second when she wondered if she could turn on her heel and slip away unnoticed, back into the crowd.

'Hey! It's your mummy, Dom Dom!'

Kathryn wasn't sure who had spoken, but recognised the tone.

'Yes it is,' she offered brightly. 'Hello, Dom! Hello, everyone!'

Dominic flicked his head around and groaned as he surveyed his mother in her floral cotton apron.

'Hello, Mrs Brooker!'

It was Luca who had been so very polite.

'Hello, Mrs Bedmaker!'

Again, she couldn't determine who had spoken, but presumed it was one of the lower sixth whose face was buried in a white slipover. Kathryn felt her cheeks turn crimson as heads snickered into hands and bodies shook with the exertion of trying not to burst out in guffaws. It was an absolutely hilarious situation. Her breath came in huge gulps and she felt rooted to the spot. Even Dominic laughed, but tried to bury his face into the blanket to conceal his amusement.

'I just . . . I . . . well . . .' She pleaded with herself, *Don't cry, Kathryn, not here, not now, not in front of them.* Mustering what little dignity she could, she smiled at the group and announced in a loud voice with her head held high, 'Just came to check on the score. I'll be off then. Have fun, everyone!'

Clutching her basket, embarrassed by its contents and her earlier intentions, she turned a little too quickly and stumbled on a divot. The bottle of juice rolled onto the floor. She bent to retrieve it before scurrying away. She could hear the ripple of laughter that chased her steps.

Why is it okay to laugh at me? What have I done to deserve this? I am a person, I am not invisible. These thoughts rattled around her head.

A conversation that she had once had with Natasha came to mind. The subject had been sprung on her unawares as they walked in the grounds one autumn day.

'Do you know that your nickname is Mrs Bedmaker?'

Kathryn had answered carefully. 'Yes. Yes, I do know. The kids say it to me when they think that they can get away with it. It's almost like an initiation, a positioning on the bravado scale. They always do get away with it of course, because I let them!'

'Why is that, Kate?' Natasha held her arm.

'Well, because they are only children and most of them are actually very sweet indeed and they are far from home. I have known them all for a long time and I think it would be more harmful or awkward to pick them up on it. I mean, it's only a bit of harmless fun and I know that they don't mean anything by it.'

'No, Kate, you misunderstood me.' Natasha shook her head. 'I mean, why is it that they call you Mrs Bedmaker? Why do you wash your bed linen so frequently? I know it's none of my business, but it is a little . . . odd.' She twisted her mouth into a comic grimace, trying to make light of the situation.

Kathryn had looked into the face of her friend. A little voice in her head had said, *Tell her, Kathryn, tell her now, she cares and she can help you! Tell her what he does to you, tell her what he has always done to you, tell her how you are trapped, tell her how you have to stay or you would lose your children and the thought of that is even more unbearable than the life that you are forced to lead.*

Instead, she opened her mouth and a sound popped out that would change the parameters of their relationship for a very long time. It was the sound of a very heavy door shutting, the sound of a barrier closing, the sound of a boundary being put in place, a limit, a threshold, a constraint. It was these ten words: 'You are quite right, it is none of your business.'

She often thought about that conversation and the missed opportunity. What did it matter now? Natasha was teaching at the other end of the country. Kathryn doubted she would see her again, more's the pity. The two had shared a wonderful friendship.

Kathryn thought about Dominic and Lydia's behaviour. She had tried their whole lives to make them into decent human beings, showing them the importance of having respect for themselves and other people. This sounded ironic even inside her own head: how could she teach or show them how to have respect for themselves when she had no respect for herself? She was a sham. Her whole life was a horrible pretence.

She knew that at some level her battle to make them into rounded and likeable people was futile. How could they ever grow up with any sense of 'normal' when what went on under their roof every night was so very far from normal, no matter how much she tried to convince herself otherwise?

They were embroiled in a battle that they did not even know they were fighting, playing a game in which over half of the rules and players were hidden. It was unfair on all of them.

Kathryn breathed a heavy sigh of relief as she walked up the back path that wound its way between the playing field and their private garden. Here she could hide until the match had finished.

She spied Mark's head, bent over a garden chore on the other side of the hedge. He was wearing his gardening hat. He insisted it was a panama, but to Kathryn it looked more like a Stetson, which made her chuckle on the inside.

Kathryn paused and looked beyond the gate into the garden. At first she couldn't identify the strange haze that loitered over the top of the roses, the shimmering distortion of the grass and flowers. The house bricks flickered and the air seemed to flex. Then she realised that she was looking at the house through a wall of heat. Something was burning.

She sniffed the air and recognised the distinctive smell of a bonfire. The bitter, intoxicating smell transported her to her childhood, her dad in his black wellington boots, holding a garden fork as he skewered leaves and wrappings onto the burning pyre. His 'bonfire' was a permanent fixture: within a wheelbarrow's leap of the compost heap, he had constructed a ramshackle box out of chicken wire and an old metal gate. The whole thing was supported by two bricks at each corner. He would always make out that it was an arduous task, but she and Francesca knew it was one of his greatest pleasures. In fact it seemed that most men loved the almost primal task of starting a fire and watching the heat of the flames destroy things.

Kathryn stepped inside the gate. She watched Mark as he bundled up paper and cardboard then threw the pile onto the fire and stood back, hands on hips, to admire his handiwork. Unlike her dad, Mark would be burning things out of necessity, to clear away mess; he would not have secreted a handful of foil-wrapped spuds at its core, for retrieval and eating with butter at dusk. She thought back fondly to her and Francesca in their frog-eyed wellies and hand-knitted Aran jerseys, sitting with their father on upturned milk crates, with buttery chins, burning tongues and cold, prune-like toes . . . Happy, happy days.

She walked down the path towards the house. The black smoke swept across the garden with ferocity and she was thankful that she had taken in the washing earlier.

'Ah, Kathryn, there you are.'

He smiled at her. He probably required something: a cold drink, sandwich, chair, punch bag, who knew.

She said nothing, but smiled back, nodding her head slightly to indicate that yes, there she was.

Kathryn moved closer to the fire, enjoying the warmth it radiated despite the summery temperature. She quickly became transfixed by the flames. She was fascinated by the colour palette within the blaze: yellow and orange flickered to purple and green with the brightest blue leaping at certain points; it was beautiful and captivating. Kathryn not only loved the sight and scent of a fire, but also the noise. It was distinct and evocative of cosy nights in, romance and snuggling under blankets on a cold winter's evening; it was a good book and lamplight; it was comfort for aching bones.

She stood silently for some minutes as Mark jabbed at the flames with a long branch. As she focussed, she could make out an empty tissue box, the front cover of an old cardboard file and some peanut shells. As she continued to stare, her eye was drawn to some lettering that jumped out at her from the burning matter and punctured her vision. It was just a few letters that weren't immediately decipherable: *g . . . u . . . d . . . i . . . gudi.*

Kathryn knew at once to what those four letters referred: *Tales from Malgudi! Oh no! Oh no!* Her breath quickened as her heart thudded inside her rib cage. She began to shake. She screwed her eyes into slits to better withstand the acrid smoke, and, taking one step closer, she looked deep inside the flames.

They were all there: *Tom Jones*, *Portrait in Sepia*, *The God of Small Things*. All of them. She pictured her husband tearing through the house, a whirling dervish in search of all her concealed treasures, saw him gathering them into his crooked arms and tearing down the stairs in his haste to throw them onto the flames. Would it have brought him joy to know that he was destroying her secrets? Yes, yes, she knew that it would.

Her mouth hung open. Putting her hand to her forehead, she looked at Mark, who returned her gaze with an unwavering, expressionless stare.

All of her books that she had hidden about the house – her friends, her distractions, her joy. He had found them and he was burning them. The discovery may not have been made today; he may have known about them for some time and had simply been biding his time, waiting for the right moment to execute his plan.

That moment was clearly now and her books were nearly gone; seconds of life remained in one or two untouched words. He was burning her novels. *Burning her books . . . Burning her books . . .* It didn't matter how many times she repeated the horror inside her head, it didn't make it any less distressing.

Kathryn dropped her basket, indifferent to the lemon drizzle cake that spilled onto the grass and the bottle of juice that skittered off the path, coming to rest under a shrub. She sank to her knees, unaware that dirt and soil were seeping through her skirt and discolouring her knees. She looked again at her husband, but no words came. There were no words, nothing to adequately convey what she was feeling or that would make him understand. She wanted to use words like bereft, anguish, sorrow and heartache. She knew, however, that to him they would feel like an exaggeration, a taunt, and so she could not speak them, not with it being only a couple of hours until bedtime.

It was while she sat mourning the loss of her books and her only means of escape that something else caught her eye. Sticking out from the corner of the fire was a rounded wooden knob. It was about a centimetre in diameter. Once her eyes had identified it, she quickly spotted the split legs of another and the head of another and another . . .

Kathryn slumped forward until her head was on the soil. She beat the ground with clenched fists, then ripped at the grass with her fingers. The sound she emitted was part cat mewl and part wail, animalistic and desperate.

'No! No! No! Please, no!'

He had burnt her grandmother's pegs, severing the last tangible link she had with her mother and grandmother. He had destroyed part of her history and part of Lydia's future, removing the only things that made her whole pitiful laundry routine bearable. These little dolly shapes were her one diversion from the abuse she suffered. Whilst pegging out her bed linen, these little wooden objects enabled her to think of her grandma and of summer days in childhood, of homemade cakes and garden picnics and not the fact that she had once again been forced to remove the evidence of her husband's torture.

Tears slid from her eyes and down into her open mouth. She sobbed without restraint. Kathryn had mastered the art of crying silently and discreetly and could even cry on the inside, allowing tears to slip down the back of her nose and throat without breaking her smile. Today this was not possible; her distress was overwhelming and all consuming.

She cried loudly as she fought for breath. Burying her dirt-covered face in her hands, she sobbed and sobbed. Every time she peeked between her fingers and glimpsed the glowing, charred remains of the little wooden splints, her tears would flow again. He had burnt her grandmother's pegs . . .

She continued to sit statue-like on the dewy grass long after the flames had disappeared. In their place was a pile of smoking charcoal. Occasionally a small defiant flame would fizz and flare, but this display was always short-lived and feeble.

Kathryn became aware that it was growing dark and that she was dreadfully uncomfortable, damp, aching and covered in dirt. It hadn't occurred to her to finish off supper or attend to her chores; she could only focus on her distress. Standing slowly, she looked into the kitchen window and into the face of her husband, who stood on the other side of the pane with a glass of wine in his hand.

Her soot-smeared face was streaked with the paths of tears that had long since dried, leaving only tracks of salty residue. Slowly Mark's mouth twisted into a smile and his eyes creased accordingly. He was smiling at her, but she couldn't even pretend. She couldn't find her happy face or her happy voice. She felt broken, broken and beyond repair.

> *Hey, little girl,*
> *Comb your hair, fix your make-up.*
> *Soon he will open the door.*
> *Don't think because*
> *There's a ring on your finger,*
> *You needn't try any more*

Next morning, Kathryn felt surprisingly numb. Each time she closed her eyes, the nightmare of her burnt pegs leapt into focus. She could picture nothing else; the images consumed her every thought. She felt strangely disconnected from her surroundings and stacked the breakfast things into the dishwasher slowly.

'You okay, Mum?' Her son's tone was one of concern.

Kathryn couldn't find any words of response or her happy smile, so she simply nodded.

The chapel was busy; each boarding house occupied its usual pew. Invited parents in their finery crammed into the narrow seats, each mummy trying to out-yummy the next. Pinstriped dads shook hands and slapped each other's backs in congratulations at all that they had achieved: a smart suit, flash car, expensive watch and gorgeous wife. Game, set and match.

Governors and staff were dotted among the congregation, wearing their dusty graduation gowns and university colours with pride. The organ music boomed and invigorated, giving everyone who sat staring at the ornate domed ceiling a feeling of self-importance and belonging: our history, our tradition, our money well spent.

Kathryn felt all eyes scan the headmaster and his wife as they settled into their seats. She had to resist the temptation to stand and shout at the appraising eyes, *'Yes, I know I am wearing the blue jersey and pleated skirt again, but truth be known it's my "chapel outfit" and you will all be seeing it for at least this year and probably the greater part of next.'* She was wrong; no one at chapel that day would see this outfit again.

Kathryn glanced over at the masters sitting with jutting chins and narrowed eyes in their allocated seats. She knew that at least three of them would be dozing within minutes, using the ruse of deep prayer and concentration with eyes closed to catch up on sleep. They fooled no one, least of all the children, who would point and nudge at the lolling heads.

Kathryn had almost given up on the God to whom they all paid homage, but it was important that she attended nonetheless. Not to do so would be bad manners and she did enjoy the beautiful surroundings, the singing and the sight of her children, whom she watched surreptitiously from across the aisle. She wondered if every mother felt the same swell of love and pride when they studied the perfect faces of the humans they had created.

Unaware that they were being scrutinised, Lydia and Dominic looked relaxed and natural. Dominic twitched his nose involuntarily; a tiny act that transported Kathryn back to when he was a baby. It amazed her that this boy-man was only ever a minor flinch away from the baby she had held in her arms. If she closed her eyes and breathed deeply, she could still invoke his newborn scent, a unique and intoxicating combination of baked bread and new human. Lydia had smelt quite different: fresher, with an almost citrusy tang, like a warm lemon muffin.

Kathryn watched Lydia put the nail of her index finger into her mouth and start nibbling. It made her wince. Lydia had the beautiful hands of an artist: long, tapering fingers and almond-shaped nails. It was a long-standing family joke that if she sat on her hands she would be unable to communicate; she was so expressive with them, using her palms and fingers to illustrate and emphasise every point.

Dominic sat with his fingers interlaced in his lap. His gaze was steady in the direction of the chaplain. A casual observer might think that he was transfixed by the words being dispensed from the lectern, but Kathryn knew different. From her privileged vantage point she could see that Emily Grant was sitting slightly to the right of the chaplain and was busy returning her boyfriend's gaze with not so subtle nods, gestures and raised eyebrows. Kathryn smiled to herself, feeling like a secret had inadvertently been shared with her.

The chaplain, Tim Cattermole, was warming to his theme. He grasped both sides of the lectern, as if to add extra gravitas to his words.

'"I know the plans I have for you," declares the Lord, "plans to prosper you and not to harm you, plans to give you hope and a future." Boys and girls, staff and parents, I would like you to think about that quote from the Bible while I give my address today, the theme of which is "protection". I want to talk about our duty to protect all that is precious and important to us, including our wonderful school and all that is in it, but also the need to protect each other, to keep each other safe from harm . . .'

He spoke at length about how bullies and people that harm others were the opposite of protectors, how they were in fact 'destroyers' of all that was good and worth protecting. Most of it went over Kathryn's head, for she was greatly distracted by a single thought that rang out like a clear note, high and visible above everything else – that the right thing to do was *'to prosper you and not to harm you'*. Tim Cattermole was spot on: she should not be harmed, she should not be harmed any more; this was not why she had been created, not what her parents had raised her for, not why she had been blessed with children. Enough was enough. Kathryn Brooker did not want to be harmed any more.

She closed her eyes as the chaplain's words rose up and danced about the keystones of the arches, waking the slumbering carvings and gargoyles. For the first time in a very long time, she prayed. *'Help me, please help me. I am so lonely, I am alone. I am lonely and alone amongst all of these people; I am always alone. Wherever I am and whoever I am with, I am always alone. I am asking for strength because I want to give up. I don't think that I can do this any more. Help me, please help me . . .'*

In a moment of epiphany, Tim Cattermole's words pierced her prayer and spoke directly to her. He was quoting the answer, he was giving her the solution, he was answering her prayer:

'Thou shalt not consent unto him, nor hearken unto him; neither shall thine eye pity him, neither shalt thou spare, neither shalt thou conceal him: But thou shalt surely kill him; thine hand shall be first upon him to put him to death.'

The words replayed in her head until she had little choice but to give them consideration.

After chapel, the great and the good gathered in the refectory for drinks. Kathryn was in no mood for jovial interaction with strangers, but as usual she had little choice. Mark was chatting to Dom and a group of his peers, holding court, making friends. Kathryn caught the tail end of Luca's story.

'. . . the nasty little poof.'

She correctly concluded that the boy under discussion was Jack Hollister, who had recently left school after being outed on the web by his tutor group. She had found the whole episode disgusting.

'I don't think you should be talking about anyone in those terms, Luca. It isn't very nice.'

The group stared in surprise at the unusually opinionated Mrs Bedmaker.

When the last of the assembled parents and masters had scoffed enough plonk and vol-au-vents, Kathryn and Mark found themselves alone.

'Thank you for your valuable input on the Hollister boy incident earlier, darling. Your insights will I'm sure prove most enlightening to the boys as they venture forth into the world. I find it odd that you felt the need to comment at all. It can't be news to you that the world is indeed "not very nice" and my personal view is that he is better away from a school of this calibre. We have no need of his sort here.'

'His sort?' Kathryn could not keep the horror from her voice.

'Yes, his sort. Do I need to remind you that I am an educator and therefore fully aware of exactly what a subversive influence in a small group can do? For future reference, if I need advice on what polish to use or the best way to get the dishes really clean, I'll ask you, but in the meantime kindly don't offer your views on matters about which you have absolutely no knowledge and that I or anyone else have absolutely no interest in hearing. Is that clear?'

Mark smiled throughout his lecture, but the tone in which it was delivered left Kathryn in little doubt that she was in deep trouble. Before she had a chance to respond, the kids popped their heads around the refectory door.

'Can we please go home? Some of us have lives outside of school!'

'God, kids, can't we have a little smooch without being hounded by you two?'

'Oh, gross, Dad!' Dominic shook his head.

Kathryn stared at her husband. His capacity to lie and smirk in unison knew no bounds.

Once the chaplain had been congratulated, the choir thanked and the pupils dismissed, the Brookers walked along the path back to their house. Dominic and Lydia strode ahead, loosening their chapel-smart ties and rolling down their socks, impatient to shake off 'geek' and become 'cool'.

Kathryn watched Mark saunter along the path

with his hands clamped behind his back. His gown billowed behind, giving him a bat-like quality.

'I thought it went rather well this morning,' he said. 'I think people found my address interesting; some were clearly captivated.'

'If you substitute "long" for "interesting" and "bored" for "captivated" then I couldn't agree more, Dad!' Dominic shouted back along the path.

Kathryn watched her husband laugh loudly as he tipped his head back. It was incredible how he allowed – appreciated, even – such frankness and deprecation from the children and yet reacted with such wrath to even the slightest transgression from her.

'I agree with Dom,' Lydia interjected. 'You go and on and on, Dad. Blah, blah, blah. I stopped listening after the welcome bit.'

'Right, I get it. My children are finally learning the power of combined effort. Well done, kids. Two is definitely better than one when it comes to brain power.'

Dominic and Lydia high-fived each other in a rare moment of camaraderie.

'Hang on a mo though, kids. Your celebrations may be a little premature. You seem to have overlooked the fact that I am not necessarily outnumbered here. I do have my good lady wife on hand to boost my team numbers.'

'Actually, Dad, sorry to disappoint you, but I have to say that I saw Mum's face during your performance today and she looked bored shitless like the rest of us!'

'Is that right?'

Mark stopped walking and turned to face his wife.

'Come on, Kathryn, enlighten us. Which were you? Captivated or bored shitless, as our offspring so succinctly put it?'

The three stood facing her. Her children's faces were open and smiling, but Mark's eyes were thunderous, his mouth set.

'Yeah, come on, Mum. Bored shitless or captivated?'

Kathryn studied the trio around whom her world revolved. She practised the correct phrase in her head, mentally forming the words that would placate her spouse and disappoint her children.

It was a split-second lapse of concentration. The briefest of moments when her words leapt from her mouth unfiltered and uncensored. It was done in error.

'I was absolutely bored shitless.'

Dominic and Lydia doubled over, each laughing hysterically at this unexpected turn of events and delighted that at last their mum was joining in the fun. Dom wiped the tears from his eyes as he put his arm across his mother's shoulders.

'That is classic! Bloody classic!'

Lydia put her arm around Mark's waist, evening out the teams.

Kathryn held her husband's gaze, which was

unwavering despite the physical distraction of the kids.

'Is that right, Kathryn? Bored shitless, eh?'

Mark narrowed his eyes, trying to better understand his wife's dissent. He stared as if trying to fathom where this new-found confidence had come from, what had shifted in their universe that meant she felt able to openly go against him. He wasn't accustomed to being disagreed with and he didn't like it. He didn't like it one bit.

She sought words of solace, tried to find the right words of retraction that would prevent severe punishment later. Try as she might, they remained obstinately hidden, as though a greater force than she was controlling her tongue.

'Looks like you're finally outnumbered, Dad!'

Dominic was delighted with the small victory.

'It would appear so!'

Mark laughed as he released his daughter's grip. The family continued along the path.

Kathryn felt an overpowering rush of longing for her children. It felt wonderful to be on the same side. She surged forward and put her arms around her children's backs, clutching at them with outstretched arms and splayed fingers. They chorused in unison, 'Get off, Mum!' and 'What are you doing?' She didn't care. The trio stood on the path.

'I love you both so very much. I am so proud of who you are and I am proud of all the things that I know you will achieve. You are both amazing, my amazing kids! Promise me you will always make good choices.'

Dominic shrugged himself free of his mother's arm.

'Sure, crazy lady.'

He did, however, peck her on the cheek before jogging ahead and home. Lydia took her mother's hand and the two continued along the path, with Mark not far behind.

'I love you too, Mum.'

Kathryn beamed. 'Thank you, darling.'

'Do you remember, Mum, when you asked me a while ago if I would like your life and I said no?'

'Yes, yes I do.'

'Well, I should have added that even though I wouldn't like your life exactly, I would like to be like you. You know, sweet and kind and lovely all the time. I really would like to be like that.'

A single tear rolled down Kathryn's face.

'Thank you, Lydia. Thank you.'

Mark opened the gate and stepped back to allow his wife into their garden; ever the gentleman. Kathryn slowed as she walked past him, her eyes cast downward. The earlier moment of euphoria had passed quickly.

'I will kill you.'

His expression belied the fact that he had spoken. It had been little more than a whisper and was so softly offered that she couldn't be sure she hadn't imagined it. Maybe she had.

★   ★   ★

Kathryn tied her floral apron about her neck and waist and put the kettle on to boil. She tried not to focus on the invisible gap on the shelf between *Jamie's Italy* and *Jamie Does* . . ., where until yesterday her secret copy of *Tales from Malgudi* had rested, awaiting a snatched moment while the kettle boiled or the dishwasher whirred through its last cycle. Her precious books were all gone, burned. She still couldn't think about the bonfire without a lump forming in her throat. She tried to soothe herself with the mantra that 'they were only things, objects. None of it matters . . .', but the truth was that it did matter, it mattered a great deal.

In the seconds that it took her to fill the kettle with fresh water and plug it in, the children had changed and were now thundering down the stairs.

'Bye!' they yelled in unison.

'Where are you going, kids? When will you be back? Are you here for supper?'

Dominic paused in the doorway and flicked his long hair from his eyes.

'Which one should I answer first?'

'Erm . . . I'll take them in order please.'

She smiled at her boy, her smart, sarcastic, funny boy.

'Barbecue at Amy's. Late. No.'

'Have fun and be safe!'

'Which one?'

'Which one?'

'Yes, Ma, you can't have both.'

'In that case I will go for safety.'

'Boring.'

'That's me, Dom. Regular, boring old mum!'

Dominic let go of the door handle and walked back into the kitchen. He strode over to his mother, took her in his arms and hugged her tightly.

'Yes you are, but you are *my* regular, boring old mum and I love you.'

With the embarrassment of youth, he quickly released her and ran from the house. That one embrace with its sincere sentiment was something Kathryn would ponder time and again. Neither could have anticipated its significance.

With the early start of chapel and all the preparations that it required, Kathryn had neglected to make the bed that morning. She selected a clean set of white sheets from the linen cupboard and made her way to the bedroom. She half unfolded the sheet, placed it over the bed, and shook it open. As she watched the white rectangle billow in front of her, she heard a small thud. There, lying on the bare mattress, was one of her grandmother's pegs. Correction, the last of her grandmother's pegs, and not just any peg; it was Peggy.

She allowed the fabric to fall and scooped the wooden splint with its felt-tipped eyes into her hand. As she sat on the edge of the bed and held the precious talisman tight, relief flooded through her. She caressed it, her most cherished peg, rolled it between her palms and sighed.

'Thank you,' she whispered into the ether.

'Who are you talking to?'

Mark had suddenly materialised in the doorway.

'No one.'

'I see. Were you delivering one of your insightful speeches on raving homosexuality and niceness?'

She shook her head. Any previous confidence had now evaporated, as it always did within the four walls of their home.

Mark lunged forward quite suddenly and with his open palm hit her across the side of the head. He used such force that Kathryn tumbled off the edge of the bed like a discarded rag doll and landed in a heap on the floor. Her right ear rang and her face hurt. She opened her eyes wide and blinked, trying to restore her vision and balance.

'You see what you made me do? Do you think I like having to control you, Kathryn?'

This she knew was a trick question, because yes, he clearly did like having to control her.

'Get back on the bed.'

She obeyed his instruction, hauling herself back on to the mattress.

Mark took a step towards the tallboy, where his weapon of choice was neatly wrapped in its waxed paper. He stopped abruptly and turned back to his wife. He was smiling.

'What is that in your hands?'

'It's nothing,' she whispered.

He smiled again and a small laugh escaped his lips.

'You have given me two interesting answers,

Kathryn. "No one" and "nothing" – a thought-provoking combination. I am a teacher, Kathryn, an educator of young minds. Do you think that you are the first person to utter those two words to me in an effort to conceal and deceive?'

She shook her head. 'No, Mark.'

'You would be right, Kathryn. You are clearly not as thick as you look.'

Kathryn felt her body tremble as he approached her, not through fear of what he would do to her, but because she did not want to give up the precious thing that she had found, the one item she owned that had belonged to her grandmother and that her own mother's hands had touched.

He stroked her hair, rubbing the silky tendrils between his fingers.

'You will not leave this room until the children get home and need feeding, do you understand me?'

Her response was delayed as her mind processed her options. What could she do to conceal Peggy?

The next time he spoke to her it was through a clenched jaw, with a snarl.

'I said, the next time you will leave this room will be when the children get home and need feeding. Do you understand me, Kathryn?'

His hand went from stroking her hair to slowly winding his fingers into her roots. With a firm grip, he yanked a hunk of hair from her scalp. She flinched at the intense pain but made barely a sound.

'Yes, Mark, I understand.'

'You understand what?'

She looked him in the eyes.

'I understand that I will not leave this room until the children get home and need feeding. I promise.'

'Good. Now give me what is in your hand.'

'Please, Mark, I—'

'Do not ever use the word "please". It is akin to begging and is therefore degrading to us both. Have some pride, have some dignity. Now, give me what is in your hand or I shall break your wrist and take it myself.'

His threat echoed around the room. She knew in fact that it wasn't a threat; it was a promise. She unfurled her fingers and revealed the dolly peg lying flat against her palm. He slowly reached out and pinched it between his thumb and forefinger.

'Well, well, well, I must have missed one. These make truly excellent kindling!'

He stood in front of her as she sat shaking on the edge of the bed. He held the splayed legs of the peg and began pushing the tips of his thumbs up under each splint.

'Look, Kathryn. Watch.'

It was a command. She raised her eyes and watched. Mark held the peg just inches from her face and continued to apply pressure to its base. Kathryn's bottom lip trembled and her tears flowed. A small creak was followed by a hairline fracture, which quickly became a larger split.

The crack of her grandmother's peg finally breaking in two tore through Kathryn. Shaking uncontrollably, she gripped her apron pocket to try and stem the tremors. Her fingertips bumped against something hard – her paring knife, left in there from yesterday. Quick as a flash she withdrew the knife and plunged it hard and deep into Mark's soft belly. Mark bellowed as the blade punctured his spleen and lacerated his liver. He sank to his knees at the foot of the bed and crumpled over in the exact same spot where Kathryn had cowered under his command, night after night.

In her head, Kathryn heard the words that the chaplain had spoken earlier that morning. *'Thou shalt not consent unto him, nor hearken unto him; neither shall thine eye pity him, neither shalt thou spare, neither shalt thou conceal him: But thou shalt surely kill him; thine hand shall be first upon him to put him to death.'*

Suddenly she knew that this was the answer: her path to freedom, her salvation. It was instant and obvious. *'Thou shalt surely kill him . . . .'*

Kathryn rose from the bed and calmly gathered up the two pieces of peg from the floor.

'I think I can fix this,' she said.

She pondered the broken splints, rotating them to see if there were any joins that wouldn't marry up. Her husband's gasping made her look up. She placed the peg on her dressing table and turned her attention to Mark.

'Come on, let's get you up onto the bed.' She spoke with a sing-song quality to her voice, like a well-trained nurse.

She put her hands under his armpits and yanked him upwards. He screamed.

'Ssshh! Goodness, Mark, is there really need for such a noise!'

She dragged him onto the mattress. The linen sheet was bunched up beneath him and his head lay at an odd angle on the pillow. She casually reached over and pulled the knife from his stomach. Again he yelped. She tutted. Removing the knife had uncorked the incision and Mark's blood now spewed out in pulses. It ran through his fingers as he instinctively tried to hold his wound together. It ran over his legs and stomach, staining everything scarlet and giving off its familiar metallic scent.

'Golly, Mark, that is very deep. How many points do you think warranted an incision like that?'

He tried to whisper something.

'I can't quite hear you so I am going to have to guess. I would say thousands and thousands of points.'

She watched his complexion start to lose its handsome blush and turn ashen.

'God, you look awful. And look at the mess on those sheets – they will be ruined!'

'Please . . .'

His breath was laboured and his voice only audible because of the supreme effort that he put into trying to say something.

She breathed in sharply and put her palm to her breastbone.

'Mark Brooker! Did you say "please"? Do not ever use the word "please". It is akin to begging and is therefore degrading to us both. Have some pride, have some dignity. Have some dignity in death, Mark. Anything else would be most unbecoming.'

'Get . . . help . . .' he murmured.

'Now, Mark, how long have you known me? Don't try and answer. I will tell you. Nearly twenty years. And the one thing that you should have learned about me in all that time is that I never, ever break a promise. Never. What did I promise you, Mark? Again, don't try and answer that. I will tell you. I promised you that I would not leave this room until the children got home and needed feeding – and, Mark, a promise is a promise.'

Kathryn pulled the ladder-backed chair to the side of the bed, walked to the wardrobe and opened its doors wide. She tore clothes from hangers and left them in a careless pile on the floor. When she had made an adequate gap, she reached into the wardrobe and grabbed from the top shelf a book that had been concealed by several jerseys. It was Louis de Bernières' *Birds Without Wings*. She smiled at her husband.

'You must have missed this one.'

She cracked open the spine of the book and cast her eyes over the first chapter.

> *It seems that age folds the heart in on itself. Some of us walk detached, dreaming on the past, and some of us realise that we have lost the trick of standing in the sun. For many of us the thought of the future is a cause for irritation rather than optimism, as if we have had enough of new things, and wish only for the long sleep that rounds the edges of our lives.*

She paused from her scanning.

'I was just thinking, Mark, that this is probably a good opportunity for me to ask you some questions, to tell you how I feel, to tell you how you have made me feel. In fact my only opportunity, my last opportunity. What I want to say to you is this: I think that you are quite mad, Mark. I think the real you is the one that I get to see every night and the charade is what you present to the rest of the world, the smiles and the joviality. You may have fooled the rest of the world, but not me, not for one second; maybe I'm not as thick as I look. Did your treatment of me bring you joy or sadness? It has brought me sadness, Mark; it has brought me great sadness. You have taken the person that I was and you have slowly dismantled me over the years until I have become almost invisible. Why me, Mark? Why did you pick me? I had so much to offer, I had so much to give. I had a life. You took my life, slowly and piece by piece, and so now I am taking your life, do you understand?'

He nodded with eyes wide.

'I want you to know that I will reclaim myself, Mark. I will gather up all the little pieces that you have chipped away, hidden in drawers, swept under the carpet and shoved behind cushions and I will rebuild myself. I will become all of the things that I thought I might. All the dreams I considered before you broke me, I will chase them all and you will be but a distant, sad reflection. It is important for me that you know that. Important for me that you know you did not win.'

The blood flow seemed to have slowed, either due to clotting or some other reason, she didn't care. She sat and read through the afternoon, occasionally glancing at the vacant face of her husband. His skin was grey and he seemed sleepy.

'Are you still with us, Mr Sleepyhead?' she asked once.

It was some time later that her reading was disrupted by the sound of footsteps thundering up the stairs. It seemed to rouse her husband from his stupor. He tried to reach out his hand, beckoning to his children through the wall.

'That is pointless, Mark. Take it from one who knows: wishing for help, reaching for help, praying for escape – that doesn't work. But don't you worry, Mark, I've got it.'

She rose from her chair, turned down the

corner of the page she was reading and carefully closed her book. She padded across the carpet, opened the bedroom door a crack and popped her head through the gap.

'Hi, kids!' she shouted.

'Hi!' came at least one response.

'Dad and I are having an early night, but I am happy to come out and feed you. Are you guys hungry?'

'No.' This time Lydia's voice was distinct. 'We ate at Amy's.'

'What about Dom, is he hungry?'

'No, Mum, I told you, we both ate at Amy's!'

'So no one needs feeding?'

'No! For God's sake stop fussing.'

'Righto, if you are sure. Goodnight, Lyds.'

'Goodnight, Mum.'

'Goodnight, Dom!'

'Goodnight, Mum – you lightweight, it's only half past seven!'

She closed the door and walked back across the carpet to where her husband lay centrally on their marital bed.

'Well, looks like they don't need feeding, Mark, and a promise is a promise. I will not leave this room.'

She lifted a glass of water from the bedside table and raised it to her lips, sipping slowly. Mark eyed the glass.

'Are you thirsty? Would you like a drink, Mark?'

He just about managed a slight nod. She smiled at him.

'Oh, I bet you would, but no drinking for you tonight, mister.'

The memory of her sock-stuffed mouth and swollen lips came to mind. She replaced the glass on the bedside table and let out a deep sigh before returning to her novel.

Kathryn must have nodded off. She couldn't remember falling asleep, but was suddenly conscious of waking. She had been disturbed by her husband's breathing, which sounded rattly and loud, almost gurgling. She glanced at the bedside clock. It was 2 a.m.

'Well now, is this it, Mark? Are you off? Off to be judged, if you believe in such things. Off to a dark place whence there is no return? I think so, I think it is time. Are you afraid? Are you scared of what might come next?'

The staring, widened eyes told her that he was. She smiled and bent low over his face.

'You should be.'

'I haven't got long.'

His voice was a waning whisper. His final words coasted on fragmented last breaths.

'Too slow, painful. You'll pay.'

She mentally erased the words before he finished. She would not share, recount or remember them.

'Oh, Mark, I have already paid.'

Bending low, with her face inches from his, she breathed the fetid air that he exhaled, sharing the small space where life lingered until the very end.

Kathryn watched the life slip from him, convinced she saw the black spirit snake out of his body and disappear immediately through the floor, spiralling down and down. She sat back in her chair and breathed deeply. She had expected euphoria or at the very least relief. What she couldn't have predicted was the numbness that now gripped her.

She had expected to feel more.

Having changed into jeans and a jersey, Kathryn calmly stood by the side of the bed where her husband's pale corpse lay. With great deliberation and for the first time in her life, she dialled 999.

ONE MONTH AGO

Kate sat at the breakfast table filling out more dreaded forms. Tanya had been back at Prospect House for three weeks now, and Kate had only just got round to doing the requisite paperwork. The girl had walked in as though she had never been away, turning up one Wednesday morning with her holdall and asking Tom what was for lunch. It was a relief to have her back.

'Who's Lydia?'

Kate turned round in surprise. She hadn't heard Tanya come into the kitchen.

'Sorry?' The question had caught her off-guard.

'Who is Lydia? You were shouting her name out last night. I thought about waking you and packing you off to bed, but you looked so snug on the sofa.'

'Oh, well, thank you for not waking me, Tanya, that was very sweet. I must have dozed off while watching some rubbish on the telly.'

'So?'

'So what?'

'Who is Lydia? You never said.'

Kate inhaled sharply.

'Lydia is my daughter.'

'Your daughter? I never knew you had one. Where is she?'

Kate swallowed the hard ball of tears that sat at the base of her throat. Imagine that. Tanya did not know that she was a mother to the most beautiful girl and boy on the planet, did not know that every time her hand touched the stretch marks on her lower abdomen, she was reminded of the joy of having carried another human. They were her greatest achievement and Tanya, who lived under her roof, did not know that she was someone's mum.

'I . . . well . . . she lives in Hallton in North Yorkshire, near her aunt, my sister.'

'Do you ever see her?'

Tanya's questioning was typically frank. Nothing was taboo in her world, no feelings too precious to trample on. *'Are you using? Pregnant? Infected? Where is the bitch?'* For her this type of talk was just routine.

'Not really. In fact, no, not at all, not for a while.'

'It's weird isn't it.'

'Yes. Yes, it is weird.'

Kate could only concur. But Tanya was not finished.

'I mean, here's you, being a mum to me and anyone else that needs one and yet you don't see your own daughter!'

'Oh my goodness, Tanya – if words were daggers . . .'

Kate put her hands over her eyes; she wanted to hide from the world.

'Oh God, Kate! I'm sorry. I didn't mean to upset you. God, I keep doing that, don't I? It's just that I sometimes say what I think without checking with myself first.'

'Don't be sorry. It's not your fault. It's just how it is – a horrible situation that haunts me every minute of every day. I miss her, Tanya, and my son, Dominic. I miss them both dreadfully.'

'I can't understand it. My mum is totally rubbish and I can see her whenever I want, which I don't. But you're completely brilliant. If you were my mum, I'd want to see you all the time!'

'Maybe your mum feels like me, did you ever think of that? Perhaps your mum would love to see you. You can call her any time you want, Tanya, you know that. Or you could write to her? She's more than welcome to visit; we've got plenty of room.'

Tanya's gaze was steady and the seconds ticked by in silence.

'The last time I saw my mum was the night I got arrested. The police knocked on the door and she screamed at me cos she'd been woken up. I went into her bedroom; it stank and this filthy, hairy pig was starkers and out for the count in the middle of her bed. They'd both been using and he was out of it. I noticed the ashtray on the floor had a long sausage of ash that was still attached to the fag; you know, where it's just been left to burn and gone out because you forget about it. This bothered me because I could see her burning the bloody place down; she's not careful with stuff like that. I don't know what I expected from her, but I knew I was in serious shit. I'd got away with stuff before, but I knew this time I was going down and to be honest, Kate, I was scared. I said to her "Help me, Mum" and do you know what she said? She lit a new fag and she said, "Shut the fucking door on your way out!" I haven't spoken to her or seen her since. She has never been there for me or helped me and I'm really pissed off with myself for asking for her help on that night. So I don't think that she sits waiting for me to call or hoping for a visit. She couldn't give a shit, Kate. She never did.'

There were a few seconds of silence while both of them took stock. Kate had never wanted for maternal love, but she did understand cruelty and could not blame Tanya in the least for wanting no more of it.

'Well, even though I am not your mum, I can tell you that I am truly proud of what you have achieved. Only months ago your life was falling apart, Tanya, and now the whole world is out there for the taking. Whatever you decide to do, I know you will achieve great things.'

'I don't want to achieve great things, Kate. I just want normal. I'd settle for a bit of peace, a little flat, a job. And I'd really like one of those posh coffee machines they've got in the pub; I could drink that stuff all day!'

'And you shall have that, Tanya, all of it.'

'Gooooood morning!'

Tom came through the back door with a basket chock full of fresh vegetables.

'Today I make-a my leeegenderrry vegetable lasagne!'

His Italian accent was appalling. They all laughed.

'Just bumped into Rodney on the harbour. He's tarting up his boat as usual. I managed to snaffle all this veg off him at cost! A good day's work, if I do say so myself. Fancy giving me a hand, Tanya? This lot won't chop itself, you know.'

'Sure.'

Tanya slunk off her chair and took the little paring knife gingerly into her hand.

'I'm not very good. Nearest I've ever come to cooking is watching *Ready Steady Cook*.'

Stacey came down the stairs, heading out for her morning constitutional. She caught the tail end of the conversation.

'*Ready Steady Cook*? God, that reminds me of one of Nathan's old ladies who was obsessed with it, and she couldn't cook either! He used to tell me about her and have me rollin'.'

She smiled at the happy memories.

'Well, I'm going to teach Tanya, so at the very least she'll be able to conjure up a decent lasagne. There is really nothing to it. By the time we've finished with her, she'll be creating masterpieces that she can rustle up in her own kitchen.'

The trio looked at Kate. Tom winked at his boss.

Tanya beamed. This only reinforced the idea that one day she would have her very own kitchen and she would prepare the dishes that Tom had taught her. She couldn't wait.

Kate had gone for an afternoon nap. Her head was filled with thoughts of Lydia, imagining what tomorrow might bring. Even though the trip to Bristol was all arranged, she was still in two minds about whether she should go to the exhibition. There were so many things that could go horribly wrong.

A nightmare wrenched her from her rest. The song that she thought she had banished forever swirled in her head.

> *Hey, little girl,*
> *Comb your hair, fix your make-up.*
> *Soon he will open the door.*
> *Don't think because*
> *There's a ring on your finger,*
> *You needn't try any more*

The relief upon waking had been instant and sweet. It was just a horrid dream and she was safe. Mark was gone and could not hurt her any more. She sat up in the bed and wrapped her arms around her bunched-up knees. The fingers of her right hand snaked to the back of her thighs, where they ran over the bumps and dents of her scars, never more than a fingertip away. She shivered.

Whenever Kate dreamed like this, she always spent the next few hours with a slight tremor to her hand and a quiver in her voice. The memories of her old life sat like a tiny echo at the base of her thoughts. They unnerved her.

After gulping down a wake-up coffee, she welcomed the sun against her skin as she wandered the garden. The meandering paths that led nowhere in particular and the cottagey feel of the disorganised, mismatched planting suited her much more than . . . she suppressed the image of the school grounds, its manicured lawns and the regimental roses. A shudder ran through her. At the washing line she brushed her hand over the soft pale lilac sheet that pulled against its anchorage like a spinnaker in the Cornish breeze. Kate had not washed a sheet for many years. It had been one of two unshakeable resolutions, the other being to wear jeans every day.

She negotiated the steep path down to the sea and spread her blanket on the sand. *The Life and Loves of a She Devil* fell open against her palms, revealing her bookmark. Every time she looked at the saccharine pink, glitter-coated rabbit, her breath stuttered in her throat.

Kate ran the pad of her index finger over the scrawled text inside the card: 'happpy birday mummy'. Her heart swelled with pride and sadness in equal measure. How she had loved being called Mummy. How she missed it. Lydia's signature was surrounded by an oval of kisses, an unbroken chain, created when everything in her daughter's world had been perfect. A time when her little girl lived unaware of the wolf baying at the door, before Kate had broken everything.

The words of their telephone call floated to the front of her mind, always there for perfect recall. *'Sometimes, Mum, I pretend that you are both dead, and that makes it easier somehow. I pretend that you were both killed in an accident and then I don't have to think about you doing something so horrible to Dad or about the horrible things that Dad did to you. I don't like to think about it, Mummy.'*

She looked towards the horizon and studied the sun diamonds glinting on the water, framed by the rocky cliffs on either side of the bay. It was as good as any beach anywhere. Maybe not as stunning as her St Lucian horseshoe paradise, but better in some ways because it was her beach, her special place. Somewhere for her to think. And no one was going to sell it from under her feet.

Bristol was buzzing and busy – or maybe Kate was simply transferring her own excitement and energy onto the city in which she found herself. Life in Penmarin was calm and quiet, just as she liked it. Bristol was entirely different. She enjoyed observing the university students clustered together in the entrances to buildings, in the way that only the young and carefree are happy to do. She laughed at how they had left school and abandoned their uniforms only to all dress the same

345

now. And soon they would evolve again, perhaps joining the tribe of glamorous women who paraded the pavements clutching stiff paper bags stuffed with the day's booty.

The three friends had agreed to meet at Browns restaurant, a prominent landmark on the Bristol skyline. They sat outside at a table at the top of the steps. Apron-clad waiters bought them a cold jug of Pimm's and salmon fishcakes with stick-thin golden chips. Nothing, however, could distract Kate from what lay ahead. On at least two occasions her heart skipped a beat at the sight of a dark-haired young woman on the opposite side of the street – for a split second they looked like Lydia and she had to quell the temptation to cry out. She was impatient to finish lunch and get to the gallery, wanting both to linger over her daughter's work and to get the whole thing over with.

'How are you feeling, mate?' As usual, Janeece was more than in tune with her friend's anxiety.

Kate hesitated. How *was* she feeling?

'I'm nervous, excited, scared and then nervous again.'

Natasha placed a hand on her friend's arm. 'You'll be fine, we're right here with you.'

Kate nodded, but Natasha's reassurance did little to ease her angst.

'She could be close by right now. I might be a few steps away from her . . .' This Kate whispered, more to herself than anyone else.

★ ★ ★

Janeece strode on ahead to check that the coast was clear, leaving Kate and Natasha to hover further down the street, waiting for the sign that they could proceed. It felt like an eternity, but it was in fact only minutes before she reappeared.

'Right, had a word with a Mrs Ladi-dadi-da-pants in reception, who informs me that the *artiste* will be attending on Wednesday evening for the formal opening and then on Thursday only. So as today is Tuesday, I reckon we're good to go!'

Kate beamed. 'Right. Let's do this.'

'You sure you are okay, honey?'

Natasha knew only too well how revealing art could be and was worried that it might not be the positive experience her friend was hoping for.

'Yep, I'm more than okay.' Kate walked ahead alone.

The building was beautiful: grand and full of marble, with Corinthian columns and a wide, sweeping staircase. Kate marvelled at the vast, ornate oils that lined the walls. Her little girl was in fine company. Imagine her daughter holding an exhibition in a place like this. Pride swelled in her chest and made swallowing difficult. *Lydia* . . .

She lingered at the poster in the upper foyer – a blown-up version of the flyer that currently nestled in the bottom of her handbag. Lydia's flawless complexion and liquid eyes were stunning. Kate breathed in sharply, realising how much she had missed. Although Francesca had emailed her the odd blurry snapshot over the years, this PR shot was of a different order altogether. The Lydia in her memory no longer existed: gone was the teenage skin and the wobbly application of heavy eye make-up. Now twenty-five, Lydia had found her style and become a woman.

Kate studied each one of Lydia's pictures intensely and read the titles carefully. Titles like *Come Undone* and *Life Interrupted*. Lydia was clearly talented; she had honed her skills considerably since Kate had last seen any of her work. Kate approached each piece with a mixture of pleasure and intrigue, even if she didn't fully understand them.

It was a strange and unique experience. Kate was certain that she would have known her children's handwriting from the tiniest scrap, would be able to identify their voices from just one word spoken within a group, would know of their presence by nothing more than a cough. What she hadn't considered was Lydia's personality being so easily identifiable with every stroke of the brush. The bold colours and contemporary themes were as much elements of her character as her voice and humour. Kate could see that this work was the progression of all the sketches and paintings that had come before, going back to her childhood.

When Janeece and Natasha caught up with her, Kate was transfixed by a large canvas, about fifteen feet square. She studied every square inch with a wide grin. Her hands fluttered at her chest. She wanted to whoop with joy!

Natasha read the title. '*My Background Noise –* it's an interesting title, what do you think it means?'

Kate turned to her friend, the art expert, and with eyes brimming was able to interpret the meaning of the piece with confidence.

'It means me, Tash. I am her background noise. Not cool, but like jam or a favourite pillow!'

Kate ran her fingers over the daubs of paint that depicted a set of speakers with flowers, strawberries and dolly pegs coming from them in every shade of the rainbow. It was beautiful and it was a message that Kate read loud and clear. Happiness swelled in her chest.

'Oh, Lydia, my clever, beautiful girl! I will be waiting for you.'

As Natasha and Kate pulled into the driveway of Prospect House, they were still discussing the minute aspects of Lydia's work. Kate knew that she would analyse and reinterpret what she had seen, time and time again. She felt close to her little girl; her hand had touched the paint that her daughter's hand had applied. It was wonderful. But the state of excitement was not to last long, once the front door had been opened.

'Ah, Kate, I'm so glad you're back. We've got a bit of a situation on our hands.'

'What kind of situation, Tom? Is the house burning down and you have forgotten the number for the fire brigade? Or have we run out of biscuits and cake will have to suffice? I'm really hoping that it's closer to the latter; I don't want anything to spoil my lovely day!'

Tom shook his head and held open his palm, in the centre of which sat a plastic bag. Her time in jail and her work in the field of rehabilitation meant that she could instantly identify the irregularly shaped, off-white rocks as crack cocaine.

'Oh please God no, not that! Is it Tanya's?'

'Well I think we can assume so, Kate, unless you have taken up the habit?'

'Oh, don't tempt me, Tom! Right, leave it with me. Where is she?'

'In her room. I haven't mentioned it to her.'

'No, you did right. It would be today, wouldn't it; the one day I am away.'

'How was it, boss?'

'Oh, Tom, it was magnificent!'

'I'm glad. If that's all, Kate, I think I'll call it a night. Been quite a day. Stacey got off okay; phoned to say that she'd arrived at her mum's and was doing fine. Said she'd be back in a few days.'

'That's good. Night, Tom, and thanks for today.'

Kate saw the lamplight shining from beneath Tanya's bedroom door. She knocked and waited.

'Yeah?'

'Can I come in, Tanya?'

It was unusual for Kate to visit at this time of night, so Tanya instantly knew that something was up.

'Sure.'

Tanya was in bed, propped up on several pillows

and cushions, reading a magazine and doodling in the margin with a biro. Kate noticed that she had drawn rolling waves over and over, making a frame around the article that she was reading.

'Hey, Kate, how was it?'

'Good, thanks, Tanya. Amazing, in fact.'

Kate let out a long sigh.

'Everything okay?'

'Not really, Tanya, no. I'm sorry to have to ask you, but do you know anything about this?'

Kate opened her hand to reveal the plastic bag with the drugs nestled inside.

Do I know anything about it? I would say you have found someone's candy. Judging by the colour, a good grade, not too cut. An eight ball probably enough for fifteen hours of bliss with a comedown so bad that whoever is using it would give anything, even sell their grandma for another high. That's all I know about it.'

'This isn't funny and that wasn't what I meant, Tanya, and you know it. Is it yours?'

'Well it wouldn't be Stacey Goody-Bloody-Two-Shoes, would it?'

Kate sat on the end of Tanya's bed. She rubbed her temples and ran her fingers through her hair.

'I give you a lot of freedom, Tanya, because I think that's the right way for you to explore where you are going and where you have come from. The one rule I have is no drugs and only moderate alcohol, you know that. This is a serious breach of trust. I'm really disappointed.'

'Well welcome to my world. Now you know what it feels like to live my life. I am permanently bloody disappointed! Although let me tell you, Kate, that if the worst disappointment you have to face is the fact that I have a small amount of rocks in my pocket, then your life ain't too bad!'

'I'm not the one being reprimanded here, Tanya. You broke the rules. It's not as though we have that many. And it's not like you've snuck in some booze or are smoking out of the window, its crack cocaine! This is on another scale. People have been asked to leave Prospect House for much less.'

'As I said, yet another disappointment for me. Go on, ask me to leave. I couldn't give a shit. At least if I go, I'll be able to eat what I want instead of all that organic shit Tom makes, and I'll be able to smoke what I bloody like!'

'Well, that is up to you, Tanya. I'm not asking you to leave; I'm just asking you to think about what you are doing.' Kate held up the bag. 'This is not what I want for you Tanya; you can do so much more than look for answers in this muck. You have to observe our rules. It's how we keep you safe.' She paused, not knowing quite how to wrap up this horrid end to an otherwise perfect day, 'Quite frankly, it's too late for me to deal with this right now. We can talk about it tomorrow when we are both less tired.'

Kate walked to the door.

'Good night, dear.'

Tanya mumbled her response. Most of it was

inaudible, but Kate could just make out the words 'cow' and 'off'.

'Pancakes, Tanya?'

Tom stood by the stove and waved the spatula in the air, indicating that he at least was in a jovial mood. A debate raged from the tinny radio in the corner: the voices were barely audible, yet it was enough of a noise to make the place feel like home.

Tanya shrugged her pointy shoulders inside her oversized sweatshirt and let her fringe hang over her face as she addressed the floor.

'Don't know if I'm allowed pancakes. I might be on gruel rations if ma'am has anything to do with it. Or, worse still, no breakfast at all before I'm turfed out.'

She was only half joking.

'I'm sure it's not that bad, Tanya. Kate's got a lot on her mind, that's all. She wouldn't turf you out, love, I'm sure. She ain't a pushover, but she won't give up on you. I know that.'

'Don't know if I really give a shit actually, Tom. I was thinking that maybe I'd be better off heading back to London. It's so bloody quiet here, it could drive you mad. Plus I've got things I should be getting on with, people that I should be seeing. I was thinking I might go and get a job, sort a few things out, stay with a mate for a while. Y'know . . .'

Tom smiled. No, he didn't know, and he had seen enough of Tanya and her slumped posture, nervous hair flicking and nail biting to see that she didn't really know either.

'You need to talk to her, Tanya. It'll all come out in the wash, you'll see. That's one thing I can tell you about Kate and Tash: they only have your best interests at heart, love. I see how they worry and how they discuss the best way to help everyone that stays here. They're good people.'

Tanya shrugged with indifference and simultaneously curled her top lip to show aggression and dislike in two simple moves. This was in fact the exact opposite of how she was feeling. She wanted to sob, to apologise, to lie wrapped in the soft pink lambswool blanket with her head on a cushion in front of the fire. She wanted to be told that she could stay for ever and ever.

'Whatever.'

She wasn't even sure who the bravado was intended for any more; it was a habit that she didn't know how to break.

'So is that a yes for pancakes or a no?'

Tanya cracked a smile in spite of her best efforts. Her tummy groaned as she inhaled the buttery, vanilla scent of the batter that wafted from the hot pan.

'Well, as you're making . . .'

It was a beautiful, clear Cornish day in the early flush of summer; one of those days when weather and mankind conspire to make a golden day of perfect memories. The sun was hot against bare skin, the sky bright blue with the merest wisp of cloud, as if painted by an artist's brush stroke. The air was warm with a gentle breeze that lifted the flower heads just enough to show off their true beauty. Toddlers dozed in pushchairs, couples held hands and strangers smiled, each playing their part.

Kate mooched around the harbour, taking time with her chores and enjoying the moment. Every time she closed her eyes, one of Lydia's paintings came into focus. She felt closer to her somehow. Seeing her daughter's work had been like peeking into her diary, offering wonderful insights into her darling girl's mind. She was so glad that she had gone to Bristol, despite her initial worries. Kate also had to acknowledge the tiniest hint of disappointment. Deep down she had secretly hoped to catch a glimpse of her daughter; it had been difficult not to envisage a full-blown running-with-arms-wide reunion.

She wondered how Stacey was getting on at home and hoped that she would simply come back to Penmarin, collect the rest of her things and return to her mum and brother. As much as she would miss her, Kate knew that was where she belonged; it was the best thing for her long term.

The previous night's showdown with Tanya weighed on her mind. She would call Janeece and get some advice. Drug use and addiction were Janeece's specialisation, although where Tanya was concerned, Kate suspected it was more a recreational habit born out of boredom than an addiction. She needed to occupy her more: maybe a job in the village, the pub? No, not the pub, silly thought. Bloody Rodney Morris; even the thought of him brought a fresh wave of anger.

She would give it some thought and they would find a way through, whatever happened. Kate loved Tanya's spirit, even if her energy was a little misdirected at times. In the cold, bright light of day Kate laughed to herself at the detailed description Tanya had given her of the small bag of drugs. Cheeky girl. She'd go back and talk to her now, so that they could all return to calm waters and move forward. Kate inhaled the fresh sea air. Life felt good.

Tanya locked her bedroom door, turning the heavy key until the satisfying clunk told her it was safe to proceed. In her bathroom she removed her purchase from the white plastic bag. She unwound the thin strip of coloured cellophane, then peeled the wrapper off the rectangular box. With her jeans and pants bundled around her ankles like a nest, Tanya gave little thought to the task in hand. By mentally transporting herself somewhere else entirely, she could pretend for a little while longer.

Job done, Tanya washed her hands meticulously, taking care to scrape under her nails and lather between her fingers. She patted her palms dry on the thick white towel and then, as she always did, inhaled the fresh scent that the liquid soap left on her skin. She breathed deeply, intoxicated by the floral tones that filled her head. She cherished this small ritual; there had been so many times that she had been without soap and the means to get clean.

The spatula-like stick sat on the glass shelf above the sink. Tanya felt slightly faint when she considered what was at stake. There was the slightest tremor to her grip as her fingers rolled around the plastic. The truth was she had known the result before looking. She knew because her instinct had been screaming at her for the best part of six weeks. The slight sway of nausea, the fatigue, the heightened emotion – it had been very easy to explain away each of these elements. It could be the change of environment or Tom's unfamiliar food; even the sea air had shouldered some of the blame. It had all sounded plausible, reasonable. Yet deep down Tanya knew that the symptoms would have been exactly the same had she stayed in London or ended up in Timbuktu.

She could recall the hour, if not the very minute of conception. It hadn't been beautiful, romantic or considered. It never was. She had gone to say goodbye, explain that she wanted a fresh start away from him, away from that life, away from temptation. He had been quiet and surprisingly understanding, leading her to believe that he never had really given a shit, or that her replacement had already been lined up. Whichever, it mattered little now.

One drink, two, maybe three later and they had done what was natural and familiar to them both, for old times' sake, one last time. His deep blue eyes with their penetrating stare still fascinated her and drew her in. She had relished the comfort she found in his arms, loved the feel of his skin against hers. This dark, brooding man who had shown her both the height of ecstasy, sending her spirit skywards, where it would dance among the stars, and also the depths of despair, where she would beg to be shown the merest crumb of affection, for which she would be deeply grateful. This man, whom she would jump through hoops for, follow to the ends of the earth, even take the rap for. They were cut from the same cloth: two individuals whose life experiences and surroundings were so similar that their connection went way beyond physical attraction; theirs was a deep yet destructive union. It was almost impossible for her to distinguish between the need for the man who wrought so much influence over her life and the drug that he supplied, the two were inextricably linked. One thing she knew for certain was that he would always be the love of her life.

After wiping around the sink and flushing the loo, Tanya returned to the bedroom. She looked out of the window and not for the first time marvelled at the fact that if you could swim far enough you could get all the way to Canada. She would like to go to Canada. What did she know about it? They ate a lot of maple syrup; they had big bears and even bigger mountains. Something in the back of her mind told her that they spoke French, was that right? This made her laugh. Imagine that, swimming all the way to Canada and not being able to speak French.

Tanya made her bed. She pulled the sheet taut and smoothed the creases from the duvet cover. She plumped the pillows and piled them just so, before folding the soft blanket over the base, just as she liked it. There was something quite wonderful about climbing into a bed that had been so beautifully made.

'*Bonjour!*'

She laughed as she tested out the foreign word, then walked over to the mirror above the fireplace.

'*Bonjour*, I am Tanya, Mr Mountie. Can I have some maple syrup *s'il vous plaît*?'

This made her laugh even more. She giggled until tears gathered in her eyes. Who would have thought it? Thick old Tanya Wilson, if she swam all the way to Canada, could actually speak a bit of French to the Mountie who would hand her a towel on the beach. Now that was amazing.

She switched off the bedside lamp and opened the sash window, just enough to air the room. She cleaned her teeth and patted her face dry with the soft white towel before replacing it carefully on its hook. Tanya placed her forehead on the cool glass of the window and could hardly draw her eyes from the sea that stretched out before her, a vast never ending blanket of black. Her fingers lingered on the sprig-patterned curtains, feeling the tiny bunches of lavender embroidered beneath her touch.

'Off for a walk?' Tom enquired as she trotted past the kitchen. Tanya nodded.

'Well it's a beautiful day out there. And at least you won't have to rush back for lunch. How many pancakes have you put away, girl? You must have hollow legs!'

He shook his head in genuine astonishment.

'Thank you for teaching me how to make lasagne, Tom. It didn't taste too bad, did it?'

He laughed, wondering how they had got on to that topic.

'You're welcome, love. Between you and me, I was a little bit worried for me job – it tasted superb. You're a natural!'

The cliffside path leading down to the beach from Prospect House was sheer and precarious. It meandered down the steep slope like a giant snake, with no apparent logic to its route. Rotting, half-buried steps punctuated its course and tufts of coarse grass grew at the edges in thick, ankle-turning clumps. Tanya's smooth-soled sneakers skidded and slipped on the loose stones, making her stumble then wobble until she regained her balance. She removed her shoes and held them aloft in her right hand, as though protecting them from further scuffing. An image of herself tumbling off the cliff, limbs flailing, filled her head. That

360

would be just typical of her life – nothing ever going according to plan. Though the note in her pocket would apply just the same.

When the path finally flattened out and the stones gave way to sand, Tanya's faltering steps turned into strides. The beach was empty. She ran the last few metres with a smile on her face as the salt-tinged breeze lifted her fringe and buffeted her chest.

Tanya shrugged her arms through her cardigan and folded it neatly with arm holes and hems together, before placing it on the sand. Next she slipped out of her jeans, which she placed with precision on top of her cardigan. She unhooked her bra and let the straps fall along her thin arms, and finally she stepped out of her pants. Her clothes sat in a neat little pile, like laundry waiting to be collected and put away on wash day. On top of her discarded apparel she placed her room and front door keys; just beneath them she positioned the pale cream envelope, twisting it to make sure it was clearly visible. She was done. She turned her face skywards and savoured the rays of sunshine that pierced the Mediterranean blue of the day. It was quite exquisite to feel the warmth on her naked skin.

Tanya stopped as she approached the water and winced in sudden pain. A small shard of glass, not yet smoothed into opaque sea glass, had sunk into the white flesh of her sole. She lifted the foot onto her opposite knee, gripped the tiny splinter and prised it free. A trickle of blood ran thick and red down her bare leg but she didn't try to stem its flow; it mattered little compared to the journey she was about to undertake. She wasn't sure why she had even bothered to remove it; what did it matter? A second or two of foot pain meant nothing in the grander scheme of things.

She walked forward to the dark shadow on the sand where the water lapped, staining it the colour of dark tea and pitting it with fizzing holes in which small worms and crabs bathed.

Tanya trod gingerly, feeling the shock of the icy current on her exposed flesh. It was her first time in the sea and wasn't quite the warm bath that she had anticipated. She took tiny, cautious steps at first, until she was knee deep. Then she found her courage and strode further out.

She allowed the tiny waves to lap her with their salty tongues. She turned and faced the shore, stepping slowly backwards until the sea covered her shoulders. Her teeth chattered in her gums and her limbs jerked involuntarily, trying to counter the effects of the cold.

She gazed up to the top of the cliff for one last look at Prospect House. This was the one place that she had been happy, the one place she had been comfortable and felt wanted. She pictured the shiny bathroom, remembered the comfort of her clean, white bed and its blanket tucked around her shoulders on chilly nights. Her heart had ached at the thought of being asked to leave. She had messed up and she knew it. It was to be expected; she always did mess things up. It was as if she was programmed for self-destruction.

She remembered a Christmas from her childhood when she had been given a Furby toy. Presents were thin on the ground in their house and she had loved the furry creature that opened its eyes and mouth when it sang, loved it more than anything she had ever owned. She couldn't believe that something that brilliant had been given to someone like *her*. She sang with it, stroked it, slept with it and held it close. Then, one night, her mum, in an even fouler mood than usual after a drunken spat with her latest bloke, had threatened to stamp on her Furby to 'Shut it the fuck up!' The thought of having to witness her beloved toy being destroyed was so unbearable that a little while after her mum's rant, Tanya had taken her Furby out into the cold, damp night and stamped on him herself. With tears in her eyes, she threw his battered, broken body into the communal skip. It was far easier to cope with his loss than to live with the threat of his destruction hanging over her.

Tanya knew that life at Prospect House was as good as it got. There would never be a flat or a little job for someone like her; she would never go to Canada and never have a coffee machine like the one in the pub. But at least this way, she would never be separated from her baby, never know the pain of having to choose between her drug of choice and keeping her child, never wonder through heavy lids on a comedown who was feeding and bathing her little one, while she reached for the arms of the man that would feed her poison. The clifftop house was a wonderful sight. Her last vista could easily have been something quite different – a stained ceiling, the peeling wallpaper on a damp toilet wall or the slimy bricks of a deserted alleyway. This was better, much better. She liked the fact that she had decided. She was in control.

She placed her shrivelled, prune-like palm against the flat of her belly and rubbed in small circles. She was not alone; she would never be alone again, but would forever be at peace with her little secret safe and snug inside her.

'You'll never be afraid of the water.'

She spoke the words in her mind, to be heard by the small kernel of a human that had been conceived with love and was beginning inside her. The idea gave her a huge amount of comfort.

Her body had gone numb with extreme cold and her skin was peppered with a million goosebumps. Her fine hair floated like orange seaweed around her head. Still with her eyes on Prospect House, Tanya took two deliberate steps backwards. The soft sand beneath her feet gave way to nothing and she went down and down, under the sea, like the mermaid she had imagined so many times.

The cold water filtered into her airways, slowly at first, as her natural reaction was to close her mouth and hold her nose, but once she relaxed it gushed in, filling every space with thick salt water. When her brain registered that her gag reflex was futile, she was overcome with a beautiful calmness. A pinprick of light shone above her. She smiled. Then she slowly closed her eyes and embraced the peace and escape that lay ahead.

As Kate pulled into the driveway she was aware of Tom hovering by the back door. He was passing the checked dish cloth from hand to hand and was clearly agitated.

'Oh great, what now? What drama awaits me – please not more drugs.'

She spoke to the mirror of her sun visor, hoping for a 'run out of carrots' catastrophe, but fearing something much worse. Maybe Janeece was right and she was getting old, possibly too old.

Kate scrambled down from the jeep with her shopping basket in one hand and the local paper in the other.

'Everything all right, Tom?'

'Everything's just fine, Kate.'

Despite his answer, he continued to twist the cloth in his hand, indicating quite the opposite.

'Oh good. No minor catastrophe awaiting my attention?'

'No, nothing like that. It's just that you've got a visitor.'

'Oh, well, I'll be right in.'

Judging from Tom's twitchy stance, it could be an unexpected house guest, as had happened once before when poor communication and slow post had meant a girl had turned up for a short-term stay without warning. It didn't really matter – they would cope, they always did. There was plenty of room and as soon as a nice cuppa and words of kindness had been issued, all would be well. Or it might be a surprise visit from social services, a much less palatable scenario. Kate hung her head at the very thought. Her spirits sank; why today on this most perfect of days? Not that she had anything to hide, far from it. They had an open-door policy, but it would be tedious and time-consuming and she would have liked to have had her paperwork in slightly better order.

Kate entered the kitchen with a cheery 'Hello!'

And came abruptly to a halt.

The paper fell to the floor as her hand flew to her mouth. Her heart beat so quickly that she felt quite light-headed. Sitting at the table was her son.

Tom deposited a mug of tea on the table to match the one he had already served Dominic and quietly disappeared.

'Hello.'

'Oh, my! Oh, Dom!'

Kate walked forward and ran a hand across his back; with the other she cradled his head into her form. Her touch was gentle, tentative, not only because she was unsure of how she would be received, but also because of the very real fear that he might vanish. She had pictured this scenario so many times that she thought it might be a dream. It wasn't. He was solid to the touch, he was real and he was in her kitchen.

She inhaled his scent, familiar and intoxicating.

'Oh, Dom, look at you! Look at you! This is wonderful, this is the best moment . . . I have *missed* you!'

It felt like the grossest of understatements. Words could not describe what the absence of her kids had meant to her – they were all far too meek, thin and inadequate.

'You're squashing me.'

'Oh, I'm sorry, darling.'

Kate took the seat opposite her child.

She surveyed the man sitting in front of her. He was wearing jeans and a thick, white cotton shirt and he really did look wonderful. His muscly fore-arms were covered in a mat of dark hair. She squinted and superimposed from memory the gangly arms of her boy, covered in paper-thin Spiderman tattoos that had come courtesy of a packet of bubble-gum. She could picture his skinny, freckled limbs poking from beneath a striped T-shirt sleeve that gaped in the absence of biceps or triceps. *How long ago was that? Ten years? No, twenty years. My goodness, where had that time gone?* She noted that the contours of his teens had now bulged into muscles, the hair had sprouted thicker and darker than she had seen it last and all his sharp angles had been replaced by rounded solidity.

The physical changes were huge, but Kate could also see that he had some time ago vaulted the line between lackadaisical teenager and careworn man of the world. His eyes no longer held a subject in languid fascination; instead his glances were hesitant, furtive. His leg jumped, his heel beat time and his fingers drummed. He was edgy, nervous. He spoke a little too quickly and his humour was biting. He made Kate think of an animal backed into a corner, ready to pounce.

'I can't believe you are here, I really can't. There is so much I want to say, Dominic, but I almost don't know where to start – which is crackers because I've practised every day since I saw you last. I am so happy. How long can you stay?'

Already the fear of him leaving was eating up their precious moments together.

'I've got rooms made up already; we can have a proper catch-up. Are you hungry? How did you get here? Did you drive? Francesca said you had a little runaround. I feel like a kid! I am so excited! How's Lydi?'

The words burbled from her like water.

'No, I can't stay, but thanks. Lydia is great, thank you. Quite the little artist, getting rave reviews for her work and she thoroughly deserves it; she's very talented.'

Kate hated the way he had thanked her – politely, as if she were a stranger. There was no warmth in his response. The tone in which he talked about his sister was protective, with an underlying sneer that seemed to ask, *What has it got to do with you?* Kate decided not to tell him that she had seen some of Lydia's work and that yes, she definitely did deserve all the rave reviews.

'And what about you, Dom, what are you doing? Still working with Luke and Gerry?'

'Yes, we have a property business actually – buying and selling, renovation, interior design, that kind of thing. It's going pretty well.'

'Oh my goodness, that sounds great! And it sounds so clichéd, but you have grown, you look wonderful. You are so beautiful, Dom, such a good-looking man. I always knew you would be. Do you have a girlfriend?'

His response was vague. An image of a recent conquest came into focus, but it was futile. What girl would stick around once they knew his story? He had no intention of confiding in his mother. Instead, his eyes assessed the room in which they were sitting.

Kate had known that their first meeting might be this way, but it didn't make it any easier. She wanted so badly to hold him tight.

'I can't tell you how very happy I am to see you.'

He ignored her words.

'This is a nice set-up you have here. The house is interesting . . .'

Kate nodded. She didn't want to talk about the house.

'Dom, I have missed you dreadfully.'

'Well, you knew where I was. If you missed me that much . . .'

She held his eye.

'Darling, that's not fair. You made it quite clear that you didn't want to see me and I respected your wish. I figured you would come to me when you were ready.'

Dominic laughed, but it was an insincere chuckle that for a brief moment put her in mind of Mark.

'Well, clever old you. All that amateur psychology is obviously paying off, here I am! You once told me that I could always talk to you, that you would listen. You said it was your job.'

Kate smiled. Yes, she had said that.

'Well, you've been doing it really badly and I am majorly pissed off with you, Mum!'

He sounded like a little boy; it made her heart constrict. She pictured him using the same tone to protest about bedtimes or having to eat Brussels sprouts. But he had called her Mum! How she had missed that.

'Dom, it's been too long that we have been apart. I don't want to spoil it by fighting.'

'Maybe it's not all about what you want. Maybe there are things that I want, that I need.'

'What things, Dom? Tell me what they are and I will do my best to help you. I love you so much. I don't want to see you hurting.'

'Hurting?' He put his splayed hand over his mouth and gripped his chin and cheek, again stifling that incongruous laugh. 'Christ, you have no idea about hurt.'

'Oh, Dom, I think I have more than an idea.'

She swallowed the words that bubbled on her

tongue. *'Your father was a monster. You have no idea how I lived; I was tortured for eighteen years, but I put up with it for you and Lydia.'* But she kept them to herself, not wanting to burden her son still more.

'I don't expect you to understand, Dom, and I do know what my actions have put you through—'

'Do you, Mum?' He interrupted again. 'Do you really know what your actions have put me through? Have put Lydia through?'

Kate cast her eyes downwards and awaited the onslaught that she knew was coming; the one she had been waiting the last ten years to receive.

'Mountbriers was all I'd ever known. Those people weren't only my friends, they were my family. I loved being part of it. I used to feel so proud putting on that uniform and walking through the stone archway every day. It made me feel so special; it was everything to me. I was working hard, doing great, planning for the golden future that you kept telling me I would have. But you were lying, weren't you? You had other plans for my future, for all of our futures. And it wasn't as if I left in the way that other kids did. I didn't win a scholarship and flit off to another school; my parents didn't run out of fees and send me to the local comp. Plenty of kids did that and it was okay for them; they could still be part of it, if they wanted to. But not me. I couldn't keep in touch or pop over for weekends, or even finish off the bloody term!'

'Dom, I—'

'No. Let me finish. The police questioned Lyd and me for hours, did you know that? We were in separate rooms full of bloody strangers in a police station while they asked if Dad had ever touched me, hurt me? Can you imagine? My head was totally fucked. One minute I was at a barbecue with my mates and the next my whole world had turned to rat shit and there's this bloke asking me if Dad had ever . . .'

Dominic breathed deeply, to slow his heart and stop the tears of frustration that threatened to fall. He wasn't done.

'Dad never laid a finger on me or Lydi; he would never have. He was a brilliant dad, whether you like it or not. He was brilliant and I loved him. He was smart, funny, clever and I used to hope that one day I'd get married and have kids and be just like him! How funny is that? Imagine wanting to be just like *him* . . .'

'Dominic, I can only imagine—'

He didn't allow her a response, wouldn't stop until he had exorcised it all.

'We weren't allowed anything from the house, nothing. Did you know that? They took my computer, my photos, my phone, clothes, everything. Everything I had ever owned or known was wiped out. My home became a crime scene and the crime that had been committed wasn't burglary or assault, it was murder. My father was stabbed – not by some nameless attacker, but by my mum.

372

By you! I lost my school, my friends, my possessions, my home, my parents, everything! I lost my whole fucking life. Can you imagine that? And worse still, it wasn't some stranger that did that to me, it was my own fucking mother! You took it all from me, from us!'

His tears fell freely now and Kate felt a strange sense of relief, his tears cathartic.

She reached across the table top – a matter of inches, but to mother and son it represented miles and years. Kate took her son's large hand and encased it inside both of her own. She felt the flex of his fingertips as they curled to sit against hers; a small act of enormous significance.

They sat in silence until his tears abated and his breathing had steadied. They had all the time in the world.

When he next spoke his voice was calmer, quieter.

'You did that to us, Mum. I'm not only blaming you; it was you and Dad. You were both liars and you made our whole existence, our whole childhood, into one big lie.'

Kate remembered Lydia's painful words, across the miles via a telephone wire. *My whole life and the people I trusted, it was all pretend.'*

Dominic wasn't done.

'I think of all the times we sat at the breakfast table, Dad making jokes and chatting and you smiling while you cooked bloody bacon; and yet only an hour before . . . Who was the best liar,

Mum? I'm not sure. I know Dad started it, he was a shit to you. But you finished it and I can't decide which is worse. It's okay for you, you have become Kate Gavier. I can't do that, I can't become Kate Gavier. I am stuck being Dominic Brooker. I give people my name and I watch them mulling it over, trying to work out why it's familiar . . . and then their eyes widen as they place me. *Ah yes, Brooker. Spawn of bastard Mark and psycho Kathryn.* And you ask if I have a girlfriend? What do you think? How would the "meet the parents" conversation go? It's a fucking non-starter.'

'I'm sorry, Dom.' It was an inadequate, automatic response.

'And then you disappeared. Firstly prison and then here, to immerse yourself in other people's problems so that you wouldn't have to deal with ours. Like we didn't count any more, like we didn't count enough.'

'Dom, you have always counted; you have been the one thing that does count. You are the reason I keep going. I love you and Lydia more than you can imagine, more than you will ever know. I haven't been hiding from you! I've been waiting for you. Every minute of every day and with every breath in my body, I think of all the possible ways I might be able to see you or be near you or contact you without causing you more distress—'

He cut her short again.

'I think about that night, Mum. I think about it a lot. I wish I didn't. We were in the room next door; we were only in the fucking room next door! Just metres away from what was happening. And you were cheerful. I remember, you sounded very cheerful. That's what I told the police and yet all the time Dad was on the bed . . . I bet he wanted me to help him, I bet he felt frightened and alone. I wonder if he called out to me, Mum. Did he want me to help him? I can't believe I slept soundly next door, Mum, with my head full of the barbecue and Emily Grant, while you . . .'

'Oh, darling. Oh, Dom. You mustn't do that. There's no point; it will just destroy you.'

'Ya think?'

His sarcasm warbled through his contorted mouth.

'I never sleep deeply now, not once since it happened. I lie with one ear cocked in case someone needs my help, in case Dad might need my help . . .'

Kate rubbed at her closed eyes.

'I am sorry, Dom. I am truly, truly sorry for all the hurt that I have caused you both and one day we will talk about fear and being alone and the reasons why, but not today. Not today, Dom. It's important that you know that I always, always put you first. I—'

Kate never finished her sentence.

The kitchen door slammed against the wall, causing them both to jump and jerk their heads in the direction of the bang.

Rodney Morris stood with one arm outstretched, flat-palmed against the open door. His body was not used to the speed with which his adrenalin had propelled him up from the beach. He panted and sweated, his face scarlet. His other hand was crooked against his chest and in the space between he held what appeared to be clothing. Keys dangled from his finger.

Kate let her son's hand fall onto the table top as she rose from her chair.

'Rodney! What's the matter? What's going on?'

Slowly he raised his head until his tear-filled eyes were level with hers.

'Tanya . . .' he stammered.

He passed Kate the opened cream envelope that had been tightly scrunched inside his palm.

Kate put her arm around him and steered him into a chair, the bad blood between them evaporating in the face of his obvious distress.

She pulled the sheet of paper from the envelope and hurriedly scanned Tanya's words.

'Where is she now, Rodney?' she screamed. 'Is it too late?'

Rodney rocked slowly in his chair and rambled incoherently.

'Oh no! Oh please God, no!' Kate howled, bordering on hysterical.

'Beautiful . . . so young . . .' mumbled Rodney through his tears.

Kate read and reread Tanya's note, transfixed by the ten lines, trying to absorb their meaning.

Her breath came in gulps. The pain in her chest was hard and instant. She looked up and sought the face of her son, seeking comfort and reassurance, but he was gone.

TEN YEARS AGO

During her trial, Kathryn felt as if she were living underwater. Day and night were indistinguishable; hours were bunched together and blurred, punctuated with catnaps and the occasional intake of flavourless food that tasted wooden in her mouth. Words were somehow distorted, colours muted and sound muffled. She felt something akin to weightlessness. Of the throng of people that peered in her direction, only Lydia and Dominic stood out, distinct and recognisable. Their faces pinched through grief, expressions blank, numbed by their ordeal.

As she listened to the droning voices dissecting and analysing the most minute aspects of her life, it felt as if they were talking about a stranger. She felt disconnected from the proceedings, unable to fully grasp the process. People she recognised sometimes stood in the dock; she was vaguely aware of Judith sneering at her as she placed her fat hand on a Bible.

To Kathryn, the facts were straightforward. Mark had hurt her for a long time and one day, under extreme provocation, she had enough and killed him. No more, no less. Whilst she wouldn't go so far as to call what she did justified, she knew that extreme scrutiny and debate would not change the situation. It was what it was. The twelve men and women of the jury pronounced her condemned, just as she had known they would. The sentence however was fair. Eight years, of which she would serve five with good behaviour. Kate felt some justification, these strangers selected at random had conceded that his acts against her were monstrous and for that, at least, she was grateful.

Kate – not Kathryn any longer – lay on the hard prison bed and tried to familiarise herself with her new home. She was relieved that her sentence had finally begun. Like a marathon race, the sooner she started, the sooner she would finish.

Marlham Women's Prison was centred around an atrium encircled by metal walkways with Plexiglas sides and decks with rows of cells on each floor. It was ugly and noisy: even the lightest touch to a railing sent up a loud clang, like a sneeze in a silent church. It had been built originally as a sanatorium but now sprawled under a mass of fiddly red-brick extensions.

The cells were far more homely than the communal areas suggested. Not chintz and soft lighting, admittedly, but nor was it all shiny magnolia bricks and metal bars, as *Porridge* had led Kate to expect. It was more like a youth hostel, functional and sparse.

A tiny rectangular window sat high on the outside wall. The safety glass was frosted and there was no mechanism for opening it, but it still had four metal bars across it for good measure. Kate tried not to imagine the world beyond the window; it was easier. In her mind, there was her old life and a new future life waiting for her. This was the period of transition in between – limbo-like and necessary.

She wished she could tell the kids that she was all right and that it wasn't as horrendous as they might have imagined. She had a cell to herself and was quite comfortable and warm. It could have been a lot worse. Unlike most new inmates, Kate wasn't longing for her mattress at home. Quite the opposite. She felt cosy and safe in her new environment, enjoying the solace of a single bed.

Her musings were interrupted by a burly guard who came to her cell and unlocked the door that had only minutes before been locked; Kate didn't yet understand the protocol.

'Up you jump!' The instruction was delivered as a friendly request more than an order.

Kate slipped off the bed and popped her feet into the open-backed, rubber-soled slippers that she had been issued with.

The guard strode ahead of her, using a combination of key and swipe card to gain access from one corridor to another. They criss-crossed several walkways until she found herself in a grey, cold, clinical bathroom. There was a single dull light bulb contained in what looked like a small cage. The sink was cracked with rust-coloured water marks running towards the plug hole. The atmosphere was damp, fungal.

'You can shower, Kate.'

Kate smiled at her. 'Thank you, I'd like that. How long have I got?'

The warder's tone was pleasant. 'Take as long as you need, my love.'

'Really?'

The woman nodded. 'There's not much going on tonight. You take your time.'

Kate replayed the guard's words over and over. *'Take as long as you need, my love.'*

She couldn't believe it; those eight words were like music.

Kate stepped into one of four identical cubicles, noting the peculiar dairy-like smell of changing rooms and communal bathing. As she let the water pour over her head and body she laughed into its cascade. This quickly turned to crying. Her tears, however, were of relief, not sadness. She had already vowed never to shed a tear for Mark or for what she'd done to him. Never. Leisurely, she soaped her skin and shampooed her hair – twice! She stood in the small square confines long after she had finished washing and let the water pummel her skin just for the sheer joy of being able to.

Then she closed her eyes and catalogued this brand-new sensation. This was what it felt like to take a shower without a hammering heart, without setting a mental timer, without listing the chores to be done inside her head while her shaking hand fumbled for shampoo or soap under a too hot current.

She giggled. For the first time in over eighteen years, with a warder standing on the other side of the door and about to retire to a cell where she would be locked in for the night, she knew that she had been liberated from her own private hell.

'Better?' the guard asked as Kate stepped from the bathroom.

'Oh yes, much.'

The tears came an hour later. The sobs from Kate's cell could be heard along the corridor. There were several shouts of 'Shut the fuck up!' and a couple of more empathetic responses.

The guard on duty lingered at the end of the walkway. It wasn't unusual for this to happen once the drama of the trial had faded and the realisation dawned on new prisoners that this was it for the next few years. She waited. Kate's distress was evident. The warder was a good judge of character and after just a few hours in her company could tell that Kate was not here to make trouble.

'Lights out, ladies!' The warder flicked the switches on the outside walls. 'And let's try and keep the noise down please!'

She heard the unmistakable sound of a pillow rustling and guessed that Kate was trying to muffle her sobs.

An hour later she did the rounds to check all lights were out and everyone was where she'd left them. She found Kate sitting on the edge of her bed. Her hair hung forward over her face.

'How you doing?' the guard whispered.

'Okay, thank you.'

Kate smiled at the shadowy figure. Her voice stuttered between dry sobs; her breathing had lost its natural rhythm. She sounded like a toddler that couldn't speak after a tantrum.

'Actually . . .'

'Yes, Kate?'

It was not unusual at this time of night for the inmates to initiate conversation or make a request.

'I was wondering if you could help me with something.'

'What's that?'

The guard's tone was suddenly stern, prepared for a verbal assault or a ridiculous demand. Both were the norm on night rounds.

Kate raised her left hand and held it up to the small grille at the top of the door.

'I need to take off my wedding ring. My solicitor said I should keep it on during my trial, but that's over now. I hate wearing it, I really do, but I can't seem to get it off. I've been sitting here trying and I can't get the bloody thing off. I don't want to spend another night with it on my finger, not one more night.'

Kate was desperate to remove the symbol of her misery. When the band of gold had been placed on her finger, she had been young, hopeful and full of passion for life. The middle-aged woman who now pulled and pushed at the third knuckle of her left hand had joints and fingers that were swollen through hard work and abuse. She felt as if a time-thief had come along in the dead of night and erased decades from her life. It was a cruel trick, the cruellest.

Her tears fell thick and fast.

'I really don't want this on my finger any more. Please . . ..'

It was the first and last time that the warder would see such a display from Kate, and she felt moved to help her. A few minutes later she returned with a bowl of warm water and a bar of soap. Unlocking the door, she handed them over to the mild-mannered lady who was in such distress.

'Thank you so much. I'm very grateful.' Kate smiled through her tears.

She vigorously soaped and wiggled and pulled until her finger bled. This only made her more determined; she reapplied the soap and tried again. On the third attempt, and ignoring the agonising swelling that made the job that much harder, Kate succeeded. She plopped the ring into the bowl of water along with the soap and studied the groove that still marked her finger.

'How long do you think it will take for this to disappear?' she asked when the guard made her next round.

'I don't know. I'd guess a few months.'

Kate nodded; she could wait a few months.

'What would you like me to do with this?' The guard had fished out the shiny gold ring and held it between her thumb and forefinger.

Kate flapped her hand in the direction of the window. 'Oh, I don't care. Anything! Throw it away please.'

She nodded before returning her attention to her finger, flexing it and admiring her naked hand. She might have been referring to the soap, so nonchalant was she about its disposal.

Kate slipped between the stiff, starched sheets and knew that she was finally free. That was her final thought as she drifted off into a deep, sound sleep. It was a whole new quality of sleep and one that she had forgotten was possible.

When she woke in the morning with the sun filtering through the prison bars and streaking her grey blanket, she had a smile on her face and peace in her heart. She had done it: she had escaped and was at peace. Kate grinned. It felt utterly wonderful.

TODAY

The house was eerily silent. Natasha and Kate sat at either end of the sofa in front of the fire. Both had neither appetite nor energy. It had been a gruelling day, a gruelling month. The two women had been preoccupied by their grief, exhausted in their distress, and organising the funeral had been all consuming. Now it was time for quiet reflection, time to catch the many breaths that had stuck in their throats since the day Tanya took her life.

Kate replayed the funeral in her head, as if by making it familiar she could dispel some of the horror. Dark, thumping organ music had reverberated through Penmarin's small church as she and Natasha arrived – much too sombre a piece for a young girl like Tanya, Kate thought; it should have been something light and ethereal.

The pews were packed. Janeece and husband Nick were already in situ and Kate recognised people that she was on nodding terms with from the pub, as well as various local shopkeepers and suppliers to Prospect House. The back rows were taken with a few of Tanya's friends and acquaintances from London. At least one of them could have been the ex-boyfriend, a curly-haired youth with deep blue eyes. Kate smiled at him, trying to make him feel comfortable in this alien environment on the saddest of days. She was glad for Tanya that they had made the journey, which was neither cheap nor convenient without a car. The boy smiled back awkwardly in her direction, thrusting his hands into the pockets of his leather jacket, the only black thing in his wardrobe. He continued to glance furtively at Kate – how much did she know? Enough to know that a sweet girl had taken the rap for him and had deserved better.

Tanya's mother had declined to attend, saying it was 'best that she didn't'. *Best for whom?* Kate wondered. Ironically the woman was probably right, as neither she nor Natasha could have guaranteed civility, and that was a battle they were too weary to undertake.

Rodney had paid for the whole funeral, his way of apologising, no doubt. It was too little too late as far as Kate was concerned. What was it he had said? *'Where Tanya is concerned, my curiosity is more than satisfied.'* The bastard.

There were many 'if onlys' bouncing from the Norman joists. Rodney thinking if only he had walked the beach early enough to catch her in the act. Natasha wishing that she had pushed Tanya a bit harder in her art classes. She had already identified her as extremely vulnerable; if only she had delved deep enough to uncover Tanya's plan and prevent it.

Tanya's body hadn't yet been recovered. That was a good thing, Kate thought, allowing them all to remember her freckled form and ready smile. The bodyless coffin stood on its trestle at the front of the church.

Kate thought about the day of Tanya's arrival in Penmarin.

'I have been reliably informed that if you swam as far as you could, the first country you would hit would be Canada.'

'Canada near America? You're shitting me?'

'No, it's true – if you swam until you hit a beach, you'd probably be handed a towel by a Mountie! Imagine that.'

'I can't swim.'

'Would you like to learn?'

'No.'

Tanya's answer had been loud and emphatic.

She thought about the last few days prior to Tanya's death. Had she taken her eye off the ball? Been too hard on her? She should have handled things differently, offered support and understanding instead of reprimand. What wouldn't Kate give to have Tanya here now, high as a kite, but still here . . .

She looked up at the open-armed, smiling saints that filtered the sunlight through the stained glass windows, allowing it to fall in shades of green and teal across the congregation. Some of the words from Tanya's final letter played over and over in Kate's head:

I've always messed everything up, Kate, and I'm sorry that I let you down as well. Carry on without me. The world won't miss Tanya Wilson – who was she anyway?

Kate whispered into the ether as the congregation mumbled in familiar prayer.

'I will miss you Tanya Wilson, I will miss you always.'

Kate shook her head to clear the image. She wished she could stop thinking about the funeral. She wanted to remember Tanya with her flame-red hair and air of mischief, not this sad occasion that summed up their biggest failure. Maybe in time . . .

Her words cut through the silence and were unexpected.

'I'm closing Prospect House, Tash. I don't want to be here any more.'

Natasha was silent for a full minute.

'I think it's too soon for you to make a decision like that, Kate. You need time to let your thoughts settle. See how you feel when things are more back to normal.'

'Back to normal? I don't think things will ever go back to normal, whatever "normal" is. And actually I'm not sure I want them to. No, I've decided.

Surprisingly, it's quite an easy decision for me. The fact is, I thought I could make a difference, but I can't . . . I didn't . . . or she would still be here and that is that.'

'It doesn't work that way, Kate, and in time, with a clearer head, you will see that. You have helped a lot of girls, most of whom are now thriving, and have changed lives because of you, because of us. Don't lose sight of that.'

Kate studied the mug of strong tea between her hands. The only thing that eased her shivering core was the constant, slow sipping of hot tea.

'I keep thinking that I should have handled the drugs thing differently. Maybe I was too aggressive or dismissive. If only I had been a tad more understanding. It was because I was tired and my head was whirring with all that I'd seen at the exhibition. I can't even remember what I said exactly, but I wish I'd done it differently. What Tanya needed was my help and yet I went into her room, played the heavy. Maybe if I hadn't . . .'

Natasha smiled grimly. 'Kate, you wouldn't know how to play the heavy if your life depended on it and the girl had crack cocaine in our home – that is not a small thing. What was the alternative, not mention it? Of course you had to. You can't beat yourself up about this, Kate. You can miss her, yes; grieve for her, of course, but please don't blame yourself. It won't do you any good and it won't bring her back.'

'Do you think I don't know that, Tash?'

'Yes of course you know that, but my job is to remind you that Tanya had a whole stack of problems before she ever came into our lives, problems that you and I can't begin to fathom, especially with so many pieces of the jigsaw missing. It is never, ever one thing that pushes someone to make a decision like that. It's something that simmers and grows over time; the decision might have been made long before she even met us.'

'I know that sounds logical, but she was making such good progress. She was happy here, I know she was.'

'Yes, she did seem happy, but we were only just beginning to scratch the surface and you know as well as I that often what we see on the outside is not always a true reflection of what is going on inside.'

Kate pictured herself at Mountbriers, painting on a bright smile, pulling back her shoulders and trying to convince everyone that all was well with her world. She continued as though her friend had not spoken.

'I think Dom was right: I'm an amateur psychologist hiding away down here. It's no good. I just don't want to be here any more.'

'Did you see the letter Stacey sent? If nothing else, then look at what you did for her. She's back home, she's on the road to full recovery and you did that!'

'Or maybe she would have bounced back anyway; maybe I'm just muddling in where I shouldn't.'

'Look how far *you* have come, Kate. Look how different *your* life is!'

'Oh it's different, granted, but recently I've been feeling as if I simply got off a rollercoaster and onto a roundabout and I've had enough.'

Natasha shook her head. She had never seen her friend this negative.

'Why don't you take a trip? A change of scenery might put things into perspective a bit.'

'How much more perspective do you think I need, Tash? We've just had Tanya's funeral, just buried an empty coffin that represented her pointless little life! All she wanted was a bloody coffee machine. It wasn't much to ask, was it?'

She instantly regretted raising her voice.

'I'm sorry. I'm not shouting at you.'

'I know that, honey. It's fine, you can shout as much as you want to. I just think that maybe you need to get out of this environment. Why not go and see Simon? You've been talking for a while about going and seeing the mission's new building.'

'No, that's the last place I want to go. I don't need reminding of all my good intentions when I started here; it would make it worse somehow.'

'Well, I'm going away, Kate. I'm taking a month to go up to the Lakes to walk and paint. I'll stop off at Fran's en route. Why don't we talk about this again when I get back? But please don't make a decision until then. I think we both just need a bit of time.'

'*Stop off at Fran's . . .*' Kate tucked her lips over

her teeth and bit down. The casual aside that Natasha would be going to see *her* children did nothing to cheer her. It was as ever a dagger that cut her heart . . . *My children.*

She nodded, more to placate her best friend than in any belief that things might be different with the passing of four weeks.

'Okay, Tash, we'll wait a month, but I think my mind is made up.'

'More tea?' Natasha raised her empty cup for the fifth time that evening.

Kate nodded. Yep, more tea . . .

Tom made a big show of lugging his small suitcase along the path; he really did not want to go.

'Are you sure you don't want me to pop in and prepare you some food each day, Kate? I wouldn't mind at all. I'm around anyway and truth be told I feel a bit redundant.'

'That's very sweet, Tom, but a holiday means a holiday – enjoy it! A whole month to yourself. Do something great! Go somewhere!'

'I feel guilty though, being paid and not working.'

'Don't. Otherwise what's the point of a break? You won't enjoy it.'

'I was thinking I might and go and visit me sister up at Bodmin, spend some time with her and the kids, if you sure you don't need me?'

'Tom, give me your house keys; it's the only way to stop you nipping in and force-feeding me lasagne!'

He reluctantly handed them to his boss.

'Good. Now go! Don't make me change the locks!'

Tom sauntered off down the drive, leaving Kate alone. She locked the door and slid the bolts before pulling down the blinds and drawing the sitting room curtains. She wanted to be alone and in the dark. She wanted to curl up and withdraw from the world, just for a bit.

She glanced at the clock on the mantelpiece. Tash would have just arrived at Francesca's en route to the Lake District. She would probably be conversing right now with Lydia, talking about art or simply passing the time of day. She swallowed the bile that threatened to rise in her throat. Life could be bloody unfair.

Paying no heed to the time of day, Kate climbed the stairs and headed for 'Wish'. She stepped into the room and stripped down to her underwear. Pulling back the duvet, she slid between the crisp white sheets and fell into a deep slumber.

It was approaching midnight when Kate was jolted from her sleep. Whether awake or dreaming she wasn't sure, but she had heard the voice of her husband as surely as if he was standing over her.

'Hello, Kathryn.'

She jumped and simultaneously yelped. Her head smashed into the headboard as a fine film of sweat covered her skin. Laughing with relief, she rubbed her scalp. It was just a horrible dream. She settled down once again with the duvet pulled up under her chin. She shivered despite the warmth of the room; he still had the power to do that to her.

At 3 a.m., Kate reluctantly woke once more. Her pillow was wet from tears shed in her sleep. Her eyes were swollen, her throat dry. She didn't know why she had been sobbing, but it felt horribly familiar, reminding her of so many mornings in the headmaster's house at Mountbriers. There she had often woken in floods of tears at the utter misery of her life. She would cry for the night she had been forced to endure and for the day ahead that she was yet to experience, all the while painting on her smile and stepping outside with her basket of linen.

She decided that a slug of whisky might be just the thing to send her back to the land of nod. Tom had a bottle squirrelled away at the back of the larder. Like his afternoon siestas in his van, it was another thing that she feigned ignorance of. Bless him.

Kate poured a healthy measure and carried it to the sofa. It tasted foul. She could stomach the odd glass of plonk, but this was something else. She carried on sipping and surprisingly after her first glass the taste was almost palatable. Gradually it warmed her throat and started to numb her pain. She welcomed the escape. Her head lolled forward, against her chest. When she opened her eyes, Mark was sitting in the chair opposite her.

'Hello, Kathryn.'

It was once again the unmistakable, polished tones of her husband.

He was wearing his dark grey suit, a starched white shirt and a pale blue tie. His legs were crossed, his slender trouser leg hitched up just so to reveal a pale blue silk sock. His interlaced fingers formed a pyramid shape and rested against his chest. He looked tanned, relaxed and happy. He was smiling. Her nostrils filled with the unmistakable scent of Floris No. 89. Her breath came in short bursts. She was trembling. She closed her eyes, hoping that when she opened them he would have disappeared. He had not.

'Are you not talking to me, Kathryn?'

'Go away. You are not here any more!'

'Kathryn Brooker, did I teach you nothing? Where are your manners? It's only polite to converse with a guest that comes into your home, whether invited or not.'

'I can't talk to you because you are not here any more!'

'Is that right? Then who are you looking at, silly girl? Who is it that is in your sitting room right now?'

'I don't want to talk to you! I don't want to talk to you ever again!'

'Ah, sweet Kathryn, but you are talking to me!'

'I'm Kate now.'

She was aware that her words were slightly slurred. He chuckled.

'Is that right, darling? And how long have you been Kate?'

She considered this.

'I have always been Kate, but I wasn't allowed to be for a while, not until you were gone.'

His voice was steady, unwavering.

'No, darling. You will never be Kate. Never, not properly. But you know that deep down, don't you, Kathryn?'

'I *am* Kate, not Kathryn, and you are gone, Mark. You can't hurt me any more!'

She thrashed her head from side to side, trying to make him disappear. Mark laughed quietly. He leant forward, his voice barely more than a whisper.

'You don't really believe that, do you?'

'Yes! It's true. You can't hurt me now. I am free of you, Mark.'

'Oh, Kathryn. What was it you said to me? *I will become all of the things that I thought I might* . . . Have you achieved that, darling? Have you become all the things you thought you might? Did you think you might become lonely, old and childless? Is that what you thought? And as for not hurting you, we both know that I still hurt you every single day, despite all your brave words. It would take more than throwing on a pair of jeans and not making a bed to get rid of me! I am lurking over your shoulder when you look in the mirror, I am breathing down your neck before you fall asleep and I am the reason that the kids hate you. You've lost them, Kathryn. But you know that too, don't you?'

Her sobs were loud and unrestrained.

'They do NOT hate me! That is a lie. They are my children, they do not!'

'Then where are they, Kathryn? Where are they right now? Why have there been no responses to all the pathetic letters you write? How hard is it for them to pick up the phone? Why didn't they ever visit you? Why don't they now?'

She shook her head.

'I don't know why and I don't know where they are.'

'And Lydi surprises me still. I would have thought that in her you had found an ally, especially with your life experiences being not that dissimilar.'

'Our lives were never similar!'

'Were they not?'

Mark raised his eyebrow, his smile widened.

'Think about it, Kathryn, think about it logically.'

'Mark, if you touched her, I swear to God . . .'

'What, darling? What will you do? Kill me?'

He laughed loudly.

'I only stayed with you to keep them safe, and if they weren't safe . . .'

'That's right, darling – it would all have been for nothing. Ironic, isn't it? Oh, Kathryn, what a price you have paid. Was it worth it, *amor vitae meae*?'

Kate slid down onto the floor. Her tears snaked into her mouth.

'NO!' she screamed into the ether. 'It was not

worth it! I want my kids back! I want my children and I would go back to that life in a heartbeat if it meant I got to see my babies every day! It was NOT worth it, Mark! You have won! Are you happy? You have won!'

Her throat was raw from shouting. She lay in the small gap between the sofa and the coffee table and she slept where she fell.

Kate busied herself with tidying the mess from the night before, vacuuming and plumping the cushions in the sitting room. She couldn't control the tremor that dogged her right hand as she wrote out cheques in the study. That was all the bills up to date. A few more lines were penned and sealed in envelopes and she was all set. Dishwasher on. Loos cleaned. Plants watered. Laundry folded. Bed made.

Kate pulled the front door behind her and relished the feel of the morning sun on her cheeks. This had always been her favourite time of day. As the path flattened out and the stones gave way to sand, Kate's faltering steps turned into strides. She ran the last few metres with a smile on her face as the salt-tinged breeze lifted her fringe and buffeted her chest.

Kate removed her T-shirt, folded it neatly with arm holes and hems together, and laid it on the sand. Next she slipped out of her jeans, which she placed with precision on top of her T-shirt. She unhooked her bra and let the straps fall along her muscular arms and finally she stepped out of her pants. Her clothes sat in a neat little pile, like laundry waiting to be collected and put away on wash day. She was done.

Kate felt the bite of small stones and shells on the soft soles of her feet. She did nothing to ease the discomfort, figuring that it mattered little compared to the journey that she was about to undertake. A second or two of foot pain meant nothing in the grander scheme of things. She ran her palms over the backs of her thighs; she'd had worse. *'Good morning, Mrs Bedmaker . . . Good afternoon, Mrs Bedmaker . . . Mrs Bedmaker . . . Mrs Bedmaker . . .'* She always noticed, always.

She walked forward to the dark shadow on the sand where the water lapped, staining it the colour of dark tea and pitting it with fizzing holes in which small worms and crabs bathed.

Kate trod gingerly, feeling the shock of the icy current on her exposed flesh. It was colder than she remembered for the time of the year. Her mind flitted briefly to the warm Caribbean Sea that had caressed her under a hot sun all those years ago. She remembered throwing herself into the balmy current and feeling the heat smooth the knots from her muscles; she remembered dancing in the rain at Carnival and wearing green feathers. She recalled being held in strong arms with nothing but a towel between her nakedness and a beautiful man; she remembered a kiss that had been full of love and promise. That had been a perfect day.

The man reversed on the winding lane and struggled with the unpredictable gearstick of the hire car as it crunched and whined in protest. He pulled into a lay-by to allow the caravan and hefty 4x4 to pass by. His female passenger winced and squealed, closing her eyes against the impossible manoeuvre. The man exhaled loudly through puffed out cheeks; these roads were going to take a bit of getting used to. Relief and laughter filled the car.

Kate strode further into the water and allowed the tiny waves to lap her with their salty tongues. She turned and faced the shore, stepping backwards until the sea covered her shoulders. Her teeth chattered in her gums and her limbs jerked involuntarily, trying to counter the effects of the cold.
The man pulled the car into the driveway. This was it. Bulky luggage and a partly defrosted shepherd's pie were quickly retrieved from the tiny boot and lugged to the front door.
The girl shielded her eyes from the sun and looked out over the ocean.
'I am so going to paint this!'
The man put his arm across her shoulders.
'Nervous?'
She nodded and bit her bottom lip.
'Me too,' he said.

Kate gazed up to the top of the cliff for one last look at Prospect House. This was the one place that she had been happy, the one place she had been comfortable and felt needed. Kate knew when she was beaten. Mark was right, he had won. She would never be free of the memory of what he had done; her scars ran too deep and the pain hovered too near the surface. There would never be peace for someone like her; she was too broken. The prospect of a life without her children was one that she could not contemplate. Deep down she had always known this. She would rather bow out than face that reality.

Prospect House looked beautiful. She thought of how easily her last vista could have been something else – Mark's grinning face, the underside of a pillow at Mountbriers, a reflection of her own face, begging. This was better, much better. She liked the fact that it was by her own hand and not his. She was in control.

Kate's body had gone numb with extreme cold and her skin was peppered with a million goosebumps. Her fine hair floated like brown seaweed around her head. Still with her eyes on the shoreline, Kate took two more steps backwards, until the soft sand beneath her feet gave way to nothing and she was treading water, preparing to go down, under the sea.

As the cold water began to engulf her, she was overcome with a beautiful calmness. Kate smiled at the prospect of the peace and escape that lay ahead. She would just take a moment . . . prepare.

Her eyes scanned the sand; she saw an image of the kids. They were toddlers with fat little tummies and chubby, splayed feet. They trudged up and down the beach carrying little red buckets filled with water that sloshed and slopped so that when they eventually reached the sandcastle moat there was nothing to tip. She laughed into the water and closed her eyes. When she opened them again, the kids were nine and ten. Lydia, resplendent in oversized yellow sunglasses and her first bikini, lay on a beach towel, trying to be so grown up. Dominic, sneaking up behind his sister, held a clump of wet seaweed that in a matter of minutes would be deposited on her stomach.

Her precious memories would go with her. It had been an unfortunate life in one sense, but Kate could safely say that she would go through it all again, just for the sweet joy of being a mother to two such exceptional human beings. They would always be her greatest achievement, her legacy and no one, not even Mark could take that away from her.

Kate took a deep breath and prepared to submerge. She squinted at the shoreline, slowly exhaling, blinking through saltwater lashes to try and better focus. Another memory, only this felt different . . . The kids looked older and try as she might to search the crevices of her mind, she couldn't remember it. It was more like a premonition. Here they were, adult at last. Dominic standing tall in a white open-necked shirt with his arm across Lydia's shoulders. They were shouting, waving. Had they come to say goodbye? She strained to catch their words, but only Simon's lilting tone filled her head. *Try and remember that hope comes in many forms; sometimes it's a place and sometimes it's a person.*

Lydia and Dominic stood on the shoreline. This was no memory, they were real and they had finally arrived. Standing arm in arm now, the siblings waited tentatively at the water's edge. What on earth was she doing? They held her bundled clothes and beckoned her inland with open arms.

'Hurry up! Some of us are desperate for a cup of tea!' Dom bellowed in her direction.

Kate smiled and wept into the current.

Or people, she thought. *Sometimes it comes in the form of people.*

Kate began to swim, towards the shore, towards the hope that had been there all along, towards a future, a future with her children. She knew that she was free. Finally she would be able to tell her children the story of Mrs Bedmaker without fear.

'I *am* Kate!' she shouted. 'I *am* Kate!'

She had won after all.